GW00836367

WORK WIFE BALANCE

Jo Edwards

Published by Weasel Green Press

This book is a work of fiction. Names, characters, places, and incidents either are products of the author's imagination or are used fictitiously. Any resemblance to actual persons, living or dead, events, or locales is entirely coincidental.

WORK WIFE BALANCE

Copyright © Jo Edwards 2012

Cover Art by Regina Wamba of Mae I Design
Edited by Mike Rose-Steel
Interior Text Design by Tricia Kristufek

ISBN-13: 978-1479188345
ISBN-10: 1479188344

All rights reserved.
No part of this publication may be used or reproduced in any manner whatsoever without written permission, except in the case of brief quotations embodied in critical articles and reviews. Requests for permission should be addressed to admin@weaselgreenpress.com

First Edition:
10 9 8 7 6 5 4 3 2 1

DEDICATION

For Mum and Dad

CHAPTER ONE

Someone was in the bedroom. A tall, shadowy figure stood over me. I tried to scream but fear froze it dead in my throat. I whipped back the covers, braced for an attack, but the figure didn't make its move. It couldn't move. It was my grey trouser suit, hanging on the wardrobe door. *You idiot.* Heart pounding, I pulled the covers back over myself. That would teach me for trying to be organised for a change. It was one of my resolutions - select the next day's outfit the night before, thus avoiding the 6.00 am gazing-into-the wardrobe-in-bewilderment routine. I hadn't realised this foresight could potentially lead to heart failure.

I was determined that this year was going to be different. I would leap out of bed like a salmon, thankful to be alive and full of zesty energy for another new day. I would eat a healthy and nutritious breakfast; something with whole grain in it for my bowels, and arrive at work with a glowing complexion and a cheery smile. Nothing would get me down. Nobody would grate on my nerves. My team would do what I asked them to do without me having to issue death-threats. I'd even be nice to that officious little twerp on reception, Stalin Stan, and stop sending him bogus emails requesting parking spaces for fictional visitors just so he'd have to go out in the rain to put the cones out. Anyway, I needed to drop off again smartish as I'd resolved to get a minimum of eight hours sleep a night - if only my pulse would return to a normal

1

speed.

The alarm was like a pneumatic drill going through my skull. I peered at the clock in disbelief. *No no no* - surely it was still the middle of the night? The clock said 5.30 am, but it just couldn't be true. I heaved my body out of the warm covers and sat, stunned, on the edge of the bed. *Bloody hell, it's freezing.* My stomach hung there like a roll of pastry, reproachfully squashed between my thighs and my rib cage, an unattractive reminder of Christmas. I wished I hadn't eaten my own body weight in cold roast potatoes. And why had I drunk those glasses of Baileys last night? I don't even like Baileys! I'd seen it on the adverts during The Great Escape and had suddenly fancied some. Why hadn't I taken some exercise over the holidays? I could have gone for some bracing country walks in the crisp fresh air and had firm, walnut-cracking thighs by now. Apart from chasing a cat out of the garden (demented arm-waving, foul language) I'd hardly moved. Oh God, here I go again; the daily morning self-loathing ritual. *Stop it.* This was a brand new year, a fresh start. A chance to do things differently. I had to stop beating myself up, start being positive and make good things happen. *I can do it.*

I dressed in my grey suit, having to inhale drastically before I could do up the trousers. Why did I suck my cheeks in when I did this? That wouldn't help. I wasn't convinced that the button would survive the day. I did have an elasticated skirt somewhere for bloating emergencies, but I'd never find it, as I was having to get dressed in the dark so I didn't wake The Husband, who didn't have to go into work until later. I got one leg caught up in my tights and hopped around like Long John Silver, before crashing into the dressing table. The Husband stirred and irritably muttered "For Christ's sake..." I couldn't win. If I'd put the light on he would probably have accused me of trying to blind him. He'd been a bit quiet over Christmas and particularly grumpy over the last few days. I didn't think he'd fully recovered from New Years Eve, a fancy dress party at a friend's house. He'd gone as Che Guevara, but everyone thought he was supposed to be Frank Spencer. People kept coming up behind him and shouting "Ooh Betty!" or "The cat's done a whoopsie!". He'd initially pretended to laugh it off, but had eventually experienced a major sense of humour failure and spent the evening sat sulking on the stairs with Cleopatra. Or it might have been Boy George.

My car was covered by a thick glistening layer of ice. I started it up and went inside to boil the kettle, munching on a strawberry Pop Tart as I waited. Were Pop Tarts whole grain? They looked a bit granular so they were probably ok. When I tipped the hot water over the windscreen, the wipers came on and swept the water back over me. I gasped in shock - I was drenched! I could hear my next-door neighbour howling with laughter, even from the other side of his triple-glazed windows. I couldn't face having to change, so with the heater on full blast in an attempt to dry out my blouse, I drove the 23-mile journey towards Cheltenham that I had made for the last 12 years. The beginning of the route was quite attractive, initially passing by fields and hedgerows, and as long as I remembered to hold my breath passing the sewerage works it was a very pleasant drive. The countryside eventually dissolved into busy, impatient A-roads, lined with non-descript industrial units. I had read in the paper that in order to challenge your mind and ward off dementia you should regularly change your route to and from work. I mentally added that to my list of resolutions; I'd start from tomorrow. I put on my iPod and selected "Eton Rifles" by The Jam, turning up the volume to maximum. It was one of my "kick-arse" songs to uplift and inspire me before the day ahead. I sang along loudly, thumping the steering wheel and visualising myself sweeping into work, radiating positivity, sharing a few jokes with my happy, motivated colleagues and high-fiving down the office as I bounded to my desk. I plastered a broad smile onto my face as I turned into the Kingfisher Business Park, noticing that the "Welcome to Perypils Insurance" sign didn't look quite right. It had, rather unfortunately, lost the "l" in Perypils.

The Cheltenham site of Perypils Insurance shared its premises with a health insurance company called "Insight Health" which our guys referred to, somewhat predictably, as "In Shite Health". They had the first two floors and we had the third and fourth, with a shared canteen (which I referred to as Sam 'n Ella's) on the ground floor. I prepared to give Stalin Stan a beaming smile as I walked into reception but he was fully occupied, interrogating poor old Mary Miller who had forgotten her pass. "Of course I can't just let you in, you could be anyone!"

"But I've worked here for over twenty years," she pleaded, "You see me go in and out every day. And I go to bingo with your wife on Tuesdays, you drive us there..."

I scurried on past and up several flights of stairs to my department of approximately 100 heads, which occupied half of the fourth floor. It was as quiet as a morgue when I walked in, and about as cold. Some of the guys on the telephony early shift acknowledged my cheery "Morning all!" through hollow eyes and with grouchy grunts. Even the tinsel looked like it wanted to be at Beachy Head.

As I was removing my coat, I saw a familiar anorak-clad figure enter the department, clutching an Asda carrier bag which, I knew, would contain exactly four Dairylea cheese spread sandwiches, a packet of ready salted Hula Hoops and a Cherry Bakewell. I referred to Martin as The Drain because he had the tendency to suck any reason to live out of a room. He was on his way over to me, which surprised me. Usually it took him at least an hour and several cups of coffee before he felt mentally strong enough to be able to converse with anyone in the office. He looked at my still-sopping wet blouse but didn't pass comment.

"Morning Martin," I said brightly, with a big smile. "How was your Christmas?" *What a mistake.* Why did I ask? I got the lot.

He'd had an argument with his butcher on Christmas Eve over the exact weight of the turkey, and ended up leaving the shop without it.

He'd served (previously frozen) Asda chicken drumsticks for Christmas lunch, which his visiting parents had called "feral".

His wife got very drunk on cooking sherry and accused him of being "an anally retentive dickhead".

His hard of hearing father had the telly on so loud it had triggered Martin's tinnitus and labyrinthitis.

His eight year old daughter had a tantrum when presented with her new bike. She'd wanted a 42-inch, 3D HD Plasma TV.

His five year old son had left a letter out for Santa telling him that all he wanted for Christmas was "to be fostered".

Martin's irritable bowel syndrome had flared up as his nerves were "shot to shit".

The dog had diarrhoea, probably for the same reason.

My positive resolve began to crumble under the weight of his litany of misery. I wasn't required to respond, but waited until he'd paused for breath, then interjected with an upbeat "Well at least it's all over for another year!" hoping that he'd bugger off so I could start some work. Had he asked me about my own Christmas, I would have told him that my day, spent at my parents, had passed without particular incident, although lunch was over three hours later than expected because my mother kept taking the turkey out of the oven, attempting to carve it with a butter knife, and declaring it wasn't quite ready.

The Drain was still hovering.

"There was something I needed to talk to you about, Kate." *Oh God, what else?* He scratched at his bald patch. "I want to make a complaint - about my team, and er, the Secret Santa gift they gave me."

For God's sake, not this again - every year, every single sodding year, Secret bloody Santa upsets someone.

"What was the gift Martin?" I asked wearily.

He sniffed. "It was a lady's flannelette nightie and a pair of support tights. American Tan," he added, as if the colour was of great significance. He paused. "And they were wrapped in an Asda carrier bag."

Mustn't laugh, mustn't laugh, mustn't laugh.

"I'm deeply offended," Martin continued huffily. "They're clearly insinuating that I'm an old woman and I think it's totally unacceptable. I feel they've questioned my sexuality, which completely goes against company policy. I'm very upset; I want something done about it."

I assembled my face into a mask of concern.

"Well Martin." I said, "I'm sorry this has happened. Of course you can make a formal complaint, that is your right. But that course of action could cause you a great deal of personal angst," - *and a huge amount of paperwork for me* - "so perhaps you should consider something a little less formal."

He crossed his arms and looked sulky. I tried again. "Maybe you could talk to your team and tell them how they've made you feel," - *although I very much doubt they could give a toss* - "or perhaps you could even, well, attempt to laugh it off." It was unlikely he'd go for this option, but it was still worth a shot.

The Drain pursed his lips and tugged at his belt in a futile attempt to pull his trousers up over his belly. He sniffily informed me that he would be considering his options and returned to his desk. I knew exactly what he would do: sulk for a few days, maybe even a week, be very curt with his team in an attempt to make them feel guilty (although he wouldn't directly address the issue with them, they'd have to guess why he was sulking), hopefully they would eventually take pity, start to be nice to him and then he would get over the whole thing. *God, he was such an old woman.*

At last I could log in and attempt to start some work. This was always a tense moment after a period of holiday - just how many emails would I have received since Christmas Eve? And how soon would it be before someone asked "Kate, have you read that email I sent you?". Even though they would have received my out of office message saying I wouldn't be back until today, they'd still think I possessed the super power to have read and absorbed hundreds of emails in

7

3 seconds flat. I clicked on the inbox, narrowing my eyes into slits to protect myself from the horror. It opened up at 63 unread emails - wow, that wasn't too bad at all! I could cope with that. Oh, no, it was still receiving - not a good sign. I flicked into my calendar. Bugger - the first meeting of the day started in 10 minutes. Too late to do any prep now, I'd have to wing it.

Emails were still coming in. Up to 184 and rising. There were quite a few from Brett The Boss. He'd obviously been working all over Christmas. I doubted any were to wish me a Happy New Year, as he hadn't managed to wish me a Happy Christmas, nor had he been down to see the teams in months - and didn't they just love to whinge about it! He did cover four sites, but even so, I felt he could have made the effort. I did call him on Christmas Eve - the background noise of raucous laughter, thumping music, smashing glasses suggested he had already left the office. He kept shouting "Kate? Kate who?" even though I've worked for him for over a year.

I had wished him a Merry Christmas and asked how he was planning to spend Christmas Day.

"Depends if the bitch lets me see the kids or not."

Ooh, that was awkward. I attempted a joke about hoping he got a Batman outfit for Christmas just in case, but I don't think he got it, so I said "Merry Christmas, then!" and quickly rang off.

I still felt a bit raw that he hadn't got me anything at all for Christmas. Well, actually, very raw. I had got my guys a bottle of wine (each, not between them), tins of chocolates, mince pies and Bucks Fizz *and* held a Christmas raffle for them. (Top prize an iPod, bottom prize lunch for two in the canteen, Immodium supplied.) I had received precisely Jack Shit. I wasn't expecting a Harrods hamper, but just *something* would have been nice, even a chocolate orange, just to say "thanks for working your tits off all year love, it's much appreciated".

I *had* received a Christmas card from The Boss. On it was a picture of Rudolph standing in front of a group of embarrassed-looking reindeer. He was saying: "Santa, we've got a case of syphilis in the herd". Santa replied: "Thank God - I'm sick of the Beaujolais!" Inside Brett had written:

> *To Keith, saw this and thought of you!*
> *Hope you get the all clear in the New Year!*
>   *Cheers, Brett.*

I didn't know who Keith was, but he was obviously someone to avoid for a while.

The email avalanche had stopped at 268. *Bloody hell.* It was going to take me days to get through that lot - I'd have to work evenings as well this week. I texted The Husband to let him know I would be late home. He texted back: "Don't 4get we r going to Deb & Pauls tonight". I gave an inward groan - I had forgotten. Who has people round for dinner just after Christmas, for Christ's sake? And on a school night? Obviously *they* were still on holiday and didn't have to get up for work tomorrow. *Sadists.* Debbie worked with The Husband and had become his New Best Friend, having joined his company last year. I'd met her a couple of times: once when we'd been in Cafe Nero she was passing and joined us for a cup of coffee, and once when we'd been in our local pub, she'd been there too and joined us for a glass of wine. She was ok - very talkative, and of course like most people that work together, she and The Husband talked shop

9

all the time, which is fine for them, but excludes everyone else. I'd never met Paul, but knew he worked in IT. What was I going to talk to him about? The joys of Alt, Control, Delete? That was about the limit of my IT knowledge. They also had a young daughter but The Husband, typically, didn't know her name or how old she was.

I went for a quick walk round the department to say "good morning" to my team. A number of the staff were making very loud "brrrrr" noises for my benefit and rubbing their arms across their bodies with huge exaggeration. Who did they think I was - a bloody heating engineer? I knew that once the heating system got up to temperature the exact same people would be fanning themselves vigorously, gasping for breath, on the very verge of heat-stroke. I noticed that The Lazy Shit George quickly shut down a screen as I approached, and moved his arm in an attempt to shield his iPhone from my view. *Hmmm, what was he up to?* The Rock was cradling her phone between her neck and shoulder, whilst typing something onto her screen with one hand and holding a half-eaten prawn and mayo baguette in the other. The Snake, Hissing Cyn, was talking in hushed tones to one of her team and stopped abruptly when I went over, looking up rather shiftily. Someone's ears would be burning. Mine felt quite hot.

I went to find The Climber. She wasn't in her team (no surprises there, as that's where any work was likely to be) and I eventually found her perched on Big Andy's desk, laughing her silly, annoying laugh and flicking her long brown hair around. She reluctantly peeled her backside off Big Andy's jotter pad when she saw me coming. She had an extremely short skirt on so I think Big Andy may have seen more than he'd bargained for as she got down. He looked at me and pulled a face of mock horror as her back was turned.

"Hello Katie old girl!" he boomed, as cheerful as ever. "A happy New Year to you! We'd better get our arses in gear, the meeting's about to start. And did you know you'd wet yourself? Or were you trying to make your blouse see-through? Hoping for promotion are you? By the way, have you read that email I sent you?"

CHAPTER TWO

I wasn't at all keen to go to Debbie and Paul's for dinner, but I couldn't tell The Husband that. The last time I'd said I didn't want to go to dinner with one of his work colleagues it had sparked a huge row. He accused me of being unsociable and not wanting to go anywhere or meet anyone new. That wasn't true. I hadn't wanted to go to dinner with this particular colleague because he talked whilst his mouth was full and his laugh sounded like a donkey being interfered with.

I had my work lap top open as I sat on the sofa at home, leaving getting ready until the last possible moment. When the Husband came in he'd said:

"Is this how it's going to be again this year, your head in your lap top night after night?" That was a bit rich coming from him, a man so attached to his iPhone that I had named it Camilla - the third person in our marriage. I even found the bloody thing in bed with us sometimes. I put his cutting remark down to the fact that he'd had a frustrating day at work. He had been out to give financial advice to a couple who lived in Canberra Flats, or the "Concrete Shit Hole" as he called it, and apparently they had been stoned out of their heads and thought he was from the council. They kept asking him when they could get an allotment as they were keen to "grow their own". They also kept a parrot which said "What a tosser!" every time The Husband spoke. He hadn't made a sale.

As I clicked through the endless emails, I came across an absolute turd. It had been sent very late on Christmas Eve, thus ensuring it wouldn't be read until it was too late for the recipient to challenge its content. It had also been sneakily left untitled, so it could lurk undetected amongst the rest of the shite before it got flushed out. It gave notice of the one thing guaranteed to instil bum-clenching, acid-refluxing fear into every manager - A-U-D-I-T. *Oh no, please God, no.* My department hadn't been audited for several years - why now? Why me? Normally only areas that were under-performing got audited. Everything was going pretty well, wasn't it - why pick on me? Was someone out to get me? That's all I needed - a team of suited midgets (small man syndrome) to descend on my teams and pretend to be everyone's friend - "we're here to help". Their definition of "help" would be to produce a detailed report highlighting every single flaw. No matter if there weren't any flaws, they would make sure to find some. They have to prove that their run-and-tell-tales-to-Mummy job has some value. To complete your humiliation, they distribute their help/report to every senior manager right up the line until it hits the desk of the Big Cheese Chief Exec. And then it all comes down on you like a ton of hot horse-shit.

Oh Christ. Still, there was no time to worry about that now, The Husband was circling, looking pointedly at his watch. I needed to get ready to go Debbie and Paul's. I'd made the mistake of getting comfy on the sofa, so it was a real effort to get up again. I was feeling quite tired after my early start, so I opened a can of Red Bull to try and perk myself up. I sipped at it, feeling a bit sorry for myself. I was

13

fed up with having to go to things I didn't want to go to. Time away from work was very precious, especially as I needed this time to be able to catch up with work. And Coronation Street. Why spend it in the company of people you didn't particularly want to see; why did I always feel obliged to accept invitations? If I thought quickly enough I would make up an excuse, but why did I feel the need to lie, couldn't I just say "thanks very much for the invite, but I'd really rather cut my own head off with a blunt spoon. Hope you don't mind". How easy is that? So why couldn't I ever say it? I'd read in a Le Carré novel that "one calls it politeness, but it's really nothing but weakness". Too bloody true.

I hadn't a clue what to wear and was out of inspiration. A dress would have been easier than having to choose both a top and a bottom, but a dress seemed a bit over the top, like I was trying too hard. Jeans were far too casual and didn't expand enough when you needed them to, so I played safe with olive green trousers and a cream jersey top. Decided cream wasn't a sensible colour to wear to dinner in case we were having spag bol, so I changed into a black jersey top. I examined my reflection in the bedroom mirror. My face looked very drained against the black so I put on a cerise scarf. That shrieked back at me from the mirror, so I changed it for a pale blue one. That didn't look right with the olive green trousers. *Oh for God's sake*, time was getting on, we were going to be late. I could hear The Husband in the hallway rattling his keys, a sure sign he was getting impatient. I took out my drawer stuffed full of scarves and tipped the whole lot onto the bed in a temper. Why couldn't I just get dressed without having a tantrum? All I needed was a scarf that went with olive green and black, and that wasn't too dark and wasn't too loud. It shouldn't be this difficult. I seized one that was a sort of black and white animal print, and tried wrapping it round my neck in several different ways, none of which looked quite right. "What are you doing up there?" called The Husband.

"I just can't tie this scarf properly!"

I thought I heard him say "Just pull it as tight as possible..." but I couldn't be sure. *Oh sod it*, I'd just leave it loose. I grabbed my handbag and went downstairs, hoping The Husband would say I looked nice, but he didn't even look at me. I said, as a prompt, "You look very smart love," hoping he'd reciprocate, but he turned to look at himself in the hallway mirror and said "Yes, I think this blazer's ok, don't you?" before heading out the front door. I felt like a puppy that was wagging its tail hoping for a pat on the head, but instead got a swift kick in the goolies.

The Husband drove to us Debbie and Paul's house, which was about twelve miles away. The plan was we'd leave the car there and get a taxi back so we could both have a drink. Hooray! I always found it easier to be social when I was a bit squiffy. I mustn't overdo it though; work tomorrow. Also, I didn't want Debbie and Paul thinking I was a sad old lush who couldn't control her drinking. Although chances were that Debbie had heard all about my performance at their office Christmas party the year before last. I'd got completely hammered with my friend, and we'd started to spin each other round on the dance floor. She'd let go, and I'd fallen off the edge of the dance floor, stumbled into the band and straight into the drum kit. The noise and carnage was unbelievable. My friend had tried to pull me up but was laughing too much, and had wet herself. Our husbands were absolutely mortified. Needless to say, partners were not invited to last year's do.

We eventually found Debbie and Paul's address after turning up a narrow country lane which we'd driven past twice and missed. It was a large detached property called "Oak Cottage", although it looked too new and modern to be classed as a cottage. Numerous lanterns lit up the driveway and I could see an enormous sparkling chandelier through the hallway window. Presumably the rest of Cheltenham was plunged into darkness each time they switched that on. Debbie answered the door. She was wearing a dark green velvet dress and black suede high heels. I immediately felt like a frump.

"Hi, you made it!"

She welcomed us inside, and we followed her clingy, snugly-fitted bottom into a rather grand hallway.

"Did you find us alright?"

"Oh yes, no problem," The Husband lied. He looked round the hallway. "Gosh, this is really nice."

"Thanks, we're making it our own, bit by bit," she trilled, spinning round with a swish of her shiny chestnut bob. "Come and meet Paul and Chloë."

Chloë? Oh, the daughter. I'd forgotten they had a kid. Surely she should be in bed by now; it was half past seven after all. Debbie led us into the sort of kitchen you only ever see on the adverts - very modern, with lots of chrome and shiny bits and with completely clear surfaces. Who has people round for dinner and keeps all their kitchen surfaces free from clutter? Paul, tall and well-built but with an ill-advised gingery-goatee-beard-effort was stood over a wok. He shook hands with The Husband and bent to kiss me on the cheek. *I'd never met him before, why couldn't I just shake hands too?* He smelt of fried onions and sweet, florally aftershave.

"You found us alright, then?" he asked. It must be their stock question to visitors.

"This is Chloë," Debbie announced proudly, holding out her hand towards the corner of the room. "Chloë, come and say hello."

A little girl, probably about 2 years old, came shyly over from where she'd set up her tea service. She was very pale, with a long nose and short blonde-white hair, which looked like it had been deliberately set in tight waves. This gave her the appearance of a 55 year old spinster, the sort that would wear a head scarf and bake sponge cakes for the WI. I suspected her first words had been: "Do have another scone Marjorie, they're absolutely super." I tried to converse with her, but I'm rubbish with kids and she just stared at me. I hoped she would go to bed soon, she was freaking me out.

The Husband inspected Paul's wine rack whilst I feigned an interest in Chloë, asking Debbie lots of questions about how old she was, what she enjoyed doing, what the schools were like round here and so on. Even though I'm good at faking, I'm increasingly isolated from people who have children. Their conversation always centres on their kids and I find it dreadfully dull. I sort of understood it though - parents were so competitive these days and the pressure on them to be perfect in every way and get everything right all the time must be all-consuming - no wonder it took over their lives. I'd once walked past a group of immaculately groomed mothers gathered at the gates of an infant school and I'd heard one of them saying; "Alicia's teacher says she is

the best in her class at paying attention." Another
immediately chipped in with "Well, Rosie's teacher says she is
the best at sitting up straight - in the whole school."

I was relieved not be a part of the mummy mafia - The
Husband and I had never wanted children. And thank God
we didn't. Guaranteed, our child would be the one that craps
in the swimming pool or shouts "Fuck it!" at play group.
We'd have been parental pariahs.

Chloë was still staring at me, so it was a huge relief when
Debbie took her up to bed. We sat down at a long oak table
in the open plan dining area of their kitchen. They had made
us a first course of a creamy cauliflower soup (which I
managed to dangle one end of my scarf in) and Paul opened a
bottle of white wine that was French and had a very posh
label. It was a bit acidic but he assured us it was a really good
one. He clearly fancied himself as a bit of a connoisseur, so I
asked him about his favourite wines while The Husband and
Debbie chatted about their work. I noticed that Debbie
sipped her soup very correctly from her spoon whilst The
Husband dunked great lumps of crusty bread into his, and
slurped them up. He used the crusts to mop up around his
bowl.

The main course was a creamy, stir-fried salmon pasta
dish, which Paul told us was his own recipe, influenced by his
trips to Asia. I had no idea which parts of Asia ate a lot of
creamy pasta, but still... He also produced some garlic bread,
which he said he'd made himself. Clearly he had time on his
hands. The acid from the wine helped cut through all the
cream, so I drank a great deal of it. Towards the end of the
pasta, I was beginning to run out of conversation with Paul.
Although "conversation" isn't strictly accurate - I'd found out

lots about him, but he hadn't asked me one single thing about myself. He'd talked about wine and his love of France, and although I told him I'd travelled extensively throughout France, he didn't show any interest in my experiences at all. He was in IT and regularly worked in Japan. I'd asked him as much about Japan as I could possibly think of, which wasn't much - mainly tsunamis, Geisha girls and with some desperation, Mr Miyagi. I'd now reached the hairdresser question of: "Going anywhere nice for your holidays this year?" and he'd launched into some long, tedious story about his luggage going missing last year when they'd gone to California. The Husband was still happily talking work with Debbie and wouldn't make eye contact with me. Why couldn't he be a bit more attentive to me, make sure I was ok? Debbie had, at one stage, asked jovially "Are you two okay down that end of the table?" and I'd nearly replied "No, I'm so bored I think my heart has stopped beating."

After three solid hours of asking Paul about himself, I'd had enough. I excused myself and went upstairs to find the loo. The bathroom was as pristine as the kitchen, floor-to-ceiling tiles all gleaming and spotless. They must have a cleaner - this level of shininess just wasn't natural. I almost felt too shabby to sit on their toilet and I wiped round the hand basin with a piece of tissue after I'd washed my hands, just in case I'd left any unseemly drops of water. As I exited the bathroom and turned out the light, I suddenly caught sight of a pale figure stood close by. I screamed in shock. The figure screamed out too. A child's scream. It was Chloë. Debbie, Paul and The Husband came racing up the stairs.

"What's happened?" exclaimed Debbie. Paul flicked on the landing light. Chloë was wailing very loudly, beside herself.

"Ooh, I'm sorry," I stammered, my heart still racing. "Chloë just gave me a bit of a fright."

"Jesus, Kate, what did you do to her?" hissed The Husband as we went back downstairs, leaving the parents to console their child, whose screams were now really quite deafening.

"Oh trust you to blame me!" I hissed back at him. "I came out of the loo and she was there, like something out of the bloody Omen."

"I suppose she is a bit of a freaky-looking kid," he conceded. We poured ourselves some more wine, and sat awkwardly at the table waiting for the screams to subside and for our hosts to reappear. It seemed to take an age.

"Perhaps we should go soon," I suggested, hopefully. "Shall I call a cab?"

"We haven't been here that long," said The Husband. *Bloody well long enough if you'd had to talk to Paul all night.*

We could hear Chloë had reached the hiccupping stage and Debbie returned.

"Paul's going to sit with her for a little bit," she told us, "just in case the poor little thing makes herself sick from all the upset."

Oh Christ, make me feel guilty, why don't you? The Husband shot me an accusing look. I hadn't meant to upset the kid! And what about me? I'd had a fright too. I'd a good mind to howl and make myself sick. It wasn't a bad idea; after all that cream they'd put in their cooking, they should supply a cholesterol testing kit when they entertained. Or at least have an ambulance on standby.

Debbie and The Husband went back to talking about

work. Tales of colleagues I'd never heard of had them
shrieking with laughter, along with stories of disastrous
appointments with customers that I didn't understand. I tried
to look sober and smile in what I thought were the right
places. I noticed we had got through nearly five bottles of
Paul's fine wine. We'd bought just the one with us - a
Chardonnay that I'd got on offer at the Co-op for £5.49. It
remained unopened on their side-board. Paul eventually
returned from the devil child, but didn't come back to the
table. He started on the clearing up.

The last part of the evening was a bit of a blur. I know
that liqueurs appeared at one stage, and we tried to make
floater coffees with Tia Maria and yet more cream. I vaguely
recall we were talking about our favourite movies and I'd said
mine was To Kill a Mockingbird. It's not, it's There's
Something About Mary. But I wasn't the only one trying to
impress. The Husband said his was Schindler's List, even
though he'd only ever watched the first ten minutes before
nodding off.

I think Paul went to bed before we left, and I don't
remember much about the cab ride home or what time we
got in. I crashed out, but for some reason woke up at 5.00
am, feeling rough but wide awake. The Red Bull must have
finally kicked in. I had to get The Husband up so he could
take me to get my car, which we'd left at Debbie and Paul's.
He growled and snarled at me, but eventually got out of bed.
We stood, fuzzy-headed, in the kitchen, as I tried to force a
piece a toast down, hoping it wasn't going to reappear. The
Husband looked grumpily round at our perfectly nice kitchen.

"Our house is shit isn't it?"

I knew he was comparing it to the splendour of Debbie

21

and Paul's. I said our house might not be as grand but at least it wasn't possessed by the spirit-child of Ann Widdecombe. That at least made him chuckle.

CHAPTER THREE

I arrived at work feeling extremely hungover and horriby conscious that I reeked of booze and probably should not have driven. I felt very sick, though I didn't know if that was caused by the effects of too much wine, or too much cream, or by fear of the impending audit. I tipped a pile of Tic-Tacs into my mouth as I walked into the building. I considered smiling at Stalin Stan but in the end I couldn't be bothered - no point wasting energy, I needed every ounce of strength today.

I didn't get the chance to tell my team about the audit as I had to undertake a colleague "Health Check" visit first thing in the morning. This is when a very poorly member of staff has a manager, to whom they've probably never spoken before, turn up at their home, question them about their condition and other deeply personal issues, whilst pretending to show concern for their well-being. All the manager really wants to know is: "When will you be back at work you shirker? You're making my absence figures look terrible."

Today I was going out to see a young lad, Lee Halfpenny. I was taking Hissing Cyn with me, as Lee's team manager, and she would be useful as a note-taker. His address wasn't in the nicest part of town, so I told The Snake we would have to take her car. She wasn't very happy about going.

"Wouldn't it be more appropriate for someone in HR to

handle these types of meetings?" she asked me, not unreasonably. "I mean, that's what they're trained for isn't it? We're not."

"They do provide us with support Cynthia," I reminded her. "They'll read our notes from the meeting and tell us what we did wrong."

"But why don't *they* come out and visit the colleague? Surely they're the ones with the expertise? I mean, they have to take a qualification in HR don't they - what's it called?"

"It's called "Difficult Colleagues and How to Avoid Them. Come on, let's go and get it over with."

I had a quick read of Lee's file whilst waiting for The Snake to come out of the ladies (I assume she was powdering her scales). Lee hadn't been with Perypils very long, and had been struggling with his performance. His attendance record was poor, and he had been signed off from work for the last four weeks with "anxiety". He still lived at home with his parents. I prayed he didn't have a skanky cat that would leave horrid clumps of fur on my suit, or a smelly dog that would try and hump my leg. Or the worst thing I'd ever come across when visiting a colleague in their home - a ferret.

The Snake began to inject me with her venom as soon as we got in the car.

"I shouldn't really tell you this," she began conspiratorially, "but Lee's recently put pictures of himself on Facebook, out on the town getting plastered. He's done this several times since he's been signed off." *Bloody Facebook.* "And there's something else..." Hissing Cyn looked like she was working up to something, I could see her coils constricting. "He also posted a comment on his Facebook wall that he hated it at work, and was looking for another job that wasn't - and these are his words of course - as dull as shit. And you'll never guess who said they liked that comment!" *No, I couldn't guess, there could be a cast of thousands.* "It was George," The Snake finished triumphantly. When I didn't react, she went on: "Well, I was shocked of course, you don't expect that from a team manager, do you?"

"No, you don't Cynthia," I agreed and added, "No more than you'd expect one team manager to drop another team manager in it."

She went on the defensive immediately.

"It wasn't me that saw it, one of my team showed it to me, they were all talking about it. I'm sure I can trust you not to tell him it was me that told you? I just thought you ought to know. As his manager." *Oh, you're too kind.* Still, The Lazy Shit was beginning to get on my nerves, I'd have to have a word with him.

We arrived at Lee's house, or to be correct, at his parent's house. I was pleasantly surprised to see that it looked quite nice; a very small but smart bungalow with a well-kept front garden. His mother answered the door; a thin, ratty-faced woman with strands of wispy brown hair framing her pointed face. She shepherded us inside and *oh God*, there was a large fluffy white cat sitting in the hall. I was wearing a navy suit - *just perfect.* We went into a tiny lounge where Lee was slouched on the sofa in front of the biggest television I had ever seen. It took up almost an entire wall. The coffee table had about six remote controls on it.

"Hello Lee," I said brightly, as The Snake and I shuffled around the coffee table to reach two armchairs on the other side of the room. I examined mine for cat hairs and it looked ok, but I still perched with my buttocks right on the edge, just in case. The cat had followed us in and was watching proceedings through its big yellow eyes.

"Turn the telly off, Lee," said his mother, as she went to make us some coffee. I could see she was trying to listen in through a gap in the kitchen hatch.

"Right, well," I began, watching the cat, which had jumped up onto the coffee table. "Thanks for seeing us today Lee. How are you doing?"

"Oh well, you know..." Lee sat up a little and pushed a floppy strand of hair away from his eyes. "Not great, really. Feeling very down, not really coping with everything."

"What are you struggling with in particular?" I asked, my face full of concern. The cat was headed for The Snake. *Watch it mate, she could easily swallow you whole.*

"Well, it's just everything really, you know?"

No I don't bloody well know that's why I'm asking! I tried again. "Your doctor has signed you off with anxiety. Can you tell me what's making you anxious?"

Lee rubbed his eyes. *Please try and stay awake, I have to.* "I'm not sleeping very well, and I feel quite tired a lot."

It was like pulling teeth. I gritted mine.

"Why aren't you sleeping?"

"I don't really know. I split up with my girlfriend a couple of weeks ago, so I've been a bit fed up about that, and I'm quite skint, so that's really worrying me."

"How long were you with your girlfriend?"

"Not sure really, about two months, on and off."

Serious stuff then.

"And you're struggling financially? Do you have debts that you can't pay?"

"No, I don't have debts as such, I just can't afford to go

out much."

"He lives here rent-free," interjected his mother who had appeared with our coffees.

"Go away, Mum," Lee said, quite rudely I thought. She went back to the other side of the hatch.

"And what support have you received from your doctor?"

Lee looked blank.

"What has your doctor suggested to help you?" I was doing my best not to laugh as next to me The Snake was trying to take notes while the cat had climbed into her lap. It kept sticking its bum in her face and swiping her across the nose with its large fluffy tail.

"He's not suggested anything," Lee replied.

"But he signed you off work for four weeks, Lee, with anxiety. Did he suggest you see a counsellor?"

"Nope."

"Has he prescribed anything for you - sleeping tablets, anti-depressants?"

"Nope." *No, he just wanted to get you out of his surgery and not have to see you again for another four weeks. Brilliant.*

"What have you been doing to manage your condition then? Good diet, exercise, been out in the fresh air?" I thought I heard a snort from behind the hatch.

Lee knew where I was headed with this line of questioning, he wasn't daft.

"I have been out in the evening sometimes. Friends have paid for my drinks," he added quickly, "and the doctor did say that I should try and do things that I enjoyed, so, you know, I wouldn't feel quite so depressed." He looked sadly at the floor. *Give that boy an Oscar.*

"Have you been thinking about returning to work?" I asked the six billion dollar question. "How do you feel about it?"

"I really want to get back to work," he said, still looking at the floor. *Not according to Facebook.* "I just feel so down though, it's really horrible."

The only horrible thing I could imagine in Lee's life of privilege was having a giant-sized Jeremy Kyle projected into the lounge from that enormous screen.

I picked up my coffee and turned to The Snake, who had managed to dispatch the cat and was busy scribbling away. She too picked up her coffee to take a sip, and as she did so, we both saw a flea jump into her mug. We looked at each other in horror. In sync, we both replaced our mugs on the coffee table. I scratched at my arm.

"Cynthia - when does Lee's pay run out, do you know?"

Hissing Cyn pretended to check her file. She scratched her leg. "Er, yes, here it is. Lee your pay will run out on Monday."

We looked at Lee.

"I'll be back on Monday" he said.

"But how will you be up to it?" I asked, sounding astonished, "You've just told us how terribly down you're still feeling - you really ought to check with your doctor first. You don't want to come back before you're ready to."

"I'll be back on Monday," Lee said, suddenly very firm and decisive. A thought struck him. "But I'll need re-training." He looked at The Snake. "I'll need a lot of support when I'm back, after all this time I've been away."

Hissing Cyn took a deep breath. I thought she was going to burst out with "but you've already been through the training twice, you little shit, and you're still completely useless. You've maxed out on your sick pay, you'll come back for a few weeks when we'll have to re-train you all over again, you'll still be useless and then you'll resign before we can sack you." But instead she said: "Yes of course Lee, we'll discuss that on Monday shall we? Sort something out for you."

We got up, me scratching my head and The Snake still scratching her leg. We called out a thank you to Mum and quickly left before she could see we hadn't touched our coffees.

Back at the office, I started to fret in earnest about the audit. I just didn't know how I was going to accommodate it right at the start of a new year, when there were already a million things to get done. The auditors were due to arrive next week - they purposely didn't give much notice as they didn't want to give you the chance to change/hide/delete or shred anything you didn't want them to see. There were also several members of staff that I really didn't want them to have any contact with. I referred to these (just to myself of course) as the Muppets, the calibre of staff you could rely on to say things like: "Oh hello, are you one of the auditors? Please do use my system if you want to, my secret personal password is Numpty, everyone knows it, and look, I've stuck it up on my screen so anyone can use my system and log in as me." Or "Are you one of the auditors? Hello. Yes, I always take our customers' personal information home with me. Is it secure? Oh yes, I keep it in my handbag, when it's not lying on the front seat of my car that is. I sometimes pass it on to a nice gentleman from Nigeria. That's ok isn't it?"

I wondered if I was allowed to insist on the Muppets taking compulsory holiday for the duration of the audit. It

was worth a try. Or perhaps I could lock them away in a
cupboard? There was a huge safe on the ground floor with a
very dodgy locking mechanism. I bet there was a whole team
of Muppets trapped in there from previous audits.

I needed to buy myself time - what excuse could I come
up with for getting the audit put back? Department hit by
bubonic plague? Staff abducted by aliens? I emailed Brett The
Boss to see if he could do anything about the date of the
audit. He emailed back:

Kate

*Just get on with it for christs sake. I've got enough on my plate
without pissing off the audit team.*

I'm here for support.

Brett.

Here for support? Where exactly? I'd not seen him in
months. With a feeling of doom, I rounded up my team
managers to break the news of the impending audit. Martin
the Drain was talking to someone on the phone. Presumably
his wife, as I heard him say: "I'm sorry about the
misunderstanding dear, but I always keep my Anusol cream in
the fridge."

I managed to herd them all round a table and did my
utmost to sell the audit as a real positive.

"It's an opportunity for us to show how good we are at
what we do and how great our people are." I thought they
might just see through that crock of shite. They did.

The Rock: "We'll need to shoot some people first."

The Snake: "The teams will wonder why we're being
inspected, there's bound to be speculation. Will they close us

down?"

The Drain: "I need to go to the toilet..."

The Climber: "Can I take the lead on the audit?"

TLS George: "Whilst we're all together, is it ok if I take some holiday next week?"

I said we had no reason to worry, which was quite a big lie, and then tried to get them organised. I asked them to make sure all their admin was up-to-date and reminded them of the need to be extremely vigilant during the audit. If they saw an auditor heading towards one of our lesser-skilled people *i.e. a Muppet*, they needed to step in and head them off. I also asked them to check all round their teams, on desks, in drawers, on the walls to make sure anything out-of-date or incriminating was removed. I was keen that we made a good first impression on our visitors, as that counts for a lot at Perypils. "You never get a second chance to make a first impression" was one of the company's strap lines. I translated this to my team as: "If you make it look nice and shiny on the surface no one will want to look any further. So make sure you sweep all your shit under the carpet."

We agreed that a departmental tidy-up would be a good idea. I told TLS George that one of his team, Scott, had an inappropriate photograph of a woman on his desk. Although she was impressively heavily tattooed, you could still see that she was naked apart from a tiny thong.

"But that's his mum!" *Oh dear God.*

I thanked The Climber for offering to take the lead, but told her that was my job. She pursed her lips together and crossed her arms, presumably unconvinced that I could do as good a job as her. I told TLS George that I couldn't let him take any holiday next week as I needed everyone's full support. He wasn't very happy but it was tough titties. Plus I wanted to put George in front of the auditors. He might not be the sharpest blade in the knife-block, but he excelled at bullshit. That's how he'd got a team manager's job in the first place. Bullshit was just what I needed right now.

I set them off into action. The rest of the week was exhausting; trying to fit in preparation for the audit whilst juggling the usual meetings and briefings, and being swamped by emails. I think everyone had been saving them up over the Christmas period and had now gone completely trigger happy. I was getting into the office at seven and leaving at seven, driving home like a mad woman so I could get some food on the table before The Husband complained. Yesterday, when I'd placed his supper in front of him - fish fingers and spaghetti hoops - he'd looked at it very sadly and said "You really have given up haven't you?"

He was going to the gym most evenings straight from the office, to work off his Christmas tummy, so I usually managed to get in just before him, nip into the kitchen, microwave a ready meal, and chuck it into the oven in a roasting dish. Serve it up with some fresh veg and it looked as if I had cooked it from scratch. I shoved the packaging to the bottom of the swing bin. Do other women fake it at mealtimes? Surely they must do. Even Nigella has a dish named "Slut's Spaghetti" because the recipe calls for a shameful amount of tin-opening. Or possibly it was because she tossed it with her breasts.

I began to worry about the amount of salt we were consuming through ready meals. I Googled "Signs that you're eating too much salt." The top five were:
- Irritability - yes definitely, The Husband was

beginning to show major signs of this.

- Confusion - possibly, I did put both feet through the same knicker leg this morning.
- Depression - well, if not now, certainly after the audit.
- Bloating - yes, I was well on my way to having four stomachs, like a cow.
- Excessive thirst - again yes, I drank a vodka and tonic in under two minutes last night.

Constantly at the back of my mind, buzzing around like a gnat, was the question The Husband had asked me over Christmas:

"Are you really happy? Don't you ever wonder if there's more to life than this?"

At the time, I'd swerved the question, laughing it off as a joke. He hadn't persisted, but I had been glued to the Wizard of Oz at the time, so he probably thought there was no point. In truth, his question had caught me by surprise; if someone asks you that sort of question, they're only asking it because that's how they feel themselves. Hopefully, he'd just come down with the Christmas Blues (after all, he wasn't a fan of the Wizard of Oz, he found the Munchkin Men disturbing) so perhaps it was just a blip and he was fine. But was he really?

I couldn't worry about that now. I just needed to get this bloody audit out of the way and then I'd give the matter my full attention.

CHAPTER FOUR

By the end of the week I was shattered, but beginning to feel more confident about the impending audit. The Chief Nark had sent through a list of the areas they wanted to focus on, and it was primarily sales. We were good at that. The Climber was chuffed - it meant they would be prioritising her team for attention. She was the only person in the world who would view that as a positive. But she craved attention, even if it was coming from power-crazed, jobsworth midgets.

As I was sat at my desk, trying to eat my lunch of three chocolate digestives and a skinny cappuccino, The Snake slithered her way over to me. I moved my cappuccino slightly closer to me, so her forked tongue didn't dangle in it.

"Kate," she said, looking all beady eyed, "it's not really my place to say this, but I just thought you ought to know, what with the audit next week and everything."

"What's that then, Cynthia?" I asked, annoyed as I'd over-dunked, and lost half a biscuit.

"Well, I'm not telling tales or anything," *No, not much,* "but it's George. I just happened to walk past his desk and glance down and, well, I couldn't believe what I saw!"

Oh God, what was it? Had he exposed himself? Surely he wasn't fiddling with himself at his desk, in work time?

"It's his drawers," the Snake continued, glancing over her shoulder to make sure no one could hear her snitching on a colleague. "They're in a complete mess. He's got reports and bits of paper stuffed away all over the place. And," she said, leaning in for the kill, "I saw customers' letters in there too. Some were dated several weeks ago."

You did have a good old look didn't you?

"You won't tell him I told you will you?" continued the Snake. "I'm only telling you because I thought you ought to know. You did say that the auditors might want to look in people's drawers. I'd hate for George to get into trouble. Well, get you into trouble." *Hmmmm.*

I thanked Hissing Cyn for her vigilance, finished my biscuit and went to have a look in George's drawers while he was at lunch. At first I thought he'd locked them, as I couldn't pull them open, but then I realised it was because they were completely crammed full of paper. *Oh my God.* Cyn hadn't been exaggerating. I sat at George's desk and pulled out all the bits of paper. A huge pile formed in front of me. I picked up one and read it. It was a letter from a customer, complaining about the amount of time Perypils was taking to resolve his complaint. It was dated three weeks ago. Quite possibly their original complaint was also in the pile somewhere, untouched. There was all sorts - print outs, holiday requests, reports, Toffee Crisp wrappers and -*what the hell?* A folder with 'Passwords' written on the front. Don't tell me he'd written his teams' passwords down? I couldn't bear to look in it.

How the hell had he let things get into this state? I picked up a couple of bits of paper, which contained a long email chain. It seemed to have involved a number of male colleagues from around the building voting on whether someone called Laura was "hot or not". The consensus seemed to be hot, except when she was wearing her "camel-toed jeans", whatever that meant. I don't know why George had printed it. But I could see from the number of times he'd contributed to the chain where his time was being spent. The audit team would have a field day if they came across this lot; what was he thinking?

The Lazy Shit returned from lunch and looked horrified to see me sat at his desk with his crap-mountain in front of me.

"I think we need to have a word George," I said, slapping my hand on the top of the pile, wishing it was his arse.

"I was just coming back to go through all that," he said quickly.

Liar liar pants on fire.

"Oh, were you really?" I said sarcastically. "I tell you what, take this pile into the meeting room - if you can carry it all that is - and I'll come and join you in just a minute." I wasn't going to bawl him out in front of his team. As it was, they were all watching and listening but pretending not to.

I went back to my desk to salvage the dregs of my coffee (full of sweet soggy biscuit, yuk) and watched George struggle towards the meeting room carrying his huge pile of paper. I noticed he'd balanced his iPhone on the top of it. What was it with men and their iPhones? They seemed to have become an extended part of their anatomy. I woke up the other morning with something hard poking me in the back. No, no such luck, it was just Camilla, who was in bed between us. I followed TLS George into the meeting room.

"I know it looks like a mess," he started, "but it's an organised mess! I know where everything is, I can always find what I need."

You couldn't find your arse if it sat on your face.

"It's not good enough George," I said. "I'm absolutely appalled by what I've found. Especially with a bloody audit starting on Monday. What on earth were you thinking? You've got correspondence from customers in here dating back weeks. Some are complaints, which have to be responded to within three working days. You know that."

"It doesn't mean they've not been responded to," said George, getting defensive. "It's just that I haven't got round to filing the letters away."

"George, don't you bloody bullshit me! You've got yourself in a total mess. And what's this folder that says 'Passwords' on it? Do you know what would happen to us if the auditors found out we'd been writing down passwords? No, don't try and feed me any more of your claptrap, I don't want to know. Just get shot of it prompto. How the hell have you let things get into this state? What's going wrong?"

"Nothing's going wrong. I just need to do some filing, that's all." He had his sulky face on. "I've been so busy doing other things, you know, coaching the team and stuff, it's difficult to find the time to do everything."

I brandished the "hot or not" email at him.

"Well you're finding time for this kind of childish crap," I snapped. "Look how many times you've responded in this email chain! You're making time for this at the expense of your other duties." He looked at it sullenly. "Not to mention the fact that its content is inappropriate, George. You are a team manager - that means you're part of the management team now. You shouldn't be encouraging this sort of stuff, it's totally unprofessional."

"What's going to happen to me?" he muttered, looking

37

down at the floor.

Well, good question, I should really report you to HR but I expect all they'll do is tell me that I have to be very, very angry with you.

I sighed. "Well, for starters you've got to sort this lot out. Today." He looked at me in horror.

"But I'm playing football at six…"

"I mean it George," I continued, "You're not leaving to kick a bloody ball around until it's all done. Sorted, filed, whatever. The audit team will be here on Monday so you need to get a move on. I'll send Martin in to help you. Give him any customer correspondence, his team can start on those. Any complaints you'll have to take round to Clare for her team to deal with, which is what you should have done with them in the first place."

He went white at the mention of Cruella.

"No, please don't send me to Clare! She'll murder me. Can't you speak to her?"

"No I can't!" *Because I'm shit-scared of her too.* "This is your mess George, you've got to take responsibility for it." I softened a little. It was Cruella after all. "You'll have to make up some excuse. Tell her a batch of letters went missing or something, and you've just discovered them. You'll think of something." *You're good at telling fibs.*

As I left the room, I scooped up his iPhone. "I'll take this George, just so you don't get distracted." He looked about to protest, but saw my face and thought better of it. I went to find Martin The Drain. I felt very disappointed in myself for wanting to know if I was considered hot or not amongst the Perypils male colleague population. I really shouldn't care about things like that. Karren Brady from The Apprentice wouldn't care about things like that, she would

38

consider it beneath her. I'd read an article on her the other day. What a woman. I must try and be more like her - well groomed, calm, businesslike. She had two young kids as well, how did she manage everything? It was a shame about her football obsession though. Still, nobody's completely perfect. But I wanted to be hot though, I couldn't help it. Was 42 too old to have one last shot at babedom? Surely not. Damn, why had I just eaten three chocolate biscuits? My waist band was digging into me. I went for a quick stride around the building to burn off the calories and the rage. *Really must try harder.*

The Weekend

I spent Saturday on the sofa with my laptop, deleting and forwarding my way through work emails. The Husband was out for the day - gym in the morning, golf course in the afternoon. He couldn't understand why, with all the exercise he was doing, he wasn't losing any weight. I muttered something inane about metabolism and kept my head down. How many calories were in those ready meals? Bloody thousands probably. Just how many had I consumed over the last few weeks? It was frightening to think about it. Everything I put on now felt tight and uncomfortable. I disgusted myself. Eat fewer calories and take more (some) exercise, that's all I had to do. I could do it; it just required determination and some self-control. I would start tomorrow. I would transform myself over the next few weeks into a honed, slim-waisted, glossy-haired goddess, full of boundless energy. I must start a list, or perhaps make a pledge to myself. That sounded more dynamic than making a list. Yes, I would make a pledge today in preparation, and start the new regime tomorrow.

I typed the pledge onto a word document:

- I will eat less: biscuits, chocolate, cheese, bread, crisps, ice cream, potatoes, pop tarts. I will stick to the recommended 1200 calories per day.
- I will drink less alcohol - I will stick to the recommended 14 units per week. (Must keep count.)
- I will eat more: lean white meat (chicken & turkey without the skin), peppers, leafy greens and pulses (full of iron for energy), oily fish and super fruits. Note - need to find out what these are. I will eat the recommended five portions of fruit and veg per day.
- I will purchase a pedometer and walk the recommended 10,000 steps per day.
- I typed "I will drink less coffee" but then deleted it. There had to be something left to live for.

I walked very briskly to the shop (counted steps - 612 one way) to buy a paper. Gorgeous women beamed out at me from the fronts of the magazines. Twiggy, LuLu, Lorraine Kelly - they looked amazing, so radiant. I was younger than them but they looked so much better than I did, it couldn't all be down to air brushing, could it? It's possible they had had expensive surgery but none of them had that startled-cat-that's-just-been-kicked-up-the-arse look about them. I had to make more of an effort to look like they did. But my morning "beauty" routine already took a considerable amount of time to perform, and a staggering array of products. I used to get away with a quick flick of mascara and a smear of lip gloss but now my routine went: cleanser, miracle skin perfector tinted moisturiser, balanced tone foundation, radiant touch Touche Éclat, t-zone shine control pore minimiser, bronzer,

blusher, cheek-bone illuminator, more bronzer. And that's
before the eye make-up, and lip liner plus lip stick, not to
mention the agonies of the eye lash curler. The whole routine
took longer and longer. If I applied any more products to my
face my knees would buckle under the weight. The Husband
just makes do with soap and water in the morning, a quick
splash and dash. Still, at least I don't have to shave every day
like he does. Not yet, anyway.

Monday morning - the day of the audit.

I arrived at work at 7.00 am after a poor night's sleep,
dressed in my best charcoal-grey power suit. I didn't know
what time the auditors would arrive and I felt very jumpy. I
couldn't settle into any real work. Martin The Drain phoned
in sick at eight thirty. He said he "literally couldn't get off the
toilet", so I terminated the call very quickly for fear of hearing
something I didn't want to. *Trust him to let me down.* I made
TLS George show me his drawers, so to speak, which were
now empty. The Snake looked a little disappointed that he'd
managed to get everything sorted away in time, although
apparently Clare had gone off the deep end when George had
presented her with a stack of out-of-date customer
complaints. He'd told her they'd been "lost in the post room"
and she'd gone storming down there to have it out with the
poor unfortunate post manager, who of course didn't know
anything about it. He was so scared of Cruella he'd apparently
just cowered in the corner, stammering "Please don't hurt
me". I didn't feel good about the wrong person getting the
blame, but I couldn't cope with Cruella's wrath just at the
moment. Lucky us to work in such a no-blame culture! At
least, that's what it says on one of the Perypils posters in the

corridor.

At nine o'clock I was watching the doors anxiously, waiting for the team to descend. My palms felt sweaty. The Rock came over to my desk, looking nervous. "What's up Jan?" I asked.

"Um, well, it's Danny and Ben. They had a bit of a late night last night, well I think it was probably an all day session, they had some friends round. Anyway, when they woke up this morning they found that their friends had drawn big moustaches on them in marker pen. They can't get it off." *Oh for God's sake.* I went to take a look at the two lads. They were both on calls, but I could clearly see great big handle-bar moustaches drawn onto their faces. They looked absolutely ridiculous. Any other day I might have chuckled, but not today.

"Jesus Christ, Jan," I hissed, "What did I say about first impressions? The first people the auditors are going to see when they walk in here is the bloody Bandito brothers! Get them off the phones and into the toilets. They've got to scrub that off."

"They've already tried, it won't come off."

"Then I suggest you fetch a scouring pad from the canteen and try that. If not, go to B&Q for some sandpaper. Just get it off. *Now!*"

The Rock hurried off and disappeared with the lads for some time. When they returned, both Danny and Ben's faces were scrubbed red raw. The moustaches were still visible, but much fainter. The Rock moved them to the back of the team and instructed them to keep their heads down. They sheepishly obeyed.

"Amazing what a bit of vinegar and a cheese grater will

do," she murmured as she walked past me.

The audit team arrived at nine thirty. They strolled into the department, four men of below-average build, but inflated by their own self-importance, armed with expensive-looking laptop bags and wearing smart suits and smug smiles. They came over to my desk to introduce themselves. Their leader, Chief Nark, looked the oldest at about forty five; small, with big ears and wide set eyes. I was put in mind of Gizmo from the Gremlins. He shook my hand and I told him a bit about the department. Whilst I was talking, he took out his iPhone and started to read a text message. *You rude bastard.*

"Oh I'm sorry, do you have something urgent to attend to?"

He said "Oh no, no", but carried on fiddling with his phone, anyway. The others were only half-listening to me; they were nodding politely, but their eyes were darting all round the department. Had I become invisible? I showed them around and introduced them to the others. They became distinctly more animated when I introduced them to The Climber. She was dressed in a short, black pencil skirt, high heels and a tight, stretchy black top. She seemed to have jacked up her wonder-bra to maximum velocity. Suddenly they were making jokes, taking the mickey out of each other, and giggling like school boys looking at rude pictures of ladies' naughty bits. They seemed delighted that The Climber looked after the sales team, and Gizmo told her that she would be their particular area of interest. They all bellowed, and she laughed her annoying laugh and tossed her hair at them. *Oh God.* I showed them to a small bank of desks which was to be their home for the week and they started to set up their laptops. Gizmo said he'd come and speak to me about the audit a bit later in the day.

I attempted to carry on my day-to-day duties as normal, but it was impossible to concentrate while keeping one eye on what the audit team were up to. However, for the best part of the day, they remained sat at their desks behind their laptops. How were they able to undertake an audit of a department without actually getting off their arses? I had to leave the department for a while in the afternoon to attend a meeting on Perypils' new cost-cutting strategies. At the meeting we were told not to: print anything in colour, travel anywhere, agree overtime, order stationery or purchase any kind of staff incentives. I asked what I should do if I ran out of paper clips, and was told I had to approach the other teams on site to see if they had any. I asked what happened if they didn't. Apparently I'd have to ask around all the other sites to see if they could send me some. There was a long discussion on holding a paper-clip amnesty. I wanted to kill myself.

When I got back to the department, the four auditors had moved from their desks and were all sat around The Climber. I hurried over to see what was being discussed. As I approached, I could hear her telling them about all the best places to go for a night out in Cheltenham. They appeared to be hanging on her every word. When I asked brightly if everything was ok, they said "Yes fine" and waited for me to go away before they carried on with their conversation. I hoped she wasn't getting too pally with them; they weren't here to make friends.

I sat at my desk and started to clear down some emails. I realised I was feeling deflated because of the lack of interest the audit team had taken in me. It occurred to me that it used to be me that turned heads when I was introduced to male colleagues. It was me that made them silly and jokey and giggly. How annoying I must have been to other women. Now, the guys had scarcely looked at me, I held no interest for them. When had that changed? When I hit forty, or before that, when I was in my late thirties? Or sooner? I remembered back to one of my first jobs as a supervisor at Waitrose. I was about nineteen, and there was a woman I had to work with who hated me. I couldn't work out why. She'd been around forty I reckoned, unmarried, no kids. I'd gone in one morning and announced my engagement (disaster, estate agent, need I say more) and she'd practically snarled in my face, refusing to speak to me for weeks. Jealous, probably. I'd reacted in a mature, positive way - by gobbing in her coffee. Had I now become like her - that bitter, dried up woman, unable to handle a flirtatious, carefree younger version? Worse still - did The Climber gob in my coffee?

The day became the evening. Gizmo hadn't been to see me like he'd said he would. The audit team were still all prodding away at their lap tops at seven o'clock, The Climber having long gone. I didn't want to leave the department before they did, just in case they started to poke around, or plant something to fit me up, but I really needed to get home so I could fake another meal before The Husband got in and heard the giveaway 'ping'. I was about to give up and make tracks when I saw them begin to pack up. *At last.* They were all staying at a hotel in town for the week. I thought they would come and say goodnight to me, perhaps give me a quick update on what they'd looked at today (apart from The Climber's cleavage) but as I looked up at them with a smile, they all walked past my desk, talking amongst themselves and left without even acknowledging me. I looked down at myself. Was I still here? I still existed didn't I? Ok, I was wearing grey - Manchester United once lost very badly when they'd played in a grey strip because they said they couldn't see each other properly. Was that what had just happened to me? I couldn't think of any other reason why someone would walk right past you and not say "goodnight". Unless that someone was a rude, ignorant tosspot of course.

I drove home feeling very down. I had to face it, I didn't turn heads anymore. Why did it matter so much to me? I was married, I didn't want to have an affair or anything like that. I just wanted men to find me attractive. *But why? Why?* What did it matter? Was it something from my childhood, did I have some deep seated need to be desired? I had been a bit of a late starter with boys when compared to my friends, but once I'd discovered Rimmel and contact lenses there had been no stopping me. I sighed. No point trying to self-analyse, I'd drive myself round the twist. The Husband's car wasn't in the drive, he must still be at the gym. Great: I had time to swing into action in the kitchen and fake another nutritious meal.

CHAPTER FIVE

The seemingly longest week ever limped on. The auditors spent the vast majority of their time either at their desks or huddled in the meeting room. One of them would occasionally appear to ask some questions or obtain some data. With the exception of The Climber and her sales team, they hardly spoke to any of the other staff or spent any time in the teams. On Thursday morning, they'd all arrived late, and looked suspiciously like they were suffering from hangovers. The Climber was also late and she too looked the worse for wear. *Had she been out on the town with them?* I'd spoken to her earlier in the week about not getting too close to them, but she'd laughed and said she was just "making sure we get a fantastic report". *Hmmm.*

The Snake slid over to my desk. "Kate," she said, glancing around, "I shouldn't really tell you this, but I thought you ought to know." *What now?* "It's not me gossiping you understand, but there has been talk in the teams about Amanda and what she's been saying to the auditors."

She fixed me with her snaky stare. I wasn't sure if she actually had any eyelids; she never blinked. "The team have heard her slagging you off to them," she said, "they've heard her doing it a lot. Well, it's not very loyal of her, is it? It's not very nice. You are her manager, and she's saying horrid things about you. I'm only telling you because I thought you ought to know."

"What sort of things have they heard?" I asked, suddenly feeling very sick.

"Well, apparently things like she doesn't think you're up to the job, and that you never show her any support for her own development. She said she doesn't think she can learn anything from you. She said it to that small guy, the older one."

I looked at The Snake with dislike.

"Have you actually heard her say anything yourself?"

"No, but..."

"Then why are you telling me this, Cynthia? Why haven't you addressed it directly with Amanda? It might not be true."

She recoiled.

"I just thought you should know what's being said in the department. It's not my place to say anything to her, you're her manager."

"Well, I don't agree. You're a team manager, you should know better. The next time you hear gossip that causes you concern, you should speak to that person. They should have the opportunity to say if it's true or not. You know that most office gossip turns out to be just that – gossip."

I waved her away and she slithered off in a huff. I thought about what she'd said, unsure what I should do about it. It wouldn't have surprised me if The Climber had been attempting to undermine me when she had such an attentive audience. It was too good an opportunity for her to miss, desperate as she was to seize my job. Was I worried? I tried to tell myself I wasn't, but I was. *Very*. Would they take note of what she said and write something derogatory about me in their report? Everyone would see it, including the Boss and the Big Cheese - I'd be finished. I didn't know what to do; I'd look ridiculous if I raised it with them and it turned out not be true. Oh hell, I'd just have to wait for the report.

Friday eventually arrived - the last day of the audit. The number of supportive texts, messages, emails, and phone calls I'd received from The Boss totalled zero. I thought he might at least have wanted to know how things were going. Only two of the audit team showed up on the last day. The other two were stuck in their hotel suffering from what sounded like food poisoning.

"Did they eat in the canteen yesterday?" I asked, innocently. Turns out they had. *Oh dear.* You should never eat in the canteen on a Thursday, not on chicken curry day. Monday was roast chicken day, so by Thursday it was best to avoid any dish with chicken in it, as it would have probably appeared in many different guises throughout the week. Perhaps I should have warned them.

The Drain returned from sick leave, a day before he required a doctor's certificate. He looked worried to see that the auditors were still around, I think he thought they would have gone by now. I took him into the meeting room for his "Welcome Back" interview. I hated doing these. Perypils HR insisted all its colleagues had a Welcome Back meeting following a period of absence. I was obliged to enquire about the illness, the symptoms, what medication had been taken or what treatment had been received, as if I were medically trained, which I most definitely am not. Plus, I'm terribly squeamish. I can't bear hearing about other people's ailments and it was often all I could do not to physically gag in front of them.

I started with the first section on the Welcome Back

form. "Reason for absence?"

"I've been suffering from the most dreadful stomach cramps, persistent diarrhoea and feeling very anxious in general."

Explore causes of absence. "What do you think is making you feel anxious?" I braced myself.

"Well, lots of things really." *Here we go.* "The thought of the audit in particular - I'm worried I'll get picked on for doing something wrong. And at home, my wife's mood is very unpredictable; she's really becoming quite erratic. Just this morning I found her sobbing into a bowl of Sugar Puffs, and all I asked her was if she'd used the last of the semi-skimmed and she flung her spoon at my head. Scared the dog half to death, and he's only just beginning to recover from Great-Auntie Jean's visit. He's still got dreadful wind. All this stress has made my irritable bowel flare up again."

Discuss and record treatment and/or medication. "What support are you getting from your doctor to help you manage your condition?"

He sniffed. "My doctor isn't being overly helpful. I went to see him and as I walked in he said "Oh Christ no, not you again" and swallowed a handful of pills."

"Do you think it might be a good idea to change doctors?"

"I've already changed doctors several times. There aren't any left at that surgery."

Agree any changes to working practices. "Do you need any support from me Martin?"

"I'll need some time off to go to the dentist now."

"The dentist? Why?"

"My diarrhoea was so bad that I broke a tooth biting

down on the towel rail."

I was glad to get out of the meeting room and away from The Drain's horrid bottom problems. I went to the canteen to recover with a cup of coffee. The Climber was in there with Gizmo, sat with their heads together at one of the tables. It looked as if their hands might have been touching, but they quickly sat up straight and looked round at me rather guiltily as I went over to them. *Jesus - surely she wasn't bonking him!*

"Oh, hi Kate," the Climber said airily, "We were just talking through the audit and how it's all gone this week. I think it's all been good, wouldn't you say so Gary?" She laughed her annoying laugh and the Gizmo smiled, showing his small, pointed teeth. He looked half-gonk half-wolf. A wolf-gonk. A wonk.

"Well, if you don't mind, Gary, I'd rather you discussed the results of the audit with me first," I said, forcing a smile to try and take the sting out of my words. "I think that's the usual protocol isn't it, to talk to the department manager? Perhaps you could come and see me before you leave today."

"Yes, oh yes of course," he said, looking a little uncomfortable, "I'll come and see you shortly." I took my enormous and over-priced cappuccino back to my desk and stirred it thoughtfully. What had they been talking about? What had The Climber been saying? I couldn't be certain that they had been holding hands, but she was obviously on very familiar terms with him - had she forgotten he was a senior auditor? They weren't the sort of people you should be familiar with. She really was becoming a bit of a loose cannon.

Gary the Gizmo came over to see me later in the afternoon.

"I haven't seen much of you this week," he said with his wolfish sneer-smile.

"No, you haven't," I replied. "But my team seem to have kept you fully occupied." He looked at me sharply, trying to glean whether I was insinuating anything, but I smiled innocently back at him.

"Well," he continued, "it's been a good week, apart from the food poisoning of course, and I'd like to thank you for everyone's co-operation - your teams have been refreshingly open and honest."

Oh shit.

"That's good to hear," I lied, trying to keep smiling. "So, er, what do you think your report is going to look like?"

He showed me his teeth again.

"We did spot a few minor transgressions in the sales reporting, but nothing too significant. I'll send you a draft copy of my report so you can have a look at the detail before it goes out to a wider audience."

That was it! I breathed a huge sigh of relief. A few 'minor transgressions' I could cope with. Hooray, we'd survived the ordeal unscathed! We shook hands and he left the building with his depleted team. I watched them out of the window to make sure they really had gone, then went to buy cakes for the department to say a big thank you. I remembered, too late, that I wouldn't be able to claim these back on expenses now because of the new cost-cutting measures. Oh well, it didn't matter, I was celebrating. I emailed The Boss and told him the audit had finished and I was expecting a good report. I thought he would reply "Audit? What audit?" but instead he emailed back "Very well done to you and your teams!". I felt quite weepy - I couldn't remember the last time anyone had said well done to me.

The Climber came over to my desk. She flicked her hair at me and examined her nails, trying to look nonchalant. "Did Gary say anything about me at all?" she asked.

"Like what?"

"Well, all the help I gave him and his team, I just thought he would have mentioned it, that's all."

"No, I'm afraid he didn't."

She pouted. "Perhaps he'll put it in his report then. I should have some recognition after everything I did to help, which was much more than, well...," *Than me?* "...than others did. Some of the audit team actually thought I was the manager of the department! Imagine that!" She laughed her fake laugh and I could see right down her throat. I wondered if my fist would fit all the way down it. "Are you going to tell Brett how much support I gave to this audit?"

I considered her for a moment. She was clearly trying to take the credit for a successful audit report, and no doubt attempt to undermine me at the same time. *Well, do your worst.*

"Why don't you email him yourself Amanda?" I suggested. "It would look so much better coming from you directly. Tell him what you did, your involvement, and copy in Giz, er sorry, I mean Gary, so he can add his own comments if he wants to recognise you."

She seemed happy with this and went off to compose her email. Would Brett The Boss take any notice of her? He rarely took any notice of me, why should he take any notice of her? It was nagging at me though, like an annoying fly that wouldn't go away. Then you realise too late that it's one of those horrible horse flies and it's bitten you on the arse.

Sunday

It was my brother Stuart's 39th birthday. Funny how when we were kids I would always crow over him as I was three years older. That changed when, well, when was it? Probably during my mid twenties when I'd realised I was free-falling towards thirty, and he'd introduce me to his friends as his 'OAP Sis'. I'd found turning forty quite traumatic. I kept reading in magazines that forty was the new twenty, but that was only ever written by women who were well into their fifties. I knew I could no longer consider myself youthful, I was showing some tell-tale signs after all:

- Looking at clothes that are sold in garden centres and thinking "Ooh, that looks really comfy."
- Frequenting garden centres.
- Rushing home so as not to miss the start of Columbo.
- Making old-people groaning noises when standing up and sitting down.
- Saying things such as "That would never have happened in my day...."
- Or "That's just what the doctor ordered" when sipping a cup of tea.
- Never heard of any of the Brit Award winners.
- Obsessed with regular bowel movements.

We were due to meet my brother for a Sunday pub lunch. He'd phoned the night before to check we were still ok for it. I'd asked him, with some nervousness, if his girlfriend (Bunny Boiler) would be there too? You never knew, they were always on and off and I couldn't remember what the current situation was. He replied rather indignantly that of course she would be there and so would Georgia, her teenage daughter. I'd only met Georgia once before, as she lived with her father. It had been a brief meeting. She was supposed to come out to a restaurant with us, but had appeared wearing a yellow tracksuit with three quarter length bottoms and heelies. Her mother had yelled at her, she'd yelled at her mother and that was that. She'd stormed back into the house and we went without her. I can't say I was all that keen to see her again.

We met at a very nice country pub which was close to my brother's house and did great Sunday roasts. We were the last to get there as The Husband had been fussing over his big toe which he thought he might have broken. He'd gone into the bedroom last night, turned on the light but forgotten that it now had an energy saving light bulb, and had walked into the bed frame when the light hadn't come on in time. *Oh, the language.* I've never heard anything like it. We then went through the ministry of silly walks, followed by girly screeching when I tried to put a bag of frozen peas on it, and finally a dying-swan-on-the-sofa performance. I eventually ran out of patience when it continued this morning, snapping "Can you move it? Yes? Well it's not broken then, is it?" He was of course now sulking, and we hadn't spoken on the drive down.

The others were seated at a long table in the cosy dining area of the pub. My parents were facing each other at one end of the table, and my brother and the Bunny Boiler were next to each other in the middle, their glasses already almost empty. Georgia was sat at the far end, her face in her iPhone. We all did the flurry of "Sorry we're late's, great to see you's, happy birthday's, mwah, mwah". I quickly sat down opposite my brother and the Bunny Boiler, leaving The Husband having to sit opposite Georgia. Serve him right - they could be sulky together.

We all ordered roasts. I really wanted the lamb but went for the chicken, trying to be good. Everyone knows that lamb is 100% pure fat. The Husband ordered the lamb and, I noticed, a huge glass of red wine; obviously making the most of his non-driving toe. My parents seemed to be on good form, although my father was not at all happy that his next door neighbours had erected a twelve foot high dovecote "They'll be flapping and shitting all over the place." I assumed he meant the doves and not the neighbours. I think my mother may have misunderstood the conversation, as she said

"They'll be after our rhubarb too won't they Frank?" I wondered if her hearing was going.

My brother made us laugh about some of the antics on his latest building job, an extension for a predatory middle-aged woman. She had taken a fancy to one of the younger builders, and had been terrifying the poor lad, following him around, backing him into corners and had even left a pair of lacy knickers in his wheel-barrow. Stu had managed to keep himself employed on general building jobs since he had left school. We all had a laugh at his expense about his next birthday being his 40th, jokes about comb-overs and M&S cardies. I kept very quiet about the fact that I was actually wearing an M&S cardy.

I recalled my 40th birthday, when, with much flourish, The Husband had presented me with an exercise bike. I'd looked at it in much the same way as I'd looked at the painting-by-numbers set my parents had once given me when I'd wanted a pony. It was my own fault, in a way, as I had not given The Husband enough clues on what to get me, just saying I wanted "a surprise". I thought every man knew that this meant something gold and sparkly. When tactfully questioning him on his choice of gift, it appeared I had apparently stated during a booze-filled evening at the pub that I really wanted to take up some form of exercise. I always talk crap when I'm drunk. They should use this as an example when giving out warnings on drinking too much. On the morning of my 40th, The Husband had got up and gone out very early. I'd thought perhaps he'd gone to collect a bouquet of flowers from the florist in the village, or to fetch fresh croissants and cappuccinos for my birthday breakfast. But no. It was to get me a card. As he only went as far as the local Londis, the choice was very limited. The card was a picture of a startled basset hound with its ears being blown around in the wind. In it he'd written:

"Hope your flaps don't do this now that you're 40!"

The Bunny Boiler, well into her second (or possibly third?) large glass of red wine had started on her favourite subject - her ex-husband. The "arse-hole" had "landed them" with Georgia for the weekend as he was taking his "tarty piece" away somewhere. Apparently, he'd never done anything nice for her when they'd been together, never taken her away anywhere, he'd treated her like a piece of crap. One of her eyes seemed to stare in a different direction to the other eye when she got worked up.

My brother patted her hand consolingly, and whispered something in her ear. She nodded, and he got up to go to the bar. *Yep, that's just what she needs, more booze.* The Husband appeared to be getting on amazingly well with Georgia. They both had their iPhones out and were comparing apps. She appeared quite animated as did he. Obviously a meeting of minds.

My brother returned carrying a bottle of sparkling wine. There was a young waitress behind him who had a tray with six champagne glasses. Stu cleared his throat. "Kirsty and I have an announcement to make," he said grandly. The Bunny Boiler giggled. *What was all this?* "Yesterday I asked Kirsty to marry me, and-" dramatic pause as he looked round the table, "I'm really pleased to tell you that she said yes!"

There was a brief stunned silence. I imagine the same thoughts flew through everyone's minds during that silence: "But you're always splitting up, you never stay together for more than five minutes; will a wedding actually happen? Is it worth me buying a new outfit? I think I'll leave getting the present to the last minute..." until we all recovered ourselves and expressed our congratulations and made noises of surprised delight. My father, ever practical, wanted to know "How the bloody hell are you going to pay for it?" but Stu was busy pouring out the sparkling wine and pretended not to hear. He said something cheeky to the young waitress who blushed and giggled - luckily for him this went unnoticed by the Bunny Boiler.

We managed to sneak a little of the sparkling wine into an empty glass for Georgia, who according to her mother, was really excited about being a bridesmaid. I caught Georgia's eye. She didn't look excited. She'd probably been told she wouldn't be able wear her yellow track suit. We raised our glasses to all chink in the middle of the table, and shouted "Congratulations!" apart from my mother who said "Happy birthday". I asked the happy couple if they had a date in mind, and Stu said probably the summer. *This summer?*

Surely everywhere would be booked already? I couldn't get any more sense out of the pair of them as they had gone all soppy and were kissing and giggling. The Bunny Boiler called him crazy, and he replied "Just crazy about you", making me fear my roast chicken would reappear. When he started rubbing her thigh under the table I quickly got up to order some coffees.

The Husband was in a far better mood for the drive home, his toe troubles seemingly forgotten. Probably numbed by the vat of red wine he had got through. He talked me through the new iPhone apps Georgia had shown him in tedious detail, being particularly taken with one called Talking Carl. This was a character who looked a bit like SpongeBob and repeated back whatever you said. The Husband said "Tit bum tit bum" into his phone and Talking Carl repeated it in a Joe Pasquale voice. I felt quite irritated and snapped "For God's sake, what are you, eight years old and giggling over rude words and silly voices?" He tried to get me to speak into Carl while I was driving, and I eventually caved in and said: "My husband's name is needle-dick the second." I did have to admit it was quite funny hearing it back. We ended up singing "You'll Never Walk Alone" into it and howling with laughter. I realised with a twinge of guilt that I couldn't recall the last time we'd had a really good laugh together; we used to laugh all the time. I really must try to be more spontaneous and fun. I must make an effort.

CHAPTER SIX

It took well over a week for the audit report to drop into my inbox. What on earth did the audit team do with all their time? There were four of them, how could it possibly take so long to knock up a draft report? As it was, the day had already started very badly as I'd arrived at the office and noticed, with dismay, that I had a "colleague coffee morning" scheduled. If only it were the kind held at local community centres up and down the country, where you turn up for your cup of coffee, a piece of homemade cake, and a nice chat about the weather and your dodgy hip. Not so. Perypils encouraged (forced) its managers to hold these sessions with a selection of colleagues once a month, so they could raise and discuss any issues or concerns in an open forum. It was always the negs and dregs that turned up for a general whinge; they never ever wanted to ask anything interesting or insightful. It was just a complete waste of an hour.

I entered the meeting room and, true to form, looking back at me were about fifteen of the department's finest loudmouths. The first question was always the same: "So when is Brett coming down?" I sighed inwardly and stirred my coffee very deliberately, looking into the brown ripples as if the answer might be found in there. If I could dive into my coffee cup and emerge somewhere else, a bit like Mr Benn, where would I want to be? Venice, I decided, on a gondola, wrapped in beautiful cashmere blankets, being serenaded by a gorgeous Italian and floating past the Rialto Bridge. Brett would be stood on the bridge ordering me to get back to work and I would raise two fingers up at him as I passed underneath.

Back to reality. When would Brett the Boss make an appearance? I really didn't know, so, as usual, attempted diplomacy.

"Well, I know he hasn't been able to get here in a while, however he does have several sites to manage and he needs to be in the ones where his support is needed most."

The question-raiser, Kathy (well-built, cropped hair, very scary) wasn't satisfied.

"But it's been months since he was here," *at least four I reckon,* "it feels as if he doesn't care about his teams on this site." *He doesn't.* "There's a lot of bad feeling about it from the staff, everyone thinks he favours the other sites over us." General nods and murmurs of approval. *Oh grow up.*

"There's a lot going on, Kathy," I said, fixing her with one of my firmest stares. "The fact that he considers he doesn't need to be here very much is a great credit to our site. It means he trusts us to get on with things," *pause for dramatic effect,* "without moaning and complaining." *Surely they wouldn't swallow that shite? They seemed to!* "Next question," I said brightly. They were:

"Are we closing?" *Always gets asked. Always truthfully reply "not to my knowledge".*

"Why is this building so cold?" *Guess what they ask in the summer!*

"Can the smoking section outside be made any bigger?" *Don't know, don't care, it's a disgusting habit, why don't you give up? It would improve your attendance and you wouldn't smell so bad.*

"Why aren't there enough parking spaces for everyone?" *There never have been, why are you still asking this after 22 years? There's plenty of parking elsewhere, you just have to walk a bit further you lazy gits.*

"Why doesn't Perypils sponsor the Kingfisher roundabout any more?" *Doesn't it? Hadn't noticed. Reducing costs probably.*

"So does that mean we're closing?" *Same answer as five minutes ago.*

"When will the windows be cleaned?" *Why would you ask me that! I'm not in charge of the cleaning! All the windows are covered in blinds anyway, what difference does it make?*

"Can the canteen make more soup? By the time the late shift gets there it's all gone." *Well go and ask the bloody canteen then!*

"There's been a dead pigeon lying in the car park for six days, when will it be removed?" *Lucky thing. I might go and join it.*

I sloped wearily back to my desk when the hour was up. Emails were piling in and I saw that the audit report was amongst them. *About time.* I opened it up. The front of the document had the word "Draft" stamped right across it. It was also headed up: Code Red. That must be a typo. You only coded a report red if there was something seriously wrong. I read the first page. *Oh Jesus.* There was something seriously wrong. The report stated that the audit team had identified an SBI in my department. That stood for "Serious Business Impact", but you may just as well translate it as "Severe Bollocking Imminent" because of the excitement they caused - and not the good kind of excitement.

With a feeling of dread, I read on. The team had apparently come across serious discrepancies in the way sales cases were being recorded on the team's database. Some of The Climber's team had told them that they often "made things up" if they couldn't find the exact information required. *Oh Jesus Christ.* The report stated that this breached the financial regulations for the recording of insurance sales and distorted the official Perypils' sales data. The report also said that the team manager, The Climber, had an extremely poor understanding of the sales process and was not close enough to her team or its methods. The report also referred to "self-inflicted poor communication" between the team manager and the department manager as being a contributing factor to the SBI.

It was a disaster. I felt sick and cold and shaky. That evil little shit Gizmo, telling me there were a few "minor transgressions" and then sending this bombshell through. I'd told everyone the report would be good, that the audit had gone well. I'd spent £33.40 on cakes to celebrate, for Christ's sake! What a tit I looked now. I picked up the phone and dialled Gizmo's mobile number. I was going to have it out with him. It went to voicemail, so I left him a message saying I was extremely disappointed to have received this report, felt that he'd misled me and asked him to call me urgently. I left a message for The Boss to call me too. He would find out soon enough; better it came from me.

I called The Climber over. I sat her down in front of my desk and turned my screen around so she could read the report. I didn't say anything else, but asked her to read it and let me have her comments. She went white, then red, then a strange greeny-grey colour.

"But I don't understand!" she wailed. "How could they have written that, after all the help I gave them! We all went out together, we got on so well. We, we, we gelled. And how could my team say that? Why did they say they make things up? I try and help them if they come to me, I always do my best for them, always!" She covered her face with her hands, got up and stumbled towards the toilets in tears. The department went quiet for a moment as everyone watched her and wondered what was going on.

My mobile rang. *Oh no, it was The Boss.* I took a deep breath and answered.

"Jesus bloody Christ, Kate" he said angrily, "I thought you told me it was going to be a good report! It's coded red for fuck's sake, fucking red! Is that your idea of good, because the last time I looked red meant fucking awful!"

"You've seen the draft copy then?" So much for it just going to me first.

"Seen it, read it, wiped my arse on it," Brett snarled. "You know I told the Chief Exec that it was going to be a good report don't you? Because you told me it would be. Now I've got to show him this shit - he's going to hit the roof. And so will my balls by the time he's finished with me."

"I'm sorry Brett," I said, cringing, "But the lead auditor told me he'd only spotted a few minor transgressions, he didn't say..."

"Well I'm going to be sorting that jug-eared little runt out, don't you worry. You just sort your team out Kate. What the hell were they thinking, telling a team of auditors that they make things up? Eh? Had they gone stark staring mad? For Christ's sake, who's using the bloody brain cell in Cheltenham at the moment?"

He had a point. I hung up miserably and went to find The Climber. She wasn't in the toilets. I eventually found her in the meeting room. She had a carton of sandwiches, a cheese scone and a Twix in front of her. She looked up at me with a tear-stained face.

"I'm comfort eating," she said. *Good. With any luck she'd get all fat and spotty.* I sat down opposite her.

"You'll be comfort-vomiting soon if you got that sandwich from the canteen." I tried to make her smile but she just fiddled disconsolately with her Twix.

"I can't believe they've done that to me."

"I did try to tell you that they weren't here to make friends," I said, as gently as I could manage. "I warned you several times not to get too close to them, but unfortunately, you chose to ignore me."

"But we all got on so well," she persisted. "They said they'd write nice things about me, bought me lots of drinks, said I really impressed them. How could they do that?" *It's called getting shafted, it's a common enough management technique.*

"You've been a bit naive, Amanda. You need to learn from this experience, and you need to learn to listen to advice."

"Have you spoken to Brett?" she asked, pulling at the sandwich carton. "I bet he blames me."

"It's not about blame." *And if you believe that you'll believe anything.* "Anyway, the buck stops with me. I'm the manager."

She looked a bit brighter. "I don't know why my team said they make things up. Why would they say something like that? I'm quite sure they don't make stuff up. Obviously they've misinterpreted my instructions or something."

"Amanda," I said, leaning forwards, "your team saw you

being friendly and cosying up to the audit team like they were your best buddies. So they felt safe with them too - they got lulled into a false sense of security and thought they could say whatever they wanted."

She didn't respond, concentrating on getting a sandwich out in one piece. The carton said it was Coronation Chicken. Chunks of grey meat fell out onto the desk. The chicken had probably been alive at the coronation.

I tried again. "This is really serious Amanda. We've been given an SBI which means all eyes are going to be on us, for all the wrong reasons. You need to focus fully on your team now, spend much more time in the process, understand what is going wrong and put it right. And for us, well, we need to talk to each other more. You need to tell me what's going on, ask for help if you need it."

"Was Brett very cross, what did he say?" She bit into her sandwich, which I noticed had begun to curl at the edges.

I sighed.

"I really don't think you're listening to me at all, are you?"

She tried to protest, but her mouth was too full.

"Never mind about Brett, that's not your concern. He's my manager, not yours. Your priority is to get stuck in and get this issue sorted out as quickly as possible. Then Brett will be happy with us both. Do you understand?"

She pursed her lips and looked about to say something else, but in the end just nodded. I got up. "And for God's sake don't eat that cheese scone. It's going green."

By the time I got back to my desk the shock waves from the report were already being felt. I could see I'd missed several calls, and emails were coming in from all directions -

everyone asking similar questions about the SBI. How, when, why - what were my plans to address it? The Perypils risk team had invited me to a teleconference at 6 pm to discuss. 6 pm - what a cheek!

My working day finished at 5 pm. My paid working day anyway. Managers didn't get overtime. I'd calculated that on the hours I was currently working my hourly rate was less than the minimum wage. Why was I working for nothing? Why was I such a mug?

The next few days were utterly hideous. I was placed on "daily reporting" by the sales risk team which meant a teleconference each morning during which I had to give them an update on the issue. I then had to complete a daily written report and send it to The Boss so he could send it to The Big Cheese (the Chief Exec). This would then be returned to me with numerous questions which required detailed responses from me. My responses only served to generate additional questions. I was bombarded with emails from not only the risk team for sales but also the regional risk team, the national risk team and the executive risk team. They all wanted to know something slightly different and each sent me a different proforma to complete detailing the issue. Why couldn't all the risk teams speak to one another? Why not just have the one generic form that they all shared? I would have thought that having hundreds of different forms was a risk in itself. Perhaps that's how they kept themselves in business.

By the end of the week I was close to melt down. I had shouted down the phone to someone from 'process' risk who'd called me for an update: "For Christ's sake leave me alone for five minutes can't you? How the hell do you expect me to manage the issue when all I'm doing is writing endless reports and answering the sodding phone to you idiots?" I was working until midnight in the attempt to clear down my email inbox, but by the time I'd arrive at work in the morning there would be another ten emails all relating to the same issue, all wanting additional information.

The Husband was not at all impressed with my long hours and having to cook for himself in the evenings. By the time I got home I felt too sick from stress and nervous exhaustion to eat much, so I was getting by on a bottle of wine and a marmite sandwich. He wasn't at all sympathetic to my issue, simply grunting if I tried to tell him anything about it. I knew he was being particularly grumpy as he'd been going to the gym almost every night but still hadn't managed to lose any weight. He thought it might be his thyroid.

My brother called one evening to make sure I wasn't upset about not being a bridesmaid. I said "I'm 42, so no, I'm not upset."

He explained that they needed to keep costs down, so it would just be Georgia. Was I ok with that? *Yes, I'm 42, who the hell has a 42 year old bridesmaid?*

He handed the phone over to the Bunny Boiler, who slurred some more apologies to me, told me I was like a sister to her already and that she wanted me to play a special part in their wedding. *Oh God.* She said she wanted to go shopping with me so we could look at wedding dresses and "going away" outfits. Wouldn't that be an amazing thing to do together? *No, it bloody well wouldn't, I can't think of anything worse.* Cornered, I agreed on a date to meet up in a couple of weekend's time. With a bit of luck, she wouldn't remember the conversation.

The torture at work began to abate when the Climber

eventually managed to get to the bottom of the SBI. She discovered that the sales database wasn't fit for purpose and hadn't been for quite some considerable time. Her team had therefore been making do, and where they didn't have the right information they had been 'best-guessing'. It was pretty hard to believe. I asked the team why they hadn't raised this before. They shrugged and looked blank. I asked why they'd waited until a team from audit came in before they had chosen to sing out like canaries? More shrugs. I couldn't get the theme tune from The Muppet Show out of my head.

It became apparent that it wasn't just my team in Cheltenham that was affected by the database issue - it was across the company. And nobody had noticed. I assumed that meant that everyone else's sales data was corrupt too - it was clearly a massive issue. The risk teams went very quiet for a period of time, and then I was told that the database was in the process of being rebuilt. I could consider my issue closed and was asked to destroy the audit report along with any copies I had made. It seemed Perypils now wanted to keep a lid on the whole thing for fear of being hauled up in front of the regulators. I'd heard that all the fingers were being pointed in IT's direction and they were getting it in the neck now - in this no-blame culture that we operate in.

I stared at my reflection in one of the mirrors in the Ladies. I looked grey and exhausted, with heavy, dark circles under my eyes - this whole audit business had robbed me of much-needed beauty sleep and given me many more white hairs. I could easily pass for The Climber's mother, if not her grandmother. I would certainly be on TLS George's "not" list. The "not even with a paper bag" most definitely not list.

CHAPTER SEVEN

Whilst watching a repeat of Lewis in bed last night, The Husband had asked me, during an advert break, if I could make it home at a reasonable hour tomorrow. I panicked: what event had I forgotten? We weren't going to Debbie and Paul's again were we, did I need to think up an excuse? I hedged my bets:

"Should be ok now that things have calmed down a bit, but I will have to check my diary..."

"Well, if you could try," The Husband said, a touch sarcastically. "I thought I would cook us a romantic Valentine's meal, you know, to try and get this relationship back on track."

What should have happened next was me saying: "Oh no, do you feel that our relationship is off track? I'm so concerned that you have said that, we must talk about it," and I should have got up, made us a cup of tea and we would have talked it through. But no, I was tired, Lewis was about to start again (and it was the last bit when all is revealed, after all, and I'd been following the story for one hour and forty five minutes already). So instead I said:

"Ooh how nice! What are you going to cook?"

"I'm not sure yet," he replied, after a pause, obviously not getting the response he had expected. "I've been looking at lots of recipes online, I felt quite inspired by the meal we had at Debbie and Paul's," *Inspired? It was basically just cream for*

Christ's sake, "and I thought we should really make more of an effort to try different things..." *but that takes time, and thought and planning...*" instead of some of the crap that we do eat." *Well, perhaps you could do the shopping for a change mate, instead of me doing it all the time, and perhaps you could find some inspiration amongst the rude, trolley-barging chavs and their screeching, screaming chavlings....*

He was obviously in the mood to start an argument, but I wasn't, so I remained silent and tried to focus on the end of the program. He didn't give up.

"Well, you're always watching cookery programs aren't you? Why do you bother watching so many if all you want to do is warm up ready meals?"

"I don't watch that many," I retorted, getting sucked in.

"You never miss Saturday Kitchen!" he shot back. *Yes, that's because I'm drooling over James Martin not the recipes, you fool.*

Inward sigh. Give it up, or Lewis will be over.

"Yes, you're right," I said in a soothing voice. "It would be nice to try something different for a change. I'm really looking forward to tomorrow night, can't wait." That seemed to appease him. He put in his ear plugs and picked up his book, My Shit Life so Far by Frankie Boyle.

I couldn't concentrate on the end of Lewis, nor could I fall asleep. Did he really feel that our marriage was in trouble, or was he just in a bad mood? At Christmas, he had asked me if I was happy, but he'd not said how he was feeling. Mind you, I hadn't asked him. He hadn't actually said those four little words that strike dread into the heart of anyone in a relationship: "we need to talk", so I had assumed we were ok. What do I always say to my guys at work? *Never assume.* Was I trying to duck having a serious conversation? Perhaps. I just felt too - what was the word - *sedated* to deal with it. Was that because I didn't care? My head was so full of work I didn't feel it could accommodate anything else - it could only cope with watching the telly because it didn't have to think. God, I must take control of my life; I mustn't sleep-walk towards whatever fate had in store for me. I must make an effort tomorrow evening. I would dress nicely, be very attentive and praise his cooking. I would get to M&S at lunchtime to buy some new undies; I must transform into a sex goddess. Those grey pants wouldn't do at all.

Valentine's Day was a nightmare of gigantic proportions. I walked into the office to find systems crashing and already forty customers queuing on the phones. I spent almost the entire day in teleconferences with IT, who didn't seem to have a clue how to put things right. It got so frustrating that at one stage, I had to put down the phone, go into the Ladies, scream at the wall and then walk calmly back to the phone. My poor teams finished the day shell-shocked and exhausted. Never ones to deal positively with adversity, I heard someone say: "I'd jump out of the window, but knowing my luck, I'd survive," and someone else: "If the world ended today it wouldn't really be a big loss."

Thank God The Drain was off sick, his bowels would never have coped with all this. I didn't receive a word of support from The Boss, although I had kept him updated on the issue via regular emails.

Unfortunately, I didn't get a break at all, so couldn't get to M&S and had to send The Rock out to get a Valentine's card for The Husband. Not really a fair task, but what could I do? She asked if he had a sense of humour, and I said yes. She came back with a card that had a picture of a man wearing glasses, down on his hands and knees licking a rug, whilst his frustrated wife is lying in bed saying "Brian, you really need to go to Specsavers."

I was a bit shocked at The Rock's choice of card and not sure what The Husband would make of it - it hardly set the tone for the romantic evening he seemed to have planned, but it would have to do now.

It really was difficult to get away from the office with the system problems still going on, but The Rock, sensing my anxiety, said she was happy to stay and carry on wrestling with IT. She promised to text me regular updates. I drove home like a loon and when I got in, found The Husband already bustling cheerfully around the kitchen, working his way through a bottle of white wine. I offered to help, but he shooed me out so I went upstairs to "freshen up", although I actually wanted to call The Rock to see how things were.

The mood in the kitchen began to change over the next hour. The chirpy humming stopped, and was replaced by noises of frustration, "Why won't you boil you little shit!", ill-tempered clashing of saucepan lids and eventually some seriously blue language. I kept well out of the way, except when I was asked to fetch a plaster.

The meal was eventually served at 9.10 pm (he had been planning for 7.30). I wasn't entirely sure what the dish was, but guessed it had probably started its life as a sea bass. The poor thing had been suffocated by a thick-cut rasher of bacon (apparently the recipe called for Parma ham, but he couldn't find any) and then, to end its suffering, it had been drowned in a dark sticky sauce (blackcurrant coulis). Of course, after all his efforts, I did all the right things - making sex noises at every mouthful I took, showing an interest in the making of the sauce, praising his splendid choice of wine. He wasn't very communicative, and I figured that the effort, or possibly the bottle and a half of wine he had consumed, seemed to have taken its toll. I'd thought tonight was about us having a good old talk about things, but he didn't show any inclination to start a conversation. It was like sitting opposite a stranger.

Somehow I managed to clear my plate, although my stomach was already beginning to protest even before I'd finished. The Husband retired to the study almost as soon as we had finished eating, saying he had things to do before bedtime. I assumed that meant he was eager to get to bed, so I needed to "vamp" myself up a bit. The kitchen looked like a bomb site so I started to load the dishwasher, but the bending over was too much for my stomach and it began to lurch.

I nipped up to the bathroom, hoping he wouldn't hear and just made it onto the loo in time. *Oh dear God, this wasn't pleasant.* And I was supposed to be all sexy tonight! Trust me to foul things up - literally. When it was over, I dug out some Immodium, took two, and then another two for good measure. I'd probably never go again. I also found some Rennie, so chewed on a couple of those as well. My stomach was churning again. *Oh God, please give me a break.* Just wind this time, but it was difficult to trust. How could I have sex in this condition? It could be disastrous.

Hoping things would calm down, I had a look through my underwear drawer to find something suitable to wear. *A nappy perhaps?* I found a pink and black basque-type thing at the back of the drawer. I could just about squeeze into it, as long as I didn't attempt to breathe. I couldn't find the matching knickers, but had some other black ones so that was ok. The basque had suspenders to attach stockings to. When had I last worn stockings? I could only find hold ups. Pulled them on and attempted to attach them to the straps. *Bloody impossible.* The elastic at the top was too thick and I couldn't do them up, the straps kept pinging off. I cricked my neck in the process. *Bugger it.* Could I remove the suspenders? No. Well, would just have to leave them dangling, he might not notice in the throes of passion.

I got into bed. My stomach was making a noise like a washing machine. It would probably be safer if I went on top - then I could always hop off and make a run for it if needs be. Should I put a towel down on the bed, just in case? No, that would look too gross. I still had the most awful wind. I couldn't decide whether to keep the duvet clamped down to trap the smell underneath or to waft about to disperse it. I went for clamping. Right - I must get myself in the mood, I must think amorous thoughts.

I wonder if the systems are fixed yet? No, no, no, not work, try again, think sexy thoughts. Think about James Martin oiling up a chicken breast. *Mmmm.*

Wonder when I last dusted in here, I don't think I have for a while. Must do that at the weekend. I ought to phone my brother at the weekend too, see how he is. Stop, stop. Why am I thinking about my brother when I'm trussed up in stockings and suspenders? That's just plain wrong.

Why hadn't The Husband come up to bed? I went to the top of the stairs. I could hear him talking to someone in the study. He must be on the phone. I strained my ears and heard him laughing, calling someone "buddy" and asking "how's Andrea?" Realised, gloomily, that he was talking to his friend, Chatty Dave, who lived in the States. He would be on the phone for bloody hours. I went back to bed and lay down, my stomach feeling a little calmer. I remembered I hadn't given him his Valentines card, but as he hadn't given me one (*or a card - ha ha!*) I thought I wouldn't bother now. I'd save it for next year. I tried to stay awake, but couldn't fight off sleep. Dreamt I was in a swimming pool full of giant sea bass. They were trying to eat me.

I awoke the next morning feeling decidedly queasy. My digestion had probably been impeded by that bloody basque. The Husband was still sound asleep - I hadn't heard him come to bed last night. I got ready for work very slowly, not sure whether to risk setting off or leaving it for an hour to see if I felt better. I couldn't face breakfast but knew I would have to get going; I had so much to do following yesterday's setbacks, I couldn't lose any more time. I took another two Immodium, brushed an extra layer of bronzing powder onto my pasty face and set off.

Nausea was coming in waves. I decided that some fresh air would be a good idea, so when I got closer to work I parked at the back of Tesco's and started to walk in - it was the best part of a mile to the business park.

It started to rain. Very light at first, but quickly becoming stair rods. I didn't turn back as I was beginning to feel a little better, although the exercise was causing some movement in my stomach. There's no way I could need the loo after all that Immodium! Surely everything must have turned to concrete by now. As I walked past a lay-by, I had to let some wind out. At that exact moment, The Drain pulled into the lay-by in his red Noddy car. He lent across and pushed the passenger door open.

"Kate! Jump in, you're getting soaked."

What could I do? It would just look too strange to continue walking in the pouring rain. I got in, moving the Asda carrier bag from the passenger seat onto the floor. The smell got in with me - it was clinging to my coat. We both tried to ignore it. I talked brightly, asking Martin how he was feeling and telling him about the system issues. I noticed he had pressed a handkerchief to his nose. He tried to leave it there for the remainder of the journey, changing gear and steering with one hand. Poor Martin. I have never, ever felt so embarrassed. With the exception, perhaps, of one other time, many years ago. I had just moved into my first house, a small new-build in a smart little close. I was in the front garden, bending down, putting some plants in. Several of my new neighbours were stood in the close chatting together. My boyfriend of the time was staying with me. He chose this moment to whip open the front door, break wind extremely loudly (it reverberated around the close) and quickly shut the front door again. The neighbours all turned to look at me. This felt very similar.

CHAPTER EIGHT

Saturday

The date for shopping with the Bunny Boiler was upon me. I'd exchanged a few texts with her and arranged to meet her and Georgia (oh God) in town at 10.30, outside a shop called Something Borrowed. I could only assume this either sold second-hand wedding dresses, or ones that had fallen off the back of a lorry.

I ate my porridge like a condemned prisoner, whining to The Husband that the whole outing was pointless. The wedding was probably never going to happen anyway, and why was I having to spend an entire day with someone I didn't want to spend time with? I'd had to spend the whole week working with people I didn't particularly want to work with, the weekends were too precious to waste. He told me that if it was any consolation, Georgia didn't want to go either. She'd put on Facebook "How lame is my life - a day of looking at stupid dresses with the wrinklies, kill me now." Ouch - a wrinkly! Is that what I was now? I suppose that's how I appeared to a fifteen year old.

"I didn't know you and Georgia were Facebook buddies."

"Oh yes," he replied, a bit vaguely, and studied his paper.

Hmmm. I was going to have to take a look at his Facebook site; it seemed a bit odd that a 46 year old man would have teenagers as Facebook friends. I wondered if he'd

used the same password we used for everything "Bollocks1"
or if he'd set up a different one. If it was a different one, then
clearly there was stuff in there he didn't want me to see. I'd
have to try and hack in. If it was Bollocks1, then obviously
there would be nothing worth reading. I didn't have time to
think about that now, I had to go and meet the BB and the
Baby BB.

I found the shop tucked away in a side street. It had a
massive, white, tiered wedding dress displayed on a dummy in
its window, made of a horrid shiny, crinkly material - even the
dummy looked embarrassed to be seen in it. As I got there, I
received a text from the Bunny Boiler which read: "Georgia
bein a bitch. c u l8r 11.30?" I'm not sure what was more
depressing - a mother that refers to her daughter as a bitch or
that awful text-talk from someone who's almost forty. But on
the bright side, that was an hour less in their company -
hooray! I went to Starbucks and treated myself to a
cappuccino with an extra shot, just to caffeine myself up for
the day. I then went to Boots to have a look at their anti-
wrinkle creams - my God they're expensive! I didn't get any.
I'd just have to try going bra-less and hope that pulls the
wrinkles out of my face. I spent a very pleasant half hour in
Monsoon, looking at all their lovely clothes, stroking the faux
fur shrugs and trying to work out, if the wedding was to go
ahead, which dress I'd opt for. I found myself about to
purchase a caramel-coloured cardigan but stopped myself just
in time. Let's face it, the label may have said caramel but it
was actually beige. I'm not ready for beige knitwear just yet.
But it's a worry that it's started calling to me.

I went back to Something Borrowed at 11.30. The
Bunny Boiler was there, looking harassed. She was stood

texting furiously, pushing her blonde hair away from her face, exposing dark roots underneath. She was wearing a navy maxi dress, which was a bit too tight up top. Her breasts looked in danger of spilling out. I didn't mean to look at them as I greeted her but I couldn't help it - my eyes were drawn to them. *Oh Christ, she probably thinks I'm a lesbian now.*

"Sorry Kate," she said, her face flushed, "but Georgia threw a right bloody strop and refused to come." *Result!* "She's been an absolute nightmare. She was really excited about being my bridesmaid, but I'm sure that idiot-arsehole has been winding her up about the wedding, and now she says she's not even going to come, says marriage is a waste of time." I assumed the idiot-arsehole was the ex-husband.

"I could kill him, I really could, and as for that *tart*," she spat the word out, "always sticking her beak in where it's not wanted, I know she doesn't give one shit about Georgia, I've tried to tell Georgia that over and over, but does she listen to me, no of course not, I'm only her bloody mother." *Yes, I'm sure you are Mother of the Year - that's why Georgia lives with her father.*

I suggested, hopefully, that we went for a coffee so she could calm herself down but she was determined to start looking for a dress. I told her I'd seen some gorgeous ones in Monsoon, but I was talking to her back as she was already entering Something Borrowed.

It was, as I thought, a second hand shop; not that you'd know it from some of the prices I could see. It was a long thin shop with rows of wedding dresses on either side. The Bunny Boiler told me, very loudly, that she'd sold her own wedding dress to this shop when "Fuck-Face" left her. She started to manically pull out some dresses from the racks

saying "Let's see if we can find it Kate, it might still be here."
One of the assistants started to approach us, but when she
heard The Bunny Boiler say "When I find it I'm going to
stamp all over it and kick it to kingdom come just like I
should have done with his dick!" she thought better of it,
swerving past us and going to help another customer.

I wasn't sure what to do - clearly the Bunny Boiler was
not in the right frame of mind for this expedition (or for
anything else come to that). I managed to distract her from
the task of hunting down her first wedding dress by showing
her some pretty bodices and long floaty skirts. She liked the
idea of a bodice, as she would be able to "flash a bit of tit"
which seemed important to her, but she didn't think they
were "bling" enough. When I asked her what she meant by
bling, she replied "you know, dee-amont-ee".

We found an ivory dress which had a sparkly bodice and
a big puffy skirt. She quite liked the look of it, saying she
could always "bling it up some more". We were pointed
wordlessly to a changing room by one of the shop assistants,
or "that frigid cow" as the Bunny Boiler put it.

She sat down on a chair in the changing room and
produced a small bottle of coca cola from her handbag. "Let's
have one for the road shall we?" she said, taking a few gulps.
A strong smell of alcohol filled the small room.

"Bloody hell Kirsty, what have you got in there?"

"Just some coke," she giggled, taking another swig, "But
mainly Bacardi." She offered me the bottle, but I declined,
pretending I didn't like Bacardi, so she wouldn't think I was a
boring, disapproving old fart.

I helped her into the dress. It's funny, you see this
moment so often in films: the bride-to-be tries on a wedding

dress and her friends and family are reduced to tears because she looks so lovely. The Bunny Boiler didn't look lovely. The bodice was far too tight, and flesh was spilling out all over the place, great big squashy bits under her arms and across her back and as for her chest, well, you could balance your dinner plate on her breasts. The bodice didn't come down far enough, giving her a very noticeable pot-belly. She considered herself in the mirror, turning this way and that.

"Mmmm, I do like the bodice," she said. *What??? You look like you're being squeezed out of a sausage machine!* "But I don't like the big skirt thing, it's way too plain and boring." She took another swig from her bottle, some of it escaping her mouth and dribbling down onto the dress.

I had to get out of there. I said I knew it was early, but suggested we went to get some lunch. She readily agreed and we peeled her out of the dress. Handing it back to the assistant, she told them that if she decided to have a "dull as shit" theme for her wedding she would be back. Cringing, I quickly led her out of the shop.

We went to Woody's Wine Bar for lunch. It was nearby and one of my favourite places - I had to salvage something from the day. Although it was still early, Woody's was very popular and it was already filling up. We found a table, and ordered a glass of wine each. I felt myself beginning to relax a little. I ordered a warm duck salad with a pea puree and the Bunny Boiler went for a penne pasta. I tried to keep the conversation light and cheery, and succeeded at first, but after the first glass of wine she was back onto the topic of her ex-husband and I was doomed. I looked into my Sauvignon Blanc and could see myself floating down a river. The river was called Shit Creek. There was a sign on the riverbank. It said "Paddles - sold out".

"The day he walked out," she was saying, "that very day, just after he'd left, a stray cat came into the garden." Pause, gulp of wine. "That cat was evil-looking, big and black and had this look in its eyes, like the devil. It came right up to the patio windows and looked right at me, right into my soul." *Oh my God, nutter alert.* "It wouldn't go away. Do you know what I think?" *No, and frankly I'm scared to ask.* "I think the cat was possessed by the spirit of my husband." *But he wasn't dead was he?* She sat back to let the drama of her statement sink in. I noticed that one of her eyes was beginning to wander. "I mean, it's just too much of a coincidence isn't it? That cat was possessed and came to taunt me, to mock me, I really think it had the devil in him."

"What happened to the cat?" I asked, just for something to say really.

"Eventually I held an exorcism. It never came back." *Of course, a perfectly normal way to deal with a stray cat.*

"Unlike *that tart* who never goes away-" To my horror she started to cry. "That bitch took everything from me, everything!" She slammed her hand down into the table, her fork leaping into the air. Heads swivelled in our direction.

"Well, look, don't upset yourself," I tried to be consoling, but it's not one of my strengths. "You've got Stu now, a wedding to look forward to..."

"You know she's pregnant, don't you?" The Bunny Boiler was mopping her eyes with her napkin. "He told me this morning. As if he wants to be a father again. She won't give a toss for Georgia when she's got her own kid, not a toss. Nor will he, he's so under her thumb, he just does whatever she tells him to. They'll want rid of Georgia, I know they will. That, that, that... oh." She seemed to have run out of names for her ex's partner, and picked up what she thought was her wine glass. It wasn't. It was a cocktail glass full of water which contained a floating candle. She didn't seem to notice and took a large slurp. Luckily, the candle was unlit. People on the other tables were shooting sympathetic glances at me.

I didn't know what to say. At least I knew now why she was having a mini-melt down today, but I wasn't sure if it was the news of the baby that was upsetting her or the possibility that she may have to live with Georgia. The meal arrived and I tried to get her to eat something, but she was only interested in more wine. I cheered her for a brief moment by saying that the tart would get really fat and have horrid swollen ankles, but she was soon crying again, big splodgy tears falling into her penne. Her nose was running too. I couldn't face my pea puree.

When our plates were cleared away it was to my huge relief that she phoned my brother and asked him to come and pick her up. I ordered some black coffees whilst we waited for him. He didn't seem surprised by the state she was in, he must be used to it. Poor Stu. I could understand why their relationship was always off and on. Would he really marry her? Surely she had too many issues, she couldn't possibly be ready to get married again.

I said goodbye and found myself going back to purchase the beige cardigan. Possibly the last couple of hours had aged me - the rot had started. I had to rally against it. As I made my way home, I made a mental list of the de-aging "maintenance" activities to undertake:

- Teeth whitening. *I hate the dentist, but don't trust the do-it-*

yourself kits.

- Colour hair. *Have never had to do this before, but white strands are now clearly visible and impossible to pull them all out.*
- Get my colours done. *Had a quick look on the Internet, but I'm not sure if I'm a spring or an autumn and I'm slightly colour-blind anyway.*
- Re-vamp wardrobe. *Buy clothes that actually co-ordinate, not whatever mismatched pieces I take a fancy to.*
- Lose a stone in weight. *Do not lose any more than this or face will age - it will become haggard and drawn.*
- Use fake tan? *Not sure about this one, as a tan can be quite ageing. However, would make teeth look instantly whiter without having to go the dentist, so should consider.*
- Drink green tea instead of coffee. *Yuk, yuk, yuk but might get used to it if I can get through the caffeine-withdrawal headaches. Will start tomorrow.*

Sunday

It had been a horrid day - one of those where it had rained virtually non-stop. The Husband was out playing golf, although I don't know why anyone would want to be out in this weather. He hadn't been in the best of moods when he left, having broken a piece of tooth whilst eating his breakfast cereal. He seemed to blame me because I'd bought a cereal that we hadn't had before and it was harder than he was used to. I'd thought the name "Granite Crunch" would have given him some warning. I had suggested, quite mildly I thought, that he was more than welcome to do the weekly shop himself. That put him in an even bigger strop, and he tetchily reminded me that he had put the bin out in 1938 and mown the lawn in 1955 - did he have to do everything?

I was also feeling depressed, having put on a pair of jeans I hadn't worn in a while. My bum had immediately tried to escape from them. Once I'd managed to re-capture my bum, bits of side flesh had got out. I tried to examine my reflection from behind in the full length mirror, but it was really difficult to do. In the end, I'd set up my camera on self-timer, balanced it on the chest of drawers, turned my back on it, and waited ten seconds for the picture to be taken. I examined it. *Oh my God.* That was definitely not one for the album. Where had my bum actually gone? There it was - not where I'd expected it to be. It was a lot closer to my ankles than before. Didn't it used to stand to attention a bit more? My buttocks seemed to be looking dejectedly down at the carpet, like I do when the hoovering needs doing. I was shapeless - I couldn't tell where my back ended and my bum began.

I deleted the picture with a shudder. I had to do something, get back on the diet. I'd revisit the 'pledge' I'd made to myself and try really hard this time. It was just so bloody difficult to keep count of the calories each day. I'd Googled "bum-lifting" exercises and vowed to do a hundred each morning and each evening. This time I would really be strict with myself and cut out all the crap. I decided I would start from tomorrow as I'd promised myself a cheese toastie at lunchtime.

I spent the rest of the day pottering about, making half-hearted raids on the house-work and work emails, distracted by, well, just about anything really. I was overwhelmed by a sudden desire to watch the Emmerdale omnibus, and became gripped by Ski Sunday. I'd had a long conversation with my mother, who'd phoned whilst I'd nipped out to get a paper and had got confused by the answer phone. When I'd got home, the message light was flashing. My mother's voice had recorded saying "Hello, Kate? Hello, are you still there love? Can you hear me?" I then heard her saying to my father "She is there Frank, because she answered. She can't hear me. It must be a bad line or something. It could be our phone playing up again."

I called her back and tried to explain that the answer phone message was a recorded message from BT. My mother then wanted to know if the lady from BT always answered our phone when we were out. I tried to explain again that it was a recording, but she didn't understand, convinced she'd spoken to an actual person. At one stage, her voice became very faint and distant and I could hardly hear her. I shouted "Mum, Mum, can you hold the phone a bit closer? I can't hear you." Dad eventually came on and said she'd been trying to change the TV channel with the telephone and talking to me on the TV remote. It was all quite exhausting.

I'd made myself a cup of green tea – *shudder* - and read the Sunday papers, starting with the magazines, then the gossipy articles, eventually moving onto the real news when I'd run out of all the shallow, interesting stuff. I turned a page, and there in the finance section was a huge headline which read: "Perypils Lets Down its Customers Again". There was a picture of a miserable-looking couple stood in front of their house, which was missing a large section of its roof. The story, which took up an entire page, was that the couple, who'd been "loyal customers" of Perypils Insurance for over twenty years, had suffered damage to their roof following a storm. They tried to claim on their buildings insurance, but Perypils had deemed that the bad weather did not meet their definition of a storm. Apparently, the wind speed hadn't been strong enough. I looked at the picture - there was a bloody great hole in the roof! That must have been one hell of a stiff breeze! There was a smaller caption which read "When is a storm not a storm? When it doesn't suit Perypils."

The couple's house was uninhabitable because of the damage and they were living in a caravan in their front garden. There was a picture of their caravan. It looked like a rusty, upside-down pram stood in a swamp. I read on. This "poor, unfortunate" woman suffered from arthritis, bronchitis, caravan-itis and every other itis the reporter had prompted from her. She said the stress was causing her hair to fall out. *Was that why she hadn't washed it?* There was another caption at the end of the story which read: "A customer in need is no customer of mine", positioned next to a picture of the smiling Big Cheese Chief Exec. It was a real hatchet job. I wondered how many people would read the article - millions probably. The Perypils Publicity Machine would have their work cut out spinning this one.

CHAPTER NINE

Monday morning

As I was working my way through emails (93 unread in the inbox) I noticed my teams had gone very quiet. Out of the corner of my eye, I could see that Cruella had entered the department, and seemed to be headed in my direction. I quickly picked up my headset and plonked it on my head, hoping to fool her into thinking I was on a conference call. It worked! She walked on past and through the doors. *Big sigh of relief - small victories!* I couldn't cope with her today.

An email dropped into my inbox from the Communications Team. They'd sent it to every member of staff. It had a newsletter attached to it. I opened it up and there was a picture of a woman in an anorak planting a smacker of a kiss on the cheek of The Big Cheese. He was pulling a goofy face. The headline said: "Flood Victims Thank Our Chief Exec". There was a gushing article on how The Big Cheese had sprung a "surprise" visit on the residents of Shortham, whose village had been badly flooded recently. Apparently, as soon as he stepped out of the car, our customers had "rushed to embrace him". You'd think he was the messiah. There were pictures of him in his wellies, stood looking sadly at someone's soggy garden, pretending to muck in and sweep water away from a front door and, particularly puke-making, holding up a tiny kitten that had apparently had a miraculous escape.

There was an interview with the woman in the anorak, who happened to have a severely disabled son. *Utterly shameless.* She said that the Perypils claims team had "instantly processed her claim". *Unheard of!* She was so grateful she'd said if she ever met anyone from Perypils she would kiss them. Poor woman; now she'd have herpes to add to all her other problems.

There was no mention of yesterday's article in the Sunday paper. *Let's all pretend it wasn't there!* I rubbed my temples. I had a headache starting. I was dying for a coffee; this green tea was shite, like drinking liquid iron filings. I opened another email. It was from The Boss, inviting all department managers to a team building event next month. *Oh no, please no.* It was a two-day event being held, for some reason, in Nottingham. As Perypils didn't have any sites in Nottingham, I assumed they were just trying to make it inconvenient for as many people as possible. There was an activity day, a workshop, dinner and networking. *How utterly ghastly. How could I get out of it?* The Boss had added at the end of his email that a reply wasn't necessary as "it is expected that all managers will attend". Not really an invitation then, more of a summons. *Oh crap.*

After lunch, I was sat at my desk fishing around in my hand bag looking for some polo mints, which I knew where in there somewhere. I'd had chilli beef soup in the canteen and it had left a rather unpleasant taste in my mouth, as well as a hair. I eventually found a couple of grubby looking mints at the bottom of my bag and was considering whether or not it would be safe to eat them, when I became aware that the department seemed very quiet. I also felt a sudden chill. Looking up, I saw the angular figure of Cruella upon me. Too late to feign another conference call, or to pretend my mobile was ringing. *As I walk through the valley of the shadow of death....*

"Hi Clare!" I said, giving her a pretend warm smile. *Could she smell fear?* "Would you like a polo?"

"No thank you," Cruella replied with what she possibly considered was a smile, but really didn't look like one. It was more a sarcastic smirk. She looked down her long nose at me. "I'd like to arrange a meeting with you and," she looked around distastefully, "your people, to discuss the unacceptable number of errors your team are making."

Blunt and to the point as usual. No finesse, no attempt to build any kind of rapport. Straight in, *bam*. Had she never heard of foreplay?

"They are causing a significant number of customer complaints, and creating additional work for my teams. It needs addressing urgently." She was still semi-smirking, and her pointy chin (from which a wart had been removed, I was certain of this) was stuck out defiantly.

I looked up into her dark, witchy eyes. I wondered if I threw my cup of water over her she'd dissolve, like the Wicked Witch of the West.

"Ok Clare," I replied, tapping my fingernails on the desk. "Yes, a meeting would be good. And during it perhaps we could discuss the amount of time it's been taking to hand over calls to your team. It seems to be getting worse and worse - sometimes our calls aren't answered at all. We're finding the problems this is creating for us quite, what's the word - unacceptable." *Fifteen all.*

The semi-smirk snapped off. "Kate, all I'm trying to do is support our customers in offering the best service that we can. I'm just asking that we work together to achieve this."

No, you're just petty point scoring as usual. "I'd appreciate your team's co-operation."

"Fine." I turned to my screen to show that this exchange was over. "Send an invite through and we can discuss it during the meeting."

"Fine." Cruella turned on her heel and went off to drown some puppies. Although I still felt cold from her presence, I could feel that my bum was sweating - how does that happen? Had she placed a curse on me? An email dropped into my inbox a few minutes later inviting me to a meeting. I felt like declining it, especially as she'd picked the only gap I had free in my calendar for over a week. I didn't decline it though; I didn't want to turn into a toad.

The Snake came sliding over, her eyes glinting at me hungrily. Perhaps I *had* been turned into a toad! She looked as if she was to just about to devour one.

"Kate," she said, "did you know that Lee Halfpenny had phoned in sick again this morning? Well, he said was feeling fluey, but Jane's just seen him in the Rose and Crown. He's downing pints and having a laugh with some mates."

What an idiot. Phone in sick and then pick the busiest pub in town to go into. I sighed.

"It's unbelievable really Cynthia, he just doesn't care does he? Would Jane be prepared to make a statement to confirm she's seen him, do you think?"

"Better than that," she replied triumphantly, "I've been up there myself and seen him. He didn't see me. So I can give you a statement."

Good work. "Well done Cyn, we've got him by the short and curlies."

"Can we go and dismiss him then?" The Snake asked,

hopefully. I had to laugh.

"You'd think so, wouldn't you Cynthia? But no, we'll have to have a discussion with him when he returns, document what he says, send it to HR and wait for them to arrange a disciplinary meeting."

"But that will take weeks!" she exclaimed in dismay. "He's sat up there drinking beer when he's supposed to be at work, having blatantly lied to me this morning, and you're saying we've got to wait weeks before we can get rid of him? It's ridiculous."

I absolutely agreed with her. But that still didn't change anything. I realised I was scratching my arm again. Thinking of Lee always made me itch.

Saturday

I had heard on the radio that your optimum level of happiness occurs at 12.30pm on a Saturday. This was because it took a certain amount of time to get over the frustrations of the working week and to start enjoying the weekend. It falls again at around 5.30 pm on a Sunday evening as you start to think about going back to work the next day. My mate Karen got a 'Sunday night tummy' at the thought of Monday approaching. But she is a primary school teacher, so that's understandable.

As it approached 12.30 today, I did indeed feel extremely happy and contented. I was sat with a lovely fluffy cappuccino outside the coffee shop in the village square, with my face in the sun. This was the first bit of warmth I'd felt from the sun since September, and the outside tables were all filled with smiling people. I knew I should have asked for a green tea, but sod it; it was the weekend after all. And I had resisted the carrot cake.

The Husband had been away last night at a golfing lads' dinner and he'd stayed the night at a friend's house. I'd spent my Friday night catching up on work emails. *What a saddo.* It had taken me until 1.00 am but I'd cleared my inbox and I felt so much better. On Monday I could drive into work feeling in control and on top of things for a change. I'd spent the morning being a domestic goddess. I'd tidied, vacuumed, dusted, cleaned the bathroom and the kitchen and sorted out a huge pile of post that had been threatening to topple over and bury me. I hadn't done any ironing yet, but I had matched up his socks and rolled them into neat balls, as a special treat for him. I'd do the rest tomorrow in front of a rubbishy Sunday afternoon film. I'd just bought a nice bit of lamb from the butcher so I could make us a casserole tonight - all in all, I reckoned I had earned some serious wifey brownie points.

I had texted The Husband to tell him where I was in case his friend wanted to drop him in the village. He texted back to say he was two minutes away, so I ordered him a cappuccino too. I wondered if we would go out for the afternoon; it was so nice today, I fancied a walk in the countryside and a late pub lunch. *Heaven.*

I saw him approaching across the square. He appeared to be having a little difficulty walking - had he injured himself? He spotted me and came to sit down, crashing into several chairs as he did so which caused heads to swivel in our direction at the sudden clatter.

"Hi Hon!" he exclaimed. "Wow, massive coffee, cheers." He took a big noisy slurp. "What's in your bag?"

"I got some lamb from the butcher's," I told him,

looking at him closely. He seemed a bit odd. "Thought I'd do us a casserole tonight."

"Hey hey! Casserole tonight!" To my mortification, The Husband stood up and did a little dance, moving his arms around as if stirring a massive pot, singing "Casserole tonight, casserole tonight, we've got casserole tonight!"

Everyone was staring. "Sit down," I hissed urgently. He crashed down into his chair. I leant in towards him. He reeked.

"You're still pissed aren't you?" I couldn't believe it. How much had he drunk last night? Had he been to bed at all, or just been up all night drinking?

"No of course I'm still not drunk." He looked confused, muddling his words and his jovial mood changed very quickly. "For God's sake, I only had a few drinks with the lads. God, just because I'm cheerful you think it's because I'm pissed. Well I'm not. Bloody hell."

He slurped his coffee and tried to change the subject. "So what's in your bag?"

"Still the same – lamb."

"Oh right. So what have you been up to this morning?"

"Oh you know, the usual stuff. Johnny Depp kept ringing the doorbell but I wouldn't let him in, a herd of giraffe trampled through the garden and crapped all over the lawn and Hello called again, they want us as their centre page spread next month."

"Oh right, yeah great."

The fantasy of the walk-in-the-countryside-and-pub-lunch disappeared. He would have to go to bed for the afternoon to sleep it off. What would I do now for the rest of the day? The bloody ironing I suppose, whilst listening to him snoring. *It's not fair.* My optimum level of happiness was supposed to last until tomorrow afternoon, not just ten flipping minutes.

Sunday

Whilst reading the Sunday papers, I noticed that Perypils was featured in the finance pages again.

Headline: Perypils Customers: the odds are stacked against you.

There was a picture of four studenty-looking types stood in front of a large Victorian house. Three of them looked fresh, clean cut, nicely dressed, like they'd just stepped out of an advert for fabric conditioner. The fourth stood apart from the others, arms folded, scowling, dressed in a dowdy tracksuit. The caption under the picture read: Guess which one has a Perypils policy?

The story was that the four lived in a shared house and the chimney needed repairing. Three were able to claim on their policies but the fourth, who was insured through Perypils, had had his claim declined. As well as the lead headline, the article was crammed full of lame chimney 'jokes': Perypils policies are potty, it's a clean sweep for other insurers, Perypils don't stack up... and many more. *Oh dear.* The press really had it in for us at the moment. Perypils wouldn't be winning a Pride of Britain award anytime soon.

Monday

The dreaded meeting with Cruella's Customer Complaints team was upon us. The battle-lines were drawn. I'd chosen TLS George as my wing-man (he's always up for an argument) and he'd bought a couple of his scariest team members with him: Growling Graham, who with his long beard looked like a ZZ Top throw back and Moany Mandy, who also looked like a ZZ Top throw back - for the same reason. We were armed with a vast amount of data that evidenced the Customer Complaints team's appalling performance.

Cruella bought her deputy with her, who was basically a miniature version of herself, minus the charm. She'd also bought along two heavyweights (in every sense of the word) Kim and Pat (or KowPat as TLS George named them). They arrived with a huge pile of paper which apparently contained all the errors made by my team, and dated back six months. You couldn't even see Mini-Cruella behind it when it was placed on the table.

Being a strong believer that the best form of defence is attack, I thought I might as well fire the first salvo. I opened the meeting by expressing my disappointment that it had taken Cruella's team six months to provide us with feedback. I said we weren't psychic, how did they expect us to correct issues if we were not told about them?

Cruella responded by saying that details of errors were fed back to my team every week.

I said I'd never seen any feedback; was it being sent telepathically? Cruella gave her sarcastic smirk, which told me I'd just walked into a snare. She produced, from the top of the pile, a sheath of emails which had been sent every week to TLS George. *You stupid tit George, what have you been doing with these emails? Just deleting them?*

"You can see that your team receives very regular feedback from us," said Cruella, relishing her moment, "but despite all the effort my team put into collating this feedback, nothing has improved. In fact, I would say things are deteriorating." All four of them looked at us smugly.

TLS George, who had turned flame-red, opened his mouth, presumably to spurt out some limp-dick of an excuse but I stepped in quickly:

"Well in future would you please make sure I am copied in on these emails." I'd deal with TLS George later; I wasn't about to wash our dirty colleagues in public.

We had a look at some of the most recent complaints, which made uncomfortable reading. One customer had written to complain after they had received a letter from my admin team with a word mis-spelt - the "o" had been left out of "account". *Oh dear.*

Another customer, who was transgender, had been trying to speak to one of my telephony guys. They'd given their name as Miss Clara Jones, but as they had a deep masculine voice, my advisor had a fit of the giggles and eventually had to hang up. Miss Jones had phoned to complain that "Perypils clearly has problems with my sexuality." There were numerous complaints about text-speak in letters, and one of my admin guys had actually drawn a smiley face at the end of a refund letter. *Oh God.*

To bring an end to our humiliation, I said the best thing we could do was for George to take the pile away, go through each example and come up with an action plan. TLS George looked aghast - *tough shit mate, it's called penance for making me look like a tit.* I was keen to move onto our issues. I got Graham and Mandy to talk through their experiences of trying to transfer complaint calls to Cruella's team, and I flourished some statistics that showed Cruella's call waiting time as being over 20 minutes on some days. Cruella countered this by saying her average call waiting time was much lower than this, and was usually around five minutes. But what good was an average if some customers were having to wait over 20 minutes? I said it was impacting adversely on my teams' call handling times, and asked what they were doing to make improvements.

It occurred to me that a fly on the wall would never believe that we all worked for the same company. Cruella started to talk about making amendments to their lunch time shifts and then there was an extraordinary exchange between Mini-Me and KowPat, all arguing about their teams' shift patterns. My guys sat and looked at each other in bewilderment. The scene ended with Pat bursting into tears and walking out of the meeting, saying she was "fed up with everyone picking on her".

"Oh dear, we seem to have touched a nerve," I said, trying not to laugh. I suggested we wrapped it up for now and put something in the diary for a couple of weeks' time to share progress. Cruella was fuming; there was practically smoke coming out of her ears as she left the room. Her team were for the high jump now. *Honours even I think. Deuce.*

I helped TLS George carry his pile of complaints back to his desk and asked him to show me his email inbox. He opened it up like a sulky child. It had over 500 items in it, some had been read, many hadn't. *What a mess.* There seemed to be lots that were entitled: 'Football 2night?' and 'What time u lunching?' and 'Laura lookin fit today!' All these had been read.

I told TLS George he needed to focus on his work, not his social arrangements and to get his emails read and sorted by close of play tomorrow. He started to whine that he couldn't do this as well as go through the pile of complaints so I said he'd have to ask the others to help him out; it was up to him to take responsibility and organise himself. I suggested he might need to break the habit of a life time and stay five minutes past his finish time to catch up. He looked at me like I'd suggested he spend the night with Susan Boyle, so I assumed that was never going to happen.

CHAPTER TEN

I made a start on reversing the aging process and booked an appointment at a swanky hairdressers in town during their Thursday evening opening. My stylist was a flamboyant character called Frankie. He had spiky black hair and was wearing huge nerd specs with no lenses in them.

"Let's have a look at you then, gorgeous," he said. I sat in front of his mirror. I hate those mirrors in the hairdressers. I'm sure it must be the lighting - I always look more clapped out than usual. Frankie was running his fingers through my hair, and making "hmmm" noises. "So you wanted a colour put in today did you?" he asked. "And what are we doing with the style?"

"Well, I thought just a trim, you know, just a tidy up..."

"Oh really?" he wrinkled his nose. "Well, if that's what you want. But it's not doing a lot is it, really?" *What was it supposed to do, juggle, tell jokes?* "I mean it's sort of a nothing style at the moment isn't it?" *Ouch!* But he did have a point. It was just kind of hanging there, round my face, skimming my shoulders. Frankie was getting excited and was waving his hands about: "We could cut right into here, take some of this weight out, add some layers and texturing, bring it right up to date. It will look fabulous, you're going to look like a model or something." *Or something, most likely.* He was extraordinarily confident for one so young, so I trusted him. We chose a colour from bits of hair stuck to a chart, eventually settling on

'Cinnamon Copper' which looked lovely, rich and shiny. He gave me some magazines to look at whilst he made up the colour. I told the girl who fetched me a coffee that I'd never had a colour put in before and she could hardly believe it. I overheard her say to Frankie:

"Why is she having a colour put in? Her hair's a lovely colour as it is." Frankie hissed back:

"Shut your mouth you silly cow, you'll put her off!" I started to feel a little apprehensive.

I found a picture of Cheryl Cole, with her fabulous soft shiny curls; she looked terrific. I showed Frankie and asked if that sort of style would suit me.

"Good God no!" he screeched. "No one wants to look like that ropey old dog any more!" Not much point showing him the picture of Kerry Katona's choppy bob then.

I let him get on with it. I found out all about his apartment, which was actually a bedsit but in his words "bedsit sounds a bit scummy, dunnit?", his vegetarian sister he didn't get on with - "a pube-headed carrot cruncher" - and his description of the pound shop that had opened next door: "pikey paradise".

He cut quite a lot off, but it didn't worry me too much, I was looking forward to a new style. A new me perhaps. More youthful. But the colour - *holy shit*. He removed the towel and my hair just shrieked back at me from the mirror. It was much more coppery than the coloured bit of hair on the chart had looked - much, much more. At the same time, my hair was now darker, thus making my face look drawn and very pale, ghoulish in fact. *Cinnamon Copper my arse* - it should have been called Pumpkin Explodes on a Zombie. Even Frankie knew it was not a good choice of colour, as he didn't make any comment and just quickly twittered on and on about the latest Big Brother contestants.

"Frankie," I interrupted him, "I don't like it." He pursed his lips and considered my image in the mirror for a moment.

"Well," he put his hands on my shoulders. "Tough shit babe, it will wash out." He picked up his hair dryer, "Eventually."

Why am I never able to complain at the hairdressers? Why, why? What is it about hairdressers that means I would rather run screaming into a car wash then complain to one of them? I got out of there as quickly as I could - over a hundred pounds poorer - a hundred pounds! What an absolute mug.

I arrived home, tried to ignore my reflection in the hallway mirror and went, with some trepidation into the kitchen. The Husband was preparing a salad and didn't look at me as he was telling me about his day. He'd been sorting out a mortgage for a bin man who'd come straight from work, and the smell in the room had been gross. It had been all he could do not to puke. And at the end of it "the bastard" went for a straight repayment, not an endowment, so hardly any commission in that sale. I watched him hacking up a tomato and hoped he'd washed his hands. I fixed us a drink, whisky and coke for him, vodka and tonic for me. I knocked mine back very quickly. So it's official - I have finally become invisible to men. Even my own husband no longer looks at me. I sloped off to wash my hair.

To round off a perfect day, there was a severe weather warning on the news, with strong gales and heavy rain forecast across the country. Insurers' nightmare - things were about to go bonkers at work. *Great.*

I was blown into work the next morning. I got soaked getting from the car and into the building, but for once I didn't care. It would all help wash out the Cinnamon Copper Pumpkin. The general consensus on my hair was that the "style is really nice". What was left unsaid was "but the colour is bloody awful". Several colleagues asked me if I was feeling alright, as I looked so pale, even though I had applied many coatings of bronzing powder to my face, using a broom.

The Boss sent out a "diary-crash" meeting for 10.00 to all the managers in order to discuss the weather warning. I joined Big Andy, Cruella and The Shark in the meeting room and waited for Brett The Boss to join us via teleconference. As I walked in, Big Andy had roared "Jesus Kate, where did you get your hair done, Sellafield?!" *Ha bloody ha.* We waited for Brett. Just as we were about to start without him, there was a crackle from the black squawk-box in the middle of the table and we could just make out The Boss's voice. "Brett, you're very faint," boomed Big Andy into the box. The Boss started to speak but he kept cutting out and we could only make out every other word.

"...discuss... warning... frigging... weather... claims... dicked..."

We got the gist. The claims team were based in Bridgend and always got hammered with mega-volumes of calls following bad weather. The other sites were expected to support them, and we had to find some resource to do this. Our usual bun-fight ensued.

Big Andy: "I can't give up anyone from Finance, we'll be too busy processing claims." He always says that.

Cruella: "I can't give up anyone from Complaints or we'll fall behind with our cases and be in breach of the FSA." She always says that.

The Shark: "I can't give up anyone from Operations, they've not been trained on the phones." He always says that.

All eyes turn to me - as usual. Brett was trying to say something. "...couldn't give a... just sort... what the f...."

I leant across the table and jabbed a button on the squawk-box, cutting him off. No one protested.

"Right then guys," I started wearily. "We all need to share the pain here. We can't take all the resource out of one area, so we need to agree who's going to give..."

But what about your admin team Kate," Cruella butted in, "can't we use them?" *Oh for God's sake, not this old chestnut again.*

"Yes," urged The Shark, sensing a kill. "Surely their work doesn't take priority over our customers' claims? Can't you use them to take claims calls?"

They never seemed to understand that there's a reason why my admin team do admin. Half of them are phonaphobes, having been struck down with various bizarre ear conditions, including one of them being unable to keep his headset on as his ears were "uneven" and as for the other half, well, you wouldn't want them to come into direct contact with a customer. They're not quite fully evolved yet, knuckles still drag along the ground, although to be fair, some have started to crack nuts open with rudimentary tools.

"But what about your team Ian?" I fought back. "They're also doing administrative work, and I know you say they are not trained on phones, but I'm sure they know how to answer a phone. It's really quite easy - it rings, you pick it up - so perhaps they could take messages for the claims team." The Shark fixed me with his dead eyes. The feeding frenzy had begun. Back and forth across the table we attacked, probing areas of known weaknesses, producing statistics that proved some areas were over-resourced, listening to the reasoning ("but those figures are wrong") and either re-launching an attack or moving on to another victim. It was the same old themes and arguments, all protecting our own arses and going round and round in circles until we ran out of time. At the end of the meeting we were forced to agree that we all had to give up some people, and sulkily committed names to paper. At the end of the meeting, we said as we always did, "we will put a list of colleagues together that we can call upon in the event of bad weather. That will save us having to go through this pain every time." We all agreed, as we always did, that this was a good idea. It never happened.

As I left the meeting room I passed a poster that stated "Across this company we think and act as one." *That's very funny.* The team building event was going to be interesting...

It was the policy at Perypils that in order to be impartial, managers did not hold disciplinary meetings for members of their own teams. Instead we covered each other's sites. Of course, there is no such thing as an impartial manager, but it's a nice thought and it seems to fool the staff.

Julie from the Birmingham office had battled against the elements and driven down this morning to hold the meeting with Lee Halfpenny, following his non-genuine absence. Having phoned in sick, then getting pissed in the pub in full view of his team manager meant it was going to be a bit of a no-brainer, straight-forward dismissal. I was absolutely certain that Lee would resign before the meeting, thus avoiding having "dismissed" on his reference from Perypils, but he hadn't. *What an idiot.*

The meeting lasted a surprisingly long time, well over an hour. Hissing Cyn and I kept looking over at each other, wondering what was going on. Eventually, to our amazement, Lee walked jauntily back into the department, high-fived several colleagues and returned to his desk. What was going on, why wasn't he packing up his stuff? It didn't look as if he'd been dismissed!

The Snake and I went to find Julie. She was in the meeting room gathering up her notes.

"Er, hi Julie," I started, "can you tell me what happened? Lee appears to be back at his desk."

Julie was a matronly-looking woman, dressed in a sensible dark green suit which had probably fitted her once, but was several sizes too small for her now.

"Oh, hi Kate," she said, staring at my hair. "Yes, that was a really difficult meeting." *You what?* "Lee was very open and honest with me." *He's a serial liar!* "He was very sorry for saying he was ill when he wasn't, he knows it was wrong, but he said he was feeling very down and couldn't face coming into work."

Julie saw the look of incredulity on our faces and got defensive. "I phoned HR and talked it through with them and they backed my decision not to dismiss. They said I was right to take into account his history of mental health issues."

I swallowed, hard. "He was signed off with anxiety for a short period of time Julie, that's correct, but he did not receive any treatment, medication or counselling, so he hardly has a history of issues. Because of his attendance, Cynthia has had to put him through training three times now. He is still not performing to standard and he is quite happy to lie to us whilst he sits in a pub taking the complete piss."

Julie bridled. "I've made my decision, and it's very unprofessional of you to query it in this manner." *Yes, that's true, but it was absolutely the wrong decision. You just did not have the balls to dismiss.*

She was still going on: "Managers need to show support to one another, we are one team after all and-"

"Oh really? One team are we? But it's not your problem now is it? It's become ours again!" *You've copped out and left it for us to clear up.*

"By the way," Julie ignored me and addressed The Snake, who looked like she was about to strike, "I agreed with Lee and HR that he should have weekly one-to-ones with his team manager to ensure that he is getting all the support he requires from us. I'll send you the notes through in due course, but you should schedule those into your diary."

How do you want to die, venom or constriction? I escorted Julie out of the office before she came to serious harm. I told her I'd see her at the team building event. I might have said this in a somewhat threatening manner, as she looked quite alarmed as we parted.

The first face I saw as I walked back into the department was Lee's - grinning from ear to ear. *Arghhhh.*

When I got home, I found a note through the letter box from next door. It read:

Sorry about your fence panels. Please do come round to our side if it helps you fix them.

Oh no. I went through to the back garden. Two panels lay on our lawn. Another looked very wobbly in the wind. Was it our fence? Next door seemed to think so. That was going to cost. What a pisser. I went to wash my hair.

CHAPTER ELEVEN

It was my turn to undertake a disciplinary hearing and I had to travel to Manchester to hear a persistent lateness case for them. The meeting was scheduled for 11.00 am, but I didn't want to take any chances and had gone up the night before. In the end, I half-wished I hadn't bothered, as trying to get The Boss to agree to a hotel stay amidst the current cost-cutting drive had been particularly painful. He'd tried to book me into a pub in the town centre that he knew did cheap rooms - they weren't even en-suite! He eventually backed down when I suggested it would be more practical for him to do the hearing as he lived much closer. Suddenly he didn't care which hotel I stayed at, so I picked one with a swimming pool and a fancy restaurant.

I made good time getting to Manchester and found the hotel, which was just off the M6. The building was square and rather brooding, giving me the impression of a prison, although admittedly I've never actually been to one. The Vauxhall Astra I parked next to first had one of its back windows smashed in, so I reversed and parked up as far away from it as possible.

I checked in and was given room 101 - *how typical*. 101 was the furthest away from reception, and I regretted bringing my suitcase, lap top, brief case, hand bag, umbrella and overcoat up all at once, but I hadn't wanted to leave anything in the car. Perspiring heavily, I had a total hissy-fit trying to get the blasted swipe card to swipe, but it worked on the twentieth swipe and I was inside the room.

Is there any lonelier place on earth than the inside of a (3 star) hotel room when the door shuts behind you? You're so utterly alone and anonymous. I have a routine:

- heavy sigh
- put down bags
- check the bathroom for cleanliness (this involves nervously peering under the toilet seat, having a good look round the bath for pubes, examining the shower curtain for general grubbiness/staining)
- opening all the cupboards and drawers to search for a mini bar (there never is one, but I always find a trouser press - why, why, why can't we have an iron and ironing board instead?)
- checking the eiderdown cover for any signs of, well let's just say, bodily fluids

I can never bring myself to examine the sheets or pillows, preferring instead to climb into bed in the dark so I can't see anything and pray that the sparks from the nylon sheets won't set my nightie alight. I also talk to myself - a lot.

I checked the view, hoping perhaps to see a lake or mountain or even the sea from my Manchester bedroom window. I looked down on the car park, and behind it, a river of moving white lights from the motorway. A sign stuck on the windows told me to keep them closed and locked at all times. *Nice*. There was a constant drone from the traffic, so I turned on the telly for some covering noise and a bit of company. I am certain it is a trick of the hotel trade that no matter what you press on the TV remote control, you always seem to end up about to request adult entertainment. I couldn't stand the shame of that on my hotel bill, so I panicked and turned the TV off again.

It was only 5.30 pm. The whole evening stretched out before me, long and empty. With a sudden surge of I'm not sure what - *madness, energy?* I decided I'd go for a swim. I had bought my cossie (a chocolate brown, halterneck one-piece from Boden) although I hadn't dreamt I would actually use it.

The pool was quite small, but empty of anyone else - hooray! I waded in and started breast-stroking up and down, keeping my head well above water so as not to disturb my make-up or dampen my hair - I wasn't sure what the chlorine would do to my Cinnamon Copper Pumpkin. You hear horror stories of coloured hair turning bright green.

The first few lengths were knackering - I was gasping for breath and had to keep stopping. Was I really this unfit, or could I be suffering from some ghastly respiratory disease? But I kept going and it got better - I began to feel quite exhilarated. I wondered how many pounds I had lost already, and how much flatter my stomach would look when I got out. After about twenty lengths, three rather portly middle aged men appeared at the poolside. Oh bugger off you lot, there's not enough room for all of us in here. There won't be enough water left either if you all jump in at once - ha ha. Luckily they headed for the hot tub at the end of the pool. I carried on ploughing up and down, although I couldn't help noticing that the three men were watching me quite intently. This didn't worry me too much at first - I've clearly still got it! Perhaps I would make the hot list after all. I did another 10 lengths or so but they were still watching me, *the pervs,* and I was beginning to feel a bit self-conscious and uncomfortable. I stopped at the far end and was about to get out when I looked down and saw, to my horror, that one of my nipples was hanging out. *Oh my God.*

After changing, I went to the bar to drown my sorrows. I had a large vodka and tonic - very nice. It didn't touch the sides, so I had another. I could see into the restaurant, which looked very classy and was quite empty. Normally I would stay in my room and order room service but I think the V&T's made me brave and reckless and I went over to the restaurant. I was greeted by a dark, dapper little man of European extraction.

"Yes Madame?"

"I'd like a table please."

"Have you booked?"

I looked pointedly around at all the unoccupied tables and chairs. "No I haven't."

"You haven't booked?" His lips pursed together, teeth were sucked in, he examined the bookings register to see if he could possibly accommodate one extra person into his empty dining room. I tried to peer over his shoulder at the register but he shifted his body to block it from view.

"Ok," he whirled round, "is it just for you?"

"Yes it's just me."

"A table just for one?"

"Yes, it's just me."

"Will there be anybody else joining you?"

"No, there will not." No, it's just me, on my own, with no one else to dine with. I am a sad lonely bastard, staying in a hotel on my own. Friendless, childless and probably everyone that sees me eating on my own will think that I am either some sort of weirdo lunatic with orange hair or a desperate saddo who's on the pull. Thank you so much for pointing that out.

Very red cheeked now, but unable to back out, I was shown to a table at the back of the restaurant, near the kitchens.

For anyone who eats alone in a restaurant, there are rules. The first is that you should always take with you some sort of reading matter, such as a book, work notes, magazine etc. This means you can bury your head and pretend to be absorbed in something fascinating, therefore demonstrating to others that you do not feel in the least bit self-conscious and the fact that you are dining alone does not bother you in the slightest. I did not have any reading matter. I read the menu and wine list cover to cover, but after I'd ordered, these were removed, just leaving me with a cardboard label telling me about the special offers on spirits in the bar. This I read with intense scrutiny and interest over and over whilst waiting for my starter to arrive.

The second rule is to order as many courses as your expense meal limit allows and eat very slowly. This is to elongate the experience. I got this wrong too: my plates were whisked away from me as soon as I had finished the last mouthful and the entire meal was over before I'd even managed to finish a glass of wine.

As I slunk out of the restaurant, the three guys from the swimming pool were coming in. I did not make eye contact. I thought I heard one of them say that he felt "a bit of a tit" but I could have been mistaken. They were certainly having a good old laugh about something as I passed.

Back in the room, I checked my mobile for texts from The Husband. There were none. I sent him one asking if he'd managed to sort the fence panels. I braved putting the telly back on and flicked miserably up and down through the channels, eventually settling on "It's Me or the Dog" on ITV2+2+2+2. The Husband texted back "No". That was it. One word. Got the hump because he'd had to make his own supper no doubt. What was wrong with him lately? He was so bloody moody. Possibly he was worried about his work; I think sales had been pretty scarce lately. Everyone was skint. I turned off the light and slid between the scratchy, crackly sheets, turning up the telly to drown out the sound of the couple in 103 bonking. A new low point in my life, methinks.

I arrived at the Manchester site the next morning to undertake the disciplinary meeting. The offence was persistent lateness and I read through the file. The colleague had been late on numerous occasions over the last eighteen months, and had already been issued with verbal and written warnings. Why she'd been given so many 'last chances' was anyone's guess. She was going to need to have a good reason why she deserved another.

I made my way to the appointed meeting room and met Tanya, one of the Manchester team managers who was going to take the notes for me. I asked her why this individual was still employed, given her dismal attendance record.

"I think it's because she's such a really, really nice person" was her answer. *Oh brilliant.* A sound, logical business reason then.

The meeting was set for 11.00. At ten past 11.00, I sent Tanya to look for the colleague. It was twenty past before she returned with a large, smiley lady who was probably around my age.

"This is Marcy." Tanya introduced me as they sat down.

"Hello, how nice to meet you," gushed Marcy. "I do like your hair." *She was clearly insane.*

"You're late, Marcy," I told her.

"I know, I'm so sorry I just didn't notice the time, I was so carried away with what I was doing. Sorry." She beamed at me. Surely she could see the irony of being late to a disciplinary meeting for persistent lateness? Was she very stupid or did she just have no respect at all for the disciplinary process? She'd already been through several similar meetings, I suppose; perhaps she felt bullet-proof.

I read out her offences, listing the date and time of each one, and her reasons (excuses) such as: "On the 14th March you were due to start your shift at 9.00. You arrived at work at 9.20. You gave the reason for this as you kept laddering your tights and then you got stuck behind a milk float."

As I read through the (long) list very methodically, her beam began to fade a little. When I reached the end, I asked her to explain why, despite being issued with a written warning, she had continued to fail to arrive at work on time.

"Well, I've got five children you see..." Marcy looked at me as if she was expecting some sort of congratulations. When none were forthcoming she carried on "You know what it's like trying to get ready for work as well as packing children off to school, and of course with five of the little monsters you can imagine what our household is like!" She gave a loud nervous laugh, which turned into multiple snorts. "No, seriously though," she continued, the smile gone, a sad expression replacing it, "I'm so terribly sorry about the lateness and to put you to all this trouble, I know how hard you managers work." She bowed her head and looked remorsefully up at me through her lashes. "I am a single

116

parent you know, and it's so very difficult to have to do everything yourself, looking after five children on my own. I can only just make ends meet and I rely so heavily on my job here to be able to look after my family. I do so love my job here, sometimes it's the only thing that keeps me going. The people are so lovely, they're like an extended family to me." She flashed a radiant smile in Tanya's direction. "I don't know what I'd do if I couldn't work here anymore, I rely on this job, my five children rely on this job."

I was so tempted to ask her how many children she had, as I didn't think she'd mentioned it, but I stopped myself.

"So, can I clarify Marcy - you are saying you are persistently late because you are getting your children ready for school? Is that right? Yes, you have five children, you said. Do you have anything else you wish to add by way of mitigation? I mean as a reason?"

Marcy had her sincere face on now.

"I just want to say again how sorry I am, and that I will always be on time from now on. I can assure you that I will never be late again."

I showed her the notes from previous meetings. "You've promised that on all the other occasions, too, Marcy, look. Yet you are still arriving late. You've already been given so many chances, why should you be given another one?"

Marcy, sensing she was in a bit of difficulty now, turned her attention to Tanya.

"I beg you for just one last chance, I promise you I will never be late again, never ever. I need this job to be able to feed and clothe my children, I don't know what I'd do without it, without seeing all my wonderful friends that I've made here. I will never be late again. I know I've said that before, but I really mean it this time, I really do. Please give me another chance, I beg you."

It was almost word for word what she'd said on the last two occasions. Despite some more prompting from me, she just continued in the same vein. Eventually, I asked her to wait in another room whilst I considered. She looked pleadingly at Tanya as she left. I heaved a big sigh. I could see why she had not been dismissed previously; it wasn't exactly an easy thing to do to a single parent with five kids.

I looked at Tanya and shook my head. "I'm sorry Tanya, but I really can't see that anything will change if she's given yet another last chance. She didn't offer me anything really by way of defence, or that she was prepared to make any changes that would mean she could get herself to work on time. I can see from the notes that you guys have bent over backwards to support her, well, you've bent over double I would say to support her, but even then she's still been late. I'm afraid my decision is going to be to dismiss her."

To my surprise, Tanya nodded.

"I agree," she said, "We can't keep on giving her a last chance, it's become a bit of a joke. My team places bets now each morning as to what time she's going to turn up. It's embarrassing. She's a lovely lady, and I feel very sorry for her, because of her situation, but she hasn't left us with any choice. We can't give her special treatment; it's not fair on everyone else."

We discussed it between ourselves for a bit longer, but it really was a no-brainer. I couldn't put the moment off any longer, and asked Marcy to come back into the room.

She sat down, clasping her hands to her chest.

"Marcy," I began. "I've listened to everything you've had

to say. Unfortunately, you have not offered sufficient reasoning to explain your continued persistent lateness, nor convinced me that you can make material changes to warrant another warning being issued to you. I've based this on your previous promises and subsequent behaviours...."

"No!" wailed Marcy, cutting across me. "I will change, I won't be late again ever. Not ever! Give me another chance, please, don't do this to my children, it's not their fault, they're innocent. Please don't do this!"

"Marcy, you've already had a last chance and you were late again. Several times. You need a job which offers you flexible working, and as you know, we're not able to do that. I'm very sorry, but my decision is to let you go."

I've always wondered what is must be like to witness a split personality transition, maybe Dr Jekyll turning into Mr Hyde. I felt like Jenny Agutter in American Werewolf in London when she gasps "David!" Gone was the jolly, bubbly lady and the apologetic pleader. Marcy's face darkened and her eyes narrowed into slits.

"So, you are going to let my children starve are you?" she hissed at me. "Shame on you. How can you live with yourself? Are you going to come to my house tonight and explain to my kids that they are going to go hungry? Are you going to tell them that I can't afford clothes for them anymore? No, you'll just go back to your cosy house and your cosy life and you don't care what you do to people like me." *She was taking this well.* She stood up, but hadn't finished. "I'm going to bring my children to the door of this building and wait for you to come out. You can explain to five children what you've done to them, five *father-less* children, tell them how you expect us to live now. I will leave them outside - you can feed them. You can feel what it's like!"

She stormed out of the room. I wished I could just let her go, but of course I couldn't. I had to follow her to her desk, which was slap bang in the middle of the department and make sure she signed out of all the computer systems (which took an excruciating amount of time) and take her desk keys back from her. All eyes were on us. She wasn't going quietly; slamming drawers, wailing to her colleagues that she was being victimised, thrown out for nothing, treated appallingly... the whole room had fallen silent. I then had to walk her out of the department and escort her from the building. It's never, ever going to be a pleasant task, but at least most people choose to go with dignity. Not so Marcy. She spat on the ground outside, her parting shot to me: "Don't think this is the end - you haven't seen the last of me!"

God. I drove back to Cheltenham feeling like a shit. I hated this job. I'd made the only decision I could make, hadn't I? Had it been the right one? There was nothing to feel good about, nothing at all. It would have been nice to talk to someone about it, for some support, but who was there? The Boss wouldn't be interested, he'd just say it comes with the territory. Which, of course, it does. That doesn't stop you being human though. Why was there never any support for managers? Why was it acceptable for my own manager to go for weeks on end without speaking to me? I wouldn't ever treat my guys like that. Not that they gave me any choice in the matter, the buggers never left me alone.

I was feeling sorry for myself. I didn't want to do this stupid job anymore. Perhaps the time had come to consider a career in something else. But what? I could have a look on some of those job websites that are always being advertised. Knowing my luck I'd leave Perypils and end up working somewhere with Marcy! But there's got to be something more rewarding than this. Somewhere less toxic.

I got back to the office just after four, feeling drained but prepared to face the hundred or so pointless emails that would have built up during the day. I hadn't even removed my coat when The Snake was at my desk sniping that she'd had to look after The Climber's team as well as her own as The Climber had gone missing for most of the day. It wasn't fair, she was never where she's supposed to be blah, blah, bloody blah. *Oh shut up can't you, I couldn't give a shiny shite.* I really don't think I can do this anymore.

Chapter Twelve

It was early Saturday evening. The Husband hadn't returned from golf. I'd waited in all day for someone to come and mend the fence but they hadn't turned up. I was just about to settle down with a glass of white wine and a cold chicken salad in front of another Poirot mystery (thank God for ITV3 - always something on that caters for the middle-aged middle classes) when the phone rang. *Oh bugger off will you, why does that always happen, why?* You're clutching the lovely plate of food you've been looking forward to all afternoon and the moment your bottom touches down the phone rings. I answered with a heavy sigh. It was my brother sounding very panicked, and at first I couldn't make out what he was saying.

"Stu, calm down for goodness sake, I can't understand you."

"It's Georgia," he blurted out, his words coming out all in a rush. "She's staying with us and Kirsty's away this weekend in London, so it's just me here and I just don't know what to do." I could hear something strange in the background.

"What's that noise Stu?" I asked with some trepidation.

"That's Georgia - she's throwing up on the doormat."

Euch, yuk.

"Oh blimey, has she eaten something dodgy?" A thought struck me. "She's not drunk is she?"

"Er, yes, I think she might be." *Jesus Christ, how old was she? Fifteen?* "Can you come over Sis? I don't know what I should do."

I didn't have much choice but to agree, chuck on a coat, fetch the rubber gloves from under the sink and jump into the car. It was a good half-hour drive. I kicked myself for not being drunk, too - that would have been a cast iron excuse not to go. I shuddered at the thought of what I was driving to - I hate vomit; if I see someone being sick, even on the telly, I want to be sick myself. Drinking that much, at fifteen, that's not good. I didn't want to be a hypocrite - I remembered going into a pub when I was just fifteen. My friends knew a barman that would knowingly serve under-age girls. He used to make us cocktails and then stir them with a vibrator, the dirty git. But we didn't drink so much that we threw up. Just a couple of Babychams was all we needed to make us think we were completely hammered.

On the positive side though, this situation had saviour-potential written all over it. I imagined myself making Georgia a strong black coffee, we would sit together at the kitchen table and talk, she would open up to me. She'd see me as a cool auntie type, and be inspired by my hard work ethos - my ascent from tea-girl to manager, with responsibility for 100 personnel and a million pound budget. (She didn't need to know that I was wearing odd socks under my boots and that I'd spent half the afternoon trying to unstick my thumbs following another nail-gluing disaster). We would become buddies and go shopping together, I'd introduce her to Monsoon and when she was old enough, Sauvignon Blanc and stuffed olives. I'd vet her boyfriends and give her advice on relationships and the best savings accounts.

When I reached Stu's, I went round the back to avoid the vomit-welcome mat at the front. I could hear Georgia singing what sounded like "God Save the Queen" but I couldn't be sure. I didn't think she'd know the lyrics to that one. I opened the back door and walked into the kitchen. Georgia was stood swaying, clutching a can of Red Bull in one hand and holding onto the back of a chair with the other. She was wearing black and red striped leggings under a short black tunic. Her dark eyes were glazed with smudged black make up all round them which had run down her face. It was like Halloween at New Look.

Demon eyes attempted to focus on mine.

"Oh God, look who is it," she snarled, "Mrs fucking know-it-all. What the fuck do you want?"

"Hello Georgia," I said, in a cool-Auntie-I'm-unfazed-by-drunken-teenagers-type voice, "Is Stu around?"

"Hello Georgia is Stu around," she mimicked in a stupid voice. "My mum can't bloody stand you, she thinks you're well up your own arse, she says you only care about your stupid twatty job, you don't give two shits about your husband, and she says he can't stand you either. Yeah, go on just do one, you nosy bloody..."

Feeling rather shaken by her aggression, I edged around the kitchen table and found my brother mopping the floor in the hallway. I could smell vomit and Flash. He looked worn out.

"Oh Sis, thank God you're here. What am I going to do with her, she won't listen to anything I say. She's out of control!"

"Give us some booze you tight-arsed twonk!" Georgia

shouted from the kitchen.

"She's been trying to get her hands on more booze," Stu said, "I've had to hide all my beer and Kirsty's wine in our bedroom. And the Toilet Duck."

"More booze, more booze, twonk-arsed twonk!"

"How the hell did she get in that state?" I hissed.

"It was nothing to do with me!" Stu looked alarmed. "She was out all afternoon with her mates, she said she was going to the shopping centre, and then she came back completely shit-faced."

There was a crash in the kitchen. We rushed in. Georgia had fallen backwards against the sink, knocking two mugs onto the floor. They lay in bits round her feet. She began laughing, singing "Oops I did it again." I lifted her up from the sink and tried to get her to sit down. She seemed to be running out of steam. Stu swept up the bits of crockery.

"Can you stick the kettle on Stu, we need to get some black coffee down her." I didn't know what else to suggest.

"Coffee is puke," Georgia said, now seated at the table but looking like she'd topple at any time.

"Water then," I said to Stu. He poured a glass and we tried to get Georgia to drink it. She'd gone very pale.

"Gonna chuck."

Stu and I quickly lifted her to her feet and over to the sink - just in time. She vomited copiously over the dirty plates and cups in the sink. I gagged, but managed not to be sick myself. I held her hair out of her face, while Stu rubbed her back. When she'd finally expelled it all, I left Stu to clear up the sink and got an exhausted Georgia to lie down on the sofa, and fetched her duvet. She'd crashed out before I'd returned to cover her. I realised we'd have to watch over her all night, in case she was sick again. You hear about people choking on their own vomit and dying. I couldn't leave Stu alone with her either; I could see how uncomfortable he was which I totally understood. Being responsible for someone else's child is just enormous.

He was extremely grateful I was staying and offered to make me cheese on toast. Thinking of the plates in the sink, I declined, so he fetched some of the Bunny Boiler's wine from the bedroom and we started on that. I phoned The Husband to let him know what was happening. I thought he'd be all grumpy about it, but he was surprisingly understanding and said he'd see me in the morning, and not to worry about rushing back if Stu still needed me tomorrow.

It didn't turn out to be such a bad night. Stu and I had agreed to take it in turns to watch Georgia while the other slept, but we ended up sitting up all night chatting. We talked about the wedding (they'd actually set a date for October now, but I still wasn't convinced it would happen), relationships, work, and our parents. I asked him if he felt worried about Mum at all, and if he thought she was alright.

"Yeah, she's ok, I think," but then he said that when he'd gone round there the other day, he'd found her in the back garden scattering what looked like bath crystals on the lawn. When he'd asked her what she was doing, she'd told him she was feeding the doves. She said it kept them away from the rhubarb. *Eh?*

"We really ought to get her to see a doctor Stu, she's not right."

"Oh, she's fine, she's just getting on a bit."

I wasn't convinced.

We talked about when we were younger, how we never

drank as much as the youngsters do today. We remembered Stu's 18th, when he had been to the pub with his mates for his first legal drink. They'd bought him home and left him stood with his nose pressed against the doorbell. My Dad had gone ballistic. We also remembered Mum and Dad opening the kitchen curtains one morning to find me asleep on the picnic table in the garden after a night out. But we agreed we'd never binged like they do today. As it got light, we realised we'd drunk three bottles of wine between us. When it got to a reasonable hour, with much embarrassment, I had to phone The Husband and ask him to come and pick me up. He wasn't quite so understanding this time.

Monday

I was driving to work thinking about what kind of evils the day had in store for me, then remembered with a sinking feeling that I had blocked out the day in order to reconcile the monthly departmental sales bonus and direct costs figures - a torturous job which I despised. I wondered if I could delegate this task to one of the Team Managers - a good development opportunity for one of them. But which one?

The Rock? Too busy. TLS? Too thick. The Drain? Would finish him off. Although, perhaps, that might be a good call...

I gave myself a talking to as I passed the Little Chef. I had been reading a book entitled "How to Work With People You Can't Stand", or something like that and it had just covered the Circle of Influence. Basically, this said that if you see people in a certain way, you will behave in a certain way towards them and therefore you will get exactly what you expect. So I must choose to have positive thoughts about my colleagues, and therefore I will bring about a positive result. You reap what you sow. I selected an uplifting song from my iPod – What A Feeling from the film Flashdance. I parked up at work feeling ready to burst into the office brandishing welding irons, sparks flying as I twirled to my desk.

I was preparing to start on the reports, when I received a phone call from The Drain, who said he was driving round and round the Chiltern roundabout as he could not face coming into work. The temptation to leave him doing this all day was extremely strong, but I resisted (great self-control) and told him to drive back home. *Bugger it.* That meant I was going to have to do his job as well as my own, and look after his team of moaning, whining cry-babies.

Midday. The reports were nowhere near completed, following a steady stream of interruptions from colleagues, such as:

"Kate, where shall I file this month's quality figures?"

"Try the file named Monthly Quality Figures."

"Kate, I don't understand the email you sent me."

"Which one?"

"Er, it was something to do with the new quotation process."

"Which bit didn't you understand?"

"Er, the bit at the beginning, and all the other bits..."

"Have you actually read the email?"

"Er, no, not really..."

"Kate, Susi wants Thursday off as she's competing in a kick boxing championship. What shall I say?"

"Kick boxing? Bloody hell! Just agree it for Christ's sake!"

"Kate, Glynnis has put on her health and safety form

that she finds the noise from the telephony teams disturbing. What shall I do?"

"Glynnis? But isn't she the deaf lady?"

"Kate, are you busy?"

'No of course not! I really don't know how I'm managing to fill these fourteen hour days."

2.00 pm. I received an email from Tanya at Manchester saying she'd had a letter from Marcy appealing against her dismissal on the grounds of sexual harassment. *You what?* I phoned Tanya to see if I could find out any more. She told me that Marcy was gay and that's why her marriage had broken down. I asked Tanya if she felt Marcy had any particular reason to make a claim of sexual harassment.

"Goodness no, we're quite used to her sort, we've got lots of dykey-types working here!" *Oh God.*

I emailed details of the case to HR so they could appoint a manager to hear the appeal - it was out of my hands now.

2.35 pm. Hissing Cyn slithered over to my desk. I could see the suggestion of a smile on her snake's mouth so guessed someone had suffered some kind of misfortune.

"I thought you ought to know that Joe Cooper has fallen asleep at his desk," she hissed, very quietly, obviously enjoying the moment and not wanting to wake him until everyone had noticed. "He's one of Martin's new lads." *Fallen asleep? Were you telling him about yourself?*

"Try waking him up, then."

The Snake looked aghast, like I'd suggested slaughtering her first born.

"I can't do that, we've been taught that - as first aiders -

it's extremely dangerous to wake up colleagues. The shock could kill him."

"The shock of my boot up his arse will do that to him Cynthia, for God's sake, what do you suggest we do - just let him have a nap? Shall I fetch him some pyjamas and a teddy bear? I've never heard anything so ridiculous." I was up and out of my seat before she could respond and I was bearing down on the dozing Joe when one of his quick-thinking colleagues rang his desk phone. His head jerked up and he looked around him in bewilderment until his red-rimmed eyes focused on my thunderous face, two inches from his own. "A word please, Joe."

The department fell silent as it always does for the Walk of Shame. This is when a colleague is escorted towards the meeting room. Sometimes they return, sometimes they don't. I sat across the desk from Joe, who realising the seriousness of his situation, had begun to tremble.

"Joe," I began, very calmly I thought. "You were asleep at your desk."

"Really? I don't think I was actually asleep was I? Just resting my eyes maybe. They get strained sometimes you know, with all this processing..."

"You were asleep, Joe. At your desk. Why were you asleep?"

"Well, I am very tired today. I got in very late last night you see, I met up with some friends in Cardiff, and I was driving back from Wales and the traffic on the Severn Bridge was just-"

"I don't want a travel report, Joe. Do you understand that one of the expectations of your role is that you are to remain awake whilst you are performing it?"

"Yes."

"And do you understand that if you do not remain in a state of wakefulness, by that I mean not asleep, whilst you are at work again, you will be out on your arse?"

"Yes."

"Sign here."

I got Joe to sign a ROD (Record of Discussion), and as we had to do with all RODs, I emailed a copy to HR. I did change the wording from "out on your arse" to "will be dismissed" before I emailed it, to appear more professional.

4.50 pm. I was still working on the reports. They wouldn't balance. My hair was sticking up and my eyes were bloodshot and sore. I received a phone call from Sue, an HR advisor.

"Hi Kate, I just wanted to discuss the ROD you sent through for Joe."

"Ok." *If I must.*

"It's not particularly detailed, is it?"

"What detail would you expect, Sue, for this particular scenario? He fell asleep at his desk, he agrees it was wrong, he understands the consequences if he does it again. Job done."

"Well, that's a very simplistic view of course." *You patronising cow.* "I would have expected there to have been a thorough exploration of why Joe fell asleep."

"A detailed exploration? He got in late last night!"

"You know, he may have been feeling unwell..."

"He wasn't unwell, he just got in late."

"Or perhaps he has some personal issues that he is dealing with."

"No, he hasn't, he just GOT IN LATE."

"There's no need to shout at me. You should at least have made sure he has the colleague counselling number," *Should I have wiped his arse for him as well?* "plus evidence that he understands the procedures he has breached; you should have issued him with a copy of those procedures."

"Procedures for what exactly? Show me those procedures that state that colleagues must remain awake - they don't exist! It's taken as a given that falling asleep is VERY WRONG."

"You're shouting again. So will you complete another ROD with Joe containing this detail and email it to me? When can I expect it?"

"When? I'll tell you when shall I? When hell freezes over, that's when! Stop wasting my time Sue, and go back to your knitting. I've got a department to run, you know, you may have heard of them - a department with real customers to look after. They call us, expecting to discuss their policies with advisors who are actually awake. That may seem mad to you guys in HR: perhaps you think I should go round to each one of my hundred staff every day to see if they'd mind awfully staying conscious for their shift, that's if it's not too much trouble. And if they happen to nod off, I'll offer them some counselling shall I, or fetch them one of your fluffy bunnies perhaps...."

The line went dead. Sue had hung up. I didn't blame her – I wouldn't want to speak with a ranting, demented lunatic either. I hardly recognised myself anymore; surely this wasn't the real me? I never used to shout at my colleagues, not even the ones in IT. When had I become so intolerant? I must try harder. I must be more understanding.

7 pm. The reports still wouldn't balance. Brain was fried and the noise from the hoover was driving me insane. Decided to pack it all up and take it home. I'm sure it will make more sense after thirteen V&Ts.

11.40 pm. I am sitting at the kitchen table surrounded by reams of reports which won't balance, a (now broken) calculator and an empty vodka bottle. The Husband has gone to bed, after not offering to help, even though as a financial advisor, he is supposed to be very good with figures. And the fence is still broken.

Wednesday

I finally got the reports submitted. I had to email copies to The Boss. He emailed back to ask me if I'd calculated my own bonus this quarter. *No, that's your job!* I replied not. He emailed again asking me to calculate what it should be and to let him know so he could submit it. *I'll do your job as well as mine then, shall I?* I worked it out as £412.80 and sent that figure to him. When I got home, the fence panels had been fixed and the invoice was lying on the doormat. It was for £418.50. *Great.*

Friday morning

The Boss phoned. He was on his way to Manchester to hear Marcy's appeal against her dismissal. He wanted some background information, saying he'd phoned Marcy to check she was still ok for the meeting and she had seemed like "a really nice lady". *Uh-oh.* I told him about my meeting, tactfully saying that it was all documented in the case notes. He said he hadn't had time to read the notes but was trying to look through them whenever he stopped at traffic lights. I tried to tell him about her personality change, but I'm not at all sure he was listening, given that whilst I was speaking he shouted "Get a bloody move on you tosspot, you could get a sodding bus through there!" followed by several angry blasts on the horn.

Friday afternoon

Tanya from Manchester called to let me know what had happened at Marcy's appeal. Marcy had started the meeting all smiles and had said she was very sorry and embarrassed to have to make this claim. She'd said she felt that several of her colleagues were extremely homophobic, and she'd had to put up with comments such as: "It's dress down tomorrow Marcy, don't forget your dungarees!" and "You'd better cut your finger nails Marcy; you'll never get a girlfriend with those talons!"

The Boss had said he was extremely sorry to hear that, however he struggled to see why that would contribute to her persistent lateness. At the end of the meeting, he upheld the decision to dismiss Marcy. Apparently at this point, all hell let loose.

Marcy had stood up and turned the table over on top of The Boss, scattering his files all over the floor and tipping his coffee into his lap. She then sat down in front of the door to the meeting room, refusing to move until The Boss reconsidered or agreed to foster her five children. He had to call security for help, but according to Tanya, it took him ages to get through to the security team as he was held in a queue, having to listen to a recorded message which told him his call was important to them.

When they got there, it took four of them to force the door open and remove her. She'd hung onto the door frame, screaming "Child murderer!" at The Boss. They'd had to prise her fingers open one by one. *Bloody hell.* I drove home half expecting to find Marcy on my doorstep with her five starving children in tow. That would really give The Husband something to moan about.

CHAPTER THIRTEEN

The dreaded day was upon me. I was in Big Andy's car, and he was driving us to the meeting point for the Perypils management team building day, which was a hotel in Nottingham. From there, we were to be transported to an activity centre for an afternoon of outdoor team building events. I could not think of anything worse. Then back to the hotel, quick change followed by pre-dinner drinks, networking and a motivating talk from the Big Cheese who was joining us for dinner. I was wrong; this was worse.

Tomorrow there was a classroom-based course entitled "Building High-Performing Teams", which everyone would be too hungover to give a shit about. Why was Perypils going ahead with this event, when it must be costing a fortune? We were supposed to be cutting down on costs. I couldn't even order a box of staples for Christ's sake, and yet they were entertaining around forty managers with dinner and an overnight stay thrown in. *Madness.*

I would have done anything to get out of going, literally anything, and had spent many a sleepless night trying to think up a feasible excuse. And it would have had to have been a good one: a stomach upset or sudden family crisis wouldn't have been believed. In the end, the stress of making up an excuse became worse than the thought of going, so I gave it up and resigned myself to my fate.

The worse thing was the agonising over what to wear. I

really had been quite pathetic. Even though I have wardrobes so stuffed full of clothes that I'm surprised the ceiling doesn't collapse, I have still bought new things for this event. You'd think I'd never been outdoors before. The long-range forecast had been for changeable weather, so in case of rain, I'd purchased a khaki Pac A Mac and matching wellingtons from Next. The model in the picture had teamed hers with a pair of denim shorts and bare legs, which, after three large glasses of wine I'd briefly considered (oh the dangers of drinking and online shopping, why aren't there more Government warnings) but very fortunately I'd decided to stick to jeans.

In case it didn't rain, but was cold, I had also purchased a padded brown gilet from Joules. As I was unable to find a single suitable garment in my wardrobes to wear under this, I ordered a checked shirt from them too. Total cost... I can't bear to add it all up.

The evening wear was also a challenge - the dress code stated "smart casual". *What does that actually mean?* After much deliberation, I eventually played safe with black trousers and a floaty cream top. I did buy a couple of new necklaces from Top Shop, as after all, I've only got about fifty necklaces, so am clearly in desperate need for more. Although to be fair, all fifty are tangled up together in a big mass so actually it was quicker to buy new ones.

I asked Andy if he'd had trouble deciding what to bring, but of course he hadn't.

"Jeans, jumper and a shirt," he replied, looking surprised at the question.

He said he thought it should be "an interesting couple of days". I asked him why.

"Because of all the rumours, of course."

"What rumours?"

"Oh come on, Kate, you must have heard them all flying around the company." *Er, nope.* "Sales are down and the cost-cutting drive doesn't seem to be working. Looks like there's going to be a pretty significant restructure coming up. Probably a site closure, too."

"Bloody hell!" I exclaimed in alarm. "Do you think it will be us that goes? We are the smallest site."

"I don't know, the smart money's on Bridgend, their figures are always the poorest."

"Why on earth are they forking out on this team building event, then? It must be costing a fortune."

"Ah well, apparently it's all part of their cunning plan," said Big Andy, "They're going to use these two days as part of their assessment process - to see who stays and who goes. They'll keep the ones who do the best and get shot of the others in the restructure."

No pressure then. No wonder we had been issued with a "be there or else" invitation by The Boss.

"But how can they do away with any managers?" I was aware I sounded desperately whiney. "Many of us work twelve, fourteen hour days as it is. Are they expecting the ones who are left to take on even more duties?"

"You betcha!" Big Andy exclaimed cheerfully. "For example, they probably wouldn't keep both you and Cruella. They'd just stick your two departments together and just have one of you run the whole thing. Then they can get rid of the other one."

Me versus Cruella? Oh no. She'd shred me into little pieces and feed me to her evil black cat.

"How do you know all this stuff, Andy? Where do you hear it from?"

"From Brett," he replied, "he's always wonderfully indiscreet when he's had a pint or two. He'll tell you anything." The Boys Club of course, how typical. I wondered if Cruella had heard these rumours. Probably not. She wasn't in the Boys Club either, for obvious reasons. Big Andy wittered away about his kids and his holiday, but I was only half listening. I was worried. What would I do if I lost my job? We'd really struggle to meet all our monthly outgoings, especially the mortgage. I'd get some sort of redundancy payment presumably, unless they sacked me, but what happens when that runs out? Would I be able to get another job? What if I couldn't? You hear about these people, usually around my age, sending off application after application without success. I calmed myself down - it was only rumours after all. Just rumours. No need to panic yet.

We arrived at the hotel in good time and were greeted by the event co-ordinator Jenny, a tall, stunning, bronzed-limbed lady who also happened to be Kevin the Big Cheese's PA. She directed us to a large meeting room where the others were gathering. Cruella and The Shark were already there and we greeted each other like long lost buddies to show the other sites what a great bunch we were in Cheltenham and how well we all got on. The sites were always in competition with each other, although our main rivals were Bridgend. Their staff referred to us as The Farmers and our guys, both predictably and depressingly, referred to them as The Sheep Shaggers. Originality not a strong point amongst the colleagues of Perypils.

I recognised most of the managers from Birmingham

and Manchester, who nodded a welcome, apart from Julie the namby-pamby-I-won't-dismiss-you-because-you've-given-me-a-really-good-sob story manager from Birmingham who deliberately looked away. The guys from Bridgend hadn't made it yet and there was no sign of Brett the Boss. Everyone was stood in tight groups, awkwardly clutching their cups and saucers or checking their BlackBerries, trying to look important. There were also some hangers-on from the sales and marketing teams. I bet they'd actually chosen to come. They'd show up anywhere where there was free food and drink and the potential to be around intoxicated women.

There were some real brown-nosers in the room, mainly the male managers, who latched onto Jenny The PA each time she appeared, with questions such as "How is Kevin today?"and "What time is Kevin coming tonight?" and "Can I do anything to help, Jenny?" and "Would you like me to rub Kevin down with a warm flannel when he gets here? Do you think Kevin would like to sleep with my wife later? No? What about my mother then?" *What a bunch of creeps.*

The guys from Bridgend had arrived, and I could see through the window that The Boss was here too. He was walking around the car park talking into his mobile. I was half way through my second cup of coffee when Jenny announced to the room that we would be leaving in 10 minutes and that toilet facilities were very limited at the activity centre. I put my cup down. *What sort of place were they taking us to?* I went to find the loos, dropping the swing door in Julie's face as she followed me out. *Small victories.*

They piled us onto two mini buses and we set off. After about twenty minutes we turned off the main road, and drove for what seemed like an eternity up a bumpy dirt track. I was sat next to Rich from Birmingham, who was lovely and chatty, but I found it difficult to understand what he was saying and I was too embarrassed to keep saying "Pardon?" all the time. I think I established that he enjoyed his job - "oi quoit loik it" - and that he was an avid supporter of "Berminggum Citay".

We eventually arrived at a tatty sign that said "Burrkitts Wood Outdoor Adventures" with an arrow pointing into a field. Waiting for us was a group of instructors, four men and two women, who all looked like they'd just stepped out of Sandhurst: straight-backed, clean cut, über confident. God knows what they made of us as we clambered out of the buses, unsuitably clothed, groaning, heavily made up (me), but they were probably just thinking "ker-ching!".

Rich declared he was "fookin fray-zing". It was chilly, but at least it wasn't raining. The instructors asked us to get into groups of six. Of course, everyone huddled together with their own guys. To even up the numbers as Cheltenham is a small site, the four of us were joined by Rick from Sales (loud, brash, competitive) and by The Boss, who was still attached to his mobile. We were marched up a hill to a large field for the first activity. The guys from Bridgend were doing the same activity in another field further up. Our instructor, Amy, explained what we had to do.

"This is called the farmer and his sheep. It's to start to get you thinking and working together as a team to achieve one goal. A chance for you today to put aside the pressures of your usual daily duties. And your mobiles," pointed look at the Boss, who ignored her. "One of you will be the farmer. You will stand in the middle of the field and direct the rest of your team, your sheep, around the markers and into the pen at the far end. You need to do this in the quickest possible time. The sheep will be blindfolded. The farmer will be given a whistle. You have five minutes to plan your strategy. Any questions?"

"Yes I have." The Shark was straight in. "The ground looks extremely uneven to me. Are the blindfolds strictly necessary, I mean it would be very easy to turn an ankle, or sprain a foot..." Amy cut him short.

"The blindfolds are an essential part of the activity, sorry what's your name? Ian. And we've never had any injuries so far. Any other questions? Good. Five minutes, off you go."

Rick from Sales seized control. "Righto then, who wants to be the farmer? Get off your phone Bretto, we need you in on this." *Nice work Rick!* The Boss did end his call and joined the group, but he started to read a text message instead.

As everyone wanted to be the farmer, Rick gave the role to Cruella, who clearly scared him. She agreed that she would give one short blast on the whistle for a "left turn", two short blasts for a "right turn" and then a continuous blast meant "stop".

Big Andy was to be the first sheep, and had to kneel down so we were able to get the blindfold on him. The Shark was still very unhappy about the health and safety elements of the task, but Rick told him he was being "a bloody old woman" and he sulkily shut up. Our five minutes were up, and Cruella took up her position in the middle of the field. We were off! Big Andy strode forward with big exaggerated steps like a robot, jerkily changing directions as Cruella whistled him left and right through the markers. He did really well, the only tricky bit was getting him into the pen at the end as the opening was very small, but he managed the run in

4.54 minutes. We all gave him a big cheer from the other end of the field.

The Shark went next. Gingerly stepping into the field, he shuffled his way towards the first marker, slowly turning in response to Cruella's whistle, and shuffling on a bit further. It was painstaking progress. Big Andy was shouting encouragement from his pen.

Rick, bursting with frustration, eventually shouted:

"For fuck's sake Grandma, get a fucking move on! The fucking moon will be up in a minute!" Amy the Instructor had a go at him for not being "very team spirited". The Shark finished his run in 11.32 minutes. We all cheered again, but it was a muted one this time. I was getting cold.

Brett the Boss was next. Blindfold on, he marched up the field towards the first marker. Cruella whistled two blasts for a right turn. He turned left. Cruella frantically whistled twice again. He kept going to the left. He looked like he was heading for a ditch at the bottom of the field. Cruella gave a long, continuous blast on the whistle. He swivelled to the right at last and retraced his steps virtually back to the starting point. For some reason, and without any whistled instruction, he then decided to turn left and head back towards the ditch. Cruella was running out of puff, and her whistle was being drowned out by the sound of Big Andy's laughter which was booming out across the field. Even Rick was convulsed with laughter. Amy the Instructor was shaking her head, saying "he didn't listen did he?" Amy eventually ran down to the ditch to head him off and repeat the instructions. He completed his run in 17.32 minutes. I could see across the fields that the team from Bridgend had finished and were heading off to the next activity.

I went next. I could see out of the bottom of my blindfold so it was really quite easy. I bombed round the field, although tried to make entering the pen look difficult so it at least appeared genuine. My time was 4.05 minutes. Relieved cheers.

Rick was last, and he too went round like the clappers, so I guessed he could see out too. He just beat my time, doing 4.01 minutes, winking at me after he'd removed his blindfold. Cruella joined us at the pen, looking shattered. Her lemon lips were turning blue.

Amy the Instructor tried to be upbeat. "Very well done guys! What sort of things did you learn from that exercise?"

"Ian needs a fucking zimmer frame," Rick growled. Amy chose to ignore him and looked at the rest of us.

"I think it's important to make sure instructions are clear and understood by everyone," ventured Cruella. *Creep.* What everyone really wanted to say was that you needed to listen to instructions rather than twat about on your mobile, but no one quite had the balls to say it.

Amy led us to the next activity. Heads down, we trudged to another field where the team from Bridgend were waiting for us. By the way they were flapping their arms about and hopping from one foot to the other to keep warm, I'd say they'd been there quite a while. Lots of grins and cracks of "Lost your sheep did you?" "We thought you farmers would have been right at home with that task!" *Ha bloody ha.* We returned forced smiles. Ahead of us sat two quad bikes. Amy the Instructor explained that we were to take part in a quad bike relay race against Bridgend. Brett The Boss and Rick from Sales became extremely animated and excited. The Boss, apparently, had quad biked "loads of times" and Rick, not to be outdone, said he'd once quad biked through the Arizona desert. *Really? Was that before or after you'd raised the Titanic?*

The Shark, however, pronounced them a "death-trap" and refused to take part in the activity. Amy the Instructor, tried to coax him round, assuring him they were safe and showing him a safety helmet, but he was adamant. Bridgend were getting very impatient. Rick shouted over an apology to them:

"Sorry about this guys but Granny's got her knickers in a twist again." This kicked off a furious argument between Rick and The Shark, with Big Andy having to step in to calm things down. Cruella and I, not knowing where to look, examined our feet and kicked at the turf.

As we were one man down for the relay, we decided one of us would have to go round twice. However, Bridgend were not happy with this, in case we picked our best person. There followed a ridiculous debate between the two teams about who should go round twice, with someone actually suggesting that our team did a trial run, we recorded the times, work out the average and picked the person whose time was closest to the average. The instructors were exchanging despairing glances. Eventually, exasperated, a lady from the Bridgend team said she'd drop out.

At last we were ready to go. A twisty-turny course was laid out in front of us. Bridgend's course was next to ours, laid out exactly the same. Ten seconds were added to your team's time if you missed a marker. A quick explanation on how to work the quad bikes, helmets were on and the quads were revved up. Rick from Sales was first up for us, of course. They were off. Rick was pretty good, a bit erratic and

145

wobbly for someone who had quad biked through the Arizona, but still not bad, and he finished the course neck and neck with Bridgend's rider. He handed the bike over to The Boss, who was up against Boss-Eyed Brenda from Bridgend. For someone who couldn't see straight, she did remarkably well, almost keeping pace with the Boss whilst her team yelled the directions to her. My heart was racing, I was next up. The Boss finished ahead of Brenda and handed the bike over to me.

I swung my leg over the bike and tried to set off. *Jesus, it was heavy.* I couldn't quite get the acceleration right, and started to kangaroo along the course. Over the noise of the bike I could hear The Boss and Rick shouting but I couldn't make out what they were saying. I hiccupped to the first marker and tried to turn but the bike was too heavy. I flattened the marker and started to veer off course. Next door, the Bridgend rider overtook me. I tried to steer back on to the course, but missed the next marker. The bloody thing was like a shopping trolley - it had a mind of its own. I couldn't steer it at all and ended up veering so far to the right that I found myself on Bridgend's course. Their rider looked startled to see me, but he managed to swerve round me and avoided a collision. He was haring back to complete his lap. I managed to turn the bike around by riding in a huge circle. I gave up trying to negotiate the course, and just rode in a straight line back to the start.

I was supposed to hand over to Big Andy, but he was laughing so hard that he'd had to sit down on the grass and was incapable of taking over. Scarlet with humiliation, I removed my helmet, and had to watch Cruella perform a perfect run - fast, neat and completely within the markers. It was no use though; thanks to me, Bridgend were miles ahead and they had finished by the time Big Andy got to start his lap. I felt a total fool. It reminded me of a time when I was ten years old and on a school trip to the Isle of Wight. Our class had gone to Robin Hill, and I was in Pet Corner being chased round and round by a sheep who was trying to eat my crisps. All my class mates and children from other schools sat round and laughed at me as I gradually lost all my crisps and started crying. It felt the same. No, it was worse; I'd lost the task for the whole team. And Cruella had been perfect. I felt sick with shame.

Rick from Sales gave me a hug and said loudly so the Shark would hear "Never mind Kato, at least you were man enough to give it a go." The Shark took exception to this and another row ensued. Next to us, the guys from Bridgend were cock-a-hoop, indulging in a group hug and singing 'Delilah'.

Amy the Instructor looked done in.

"Right, let's get you to the last activity of the afternoon," she said, unable to disguise the relief in her voice. This last task was clearly supposed to be the finale of the day. All four sites were up against each other. We were taken back to the first field we'd been in where some equipment had been laid out for us. Each team had four bamboo sticks, some string, strips of rubber and mysteriously, a carton of six eggs. *What the bloody hell was this?*

Amy explained the rules to us.

"Each team has thirty minutes to make a catapult using just the equipment in front of you. At the end of thirty minutes, each team will have two attempts to fire an egg as far as possible. The egg must be caught by a team member without it breaking. The team that fires their egg the furthest and catches it intact wins." We all looked at each other. Amy continued "You have six eggs, so you can have four practise runs if you want to. I suggest you appoint a team leader. Any questions? No? Ian? No? Really? Ok, off you go then."

We stood around and surveyed the equipment. Brett The Boss volunteered to be team leader as he said he used to be in the scouts. No one really understood why that was relevant, but nobody argued with him. I was appointed as time-keeper. After my showing on the quad bikes, that was the only task I could be trusted with. The Boss directed us to start tying the bamboo sticks together with the string, but it was extremely difficult to get them to hold firmly enough. It was obvious we needed the rubber strips in between the sticks to make the catapult, but it just seemed impossible to do. It didn't help that two members of the team were not on speaking terms with one another. The Boss soon lost interest and took a call on his mobile. The team from Birmingham were next to us. In what seemed like no time at all, they had put together a very sturdy-looking catapult and were firing off some practise eggs. I tried to see how they had done it, but they very deliberately blocked it from my view. *Bastards.*

Thirty minutes was up *thank God.* All the teams had to get ready for their first "live" shot. We were reminded that to count, we had to catch the egg intact. At the far end of the field, the team from Manchester went first. One person placed the egg in the catapult and the team stood in front of it, ready to catch. The egg fired, but didn't go far enough to reach a team member, and the egg smashed on the ground in front of them. Lots of groans, and I heard one of them declare "that were cack".

Bridgend were next. They all got into position, but

although it fired to a good height, their egg veered off to the right and missed all their outstretched hands. More disappointed groans.

Birmingham were next. Their firer pulled the catapult back and the egg soared miles into the air. It went straight over the top of all its team members.

Us next. We looked at our catapult. It had fallen over. Amidst some unsporting sniggers, we stood it back up and Rick got ready to fire. We hadn't done any practise runs so we didn't know how far our egg would go. We spread out, Big Andy at the rear, some twenty yards back, which I thought was a bit optimistic. Rick gingerly pulled back on the catapult. We got ready to catch. Rick released the egg - it flew backwards. Howls of laughter rang out around the field. Even Amy, who is supposed to be supportive at all times, hid her face in the collar of her jacket.

The teams were given ten minutes to make adjustments before their final shot. *Would this day never end?* We stood around and surveyed our catapult, which looked in danger of collapsing again. There wasn't much we could do in ten minutes; it was a lost cause. Rick half-heartedly fiddled with the strings and then we had to get ready for the final go.

Manchester went first again. The team spread out, ready to take a catch. The egg was fired. It was a great shot. It reached a good height, and started to fall in the middle of the team. They all rushed forwards, but the two closest ran into each other, stopping them reaching the egg in time. It fell into a gap and smashed. The two who'd collided looked like they were about to fight each other, until their instructor quickly stepped in.

Bridgend were next. They fired their egg. It sailed high

up into the air, and Boss-Eyed Brenda was directly under it. The team yelled "Catch it Brenda!" Everyone else held their breath. The egg fell straight through her outstretched arms and hit the ground. She was still looking up in the air for it.

Birmingham next. Looking cocky and confident, they stood well back, knowing their egg would travel some distance. The egg firer pulled right back on the catapult and released the egg. It shot through the air, travelling at least thirty yards before it started to descend. Julie was there. The team screeched "Go on Julie!" She was right under it. She held out her hands. She missed. The egg landed on her chest, and smashed all over her. She stood there in shock, her navy fleece covered in bits of shell and drippy, smelly egg. It had splattered her face too. Everyone else collapsed with laughter. I had to cross my legs to not wet myself.

Still giggling, we got ready for our go. Given our last attempt, we did not have high hopes. We all stood extremely close to the catapult and just hoped the egg would go forwards this time. Rick pulled carefully back on the catapult. We crouched ready. Rick fired and the egg pinged up, going about four inches high and about four inches forwards. I was stood right in front of the catapult. I made a lunge for the egg. I managed to get my hand underneath it just before it hit the ground. It didn't break! I lay prostrate on the ground, holding the egg up yelling my lungs out. The team went crazy. They pulled me up and we all jumped around in a big group hug, shouting "We won, we won!" Even Cruella said "well done", and almost looked like she meant it. I felt like an absolute hero.

The other teams looked as sick as parrots. Downcast, they slowly made their way back to the mini buses, whilst we bounded along, happily chatting away, even Rick and The Shark were sharing a laugh together. Amazing what a taste of victory can do for team spirit; for that moment we were united as one - a great, unstoppable force, champions of the world.

Back at the hotel we had an hour to check into our rooms and get down to the bar for "pre-dinner drinks and networking". I hate networking - I'm rubbish at it, and I always get trapped in a corner with some boring nerd because I've made the mistake of showing an interest in them, and then I can't get away. Of course, I also feared that some people would feel the same way about me. I thought I'd go down a bit later, just before dinner. I was still feeling exuberant, and sang a Madonna medley loudly in the shower. After I'd dressed, I phoned The Husband. He answered his mobile with a breathless "Hello?"

"Oh sorry love" I said, "are you at the gym? I'll call back later."

"No, no I'm not at the gym, I'm at home. Where are you?" He sounded a little flustered.

"I'm in Nottingham, aren't I?" I replied. *Odd - had he forgotten I was away tonight?* "I'm at the hotel, just getting ready for dinner. Is everything ok?"

"Oh yes, fine, yes fine, I was, er, just getting ready to go to the gym. You ok?"

"Yes, you could say it's been a pretty interesting day. They took us to this Godforsaken place in the middle of nowhere where we had to do these mad activities-"

He cut in "Well, that's great, really great. I'd better be off then, so have a good night and see you tomorrow? Cheers then, take care." He rang off.

I sat on the bed. He'd sounded very strange. *Cheers then, take care.* That was the sort of thing you said to a mate, or someone you'd just bought a copy of Big Issue from on the street. Not your wife. He hadn't been very keen to talk - probably just in a rush to get to the gym before it got too busy. Oh well. I felt a little deflated and in sudden need of a drink. Nothing for it - I headed off to the bar.

The bar area was already quite crowded when I got down there. I heard The Big Cheese before I saw him - booming great voice like a fog horn. He was at the far end of the bar, surrounded by a sycophantic group of cling-ons, all fully paid up members of the Boys Club, vying with each other to get as close to him as possible and laughing unnaturally loudly at his jokes.

Big Andy waved at me from the bar, and I went over to collect a large vodka and tonic from him. He was grinning at me. "What's so funny?" I asked, looking down at myself in case I'd put my top on inside out, or my knickers on over my trousers.

"Look who's over there," he said, nodding his head towards the left hand side of the room. I looked round, and did a double take. It was The Climber! She was stood talking to The Boss, holding a large glass of white wine in one hand and flicking her hair about with the other.

"What is she doing here?!"

Andy laughed. "Well, I dare say she was just passing through!" *A round trip of 168 miles?* Her annoying, silly laugh rang out around the room.

"Christ, who's the long-haired hyena?" asked Rick, who'd appeared at our sides. I warmed to him.

"She's one of Kate's," Big Andy told him. "Very

devoted, follows her everywhere."

"Bloody hell, bad luck," Rick sympathised and got me another large vodka and tonic, although I hadn't started the first one yet. I had to know why The Climber was here, and what she was talking to The Boss about, so I pushed my way over to them.

"Hi Amanda," I said, as warmly as I could manage, "what a surprise to see you here." *At a team building event for department managers, which you're not and that you weren't invited to.*

"Oh, hi Kate," she replied with a toss of her hair, "How was the quad biking?" *You bitch.* "Brett tells me you were a natural!" She laughed her stupid laugh. I wanted to grab her by her flicky hair, swing her round a few times and chuck her through the window.

"Brett invited me along for a drink as he thought it would be a good opportunity for me to do some networking. You know, with all the important people being here." I looked at The Boss. He appeared to be engrossed in a text message. Why had he been talking to her? He never spoke to me.

"Well," I said, "it's a long way to come, so I hope it's worth the journey. So you must have left the office early to get here; I don't recall you asking me if that was ok. How did your teams do today by the way, what were their results like?" She looked like she was about to say "I haven't a clue" which wouldn't have surprised me, but at that moment The Big Cheese's PA, Jenny, tapped on a glass to get everyone's attention.

"Ladies and gentlemen," she announced, "I give you our Chief Executive, Kevin Goddard!" Thunderous applause. Unfortunately, I was holding two drinks so couldn't join in.

The Big Cheese swaggered to the front of the room, clutching a pint. He opened with a few jokes: "I'm a bit late getting here today as my mother-in-law came by to see me. She said she'd decided she wanted to be cremated. I said ok then, get yer coat." Screeches of laughter. "This is a woman so mean she blinded herself just to get a free dog." More hysterical laughter. "I took her to Madame Tussaud's the other day. We were in the Chamber of Horrors. One of the attendants said to me 'Keep her moving sir, we're stock-taking'." *God give me strength.*

He started off relatively calmly, speaking about our wonderful colleagues. "The foundations of our great company are built from great people, talented people, thought-leaders in our industry." *What the hell is a thought-leader?* "It begins in this room, each and every one of you is responsible - you have the power to create an environment where our people feel inspired, motivated, fulfilled..." *Are you listening to this Brett?* "You are not just managers anymore, you need to be innovative leaders, entrepreneurs, creative accountants, skilled auditors..." *Yep that's us, Jacks of all trades, masters of fuck all.* "Don't be scared of conflict. I'm not." *You don't say.* "Conflict in a team is healthy..."

I caught Big Andy's eye and sipped my drink to hide a smile. "Use it positively, drive your teams forwards to greatness, we are on a never-ending journey...." *Are we on the X Factor?* "But I'll promise you this," The Big Cheese thumped his now empty pint glass down on a table, making everyone jump, "and this is a message I want you to take back to your people. And make it crystal clear to them. Anyone who is not on board with us can bloody well get off at the next station. I've no time for bloody passengers. And if they won't get off, we'll bloody well throw them off!" Queue some butch cheering. He was working himself up, getting redder and redder. *Is there a doctor in the house?*

"Time wasters. Disaffected followers." *Who?* "They've no place in this company." He jabbed his sausagy finger around the room. "You'll not last five minutes at Perypils if you don't perform to standard, not five bloody minutes, I'll personally assure you of that." Nervous applause from the room, everyone secretly thinking to themselves "Does he mean me?"

"Not last five minutes" - what a load of macho shit. I so badly wanted to ask if he knew how long it takes to get rid of an underperformer; do you know how many hours we spend on managing them, on supporting them, training them then re-training them, only for them to be signed off sick for weeks with a stubbed toe and we have to start all over again? Do you know that whatever action we try and take some little weener from HR tells us that we can't take it because we missed a full-stop out of the notes? I had personnel files so large you could ski down them. And then just when you think you've reached the end, and can get shot of them, some lily-livered manager called Julie Wet-Pants from Birmingham decides not to dismiss and gives them another chance! I could see Julie cowering in the corner of the room. She caught me looking at her and quickly looked away. Probably had egg on her face - ha ha!

Eventually, The Big Cheese ran out of steam, and the tirade was over. Ears ringing, we went through to dinner. The tables had name-plates, and of course, they had mixed us all up. I was delighted to be seated next to Rich from Birmingham again, although it was going to take all my concentration to understand him and my head was already spinning from two large vodka and tonics on an empty stomach. I must pace myself, or I would feel terrible tomorrow. I looked around the room but I could not see The Climber. She obviously hadn't managed to wangle herself an invitation to dinner. Was she going to wait in the bar, or was she going to drive home? That was a huge glass of wine she'd been holding, was she really going to drive after drinking that?

The wine was flowing, and by the time my fish course was placed in front of me it looked like the fish was still swimming. Rich hadn't stopped talking, I'd no idea what about, but I seemed to be nodding and smiling in all the right places. After the desserts had been cleared away, Brett the Boss stood up to drunken cheers as he said he had a presentation to make. He said he'd had a great day, and he'd learnt a lot about himself and working as part of a team. He didn't mention the fact that we'd had to surgically remove him from his mobile. He said he'd asked the instructors who had made the biggest impact during the activities and he'd like to present that person with a bottle of champagne.

My heart started to beat a lot faster. It must be me! That amazing swan dive I did at the end to win the day, it must be me. I wondered if I would be able to get up and walk in a straight line to receive the champagne. With a bit of luck, he'd bring it over to me.

"And the winner is..." Brett looked around the room. I held my breath. "Clare from Team Cheltenham!" Cruella? No way. It's not possible. What had she done? The familiar skinny figure in black got up to accept her prize amidst scattered applause. Brett said it was awarded for "showing amazing resilience when rounding up her sheep" *A guilt-award!* "And for posting the fastest lap on the quad bike - showing the boys how it's done!" From the faces in the room, I could see it was the most unpopular award in the history of meaningless trophies. So if the rumours were to be believed, it was first blood to her. Brett had already clearly pledged his allegiance to her. I asked Rich if he could reach the wine and if so, to start pouring.

Morning

Eyes opened. Unfamiliar room. Where was I? Took a moment to remember. Hotel room in Nottingham. Looked down. Oh no, I was fully clothed. Just lying on top of the bed on my back. Had taken off my boots and my trousers were undone, but the effort must have been too much for me and I'd crashed out. Sat up slowly to look at the digital alarm clock. *Oh my head.* It was a quarter to seven. I might as well get up. Staggered to the bathroom. As suspected, I still had a face full of make-up. *Yuk.* Red-rimmed eyes peered back at me. Filled a glass full of water and gulped it down. Then another. Rummaged around in wash bag for Nurofen. My ankle hurt, there was a big bruise on my knee. What time had I gone to bed? Couldn't remember. Couldn't remember going to bed.

Bits of last night started to come back to me. I could recall getting the table to play Fuzzy Duck. I could recall playing Truth or Dare. With a groan, I remembered being dared to sing "Happy Birthday" in the style of Marilyn Monroe to Market Mike, the senior manager of marketing. I'd used a tonic bottle as a microphone. Had it actually been his birthday? Who knows. I vaguely recalled leading a sing-along in the bar, but it was a bit hazy. Oh what a stupid idiot, why did I drink so much? Why? I was going to look and feel awful for the rest of the day. I'd never do this again.

I couldn't face breakfast, I felt too sick. I showered and dressed, took off yesterday's make up and put more back on. No amount of trusted bronzing powder could cover my pallid complexion. Why, in this day and age, had someone not invented a cure for hangovers - something you could take that would immediately take away the nausea, the grittiness, the headache. I made my way to the conference centre where the course was being held and slunk into the room. Tables were laid out with note pads, pens and bottles of water. There were a few people already there, most of them looked as bad as I felt.

I chose a table nearest to the door (just in case I had to make a sudden exit) and poured myself a glass of water. A guy I didn't know came in and sat down at the same table. "I'm glad to see you're ok," he said, as he poured some water too.

"Er, well yes I'm fine thanks," I said suspiciously, "Why shouldn't I be?"

"Well you took quite a heavy fall," he said with surprise. "Don't you remember? I fell on top of you. You know, during the three-legged race." *Oh my God.* That would explain the bruise.

The room slowly filled up. Everyone was very quiet. The trainer bounced in with a cheery "Morning folks!". When he didn't get a response he exclaimed loudly "Good grief, has someone died?" I know everyone was thinking "You're about to mate if you don't turn it down a bit."

The course limped along. I did feel dreadfully sorry for

the trainer who did his absolute best to drag out some participation, but no one wanted to know. It's not easy to concentrate whilst fighting off waves of nausea. It wasn't exactly new material either. Team Working in Action: comparisons to geese, shared visions, common goals and endless bloody acronyms that no one ever remembers or uses.

I think he knew it was hopeless when he started to talk about the Tuckman Model of team development which is: forming, storming, norming, performing and someone had said that the only model that worked for our teams was the FIFO compliance model. He said he hadn't heard of this model and asked, with great interest, what it was. He was told: Fit In or Fuck Off.

Mercifully, he had the sense to wrap it up early and let us get on the road. Big Andy drove me back to Cheltenham. Cruella overtook us on her broomstick. I wondered what had happened to The Climber. "Did you see Amanda again last night?" I asked Big Andy, "I wondered if she hung around waiting for the meal to finish or went home."

"She hung around I think. I definitely saw her in the bar after dinner."

"Blimey, she must have driven home awfully late." Andy shot me a pitying look.

"*If* she went home."

Had she stayed overnight then? The rooms there weren't particularly cheap, it must have cost her a fortune when you factored in the petrol as well. I was about to question him some more when a song came on the radio and he turned it up excitedly. "Remember this from last night, Kate?" It was Bon Jovi, Living on a Prayer.

"Er, no, should I?" I asked, confused.

"Of course you remember! You were absolutely rocking the bar to this one!" *Oh no, don't tell me anymore.* I closed my eyes and slumped down low in my seat. Just get me home.

Home at last. Thank God, it was all over and I could curl up on the sofa and stuff my face with carbs. To my surprise, The Husband's car was in the drive. He was home very early. He opened the front door before I could get my key out and pulled me inside, giving me a big hug and said "Hi Love, you're home! I thought I'd get back early so I'd be here when you got in and I could make you your favourite – Shepherd's Pie."

That's actually your favourite isn't it, not mine. Still I won't be churlish.

"This is a nice welcome," I said, quite pleasantly taken aback. "What have I done to deserve this?"

"Oh, you know, I'd had such a bad day yesterday, I realised I hadn't been very chatty when you called last night." *No, that's an understatement.* "I felt really bad about it, so I thought I'd make you a nice meal to make up for it!" *Fair enough - lucky me!* "Go and sit down. And I've got a lovely bottle of wine for us, shall I pour you a glass? What's the matter – why have you gone green?"

CHAPTER FOURTEEN

The Husband and I met up with our friends Karen and James at the pub on Friday night. We were all sharing the horrors of our working weeks, trying to out-do each other in the attempt to claim the title of "Shit Muncher of the Week". Karen was halfway through a story about bogeys on her blackboard when the Husband suddenly exclaimed "Oh look, there's Debbie and Paul at the bar!" and he waved them over to join us. *Great.* We all made the usual noises such as "What a coincidence" and "Great minds think alike!" and I managed to shuffle quickly round the table to position myself as far away from Boring Paul as possible. He sat himself down next to James. *Sorry mate, but I had to save myself.* I asked Debbie who was looking after Chloë (the devil child) and she said "Oh we've just left her to fend for herself!" and she trilled with laughter. The Husband joined in with a burst of phoney laughter that I hadn't heard from him before. Karen rolled her eyes at me and buried her face in her wine glass.

Despite the uninvited guests, it turned into quite a jolly evening. I tried to stick to orange juice after my ghastly hangover experience, but I soon grew tired of that and got stuck into the Rioja with everyone else. I asked everyone to name the first record they'd ever bought, going first with mine - "Rivers of Babylon" by Boney M. As soon as I said it, everyone burst into song; James even stood up and did the hand movements. Karen said hers was "Crazy Horses" by the

161

Osmonds, but we only knew the screechy bit and that practically cleared the pub. James' was "Under The Moon of Love" by Showaddywaddy, which was absolutely brilliant to sing to, and Debbie claimed hers was "Some Might Say" by Oasis. I looked at her with some suspicion and Karen pretended to cough whilst saying "Bullshit" at the same time. Paul, the boring old fart, said he couldn't remember what his was and Karen cheerfully cried "Well make it up then! Just like your wife did!" Fortunately, Debbie didn't hear her. Or possibly she chose not to.

The conversation turned to holidays and Debbie asked us where we were going this year. That was a bit awkward as we hadn't actually discussed it, so I slurred "Oh, we usually go to one of the Greek islands in September, you know, do a last minute thing."

The Husband could have left it at that, but no, he had to chip in saying "I'm so bored with holidays where you just sit on your arse on a sun lounger all day." *Since when?* "I'd like to do something exciting just for once, an activity holiday or something, you know, actually do something for a change."

I stared at him. *An activity holiday?* The closest you've ever been to active on holiday is when you once had to hop over hot sand because you forgot your flip flops. You never move from the sun lounger from ten in the morning till six in the evening, wearing your mirrored sun glasses so you can perv at all the young beach babes without them knowing. You make sure you don't drink too much so you don't have to get up to go to the loo, and you moan like buggery if I ask you just to rub sun cream on my back because it's too much bloody effort to sit upright.

"Oh yes, I know what you mean," said Debbie. "We

can't sit around when we go away, we're real activists aren't we Paul? And Chloë is too, we took her to Center Parcs at Easter and she was in her element, she did all the activities over and over." *I expect she'd scared all the other kids away and had the place to herself.* I hated Center Parcs; too many cagoule-clad, pretentious twat-couples who named their children Horatio and Portia and whose poo was 100% organic.

"We're going surfing in a couple of weeks," said Paul. "We go every year, two weeks down in Devon. My parents come too, so they can help look after Chloë whilst we're surfing." *Yes, God forbid you'd have to look after your own child on holiday.*

"Ooh!" shrieked Debbie, "I've had an idea!" *Tell us quick before it dies of loneliness.* "Why don't you all come too?" *Eh? No, no, no!*

"We stay in this massive house, there's plenty of room for everyone and we could teach you to surf! You'd love it and it would be such fun! Oh, go on, say yes, say yes!"

For a woman who'd drunk the best part of two bottles of wine, Karen's quick thinking was impressive.

"Oh what a shame," she said, "but we're off on hols ourselves shortly, so we couldn't possibly take any more time off work. What a pity." James nodded vigorously. I wasn't quite so quick on my feet, and whilst I was thinking of our reason not to go, I heard The Husband say "Oh, that sounds great! How fantastic, I'd love to surf. Are you sure you guys wouldn't mind?"

How could he - we hadn't even discussed it! Karen looked at me and opened her eyes wide. Help me, my eyes pleaded with her, *help me*.

"Wow, Kate," she said, standing up a bit unsteadily.

"Imagine, you on a surf board! Wearing one of those horrid blubber suit thingies. Brilliant, just brilliant." She tottered off to the Ladies, where I could hear her laughing out loud.

"Oh she means a wet suit," said Debbie, patting my arm reassuringly. "Don't worry, they're not that bad, you soon get used to them." *No, I won't because I'm not bloody going.* I said very pointedly to The Husband that we'd talk about it at home, and he nodded "Yes, yes" but I could see he was sold on the idea. *No way* was I going to spend two weeks of my precious holiday with the most boring man in the world and his spooky staring child, not to mention having to wear an unforgiving blubber suit and the very small matter of drowning. Surfing was for brown-limbed, tousle-haired, care free youngsters, not the likes of me. I was 42, I worked in insurance, I owned Laura Ashley gardening gloves for Christ's sake - I'd no business getting on a surf board.

We said goodbye to everyone outside the pub, and The Husband and I staggered home. He was extremely excited at the thought of going surfing in Devon and banged on and on about it. I just listened, made encouraging noises and took care not to poo-poo it straight away, as I knew that would be likely to provoke a row.

When we got in, I made us a cup of tea and opened a bag of Maltesers whilst he carried on enthusing. I threw a few spanners in, such as "Of course, you can never trust the weather in this country can you? Imagine surfing in the wind and rain, it would be horrid!" Then "Of course, we've never met Paul's parents. I mean I'm sure they're ok, but you never know do you?" and then my *piece de resistance* "Of course we'd be staying in the same house as a noisy toddler all that time, what's her name, Carrie?"

"It's Chloë," he corrected, and he looked thoughtful. I held my breath - surely that would put him off, he couldn't bear kids. It very nearly worked, but instead, I found myself agreeing to go down for a "long weekend" to see what it was like. At no point did he ask me if I actually wanted to go, which I thought was very selfish of him. As soon as I'd said "Well, um, ok then..." he whizzed off to the study to Facebook the good news to Debbie before I could change my mind. I texted Karen about the weekend.

She replied: "U shood practice dont want to look like a tit. Squeeze urself into a condom & lie on the ironing board." *Ha bloody ha.*

Wednesday

I was holding on the phone for Human Remains. I was trying to sort out a colleague's pay that they had completely cocked up. The first person I'd spoken to (after being in a queue for forty minutes) had told me that the team I needed were all at lunch, could I phone back in an hour? I said no. I asked why the team had all gone to lunch at the same time. He'd put me through to his "supervisor" - *who uses the word supervisor anymore?* She had told me that they wouldn't be able to deal with my query today as they had "other priorities". I asked her to explain to me what was more important than a colleague not being able to meet their living expenses because their salary hadn't been received. She'd said she didn't much care for my tone. I'd told her it was pretty obvious her team didn't much care about anything at all. I was now waiting to speak to her manager.

My mobile rang. I looked at the caller, it was The Boss. He never called me - it must be bad news. I let it go to voicemail and played back the message whilst hanging on for HR.

"Kate, I need to talk you. Kevin's PA has been in touch with me and Kevin wants to arrange a visit to the Cheltenham site next Monday." *Oh shit.* "I know it's short notice, but he was due to visit Bridgend and that's had to be cancelled. So he wants to go to Cheltenham instead. Can you call me as soon as possible, we need to get prepped. Cheers."

Oh my God, that was all I needed, a visit from The Big Cheese. Visits such as these had to be planned with paranoid precision to make sure that visitors only saw what we wanted them to see. I needed sufficient enough time to be able to cover up/hide/destroy any detritus - this included some of the staff. This paranoia was based on past experience of visits going a bit pear-shaped, with career-threatening "findings" being shared publicly right across the company. You rarely recovered from poor feedback dished out by a high profile visitor. My predecessor, when faced with a similar visit, had made the fatal error of saying "Oh sod it, they'll just have to take us as they find us." She was never seen again. I felt extremely concerned by the timing of the visit, what with all the restructure and closure rumours. What was the real purpose of his visit? And why had he cancelled on Bridgend? Or was he deliberately not giving us much notice so he could catch us out in some way, provide himself with the excuse he needed to close us down?

I liked the way The Boss had said "we" need to get prepped in his message, as if he was going to help. *Not a chance in hell of tha*t. But anyway, that was the rest of this week completely stuffed for me. I had a flick through my calendar whilst still holding on for HR. The next few days were completely chocka, with six meetings scheduled in for tomorrow alone. I was going to have to re-arrange what I could, and would probably have to work through the weekend to catch up. *Bugger bugger bugger.* The Husband would not be amused with that. I really did need to get better at prioritising. The trouble was, if I declined a meeting, some little weasel would be straight on the phone to The Boss saying I was being "obstructive". I ended up accepting everything and therefore totally over committing myself. I just couldn't win.

The line had gone very quiet. I looked at my phone turret - the call had been disconnected! *You bastards.*

I gathered my team managers together to inform them of The Big Cheese's impending visit, attempting to sell it to them as a fantastic opportunity to show our Chief Executive what a great team we are. Interesting reactions:

The Rock: "Whoopee! I'm on holiday next week!"

The Snake: "He never visits here, the teams will wonder why he's coming down, there's bound to be speculation."

The Climber: "Can I take the lead on the visit?"

The Drain: "I think I've got a hospital appointment...."

TLS George: "Whilst we're all together, is it ok if I leave early today?"

I wanted us to get organised. I was about to decline The Climber's offer to lead the visit, when a thought struck me. The Big Cheese was known to be a bit of a womaniser, there's nothing he would like more than to be shown around by an attractive young female. Was I prepared to pimp out The Climber? *You bet I was.* I accepted her offer and also suggested a few colleagues that we could introduce to The

Big Cheese to show him some of our initiatives and achievements. All the colleagues I suggested were pretty young females. The others didn't seem to notice this. I didn't feel at all proud of myself. In fact, I felt positively grubby.

I gave The Climber the task of organising an agenda for the day, keeping in mind The Big Cheese would also want to visit Cruella's complaints team at some point during the day.

"Stick her in after lunch," I suggested. No one liked this time of day, when energy levels were sapped and the department stank of canteen soup and oniony burps. With any luck, he'd yawn and guff his way all round her department.

I gave TLS George a task, just because he hadn't volunteered to get involved with anything, and I wanted him to pull his weight too. The Big Cheese's PA had asked for a "one-pager" to be sent through before the visit, summarising what we did at Cheltenham. I assumed that was to avoid our Chief Exec looking like a div when he turned up. I asked TLS George to put this together before Friday, with a warning not to delegate it to someone else. In front of the others, he readily agreed, saying "That's easy enough." After the meeting broke up, he came over to me at least three times to ask what he should put in the summary, and then to moan about the "value" of the task, saying "Surely the Chief Executive knows what his own teams do?" *Hollow laugh.*

Thursday morning

I went through the proposed agenda with The Climber and emailed it to The Boss. He seemed pleased with it and emailed to say he would be down on Monday to support us with the visit. The Climber was in her element, bossing

everyone around and indulging in some serious hair flicking. I
overheard her making an appointment for herself at a waxing
salon. Blimey! That's pretty impressive attention to detail.

The teams started removing all the tat from the walls,
such as out of date lunch rotas and dodgy team night-out
photos. They replaced these with morale-boosting Perypils
posters and our impressive performance statistics.

I asked the guys in facilities if they could do anything
about the blu-tak stains on the walls. They said it would have
to be a paint-job. I thought The Big Cheese would be
smelling enough "wet paint" when he arrived so I decided
just to put up more posters to cover the stains.

Thursday afternoon

Chased TLS George for his one pager at 12.30 pm, 2.00
pm & 4.00 pm.

Prepped (instructed) all colleagues (Pretty Young Things)
involved in the visit on what they should talk about and what
statistics to show The Big Cheese, plus a bit of leg or breast
hopefully, though of course I couldn't say that. They were full
of nervous excitement, the poor deluded things. *Lambs to the
slaughter.*

Planted a Tic-Tac under my desk to test the standard of
the overnight cleaning.

Friday morning

Tic-tac still there. Called facilities to complain.

Chased TLS George for the one pager at 9.30. Told him
he had until 11.00, or he would have to personally phone The
Big Cheese to explain why he hadn't received it.

Commenced frantic tidy-up. All colleagues were asked to

clear their desk areas of personal items. *Jesus, the moaning that caused.* Why are people so sensitive about their square foot of space? I only asked them to hide a few bloody gonks away for Christ's sake. One woman burst into tears because she was asked to put a photo away in her drawer. It wasn't even a photo of a family member - it was of her dog, an afghan hound. (Although at first glance it did look like it could have been a picture of her husband in the seventies).

10.58 Received the one pager emailed from TLS George. I read through his summary. It contained 67 spelling mistakes. This included 12 occasions when he'd started a new sentence without using a capital letter. I called him over, and held out a printed copy like I was holding a turd.

"George, why have you sent me this - is it supposed to be a joke and you've got the real one saved somewhere else?"

George had his mutinous face on.

"No, it's not a joke. What's wrong with it?"

"Have you heard of Spell Checker?"

"Yes."

"Why didn't you use it, then?"

"I did. Well, I thought I did."

"Do you have any problems with reading and writing? Any problems with your eye sight?"

"No."

"So you're just lazy then?"

"It was just a first draft, that's all. I'll do it again after lunch."

I took a deep breath. I felt like strangling him. "You'll do it now, George. I don't expect you to go to lunch until it's done and done properly and I certainly don't expect to have

170

to chase you twenty times just to get you to do something I've asked you to do. This visit is extremely important to us, you know that. Everyone else is mucking in - I don't want anyone letting the side down."

He went off in a huff. I would have to do something about him - I'd pick it up after the visit was out of the way.

Afternoon

The Boss emailed to say he wouldn't be down for the visit after all, as he was going to a Britney Spears concert at Wembley on Monday night. I emailed back saying I was disappointed but that I understood, assumed his daughter had been looking forward to it for some time and that he wouldn't want to let her down. He emailed back to say he wasn't going with his daughter. I didn't email him again on the subject.

The Rock finished up and left for her week in Corfu, bidding me good luck and grinning inanely. I nearly threw myself at her feet, held onto her ankles and begged her not to go. *Don't leave me.*

Chapter Fifteen

I worked through most of Saturday and Sunday, catching up with emails. The Husband was sulkily forced to go to Sainsbury's on his own, commenting sarcastically as he went: "Remind me, are we still married? It's so difficult to tell." He left behind the shopping list I'd written out for him. And he forgot his bags for life.

My mother phoned me. When I answered she said "Oh hello dear. What did you want?" I told her that she'd phoned me. She told me not to be so silly. I asked where Dad was. She said he was washing the car again. He was apparently convinced their neighbours had trained the doves to use his car as target practice.

Monday morning - the day of the visit

5.00 am. Got up (exhausted) and dug out my Wonder-bra. Put on a short purple shift dress with matching jacket. The image I was hoping for was professional, but just a bit tarty.

7.00 am. Arrived at work for last minute tidying and revision of Perypils current key objectives and favourite phrases of the moment (flavours of the month). The Big Cheese wasn't due until 10.00 am but I already felt nervous, and my bowels became very insistent at one point. Luckily there was no one else in the office that early, so I could use the loo without having to go through the rigmarole of trying to time a poo when there was no one else in the toilets, and then having to strain like mad before anyone else came in.

7.30 am. Saw that the bloody Tic Tac was still there! Facilities were really asking for it now.

8.30 am. Received a phone call from The Drain who sounded like he'd put a peg on his nose, saying he had come down with a cold and wouldn't be in. Predictable, but probably a good thing he didn't cross paths with The Big Cheese in case he shat himself.

8.45 am. The Climber arrived. I think she had dressed herself with the same image in mind that I had, just without the professional bit. She was wearing a very short black mini skirt and an extremely clingy sleeveless black top. She also had on sky-scraper heels so she was hobbling around like an old woman whenever she attempted to move about.

9.10 am. I threw an absolute hissy-fit with The Snake when I heard one of her advisors saying to a customer: "I'm sorry that you've had to complain, but we shall take it very seriously, yes, don't you worry I'm making a note of it now." Whilst speaking, the advisor was flicking through a magazine! What if The Big Cheese had seen that?

9.40 am. Getting really nervous now. Had another tantrum when I saw an advisor talking to a customer whilst rolling himself a cigarette. I got The Snake and TLS George together and told them they had to sort their people out, or I'd be shoving their magazines and cigarettes up their arses. They looked rather alarmed so I guessed my eyes were bulging a bit. I felt like I was having a meltdown.

10.00 No sign of The Big Cheese.

10.15. Still no sign.

10.30. Received a call from Jenny, The Big Cheese's PA.

She said she was very sorry but Kevin had got held up on an urgent conference call. She thought he would be with us at about 11.00

The Climber and I revised the agenda. We decided just to cut down the time on everything, rather than remove any items altogether.

10.45. Really needed another poo but couldn't risk leaving the department in case he turned up early. Would have to clench.

11.05. Where is he for God's sake? Getting seriously hacked off now. My left eye had developed a twitch.

11.15. *The ego has landed.* The Big Cheese made his entrance. He swaggered in looking like a prize-fighter with an entourage of five or six suited cling-ons plus his "executive" assistant, a small, ferrety little man who was clutching a note pad. I was immediately put in mind of Smithers in the Simpsons. I went forward to shake hands, saying "Hello Kevin." As I said the word "Kevin", a piece of spittle flew out of my mouth and landed on his tie. I was mortified. I'd gobbed on the Chief Executive! He pretended not to notice and introduced me to his cling-ons. I immediately forgot all their names and where they were from. I welcomed them and gave a brief summary of the department, and our key achievements. As I was talking, a greasy haired man in overalls wandered into the group. Everyone looked at him then looked at me. I decided to keep talking, but he interrupted me.

"What's all this about a bleeding Tic Tac? I 'aven't got time for this sort of nonsense, not when the bogs need unblocking."

I hurriedly pointed him in the direction of The Snake,

saying "I think she's the one you need" and swiftly moved the group on. I was horribly conscious of the piece of white spit which was still clinging to The Big Cheese's navy silk tie. He spotted a quotation I'd stuck up by my desk (that morning).

The purpose of a business is to keep and create customers - Theodore Levitt.

"I like that," he boomed. "Thompson! Make a note of that. Aye, we'll bloody well use that." Smithers scurried forward and started scribbling.

I introduced him to The Climber. As predicted, his eyes lit up, and his demeanour suddenly became more jovial. She showed him the agenda and took him off to meet Emma (young, tall, leggy) who was going to talk to him about our sales performance. I thought he might actually drool. *Smithers! Fetch me a bib.* The Climber did her utmost to butt into every conversation, somehow managing to personally take the credit for every success the department had ever had. I saw some of the group exchanging smirking glances. They weren't fooled.

The visit seemed to be going well, my guys were doing a great job and there was plenty of laughter. But as the group was talking to Sam (pretty, young, girlie) about our quality figures, I noticed that just slightly out of their vision, Joe Bloody Cooper in the admin team looked like he was about to fall asleep again at his desk. *For God's sake, why today of all days?* This just can't be happening to me. Joe's head was slowly nodding in a downwards direction. If any of them turned slightly to their right, they would see him.

I tried to catch The Climber's eye but she was concentrating on keeping her balance in those heels whilst pushing her chest as close to The Big Cheese's nose as possible. Keeping behind the group, I edged towards Joe. He had fallen asleep. His chin was on his chest and his eyes were closed. I didn't have long; Sam was beginning to wrap up her spiel. Any moment now the group would turn round, they'd see Joe. I got right beside him. Sam had finished. I raised my arm forwards then sharply jabbed my elbow back into Joe's chest. He woke with a cry of "Whoah! What the f..." which I managed to cover with a loud "Well then! What shall we see now?" slapping my hands together and making the group jump out of their skin.

Although it wasn't part of the agenda, The Big Cheese suddenly announced that he wanted to listen to some of our calls from customers. I had a feeling he might want to do this so I was more than ready for this request, although I made it look like I was surprised and it was spontaneous. I took him over to Lauren who had been prepped and was ready to go. She also had on the shortest skirt I'd ever seen. The Big Cheese sat next to her and I fitted him up with a headset so he could listen in to the calls. He listened to one call, then removed his headset, ready to move on. That was that then. No doubt that later, on his blog, he would write it up somewhat differently. It would probably read as though he had spent most of his day listening in, giving his readers the impression that he was a very much "hands on" Chief Executive and in touch with our customers.

It really was a whirlwind visit and when we'd done our bit he shook my hand, crushing several bones and told me it had been "great". I didn't know if this meant it really had been great, or whether that actually meant "it was crap but I'm not going to tell you that to your face, I'll wait until I've left and then I'll give some really shit feedback to your boss."

I took him and his entourage round to meet Cruella. She was waiting for him with a strange expression on her face. I realised she was attempting to smile. It looked like she had bad wind. Waiting beside her were her two heavy-weights, Kim and Pat (KowPat). *Rookie error Cruella!* He likes young blood. I could almost hear the The Big Cheese's libido screaming "I'm doomed!" Still, I bet she didn't spit on him.

Thank God it was over. I said well done and thank you to The Climber, who was removing her shoes with much relief and told the guys they could get their gonks back out again. Then I advanced on Joe Cooper.

Late in the afternoon

I was at my desk, just about to phone Joe's resignation through to HR when I received a call from Brett The Boss. *Here we go, Big Cheese feedback time.* I braced myself. His opening words:

"Bloody hell Kate, what the fuck did you do to Kevin?" Oh God, it must have been worse than I thought, it was only a little bit of spit, for Christ's sake, it was not as if he'd been water boarded.... I began to stutter something, but The Boss cut me short. "He bloody loved it! Said your girls were absolutely fantastic, and he thought that your department contained some really wonderful talent." *I bet he did.* "Well done Kate, brilliant feedback."

I almost felt like sobbing, I felt so relieved and elated. I'd had some praise, I'd actually had some praise! I rushed to tell the others, hearing the song "Walking on Sunshine" playing in my head. I felt about ten feet tall. I couldn't remember the last time I'd felt on top of the world whilst at work. I pushed to the back of mind the fact that I had no right to feel so good - I had practically prostituted out my "girls" in order to get myself a pat on the back. *How shameful that I'd done that. And how sad that it had worked.*

As I left the office, I saw Cruella in the car park. She had a face like thunder. I guessed her feedback hadn't been so good. Oh well, tough tits. Round two to me.

Saturday

Panic had seriously set in. I had less than a week before the long weekend in Devon and I needed to lose a stone in weight, get a tan and buy some suitable "surfie" clothes. I went shopping with Karen and searched for shops that sold surf-type clothes for the middle-aged. It's very difficult to know what you can get away with when you have passed the 40 year milestone. Browsing the racks, I asked myself if I was now too old to wear denim mini-skirts, ripped jeans or wet-look leggings (answers: yes, yes and hell yes). I had a vision of myself on the golden sands of Devon wearing a charming little sun dress with a matching cardy, all feminine and fragrant. We struggled with this a bit, as we couldn't tell what was a dress and what was a tunic, and therefore needed to be worn over something. *Everything was so damn short.* Karen picked up a garment in Fat Face and said "Ooh, Kate, this is a nice skirt" only for the assistant to say "That's actually a boob tube." I'd left it too late to get decent flip flops, the only nice ones left were in size 8 and above; they would only have fitted Sasquatch. As for their bikinis, well - they were no more than tiny triangular swatches. You could only fit about three pubes inside the bikini bottoms, there wasn't room for anything else.

"You are going to get a bikini wax aren't you?" Karen

asked anxiously. I told her no, there wasn't time; I was going to have to take my chances with a rusty Bic.

We ended up, as usual, in Monsoon. I picked up a lovely cream and pink striped halter-neck sundress, size 12, with a matching pink cardigan. *Perfect.* I went to try it on. It had a zip up the side which I undid and stepped into the dress. I couldn't get the zip back up. At first I thought it must be stuck, but it wasn't, it didn't even come close. *Bloody back fat, where does it come from, where?* It was such a lovely dress, but no way was I going to buy a bigger size, *no fucking way.* I slunk out of the cubicle, telling Karen "It didn't really look right on me." I ended up buying a pinafore-type dress that didn't have any zips and could acccomodate, in size 12, a small family as well as yourself.

I got a few bits from Accessorize - a beach bag and some bandos (head wraps) to keep my hair out of my face on the beach. I'd have to make do with my old bikinis and flip flops, although there might be some nice shops in Devon that cater for slightly overweight geriatric surfers. Ooh, hope they do cream teas as well.

Sunday

I went to the get the Sunday papers from the local shop. 'Celeb Beach Babes' caught my eye, a headline on the front of one of the trashy magazines. Another shrieked out at me: 'Beer Belly and Proud of it! Look at her Curves!' There were two pictures of Lindsay Lohan, with the banner 'from this to this!' In the first picture, she looked as thin as a whippet. In the second, she still looked as thin as a whippet, although very, very slightly less so. The magazine clearly saying, without actually saying, that she was now fat. She still looked quite underweight to me. *How awful.* Clearly if you're not a stick-thin tooth pick you're a fat biffer, overweight and unattractive. I flicked through the magazine. Almost the whole thing was devoted to observations on women's weight. The biggest articles were taken up by pictures of those unfortunate celebrities who they'd managed to capture in unflattering positions, perhaps showing a miniscule protrusion of a stomach. "She's letting it all hang out!" screamed the captions. I bet the editor was a man. But no, it was edited by a woman! How the hell does she sleep at night? Surely the only way women get as thin as that is because they're eating nothing but lightly steamed cobwebs? It was so cruel.

I walked back from the shop with a sense of shame. I contributed to the whole image thing, spending a fortune on clothes and beauty products, seduced by advertisements to "Look younger by the weekend", even though I know its bollocks. Did I judge a woman on how she looks? I liked to tell myself that I didn't, but I was in denial. Was that why I couldn't stand The Climber, because she was young and attractive and got all the male attention instead of me? I told myself no - actually it's because she's not very bright, she has the personality of a fence post and she simply wasn't prepared to put in the hard graft to get up the career ladder. That considered, I felt a bit better about myself. *Sod it.* I wasn't prepared to starve to death in an attempt to conform to some sadist's ideal of what a woman should look like. If I got harpooned off the Devon coast I got harpooned. As soon as I was home I went straight to the kitchen and cracked open the Custard Creams. And I didn't even steam them.

Monday

It was that time again – half-yearly performance reviews. *What a total pain in the bum.* At least it was a proper chance to sit down with TLS George and review his performance. He saw it somewhat differently to me, rating his own performance as: "Alright, I fink." I told him I thought it was below average, which seemed to surprise him. He said everything had been fine when he was working for Clare last year. *Well obviously not that fine - she binned you off onto me.*

I reviewed all the expectations of his role with him, and agreed (I told him) what he needed to do to perform to the required standards. I drew up a progress plan that documented what was required of him. Progress plans are promoted by Perypils managers as "supportive tools designed to keep our colleagues on track". Of course they are viewed by colleagues as anything but; instead they are seen as the first step to try and boot them out the door.

I captured everything TLS George needed to do to improve his performance on his plan and he reviewed it with dismay.

"How am I supposed to achieve all that?" he wailed.

"Well you won't will you? That's because you only got the job because you're young and good-looking and bullshitted your way through the interview, and some poor gullible sap fell for it. You don't have the skills or capability to do this role, and when Cruella realised that, she simply shunted you elsewhere to avoid the inconvenience of having to manage you. So now you're my problem. Ideally, of course, I would spend time coaching and developing you, but that's not going to happen is it, not when I spend all day in one pointless meeting after another and then all night trying to keep up with endless stupid emails. Perish the thought I'd have time to spend with my people, I'm only a people-manager after all..."

I didn't say that to him, of course, just in case he was recording our conversation on his iPhone - he was definitely fiddling with something under the desk. Instead, I told him he would be fully supported and we'd review the plan regularly to make sure he was on track (although I wasn't sure how, I didn't have a gap in my diary for at least six weeks). He was a bit sulky, but he had his two week holiday coming up - Majorca or Minorca, he didn't know which one, he thought they were one and the same - so at least he could "have a break away from it all". I felt like asking him how he could tell if he was on holiday or not, seeing as he did sod all, but I refrained.

There was one good thing resulting from TLS George's underperformance issues - it always cheered up The Drain when someone was doing worse than he was. He could almost be described as chirpy. Every cloud...

I wondered when The Boss would be in touch to arrange my own half-yearly review. I placed a bet with Big Andy. He went for November - next year. I went for never-ever.

I booked a last minute appointment at the beauty salon on Thursday evening. I'd never had a spray tan before, so I was feeling a bit apprehensive, having seen Ross's tanning experience on Friends. I didn't want to look like I'd been Tangoed. I was wearing a very old bikini under the loosest clothes I could find and a lovely young lady called Tina, who was wearing a white coat (how appropriate is that?) led me into a small room. It contained what looked like a tin of fence creosote with a spray gun attached to it. I tried to read what it said on the tin, thinking if it said "Radioactive Sunset" I would be out of there like the Road Runner.

Tina sprayed me all over, which felt tickly and cold, and she assured me that it wouldn't look too dark on my pale skin as the tan "naturally adjusted itself" to suit the skin tone. *Must be bloody clever then.* It didn't take long; I put on my loose clothing, paid the £35 and walked back to my car like John Wayne - I didn't want my thighs rubbing together; they still felt very sticky. I got home and examined myself in the bedroom mirror. I liked it! It looked natural (ish) and I looked healthy for once, my eyes looked whiter, not all pink and tired like they usually did. I showed The Husband, who said: "You stink. I suppose that will come off all over the sheets." *Charming.* I noticed he was wearing some coloured strips of material round his wrist that I hadn't seen before - he'd bought himself some "surfing" bracelets! I couldn't let him see I was laughing, he'd get the right hump. I couldn't help thinking that whatever beauty treatments we had and no matter what we chose to wear, we would never be able to disguise that fact that we were a couple of forty-something, mortgage-weary, office-bound farts who'd been let out on day release to go to the seaside. God help the good people of Devon.

CHAPTER SIXTEEN

We both had to go into work on the Friday morning as I had meetings I couldn't get out of and The Husband had a "dead cert sign up" which meant lots of lovely commission. We planned to set off by 3 pm at the latest so we could get to Devon for an early evening barbeque with Debbie and Paul. As it was, I was home and ready to go at 3.00, but The Husband texted to say he had been delayed. *Ha ha! Not me holding things up for a change!*

I checked the weather forecast for the weekend and it didn't look great, so I stuffed a couple of jumpers into my case. It was almost 4.00 before The Husband got home, stressed and crotchety. Apparently his "sign up", a retired gentleman or "doddery old fart" as The Husband put it, had asked a million and one questions before he'd signed the paperwork to invest a substantial sum of money, and each time his pen hovered over the "sign here" dotted line, he thought of something else to ask. The cheek of it, I said, fancy wanting to ask lots of questions when you're entrusting your life savings to someone. I got told off for being sarcastic. Then he couldn't find his sunglasses, iPhone charger or memory cards for his camera. He got more and more irate growling "Well don't bloody help me will you" when he saw me stood at the front door, waiting. Somehow, he always managed to make everything feel like my fault. Why hadn't he got his stuff ready last night like I had?

We finally got on the road at 4.30 pm, which was disastrous as we hit all the rush hour traffic. The M5 was extremely busy, and it shuddered to a standstill at one stage. We heard on the radio that there had been an accident. Fearing for the Husband's blood pressure, I suggested we swapped seats so I could take over the driving (or at least the sitting behind the wheel) whilst he texted Debbie to tell them we would be late. It had gone 9.00 pm by the time we drove into Croyde village and it was getting gloomy. We found the house at the end of a single-track, twisty country lane. It was a very impressive place, double fronted with a balcony, and what would be wonderful views across Croyde Bay if only the light was a little better. Debbie and Paul came out to greet us and helped us carry all our bags into the house.

"What a shame, you've just missed Chloë," said Debbie. "She so wanted to stay up and see you but she was so tired after being at the beach all day we thought we'd better put her to bed." *Result!* I would have high-fived The Husband if she hadn't been looking at us.

"The weather's going to change," said Paul, sounding like Eeyore.

"Oh dear," I said feigning concern, "Will that mean we won't be able to surf?"

"No you should be alright," said Debbie, "the surf school go out in most weathers." *Surf school?*

"Oh I didn't tell you," said the Husband, not meeting my eye. "I asked Debs to book a surfing lesson for us tomorrow morning, and we've got to be down at the beach by 9.30. Thought it would be a good way to start us off." *Don't you mean finish us off?* Oh well, at least it would be one hour less I had to spend with Paul.

We went to say hello to Paul's parents, Bob and Maggie, who seemed very pleasant and who were contentedly watching Taggart in the lounge. Maggie said I looked nice and brown. I liked her immediately. We sat with Debbie and Paul in the huge kitchen diner, drinking wine and eating leftover barbeque bits.

Predictably, I got stuck with Paul again, so I asked him to tell me about his week and how his surfing had been. He described every wave, every current, every grain of sodding sand in such tedious detail that my eyelids started to droop. I eventually excused myself, and Debbie showed me up to our room and pointed out where the bathroom was. *One evening over, just two to go.*

I didn't know where I was when I woke up. It took me a moment or two to work it out. The alarm clock said 7.15 am; I set it for an early time so I could get in the shower before anyone else. I looked over my shoulder, but the Husband wasn't in bed next to me, he wasn't there. Had he actually come to bed last night? I looked round the room for evidence, perhaps discarded clothes, shoes kicked off in the middle of the floor for me to trip over, but there was nothing. I opened the bedroom door and peered out. I couldn't hear anyone up and about, so I risked nipping downstairs in my nightie. I could hear a noise like a gurgling plug-hole coming from the lounge. The Husband was sprawled on the sofa asleep, his mouth wide open, snoring like a drain. A half empty bottle of brandy and two glasses were on the coffee table. He'd probably been up half the night drinking brandy with Paul. What on earth had he found to talk to him about? I went to wake him up but stopped myself. *Sod him.* Let everyone find him like that. I went to bag the shower and put my waterproof mascara on.

The morning was grey and cold with a stiff breeze. The others decided they would stay at the house for a bit, and then come down to the beach to see how we were getting on with our surf lesson. Chloë had already had two screaming tantrums: once when I accidentally stood on her favourite doll's head and one of its eyes popped out (clearly a safety hazard, so actually I did her a favour, but she didn't see it that way and my Popeye joke fell very flat) and once when the Husband pushed back his chair when she was stood right behind it and it had whacked her in the face. Paul's parents were beginning to look at us like we were some kind of child-monsters.

The Husband and I set off down the narrow lane towards the beach clutching our towels. We had to flatten ourselves against the hedgerow when a car came past us. I was wearing jeans and both the jumpers I'd packed at the last minute and one of my new bandos to keep my hair out of my face. The Husband had said "What the bloody hell have you got on your head? You look like a washer woman." I knew he was grumpy because he was hungover - he smelt strongly of brandy and looked extremely rough - *serve him bloody well right*.

We reached the bottom of the lane, crossed over the main road which ran through the village and headed towards the beach. We came to a large hut which had surf boards lined up in racks outside and long vertical Quicksilver flags flapping in the wind. Inside, there was a small group people, already in their Quicksilver wetsuits, stood around chatting. There was a couple who looked like they were still in their teens, another couple who looked slightly younger than us and two guys who were probably in their early thirties. We went up the man at the counter. He didn't look at all like my idea of a typical surfie-type, he was tall and groomed and looked like an accountant. He ticked us off his list and went to get wetsuits for us. He said it was important to get the right size as they should fit you "like a glove". He looked me up and down and handed me a "Medium" and then looked at the Husband and shouted to an assistant "where are the XLs?"

The Husband, mortified, said "No, no I'll be fine with a Large." The accountant handed him a Large, looking doubtful. We went behind some curtains to get into them. *What a nightmare, you needed to be a bloody contortionist.* Feet in first, struggle and flap like a penguin to get arms in, and then straining to reach behind to get the zip up. They were so unforgiving, showing every lump and bump and goose pimple. I sucked my stomach in, and went to see how the Husband had got on. As he appeared from behind the curtain, the accountant called out "Wrong way round mate!" He'd put it on with the zip at the front. It was also far too small, as he hadn't been able to get the zip done up and lots of flesh was escaping. He did look like he'd put on a few pounds, which I found remarkable given the amount of time he spent at the gym.

Embarrassed, he went back behind the curtain to take it off whilst I asked for an XL. I could hear much grunting and cursing from the curtain. He couldn't get the suit off, and he was sweating from the effort, which made it even more difficult. I had to ask for help from the group, and it took three of us to prize him out of his rubber casing. He was not at all happy and his face was purple from the humiliation. He got into the XL suit, but the legs were too long, so we had to roll them up for him.

We were introduced to our instructors, Dave and Tim. Unlike the guy at the counter, they exactly fitted my idea of typical surfie-types. Both were in their very early twenties, Dave was tall and thin and looked like Shaggy from Scooby Doo, and Tim was tanned, with long, bleach-blonde scruffy surf hair. They both had face paint on, Adam Ant style, even though there was thick cloud. Everything was "Dude this" and "Man that" as in: "Is this your first time surfing, dudes? That's cool man, you're gonna love it." I immediately named them Wayne and Garth.

They said they had a 100% track record of getting everyone stood up on their boards at their first lesson. I asked if that had to be in the sea. They laughed and said they weren't going to lose their 100% record today. *Wanna bet?* We all trooped outside so we could be fitted up with our boards. They said the learner boards had to be suitable for your size and weight. My God, I'd thought Paul had described his surf board as a "short" board last night when he was talking to me *at me* about surfing? These boards were massive; it was like looking up at a row of sky scrapers. Mine was really long and thick, I reckoned I could get at least five people sat on it. It wasn't a board, it was a boat. The accountant said "Have fun everyone! See you in four hours."

"Four hours?" I hissed at The Husband, "four bloody hours? I thought the lesson was an hour."

"Don't be daft, you can't learn to surf in an hour," he hissed back. "It'll go really quickly, you'll see."

"But what if I need the loo? My bladder will never hold out for four hours."

"You'll just have to go in your wetsuit," he said. "That's

what surfers do. And it will probably warm you up a bit."

"So I'm wearing a wetsuit that people have peed in? So gross."

"They wash them," he said, but he didn't sound too sure of himself.

We started to take our boards down to the beach. That wasn't easy. We had to go in pairs, one behind the other, holding a surf board under each arm. My arms weren't quite long enough to reach the bottom of the wide boards, so I ended up holding onto the fins, which were really sharp. The ground was uneven in places and we were barefoot. The Husband, who was behind me, stood on a pine cone, yelped and dropped one of the boards. I was looking ahead at the beach, and swung round to see what had happened. I caught him with the other board and knocked him over. He was absolutely fine, but made a huge girly fuss because his hands and wetsuit were covered in sand.

It felt like a very long walk to the beach, and my arms were ready to drop off when we got to the shore. The sky was a solid grey above us and big green waves reared up ahead of us before smashing down in an angry white froth. It was completely uninviting. Wayne and Garth stood and looked at the sea, discussing the best place to go for the "right sort of waves". We waited and waited, getting cold. A good ten minutes passed. They were still thinking about it when a group from another surf school ran onto the beach, picked a spot dead ahead and immediately went into the water. Wayne said "Yup, that's where we should have gone." They then walked us about 500 yards further down the beach. I was already knackered.

On the beach, Wayne and Garth went through the

concept of how you stand up on the board. It's a four step process:

1. You lie on the board. *Sounds good.*

2. You push up with your forearms onto all fours. *I'm used to that concept.*

3. Bring one leg forwards through your arms. *Sounds easy, but it's not when your stomach is in the way.*

4. Push with your arms to stand up and then stick your arse out. *Not attractive.*

Then we were ready to get into the water. *Great.* The plan was that Wayne and Garth would stand waist-deep in water as you lie on your board. When the wave breaks, they push you off so that you "catch the foam" and then you try and stand up.

The Husband said: "So they just push you off and all you've got to do is stand up, how hard can that be?" *Hmmm.* We headed into the water. It was very cold. We waded in up to our waists and I scanned the surface for dorsal fins. I struggled onto my board and lay ready for my first attempt with Wayne holding the end. A wave rose and broke, and Wayne pushed me off shouting "Go go go!" I was off. Wayne shouted "Get up get up!" and I got onto all fours, tried to bring one leg forwards but lost my balance and toppled into the sea. I came up under my board, banged my head and surfaced coughing and spluttering, my leg tangled up in the rope, only to be caught by the wave behind that thundered into my face. What a waste of Clinique Dewey Youth foundation; why had I bothered? My bando had been ripped off, and was probably half way up the Bristol Channel by now. That was £7.50 I'd never see again.

"Oh man." Wayne came to help and unwind me from

the rope, telling me that I'd strapped my board to the wrong leg, which is why I came up under the board. He said "You're gonna end up in the hack sack if you carry on like that." I'd no idea what that meant, but assumed it wasn't a good thing.

I then had to go round in a circle to await another go. The Husband was next. Lying on his board, concentrating hard, Garth pushed him off with the breaking wave. Before Garth could even shout "get up", he slid straight off his board and disappeared beneath the frothy surf. *Still confident of your 100% record boys?* I checked to see if the Husband was ok. He spat out a mouthful of salt water and said "He pushed me too hard!" I had another go. Same result. We all kept trying, but it was so frustrating, just when you thought you had your balance and could get up, you just flew off. It could be quite painful too if you caught the board when you fell or hit the water too hard. Then the girl from the young teen couple did it - she caught a wave and stood up, keeping her balance as she was swept in towards the shore. We all cheered and clapped.

"Man she really rode that one!" shouted Wayne. "Come on dudes, you can all do this!" The blokes were suddenly much more determined - they didn't want to be outdone by a girl.

I took my turn, and Wayne pushed me off as a particularly large wave started to break on me. I tried to get up on the board, but the wave was so powerful that I lost my balance and plunged in. I went under and for a moment I was completely disorientated - I had no idea which way up I was and the sea was churning me around like I was in a washing machine. It was terrifying. I was so relieved when my head broke the surface that I almost burst into tears. "Gees, you got hell-munched by that one," shouted Wayne. This time I knew exactly what he meant.

The Husband was not fairing any better. He just couldn't get his front leg through his arms to stand up on the board.

He kept saying "I always have trouble with this leg, I think it's that old muscle strain." One by one, the group were managing to stand up. I was last but one, and when I managed it I felt on top of the world. It was a smallish wave that I caught, and I didn't go far, but I got up and kept my balance.

Garth yelled "Stick your arse out!" I punched the air with delight as my wave fizzled out. I had to admit it felt brilliant. All the pressure was now on The Husband as the only member of the group not to stand up. Wayne and Garth did their utmost to get him up, but he just couldn't quite do it.

I was feeling cold and exhausted, and desperate for a wee (I could not bring myself to go in my suit) so I told Wayne I was going to go in.

"Oh no, man, you can't, the photographer's just arrived." Someone had turned up to capture our humiliation on camera. Garth instructed us to smile as we surfed in towards the photographer, which was near-on impossible when you had to concentrate like mad to stay upright. They were determined to capture The Husband stood up so they could claim their 100% record, so every time he reached the crouched position, the photographer snapped away like mad.

At last, the lesson was over; I was so happy to get out of the water.

Wayne shouted "Did everyone have a good time?"
We all shouted "Yes!"
Garth shouted "Will everyone go surfing again?" He got

a very feeble "Ye-es."

We carried our boards back towards the hut, the Husband telling me about his "muscle strain" which had led to his difficulties in standing up. I was more interested in listening to Wayne and Garth who were talking to each other about space cakes. Garth said he'd taken six space cakes home last night. His girlfriend phoned him, and whilst they were talking, his dog ate four of the cakes. It been unable to stand up, and had been stumbling about and falling over. Apparently the dog was very "mellow" today.

Back at the hut, getting the wet suits off was almost too much effort. Mine was glued to me, and as I peeled it off, I saw to my horror that my tan was coming off with it. I was left covered in patchy blotches of brown all over my body. It looked like I had some awful skin disease - I was the Singing Detective! Thirty five quid wasted. I pulled on my jeans and jumpers, which covered most of me up, thank goodness, apart from my neck. I'd have to buy a scarf.

We had a look at the photos that had been downloaded to a laptop, which gave us all a good laugh. The Husband scanned the photos and found one that made him look like he was close to a standing position so he decided to buy a disc. We said goodbye to our group and went to get a coffee to warm us up. I pulled my phone out of my jeans pocket and read a text from my brother which said "Sea Monster spotted off North Devon coast! Looking good Sis!" *What on earth did that mean?* Probably he was having a lunch time session in the pub. Another text arrived from Karen: "I don't think Quicksilver will be renewing your modelling contract with them." *Eh?* I texted her back "You what?" She replied "Facebook." *Oh no.* I asked the Husband to have a look on his iPhone. On Facebook there was a picture of me. It was the worst picture of me I'd ever seen. Even the one of me taken when I was face down on a table in a nightclub, my hair trailing in my own vomit wasn't a patch on this one. This was a picture of me tumbling off my surf board. My horrid wet sea-salty hair was sticking out from my head like snakes - I looked like Medusa. My face had this expression of gormless horror as I was about to hit the water, and my stomach was protruding from my wet suit, the angle I was at making it look even flabbier than it actually was.

"How the hell did that get on there?" I cried.

"Er, it looks like Paul and Deb posted it," said The Husband, "I saw them on the beach watching us, and Paul's got a really good camera you know, it's..."

"I don't give a shit if it can photograph through walls!" I wailed. "Take the bloody thing off." *How dare they?* I didn't ask to have my picture displayed on a public forum for people to jeer at. Seven people had already said they "liked it" and I didn't even know some of them. I felt utterly humiliated, no worse than that, I felt *violated*. I don't use Facebook for precisely this reason; my private life is private.

The Husband was hesitant. "I can't, it's on Deb and Paul's wall." He looked at me. "You're not going to make a fuss are you? It could be really embarrassing and spoil the weekend." *Oh thanks for your loyalty, you utter git.*

"It already is embarrassing - for me, your wife. You know I hate Facebook, it's not fair of them to post a picture of me without my permission, it's not bloody well on. Get it off, it's hideous."

I went to buy two coffees from a kiosk whilst the Husband made a phone call. I was furious. *Bastards*. They

195

invite us away with them for the weekend then publicly humiliate me. *How horrid of them.*

The Husband finished his call and said "It's gone." We took our coffees and trudged back to the house. It had started to spit with rain. My anger-bubble began to burst. Had I overreacted? It was a funny picture - to anyone who wasn't me. Why had I had such a sense of humour failure - was it just my own dreadful vanity? I had to admit to myself that if it had been a picture of me looking fabulous and sexy sat astride a surf board, wind gently ruffling my hair, face full of make-up, pouting for the camera, I wouldn't have minded quite so much.

Debbie opened the door, looking full of remorse. "Oh, Kate," she said, "I'm so sorry about the picture. We just thought it was so funny, we didn't mean to upset you."

I managed to force a smile. "Well you know how difficult it is when you're doing something for the first time," I said, a touch sanctimoniously. "It's not nice to be laughed at when you already feel so self-conscious."

"No, no of course not," said Debbie, looking wretched. *Good.* I went upstairs to have a hot shower. It was so lovely to be in warm water for a change and to feel clean. I rubbed at my blotchy patches of tan, but they wouldn't wash off. I tried to scrub them off with a towel, and although they faded a little, they stubbornly clung on. *How did you get this stuff off, sandpaper?* The lovely white towel looked disgusting when I'd finished; great rusty stains all over it. I took it back to the bedroom with me and hid it under my case. I Googled "How do you remove fake tan" on the iPad. The top answer was to use lemon juice. I'd have to go and buy some lemons, but that might take some explaining. I put my jeans and jumpers back on and wrapped another hair bando round my neck to hide the blotchy bits. It looked a bit odd, but then so does a skin disease.

The rain had set in. Paul's mother was entertaining Chloë, building a farm yard and doing all the farmyard noises, which got a bit irritating. Chloë shouted "Cock!" very loudly at one stage, which shocked me, but her grandmother quickly followed it up with "a doodle-doo", much to my relief. The rest of us played Monopoly. Paul, of course, got Mayfair and Park Lane and fleeced us all.

We went for an early evening pizza at a restaurant in the village. The Husband had asked me if I was going to get changed, but my only other options were dresses and skirts, which I couldn't wear because of my hideous blotchy legs. I told him it was too cold and I was sticking to my jeans. Chloë was an utter pain in the restaurant, banging cutlery, making sudden high-pitched screeches and chucking her food everywhere. Her parents were totally nonchalant about the whole thing, saying "Well it's a place for families so they've got to expect a bit of mess and noise."

I felt like saying "Yes but it's also a place for people who expect to be able to eat a meal without having their eardrums perforated." Paul's parents just smiled benignly. Proper conversation was impossible because all the attention was on Chloë. I could tell the Husband was getting irritated too; his knuckles were white as he clutched his Meaty Feast.

Even though it was still early when we got back, I excused myself and went to bed. I was genuinely shattered. The Husband woke me sometime later when he stumbled into the room and crashed into bed, reeking of brandy. I guessed he and Paul had got through the other half of the bottle. Two nights down, one to go.

The next morning, we awoke to grey skies but it wasn't raining. We were supposed to be going surfing with Debbie and Paul but I couldn't face it. I said I had a sore throat and thought I might have a cold coming. *Such a lame excuse.* I agreed to go down to the beach and keep an eye on their stuff whilst they were in the water. Chloë had a screaming fit when she realised her parents were going out without her, so it took almost half an hour for them to pacify her and for us to leave the house.

We hired a wet suit and a board for The Husband and, heavily laden, traipsed down to the shore. Debbie looked fantastic in her wet suit - although she wasn't exactly a slender woman she was very curvaceous and everything seemed to be in exactly the right proportion. She looked fit and athletic and both she and Paul were tanned (naturally, not spray-painted on) from the week of good weather they'd had before we got there.

The tide was a long way out and the wind was whipping across the rippled sand. I was surprised at how many other surfers there were today - the dark green water was dotted with black spots. The three of them went into the water and I stood guard by the towels, bags and Paul's flashy camera. I discovered that there is an activity that's colder than surfing - that's standing watching surfing. I jumped about, flapped my arms, jogged on the spot, but the chilly wind managed to invade all my layers of clothing and I felt frozen to the core. I couldn't move and leave all their stuff; I could possibly have carried it all off the beach and gone for a coffee, but I wasn't able to tell them where I was going, as they were too far out now, and actually, in amongst all the other surfers, I had no idea which was them. Hopefully the Husband would think of me stood here and pop back to check if I was ok.

He didn't. None of them did.

They were in the water for hours. When they finally emerged, Debbie cried "Oh Kate, you haven't been stood there all that time have you? But you must be absolutely frozen, and with your sore throat and everything." I smiled through chattering teeth and lied that I'd really enjoyed watching them. I joked that I could really use a brandy to warm me up.

Paul said: "Yuk, I can't bear the stuff. That's Deb's tipple." I stared at him. So he hadn't been up late-night drinking with the Husband then, it must have been Debbie. No doubt they'd talked about work until the early hours. How very dull.

The Husband was quite cock-a-hoop, as he'd managed to stand up on his board. He kept saying "Did you see me?" and I lied and said yes. Debbie was laughing and calling him Goofy, which I thought was a bit rude, but apparently it's a surfing term for someone who points their feet in the wrong direction or some boring bollocks like that. I went into the village whilst the others went back to the house to shower and change. I bought a big, steaming cappuccino and a hot tea cake and sat in the warm cafe. I was still shivering, even my bones felt cold. Middle of the English summer and I'd probably caught pneumonia.

The weekend was almost over, *thank God*, one more evening to get through and we could go home tomorrow. If we left early enough I'd be able to catch up on some work emails when we got home. I told myself off. Why wasn't I able to just live in the moment and enjoy myself like normal people do? I was either worrying about what I looked like or worrying about work. I couldn't enjoy the surfing because I was worried about sharks, drowning, frostbite, typhoid, and I couldn't enjoy the lovely house we were staying in because I'd ruined the towels and there was a devil child staring at me all the time. I guessed that a weekend just wasn't a long enough time to be able to totally switch off and relax. I'd try and get the Husband to agree to going away somewhere sunny in September - on our own.

We spent the evening at the house; Debbie made a creamy pasta dish for supper and we drank lots and lots of wine. Chloë wouldn't go to bed, and howled every time she got taken back upstairs. They were so soft on her, no wonder she never did anything they told her to. I overheard Debbie in the kitchen asking the Husband if we could stay another night, but he very quickly replied "No, no we can't, Kate's got to get back for work." *Phew.* His response was a sure sign that he'd had enough, too. We awoke the next morning and left Devon in the brilliant sunshine. *Just typical.* I asked The Husband if he'd enjoyed the weekend.

"Yes, apart from the bloody kid." We congratulated ourselves on being childless, and ripped Debbie and Paul's parenting skills to shreds, like all childless, judgemental couples do. I felt we were at one for a change - united against a common enemy - a toddler.

CHAPTER SEVENTEEN

I was slightly late getting into work because I had popped to the Dentist to enquire about getting my teeth whitened. I had accidentally asked the receptionist about "tooth" whitening and she had asked me, *the sarcastic cow*, if it was just the one tooth I wanted whitening.

The price shocked me - £273! There was the first appointment to make a mould and then the next to make sure it fitted, then you were given the whitening gel and away you go. So all they did was make a gum shield and you do the rest of the work! It's money for old rope. Or old floss. I'd have to think about it. I'd go to Boots first and look at their £9.99 kits.

Lurking in my inbox, where it had been for over a week, was a huge document relating to the new quotation system, Perypils Online Quotation System, POQS (which all the staff, of course, referred to as the pox, as in "When are we getting the pox?"). It was scheduled to be implemented next month. The document, which was 73 pages long, plus various attachments, had been produced by a Project Manager who clearly had time on their hands and the whole thing required sign off by "the business". That meant me. By asking the poor, exhausted departmental managers to provide sign off, the project team relinquished themselves from any kind of responsibility should something go tits up. Although, of course, it's absolutely a no-blame culture at Perypils

Insurance.

Deadline for sign off was approaching, so I'd printed the whole thing (killing an entire rain forest in the process) and taken it home to read. I couldn't use the study, as The Husband was in there on his lap top, sharing "Facetime" with some virtual friends.

I sat in the lounge in front of Midsomer Murders (the original with Bergerac) with a glass of red wine and the dreaded POQS implementation documents. It took me an hour and a half to read the documents, and then another hour to read them again. They were very complex, full of buggery-bollocks project speak and a vast amount of IT terminology - most of it totally meaningless to me. *How on earth was I expected to understand all this?* I didn't know which systems interfaced with each other or what bandwidth availability should be - I'm not Bill Gates for Christ's sake. I hadn't realised that as well as the 73 pages plus attachments, there were several documents embedded in the original document. *Jesus.*

John Nettles had solved the murders some time ago after randomly accusing everyone in the village, and the News at Ten was over too. There had been an item about the dangers of do-it-yourself teeth whitening kits. I'm glad I hadn't bought one now. I fired up the lap top, which seemed to groan as if to say "what the f-, do you know what time it is?" and sent an email to the POQS Project Manager, Lisa Hewitt. I'd met her a couple of times and I didn't like her very much - too young, too orange and with huge boobs, which didn't look at all real. At least she'd never need Sat Nav, I bet her nipples just followed the sun. My email asked for a detailed explanation on several areas of the document that I didn't understand. *Take that Big Boobs, you may have written this shite but I bet you haven't got a clue what it means either.*

I popped into the study to say goodnight to the Husband. He was sat talking to a "head" on the screen on his laptop - I wasn't introduced to The Head but it bid me a cheery goodnight.

10.00 am. I was waiting impatiently to start the team manager meeting. The Climber's iPhone made a noise like a duck. She read a message and threw back her head to laugh her annoying laugh. We could see right down her throat and all her fillings. I noticed her teeth were very white.

"It's from Brett," she trilled, "He is just so funny!" Why is Brett The Boss, my boss, texting her? Why? What about? He never texts me. Except, occasionally, late at night when he's clearly meant to have messaged someone else. The Rock caught my eye and raised her eyebrows. I felt quite rattled but covered it by launching cheerfully into the meeting.

I was still dwelling over the texting business at lunchtime. Why didn't I have that kind of relationship with The Boss where he felt he could text me jokey messages? We didn't have much contact at all. Maybe I should phone him more, but then equally he could phone me - but he hardly ever does. Why should I have to make the effort all the time? Especially when I'm working flat out around the clock and he's got time to send stupid messages to my team.

The Climber's annoying laugh was in my head. I phoned the dentist and made myself an appointment.

11.30 am. Received an email from Big Boobed Lisa, the POQS Project Manager, chasing me for my sign off for the

73 page-plus-attachments-plus-embedded-documents document. I sent one back saying I was unable to provide sign off until she'd responded to the questions I'd raised. I attached a copy of my email containing the questions, just by way of revenge.

1.30 pm. Received an email from Big Boobs informing me that if I did not provide sign off immediately I would be responsible for a delay in the roll out of the new system, thus meaning I would be personally responsible for causing millions of pounds of additional cost and lost revenue. There were no answers to any of my questions.

Emailed back to ask what was the value of my sign off if I didn't fully understand what I was signing off?

1.50 pm. Received email from Big Boobs saying it was entirely the responsibility of "the Business" to agree the implementation plan within the required timescales.

I noticed she was using a BlackBerry. How come she had one and I didn't? Replied saying I would provide sign off when she had responded to my questions. I signed the email from "the Business".

2.40 pm. Received a rare phone call from Brett The Boss. I answered it assuming he'd dialled the wrong number.

"Ah, Kate, the lovely Kate, how the devil are you today?" He sounded a little slurry, so I guessed he'd had a liquid lunch again. Either that or he'd had a stroke. "Now, I understand from the project team that you are being a bit awkward about signing off the impelmen, the implemen, the er... you know, that fuck-off huge project document." *Big*

Boobs had gone to the Boss behind my back! What a weasley little shit-head...

"No, I'm not being awkward at all Brett, I've simply asked some questions around areas that I need clarification on..."

"Oh Kate, just sign the bloody thing off will you? I can't be doing with the project team on my back giving me grief as well as everyone else. I just don't need the hassle. I'll tell them you're sending it over now. Everything else ok there?"

"Er, well yes..."

"Good, good, speak later." He was gone.

Oh great, I've been undermined by an empty-headed, talentless, useless, big breasted bimboid. I viciously jabbed at the keys on my laptop and emailed confirmation of my sign off, entitling it: To Weasel-Features Supergrass. (I took this out before sending it, but only at the very last minute). I sighed. I knew I had another sleepless night coming up now, as I worried about exactly what I had just signed off and agreed to.

Later on I saw Big Andy at the coffee machine and I told him about Lisa The Weasel going to The Boss behind my back. He laughed and told me that The Boss and The Weasel are "shagging each other". He said everyone knows it, the two of them go for a drink together at the Hat and Feather every lunch time and most evenings. He was amazed I didn't know. *Oh good grief.*

I was sat in the dentist's waiting room getting very cold feet. Like anyone who's seen the film Marathon Man, I had a morbid fear of going to the dentist. Jaws had also affected me in the same way. Not from going to the dentist, but from swimming in the sea. It hadn't helped that the dentist I usually saw, the nice, motherly Mrs Brown with the hairy nostrils, had retired and I'd been told that I'd been transferred to her son, Scott. I almost bottled it and got up to go, but too late, I was called in by the dental nurse, who was obviously doing this job in between her modelling shoots. Scott turned round from his computer screen to say "Hi!" as I went in. *Hubba bubba - he was gorgeous!* Not a bit like the evil Dr Szell. He had quite a muscular build, a very handsome, open smiley face and lovely even, white teeth. Which you'd expect really, being in the trade. How inconvenient - I always turned into a moron when faced with very attractive people. I'd much rather deal with munters.

Scott examined my teeth very thoroughly. My tongue kept caressing his fingers which was highly embarrassing and at one point he nearly lost one of them when I snapped my jaw shut abruptly. He declared that I had "really good teeth" and it was obvious that I did an excellent job in looking after them. I found myself welling up with emotion. I couldn't remember the last time my appearance had been praised by anyone. But that was the good bit over with. Making the mould was disgusting. He literally took what appeared to be a piece of play-dough and wedged it into my mouth over my teeth. It had to be done twice, and both times he sat there for ages pressing this hideous-tasting gunk into my jaws. Both times I gagged when he removed it. I'm amazed all my fillings didn't come away as well. *Why am I doing this to myself?* And paying for the pleasure! I must be totally bonkers. Left there saying "Thank you very much" which didn't exactly feel appropriate. Paid the first instalment. Utter madness.

I received an email from Lisa-Big-Boobs-Weasley-Pox-

Project-Manager requesting the names of the two colleagues I was sending to Birmingham on Monday to receive their system training. *Eh?*

Replied asking when I agreed to this.

Get an email straight back from The Weasel saying "It was in the document that you signed off." I noticed that she had copied in The Boss, the entire project team, and every other manager she could think of just to make me look a tit.

I scoured the document in a desperate attempt to prove The Weasel wrong, but eventually found it in an embedded part of an embedded document in one of the attachments. Can't think how I missed it.

I'd "agreed" to send two colleagues for training in Birmingham on Monday and Tuesday, (staying overnight) with the aim of them coming back to the site and training the others. I called an emergency meeting with my team managers. Thank God they are so good in a crisis. Cries of "But it's too short notice" and "But Monday's our busiest day" and "But no one will want to do it" and "But I thought we would get proper trainers" which is actually a fair point, if touchingly naive.

I supported them through this initial stage of denial:

"I'm sorry guys, but we've just got to bloody well do it." They came up with names of individuals who they thought had the required skills and expertise to undertake the training and The Rock went off to ask them if they'd be prepared to go.

She returned sometime later looking rather cagey. It appeared that everyone she'd asked suddenly had "other commitments" on Monday evening. *Like what?*

"Well, Linda has to pick up her younger brother," *Isn't he seventeen at least?* "Dave has an evening class at college," *In the middle of the school holidays?* "And Jackie just said she had personal things she had to do."

"Like what?"

"Er, she said she's got to shave her horse." *You what?* Oh well, I couldn't really blame them, I think I'd have made my excuses too if I'd been offered a night away in Birmingham.

The Rock was twiddling with the zip on her cardigan. "I did get a couple of volunteers, although they weren't on our list." I noticed she wasn't looking me in the eye.

"Go on - who?" She muttered something I couldn't quite catch.

"I'm sorry Jan, but I thought for one horrible moment you'd said Danny and Ben?"

"Yes well, they were very keen and I know they can be a bit, er, you know..." *disruptive, bone idle, pains in the arse?* "high maintenance, but their system knowledge is excellent, and, well," The Rock looked at me squarely now, "I don't think we have any other choice."

"Oh God Jan, no," I groaned, head in my hands. "Please don't tell me the entire success of this project rests on the heads of Ben and Danny, because if so we're going to come completely unstuck. Not to mention the reputation of the site when Dumb and Dumber rock up on Monday for their training. Everyone will think if that's the best we've got to offer then what the bloody hell does the worst look like... the Weasel will have a field day... Please go back and ask the others again, beg if you must, grovel on your hands and knees, promise them sex, whatever it takes."

It was no good. On Friday morning, I found myself

booking hotel rooms at the Holiday Inn and train tickets for Danny and Ben (I didn't want them to drive as they had enough trouble finding their way back from the canteen let alone negotiating a route round the Bullring). I gave the excited pair a pep talk on how they were ambassadors for the site and the importance of maintaining our excellent reputation. Ben, to his credit, asked if I wanted him to wear a long-sleeved, high-necked top to cover his tattoos. I was actually more concerned about the large bolt piercing his ear, but he said he couldn't remove that in case it sealed up. Feeling slightly queasy, I thanked them for volunteering, and wished them good luck. I really, really didn't want Monday to ever come round.

Monday

The Rock came to tell me (rather triumphantly I thought) that Danny and Ben had made it to Birmingham on time and had started the training. *That's something I suppose.*

Tuesday 5.50 pm

The Rock forwarded an email she'd received from the trainer in Birmingham. It read: "To the line manager of Danny Jones and Ben Goodman". *I'm not sure I want to read this.* "I just wanted to say how great your guys have been over the last two days. They have picked up all aspects of the new system extremely quickly and have been able to demonstrate a thorough understanding of all the training material that was used. I have no doubt they will provide you with a very successful system roll-out in the Cheltenham site".

I drove home feeling rather ashamed of myself. Had I become one of those people that once they had made their minds up about someone, they never changed their opinion? Or if someone made a bad first impression you never gave them another chance? I'd always hated people like that. Was I unable to recognise genuine talent just because it was hidden under ghastly tattoos and ear bolts? Was I holding my team back? I needed to take a serious a look at myself.

When I got home, I had a flick through a book entitled How To Get The Best Out Of People Who Are Crap, or something like that. I found a great quote, which said: "Challenge your own assumptions. Your assumptions are your windows on the world. Scrub them every once in a while, or the light won't come in." *Love it.* I typed it out and printed it so I could take it to work the next day. I would pin it up in front of me. I must look at this each time I have a negative thought about a colleague. *I must change.*

Wednesday

9.30 Said a big "Well done!" to Danny and Ben in front of their teams, and read out the email from the trainer. They were very chuffed, and received a big round of applause from everyone.

10.30 Received a phone call from the manager of the Holiday Inn in Birmingham. Rather awkwardly, he told me he was calling out of courtesy to make me aware that there were certain "additions" to the room bills that I might not be expecting.

"Such as?" I asked, as a sinking feeling hit my stomach. He listed the additions as:

- £268 phone calls to premium rate numbers.
- £143.98 entire mini bar contents - *how the hell did they get a mini bar?*

- £58 additional cleaning.
- £25 maintenance fee to put the trouser press back together.

For God's sake. I started to ask what the additional cleaning was required for, but stopped myself. I really didn't want to know.

I waited until lunchtime to see if Danny or Ben had the courage or decency to fess up, but they didn't. I took them both into a meeting room, relayed the conversation with the manager of the Holiday Inn and asked them for their comments. They looked at each other. Ben said "Oh." Danny tried "But I thought we got expenses..." I asked them for £247.50 each and told them I wanted it this afternoon, otherwise I'd be starting disciplinary action against them. Ashen-faced, they slunk out and returned after lunch to present me with piles of scruffy notes and coins. God knows who they'd robbed to get it, but at least they'd paid up - I didn't have the time for any more disciplinaries.

Thursday

My moulds had come back from the manufacturers, and Scott The Dishy Dentist fitted them both over my teeth, declaring them a perfect fit. Hooray! I could start the whitening process. First though, he wanted to take a picture of my teeth so I could see what they looked like before and after. Whilst his supermodel-nurse fetched a camera, he wedged what looked like bottle-openers into the sides of my mouth to pull my lips wide apart, exposing all my teeth. I lay there, looking like Shergar, whilst they fiddled around trying to get the camera to work. I felt my last shred of dignity leave the building.

In the evening, before bed, I squeezed the gel carefully into the teeth-moulds and placed them gingerly over my teeth. It tasted ok. I smiled at myself in the bathroom mirror. I looked like Janet Street Porter. I went downstairs and smiled at the Husband. I hadn't seen him laugh so much in ages.

Weekend

Very bored with the whole whitening process. My teeth were extremely sensitive, so much so that I had to drink coffee through a straw. No noticeable difference yet.

By the following Friday, the gel had run out completely and I still couldn't see much of a difference in the colour. I dropped into the dentist's and purchased more gel. Another thirty quid! The receptionist tried to get me to make an appointment with Scott first, but I told her I didn't have the time.

Weekend

The new POQS system was being implemented over the weekend. I'd had to attend no less than 8 "go-no-go" teleconferences throughout the weekend. My attendance was completely pointless - the only contribution I had made was to say the word "Yes" in the very last one on Sunday night, when we'd agreed to go for it. I'd no idea if this was the right word, but everyone else had said it so I did too. All the other meetings were taken up with IT and project managers squabbling with each other in a language that I believe is universally recognised as bollocks. The Husband made it even more difficult by tutting loudly every time he saw me on the phone and making sarcastic comments, such as "They do know it's actually the weekend do they?" and "Are the bastards paying you for this?" which I hoped no one heard.

We had managed to go out on Saturday night with Karen and James to celebrate Karen's birthday. We went to an Italian restaurant and had lots of lovely pasta and wine. I asked the waiter to take some pictures of us on my camera. I looked through them the next morning. My God! My eyes were immediately drawn to my image - smiling drunkenly. My teeth! They stood out a mile. They were quite freakishly white. Why had I not noticed? Why hadn't anyone said anything? I must stop using the gel; I looked like a child-frightener.

CHAPTER EIGHTEEN

Monday - 5.00 am. Awoke to the alarm clock, the most hated sound in the world apart from The Husband's iPhone message tones. I arrived at work at 6.45 am to try and get a bit of work done before the teams arrived and started to use the new POQS system. There were bound to be teething problems, there always were when IT did anything to the systems. I couldn't sign into my lap top; it told me my account had been "locked out". *Perfect start to the day.* I phoned the systems helpdesk and selected the option for account lock outs. I thought I'd got through to someone, but it turned out to be an automated voice telling me that for account lock outs I had to go into the internet site and reset myself. It then cut me off.

Just how was I supposed to access the internet site when I couldn't log in to any systems? I phoned back and selected the option for new faults. I waited in a queue for ages, before finally getting through to a human. Well, sort of. I told him my account was locked out. He started to tell me that I needed to reset myself on the internet site in such a disinterested tone that I thought for one moment I'd got the automated voice again.

"And how am I supposed to do that when I've just told you that I'm locked out of my system?"

"You need to log into a colleague's system and access the site that way."

"What colleagues? It's only twenty past seven, there's no one else here yet."

"Oh." Big sigh. "Well, I'll do it this once but next time you'll have to...."

"Yes I know," I snapped, "I'll use the bloody internet site."

There was a long silence. "Hello, are you still there?" I asked eventually. "Hello?"

"Yes," said the android, "I've reset you. Your temporary password is 'password'. You'll have to change it when you log in. In about 30 minutes time."

"Sorry, what? Why 30 minutes? Don't tell me I've got to wait thirty minutes before I can log in."

"Yes, the system updates itself every 30 minutes. You should be alright by 8.00-ish. Probably. If not, by 8.30."

Just great. I get myself up at the crack of a sparrow's fart to get a head start on the day and I can't do a damned thing. What an absolute waste of time; not even the canteen was open yet. Jim the cleaner walked through the department. "Morning Sam!" he called. "Morning Jim," I said, not bothering to correct him. He came over to tell me all about the bodily fluids he'd just had to scrape off the walls of the cubicles in the Gents toilets. *Ugh, gross. Why are you telling me this?* But at least it was interesting to know that this place was clearly exciting to somebody.

The early shift started to arrive just before 8.00. Unlike me, they managed to access their systems ok. The first calls started to come in and I hovered nervously, watching them use the new quotation system. Everything seemed to go ok - the system appeared to be working well. This could be a miracle in the making - had IT implemented a new system without any hitches? It all looked good! I felt like dancing a jig of joy around the department.

The first telecon with IT and the project team, (who I'd stupidly thought would be conspicuous around the sites today to support us with the new system - oh silly me) was at 9.00 am. I reported that all was working well. Even I had eventually managed to get into my system.

The telecon ended and I saw an email come in from The Climber, who was sat twenty feet away. *Don't get up will you, you lazy cow.* It was headed: Problem with customer details. She'd written that one of her sales team had come across a customer's policy which had information missing from the system. It was only one policy, probably some random glitch, so I emailed her back and told her to keep her eye on it. I went over to the canteen and bought a tray of whopping cappuccinos for myself and the team managers to celebrate the successful implementation and to recover from the early start. When I got back to the department, The Rock was waiting for me, looking concerned. *Oh no, what?*

"Kate, the guys have noticed a few anomalies," she said. "We've had a couple of calls from customers wanting to change their addresses and when we've gone into the system, their policies aren't showing."

"Do you mean some of their details are missing?" I asked, thinking of The Climber's email.

"No, I mean their policies aren't showing at all. They can't be found."

I felt an icy hand clutch at my insides. I asked The Rock to show me an example. She was right: she searched the system but the policies could not be found. As I was stood at her desk, another advisor came over to report the same issue.

"Do you think it's anything to do with the new quotation system?" asked The Rock anxiously.

"Well, it shouldn't be," I said, "it's a different system, but they are linked and it's too much of a coincidence that we've gone live this morning and we have these issues. I'll have to phone it in."

"What are we going to tell these customers?" asked The Rock.

"Take all the details, tell them there's a fault and we'll call them back as soon as it's corrected."

I phoned the project team and got Lisa-the-weasel. I told her we had several customers' policies that had disappeared from the system.

"Can't be anything to do with POQS," she immediately snapped. "It must be a separate issue. You'll need to report it in the usual way through the IT helpdesk, not the project team. It's nothing to do with us."

"With respect, Lisa," *you weasley little shit* "it's far too much of a coincidence for this issue not to be connected - you need to report it to the IT guys, this is a very serious issue - customers' policies have disappeared."

The Weasel refused, saying it "wasn't possible" for the issues to be connected to the project and rang off. For the second time that day, I had to phone the IT helpdesk. I selected the option "new fault" and waited in a queue - again. Whilst I was waiting, The Rock came over and mouthed at me that she'd had three more customers who had vanished. When I got through to someone, they told me I had to report the fault on the new online IT internet site. I had a complete diva-like hissy-fit melt down - and they hung up on me.

I entered all the details of the issue into the online form

on the internet site. It wanted to know the ins and outs of a duck's arse - it took me twenty minutes. Just when I'd hit submit, The Climber emailed again. Why couldn't she get off her backside and walk the twenty feet to come and talk to me? She'd had another couple of examples where policies had some customer information missing. This was turning into a nightmare.

The next telecon was due at 10.30 and by then we'd had over twenty cases of disappearing policies or missing information. When I dialled in, I told IT and the project team about the two issues. They said "Why the hell didn't you tell us earlier?" It gave me great pleasure to tell them I'd reported it to the Weasel about an hour ago. I knew she was on the telecon but she chose not to say anything. IT were initially in denial "It can't possibly be connected", followed by much disagreement, and general willy-waving until eventually someone (a woman) said they would undertake some urgent investigation.

I asked for their definition of "urgent", knowing that IT's definition differs from everyone else's, usually by about ten years or so. The woman who had spoken, Mo, said she would do it now and report back at 11.30. She sounded like she knew what she was talking about. I asked the project team what they wanted us to tell our customers. Silence. They often forgot that we had real live customers; it was so long since any of them had actually spoken with one. We agreed that my guys would keep all the details of the affected policies with the aim of calling our customers back. I reminded them that the longer they took to investigate and fix the issue, the more call backs we would have to make. I was worried this was all going to turn into a big horrible beastie.

11.30 telecon. 45 cases reported. Mo from IT told us the issues were "almost certainly" connected to the POQS implementation, but further investigation was required.

12.30 telecon. 71 cases reported. Mo from IT told us that she had identified "about 1000" policies whose data had been corrupted by the POQS system, and a load of other technical gumph that no one really understood. She didn't have a fix for it yet. The project team demanded to know how this had happened. IT didn't seem to know.

2.00 telecon. 117 cases reported. Mo from IT told us that she had identified a further 5000 policies that were affected. No fix yet. I told them that the number of call backs required was getting out of hand. There was general panic. The project team were very angry and wanted answers. IT didn't have any. I asked why this issue hadn't been picked up in testing? No one knew.

3.00 telecon. 138 cases reported. Mo from IT told us she had identified a further 3000 affected policies. From what I could ascertain from the IT-speak, she seemed to be saying that there was no fix available. Everyone agreed this was unacceptable and tempers were beginning to fray.

4.00 telecon. 156 cases reported. Mo from IT didn't join the telecon. Someone went to try and find her. The project team argued amongst themselves about who was going to give the Big Cheese the "heads up", in other words, tell him that 9,000 customer policies had gone missing. They agreed someone from IT should tell him, and decided it should be Mo, as she would be able to explain the technical detail to him.

5.00 telecon. 168 cases reported. Mo from IT said she'd found another 3000 affected policies, taking the total to

12,000. She sounded a bit weepy. She said the team were working on a fix; they'd update us at 6.00.

I phoned Brett the Boss to tell him what was going on. He said "I know, it's a shitter" before ringing off saying he didn't want to miss the start of the quiz night at the Hat and Feather.

6.00 telecon. 171 cases reported. Mo from IT said they had identified a possible fix which they were going to try to implement overnight. One of the project managers wanted to determine the "confidence level" of the fix working. Mo wouldn't commit, but he kept on and on pressing. Mo lost it in the end and shouted "I'd feel a lot more confident if you bastards shut the fuck up and let me go and sort it!" We all quickly agreed this was a sensible course of action.

Tuesday

5.00 am. Woke and checked mobile. There was a text from the IT team. The overnight fix hadn't worked. *Oh God.* There was also a text from Brett the Boss, which had come through very late last night. It read: "Do u no wot is the capitol of namibia?"

I heaved myself out of bed to face the horrors of another day. I tried to creep about quietly, but I woke up The Husband when one of my bra straps pinged off, catching me in the eye and I'd cried out in pain. He had bad temperedly muttered "For Christ's sake why are you going in at this time again?" I don't think he was expecting an explanation, so I didn't offer one.

I arrived at work to find an email in my inbox from the Communications team with a "personal" message from the Big Cheese which had been sent to all colleagues. "I am delighted and proud to announce the successful implementation of the Perypils Online Quotation System. Well done to the project team for all their hard work and superb efforts - this is a triumphant uniting of technology and leading the business through change... "

There was no mention of the 12,000 or so missing policies and I doubted my poor team would see it as a triumph. They were already calling it "that poxy system". The day staggered on as a virtual repeat of yesterday, with useless telecons with IT and the project team on the hour, every hour.

I had to get Martin The Drain to dial into one for me when I was double-booked and as I passed by his desk he put himself on mute and begged "Please kill me." IT could not seem to find a way to fix the issue. My guys were still receiving calls from customers with missing policies and by midday the number stood at 250. The customers who had called us yesterday were beginning to call us back to complain that we hadn't called them back. I asked the project team what they wanted us to tell these customers. They didn't have a clue.

I eventually managed to get hold of Brett the Boss after leaving messages all morning.

"Brett," I said "I really need some support with this one. We've got hundreds of customers we don't know what to do with; no guidance from the project team and IT can't seem to find a fix. There's 12000 policies affected, it's a monster. I need your help please, I need you to get involved."

"Right," he said decisively, like a superhero about to sweep into action, "Leave it with me; I'll get back to you."

I called my team managers together to update them with

the situation. They were all extremely stressed as call volumes
were creeping up and so were the complaints. The Climber
said the project team were "all completely useless" *pot and
kettle* and The Rock said IT were about as much use as a fart
in a thunderstorm. The Drain was in a right old flap and I
had to calm him down before he combusted. As it was he
had to get up quickly to dash to the loo, the old irritable
bowel flaring up again. I told the guys not to worry; Brett was
on the case and would help us sort this out. I received a text
from Brett. It said: "Have arranged for PM to call u."

Was that it? Was that the sum token of his involvement? I
assumed by PM he meant the Project Manager and not the
Prime Minister. My mobile rang. I answered it wearily. It was
the Weasel.

"Kate," she said, "Brett's asked me to call you, although
I don't know what I can add when you've been on all the
telecons so you know what the current situation just as well
as I do." I'd like to have spoken to the organ grinder not the
monkey's weasel.

"We need someone to take control of the situation," I
said, quite calmly for me I thought. "That's why I wanted
Brett to get involved. Decisions need to be made. We can't
just leave customers to complain, it's not fair on them or on
my guys. And why isn't anyone from the project team here on
site to support us and to see the issues first hand? It's not
good enough."

The Weasel started to mutter that they were only a small
team, they couldn't be everywhere, but I cut her short and
asked her to go back and talk to Brett. She rang off in a strop.
I dialled into the 2.00 telecon. Mo from IT broke the news
that there was no workable solution. We asked her what that

meant. She said: "It's completely buggered and can't be fixed." The project team started squawking like a load of old hens, but Mo stood her ground, simply repeating that there was no fix. I eventually managed to get a word in and asked what this meant for all the affected customers. Mo said all their policies would have to be manually loaded back on. One of the project team asked "Is that something your guys could pick up for us, Kate?" *Oh why yes of course, no problem!* Of course we can handle 12000 additional pieces of work just like that, no worries at all; if we start right away we should get it finished inside of five years. I did a quick calculation.

"Well, on average, it takes about 20 minutes to manually load a policy onto the system. So... that's about 4000 hours of additional work. My team's not in a position to support that sort of...."

"Well they could work overtime," cut in one of the project managers. *Dickhead.*

I said "Ok, but, sorry what was your name? Oh, it's Richard, is it Dick for short by any chance? Well, it's going to take ages to get through that volume of work on overtime alone, and until all the policies are loaded back on customer complaints will keep coming in. Not to mention the overtime bill, which will run to thousands, and who is going to pay for that? I certainly haven't got the budget."

"Well, it will have to come from IT's budget," said Richard, "it's their cock up."

"But we don't have any budget for this sort of thing," said Mo, "it would have to come from the project." The row that ensued was interrupted from a terrible northern roar which reverberated down the phone line.

"For the love of Jesus H fucking Christ! What kind of

inane bloody bullshit is this? I have never heard such a load of incompetent, useless claptrap in all my bloody life!" It was the Big Cheese. He had been listening in to the telecon without anyone knowing. There was a deathly silence.

"Load 12000 policies back on? You're all talking out your bloody arses, that's what you're doing. Who's using the IT brain cell today? You bloody well find a fix and find it quick, d'you hear me? That's what you're paid for, that's your *fucking job*, so if you want to keep it, you'd better sort this pile of shit out. And as for you bone idle, useless project dickheads, you get yourselves off your big fat arses and get out to the sites to see for yourselves what your fuck up has done. Do you hear me?" He was worked up to a frenzy. "So get off this fucking phone and GET IT FUCKING SORTED!"

We all hung up. There were no more teleconferences. I received an email from the Weasel saying she would be down on site tomorrow. Then I received one from Brett the Boss saying he would be down on site tomorrow. It was like waiting for a bus...

CHAPTER NINETEEN

Wednesday

I arrived at work exhausted. I had got home pretty late last night, feeling sick with stress and could only manage a few glasses of wine, and not much else. The Husband had been forced to make his own supper again, which hadn't gone down at all well, especially when he'd managed to burn the toast to go with his baked beans and we didn't have any more bread. Apparently it was my fault for dusting the toaster and knocking the heating button to max.

I had driven to work almost still asleep, which was silly and dangerous. I couldn't recall bits of the journey. I felt very light-headed. Text from IT simply said: "Overnight fix unsuccessful". So the problems continued, our calls were stacking up and my guys were totally frazzled. Lisa the Weasel and Brett the Boss arrived (together) just before 10.00, although her boobs came through the door five minutes before the rest of her appeared. We planned to get together with all the team managers at 11.00.

I found them a couple of spare desks next to the fax machine and the Weasel went to get some coffees from the canteen. When I looked up, I saw The Climber stood at the fax machine. That was unusual; she didn't normally get her hands dirty with real work. Ten minutes later she was still stood there, so I went over to see if she was ok. "Oh, I'm just waiting for a customer to fax me something, er, a policy document," she said, looking like she'd been caught out. I went back to my desk and watched her. She was obviously trying to catch Brett's attention, there was some frenzied hair flicking, but he appeared to be ignoring her, looking at his emails, his phone, anything but making eye contact.

At 11.00, the team managers and myself gathered around a table with Brett for what he called a "drains up". Lisa the Weasel had taken a call on her mobile and was walking around on her high heels, talking earnestly and trying to look important. At one point, she leant across our table, picked up Brett's coffee, took a sip and put it back on the table whilst she continued her call. We all looked at each other. Brett carried on talking about the issues. The Climber stiffened, and flushed dark red. She talked across Brett:

"Well I think this project team has an awful lot to answer for. They should have made sure that the new system wouldn't affect the existing systems. They simply couldn't have tested it properly. I hope that heads are going to roll." She looked pointedly round at The Weasel.

Brett said he didn't think there was anything to be gained from finger-pointing (*but it's so much fun!*) but instead we had to plan for the worst case scenario. He said we had to face the fact that we "might not be able to get the toothpaste back in the tube." I translated this for the benefit of the others as: if IT were unable to find a fix, we'd have to manually load 12,000 policies back onto the system. The Drain clutched at his stomach. I prayed he hadn't followed through.

The Rock reminded Brett that we had almost 400 customers who were expecting a call back, and this figure was increasing hour on hour. The Snake reminded Brett that our people were getting demoralised and were losing faith in the management. Gee thanks for that.

Lisa the Weasel finished her call and came to join us at the table. She wasn't a particularly good judge of mood, as she said airily "Here we all are then! Have I missed anything?"

The Climber went for the jugular. "We were just saying Lisa, what a disgraceful situation we are faced with, and we're all extremely upset with the project team for putting us in this mess. We're all appalled that this has happened and we hope someone is going to be held accountable."

It was the Weasel's turn to flush bright red. Brett jumped in with "We can take this offline, but for now we need to have a plan for the re-loading of the policies. That's what we're here for." He looked at me for help. I said we needed to examine the facts, and went through a back-of-a-fag-packet calculation that I'd hurriedly put together. To re-load 12000 policies over a time period of one month would require 25 full time additional staff. The cost would be around £40000. I also reminded him that it would take about six weeks to recruit them. There was silence while he tugged at his chin and looked thoughtful. The Drain's stomach gurgled loudly.

"Well," said Brett eventually, "Lisa, what budget can be found from the project for this?"

By the look on her face, she clearly didn't have the first clue but didn't want to look stupid.

"I'd have to make some calls but I think we could cover about £5000."

The Climber snorted. "That's ridiculous," she said, "Absolutely ridiculous. Kate, how many people can we get for £5000?"

"Amanda," I said, "Brett's right about finger-pointing,

it's not helpful. But to answer your question, we could only get about 3 staff with a budget of £5000..."

"Oh that's ludicrous!" exclaimed The Climber, talking right across me. "It would take the best part of a year with only three people, and in the meantime we'd still be getting complaint after complaint." She glared at the Weasel. "And will anyone from the project team be here to help us answer these complaints? Are you going to come and help us explain to our customers why you've lost their policies?"

The Weasel, still brick red from the last attack, spat back: "I find your conduct extremely unprofessional. Brett and I have come here today to offer our support and guidance, and all you can do is make negative comments. You're being very disrespectful."

"Well I'd rather be disrespectful than, than totally useless at my job!"

"Ladies that's enough!" I interjected, as Brett clearly wasn't going to. Everyone else looked horribly uncomfortable. "I'm calling a time out. Lisa, you need to find out exactly what budget is available from the project, so could you go and make some calls, please. I suggest Brett and I put our heads together to see if there is any available resource across the other sites that could support us. We'll get together again later this afternoon. Thank you."

My team managers gratefully got up from the table, The Drain heading straight for the Gents. Brett and I started to discuss the other sites and which poor bastards we could tap up to try and squeeze some resource out of. As we were talking, a commotion broke out behind us. We turned in time to see Lisa the Weasel, who had coffee all down her white top, grab The Climber's hair and attempt to punch her in the face, shouting "You little bitch!" The Climber started screaming, and one of the lads jumped up to try and wrestle the Weasel off her.

Brett and I rushed over. Brett tried to get in between them, dodging punches thrown by the Weasel who was making Mike Tyson look like a girl. The Climber was blindly and pathetically flailing her arms around to in an attempt to strike back. There was uproar in the teams. As I grabbed hold of The Climber and pulled her back, I saw Cruella walking through the department, a stupid smirk on her face. *Perfect.* "Everything alright Kate?" she called. *Up yours.* Brett had hold of the Weasel and had managed to prise open her grip on The Climber's hair. We pulled them apart, and Brett dragged the Weasel outside. I took an hysterical Climber off to the meeting room, where she dissolved into huge sobs, wailing "She attacked me, she attacked me."

I felt quite shaken myself. I tried to calm her down and asked her to tell me what had happened.

"I don't know! We were going back to our desks and I accidentally jogged her arm." *Oh really?* "She spilt her coffee down herself and she just went for me. I want her dismissed, she assaulted me."

"How did you manage to jog her arm?"

"It was just an accident!" cried the Climber. "I didn't do anything, nothing at all. I said sorry, and the next thing I knew she called me a bitch and attacked me. I want her thrown out."

I didn't believe for one moment that the coffee spillage was just an accident.

"Amanda," I said, "What's really going on here? You spent the meeting verbally attacking Lisa, incidentally you talked right over me and over Brett which I found extremely rude; I expect better from you. Is it just a clash of personalities with Lisa, or is there more to it than that?" Although technically you do need to have a personality before you can have a clash.

"I was just sticking up for us," said The Climber, sniffily, "because you don't seem to want to say it how it is." Oh that's right, I wondered when it would be my fault. "I don't know how you can blame me for this, I've done nothing wrong, nothing at all. You should be supporting me, she attacked me. I want the book thrown at her, I'll be taking advice you know, I want her out."

"So if I ask for some witness statements they won't tell me that you chucked Lisa's coffee over her?"

The Climber wouldn't budge, insisting it was an accident and berating me for not being "on her side". Brett eventually came into the room and said the Weasel had gone home. *How will you get home then, didn't you come in the same car?* He asked to speak with the Climber, so I left them to it. They were in the room for hours. I checked that all the teams were ok. The Snake looked like all her Christmases had come at once. I hoped to God that no one had been quick enough to film it on their phones, it would be a FaceTube sensation.

Brett and the Climber eventually emerged and all eyes were on them as they walked back into the department. The Climber went back to her desk and Brett came over to tell me that he'd "smoothed things over". I asked what action should be taken. He looked very shifty and just said:

"It's all done with now, we can leave it at that." I started to protest but he cut me dead saying "Just leave it now, Kate, that's the end of it," and walked off. He came back a few minutes later to ask me where the train station was.

I received an email from Big Andy entitled "Ring Side Seats" and asked if I would be selling tickets for the next fight. *Ha bloody ha.* Word certainly gets around quick.

Thursday

Text from IT: "overnight fix unsuccessful".

Email from IT informing us that Mo had left the company for "personal reasons".

Email from the Weasel saying she'd checked with the project senior manager, and there was no budget for any additional staff. She didn't offer any alternative solutions.

The Climber seemed to be ok after her "attack"; she was quieter than usual, but I did hear her snapping at one of her team "Well you'll just have to work a bit harder then, won't you?" so I guessed she was back on her usual form.

We had over 500 customers to call back. We'd stopped telling them when we'd call them back, just that we'd do it as soon as we could, but many were still calling back to complain. My own email inbox had 232 unread items in it, as I hadn't been able to get anything else done. People were starting to call me to see if I'd read their stupid emails.

The Husband texted to remind me that we were supposed to be going to Debbie and Paul's that evening. *Christ no.* I texted back to say I was too knackered, he'd have to go on his own. I'd be in the dog house but I really was too drained from this week to have to make conversation with Paul - I'd run out of things to talk to him about over six months ago.

Friday

The Husband was not talking to me. Apparently, Debbie had made a lasagne especially for me as she knew it was a favourite of mine. I didn't remember telling her that, probably I was pissed when I said it. I reminded him that Debbie may have spent forty minutes knocking up a lasagne, but that I'd worked over 60 hours already that week and I still had Friday to go. Didn't he feel sorry for me? He said it was my choice, and it didn't excuse snubbing our friends. *You mean your friends.* He could be a right snot when he wanted to be. I asked if he'd rather I gave up my job and not be able to cover the mortgage payments, and he said I was being melodramatic and ridiculous as usual and he couldn't be bothered to talk to me any more. I went to work wondering if he was going to sulk all weekend; two days appeared to be his current sulk-average.

Text from IT: "overnight fix successful". Whoopee! Oh thank God. I kissed my phone when that message came through. After all that buggery bollocks, IT had recovered the missing 12000 policies and got them back on the system. They did say there would be some "defects" which had fallen through the net, which meant we would still come across some policies with missing information, but I could live with that.

I called the team together to give them the good news and to arrange the 500 plus call backs, which we agreed to share out between the teams and use some overtime to get through them.

Everyone was happy and relieved, apart from The Snake who looked disappointed that the crisis was over. I sent The

Rock out to get some cakes for the department and made a start on my huge backlog of work. At least I had the weekend to catch up; it's not as if I'd be doing anything with The Husband now.

Into my inbox dropped an invitation from the project team for me to attend a Post POQS Implementation Review. They must be having a bloody laugh! I replied: "Here's my Poxy review: countless unpaid hours worked, one lasagne ruined, one fall out with husband, forty seven useless telecons attended, thousands of customer policies lost, hundreds of complaints received, one extremely irritable bowel (including one near miss), seventeen more grey hairs, one IT bod vanished and one punch up. But whatever I put, you'll still publish the review as "a triumph" so I really can't be arsed to attend." I deleted it in the end. I wasn't quite that brave. Not yet.

CHAPTER TWENTY

Following the POX fiasco/triumph, rumours were circulating amongst the teams about take-overs, closures and re-structures, and these were beginning to gather pace, supported by speculation whipped up in the press. The Snake told me that the word on Facebook was that our department was going to be merged with Cruella's. I told her not to listen to gossip. *Bloody Facebook.* But I was worried. If it was true, Cruella was bound to get the job over me: everyone, including The Boss, was shit-scared of her, so there was no way anyone was going to be brave enough to tell her she hadn't got the role. In addition, I assumed HR would have a say in the decision, and there wasn't anyone left in HR that I hadn't fallen out with at some time or other. What goes around comes around, so they say. I recalled a time from my previous company when I'd attended a week long training course, and had spent the entire week crossing swords with another manager who had really got up my nose. When we had to give each other feedback at the end of the week, she'd called me "flippant and destructive" and I'd called her "tedious and insignificant". Two weeks later she was introduced to me as my new line manager. *Not a good moment.* I left shortly afterwards with bridges in flames all around me.

I found what appeared to be an interesting role on the Perypils "Opportunities" website, for a Strategic Sales Manager. From the blurb, I could see that the job entailed working with sales managers across the sites to improve performance and to develop future sales strategies. There would be some travelling, but that would be balanced by some working from home. It was only a sideways move but it did have the huge bonus of not having any people to manage! Whoopee - no people! No more listening to nauseating details of health conditions, or depressing personal problems or the constant drone of moaning and whining - how wonderful it would be to be free from all that. I decided to apply. The deadline was Friday, so I had a few days to knock up an application. *No problem.*

I spent Monday, Tuesday, Wednesday and Thursday evenings trying to complete the application and update my CV. *God, why was it so difficult?* All I needed to do was list my most recent jobs, my achievements and sell myself a bit, but everything I wrote sounded so stilted, *so wanky.* I read it, re-wrote it, re-read it, tweaked it over and over but it still wasn't right.

The Husband was no help at all. He moaned that I hadn't bothered to consult him about the job (fair point) so why should he help me with the application? *Because I might lose my job and I need to find another one!* You won't be too happy if you've got to fund the mortgage on your own. I tried to explain that to him but he dismissed it again as "another ridiculous over-reaction." I knew he just had the hump because I hadn't been shopping, and the cupboards were virtually bare. He'd come home on Tuesday evening saying he'd noticed we were out of a few things so he'd "picked up a couple of bits." He presented me with a Londis carrier bag like it contained the crown jewels. What it did contain was: a massive tub of Haagen-Dazs ice cream (cookies and cream flavour), a packet of Oreos, a tin of rice pudding and a bottle of gin. I wanted to ask: "But didn't you notice we were out of essentials such as milk, cereals, daily shower shine...," but I couldn't face another row. I found a packet of fish fingers at the bottom of the freezer, scraped them free of ice and made us fish finger sandwiches out of bread slices that also required a bit of scraping. We would have to get used to living like this if we went down to one income. I'd have to start shopping at Lidls and buying clothes that were 100% viscose. *Shudder.*

I stayed up until the early hours to complete the application and I submitted it, with huge relief on Friday. I phoned Brett The Boss to let him know I was applying for another role. I suppose the reaction I was hoping for was one of dismay: I thought he'd want to know why I was applying, be very concerned that I wanted to leave and try his best to persuade me to stay. That, of course, was just a pipe dream.

His actual response was: "I wish I could bloody well apply for something else, the hours I'm bloody well working, I might just as well sleep in the bloody office."

I tried to say "Well, this is about me Brett, not you-" but he talked right over me and continued whining about his own situation. Why do people do that? You tell them something and they immediately relate it to themselves. They don't bother to ask you anything about your own feelings; they just launch in and make it about themselves or give you an example of when something similar happened to them. You shouldn't be in a management position if you can't listen. You have two ears and one mouth - you should use them in those proportions. That's what I tell my team anyway, although I doubt they were listening.

The following week I received a phone call from HR - I'd been offered an interview for the Strategic Sales Manager position! *How exciting!* But how utterly terrifying. I hadn't been for an interview in years. They were being held in Manchester, with the Head of Sales, Denise Gibbons and a representative from HR. *Bugger; let's hope they don't know me.* I'd have to do a ten minute presentation entitled "My 100-day plan" which should outline what I would do in my first 100 days in the role. There would also be some skills-based scenario questions. From what I understood, these would be something like: "Tell me of a time when..." and you'd have to give a real-life (totally embellished) example.

I had a week to prepare. There was no way I could find any time during the day, so it would have to be done in the evenings and at the weekend. In the pit of my stomach, I felt a bit concerned that the Husband would kick off if I spent even more time at home on work stuff, but I hoped he would understand. I was trying to secure a position, and that would benefit us both financially. Surely he would come round and support me? I'd better make sure the cupboards were well-stocked, that should help his mood. Right well, important things first. I needed a new suit and a "power" haircut. Book the hairdressers straight away and get myself to Next after work.

Interview Day

I was on the train heading towards Manchester. My notes were spread out on the table in front of me; a last minute run through of my presentation. It was a warm day, and I was wearing my new navy trouser suit with a white blouse. I'd had my hair tamed into a "mid length choppy bob" by the hairdresser. It looked ok, but she'd cut my fringe just a little bit too short, so I looked permanently surprised.

I was feeling extremely nervous. The coffee cart came round and I bought the largest size they had. I re-read all my notes, but nothing much was sinking in. I decided to watch the countryside go past in a blur, it was more relaxing. Anyway, it was counter-productive to be over-prepared, I'd read that somewhere. I'd been working on the presentation every evening and all weekend. As part of my preparation, I'd also been re-reading the book "The Right to be You" which was about increasing your confidence. I read a section about the importance of first impressions, and not scoring "own goals". This means that if you say things like "Oh I'm such a numpty" it gives people the false impression that you are a numpty. So even if you are a numpty, you don't need to tell people that. They will eventually work it out for themselves of course, but you may be able to blag your way through an hour's interview without it being immediately evident.

The Husband had actually been surprisingly supportive, saying he'd "keep out of my way" whilst I was preparing. He'd booked himself lots of evening appointments so he'd been getting home really late. I didn't have to cook either as he'd always managed to grab something between appointments. He'd listened to my presentation on Sunday night and timed it at 12 minutes, so I knew I was going to have to speed it up a bit to avoid running over the allotted time.

I bought another coffee as the cart went back the other way and a ridiculously overpriced chocolate chip cookie. I arrived in Manchester with an hour and a half to kill before the interview at 1 pm. The building was a short walk from the station so I found a Starbucks and took an outside table with a cappuccino and my notes. It was a lovely day. I was beginning to feel pretty excited. After all, it wasn't often you got to talk about yourself to a captive audience for an hour, and I was well qualified to do this role. I had lots of great achievements to tell them about. They'd be mad not to want me! I ordered another cappuccino with an extra shot, just to make sure I was fully alert.

I arrived at the building five minutes before the appointed time. I bounded into the foyer and announced to the startled receptionist "I'm here!" before remembering I needed to tell him my name and who I'd come to see. I took a seat, but couldn't keep still. I was jerkily adjusting my jacket, re-arranging my notes, playing with my hair and I could feel my left eye twitching. *Must be nerves kicking in.* Just after 1 pm, a thin suited woman came across the foyer.

"Kate?" she asked. "I'm Denise Gibbons. Pleased to meet you." I jumped up and pumped her hand vigorously, as if I was trying to draw water from her.

"Hi, hi, I'm great thanks, how are you?" I gushed, even though she hadn't asked me how I was. She looked a bit taken aback, and led me to the lifts. I followed at her ankles like an over-eager puppy, talking non-stop, telling her about my journey, the price of tickets, the price of cookies - I just couldn't stop. I noticed she had pressed herself back into the corner of the lift - perhaps she got nervous doing the interviews. I'd never considered that an interviewer would get nervous too. I kept talking to help put her at ease.

We entered a small meeting room where another woman was sitting. Denise introduced her as Eunice Jones from HR.

She looked like a Eunice, with frizzy dark hair with streaks of grey, no make-up and ugly glasses. The sort of woman that would have really hairy armpits. I didn't recall ever speaking to her before, which was a good start. She shook my hand saying "Hello Kate, I don't think we've ever met before have we? But I've heard a lot about you." *Oh shit.*

"Oh dear, shall I leave now then?" I exclaimed, giving a loud snort of laughter. *I've never snorted before! Where did that come from?* She asked me to take a seat and looked pointedly at my head. Yes, I know, the fringe is disastrous but take a look at your own birds nest dearie before you criticise anyone else's. Why don't you show it some kindness and introduce it to a pair of GHDs? And invest in some nose clippers whilst you're about it.

They asked me for a quick summary of my career, and I enthused about the twelve "wonderful years" I'd spent so far at Perypils, but that I now felt ready for a change of direction and how this role would be an exciting challenge for me. (I figured this sounded a bit better than the truth: I was sick to death of being a people manager as I can't stand people and I badly needed to find another job as I was about to lose my current one to someone who watched Vera Drake for laughs). Denise then said we'd start with my presentation. There was no PowerPoint available, nor was there a flip chart in the room. I had printed copies of my presentation for them, but didn't give them out.

I stood up, and launched into my 100 day plan. It felt odd to be presenting to two people in a small room without any sort of visual aids, and I wished I'd remained seated. But it was too late; I couldn't very well sit down again. I'd also read somewhere that when you are presenting, 60% of your audience's focus is on your body language, 30% is on your tone of voice, and only 10% on the actual words. I had this in mind as I spoke with great gusto about my plans for the role, trying to pitch my voice so it sounded exciting and not monotonous, using lots of sweeping arm movements and hand gestures. I had a real buzzing in my head and my voice sounded louder than normal, like it wasn't coming from me at all. It probably just seemed that way because the room was so small.

Usually when I'm presenting, I like to move around a bit, but this was difficult in such a confined space and I ended up basically shifting my weight from one foot to the other as if I needed the loo. I noticed they were sat back as far as the room would allow, presumably so they could fully observe me in action. They were listening intently - I saw that at one point Eunice put her hand to her ear, so I raised my voice a little more thinking she might be hard of hearing. They didn't interrupt, but at the end Denise asked me:

"So, do you feel this plan is really achievable?"

"Oh yes," I said, nodding vigorously, and as I did so, the room went dark. I was disorientated for a split second until I realised that my sun glasses had fallen down from my head and covered my eyes. *Oh no, how could I have left them perched on my head? Why hadn't I put them away?* I whipped them off and held them behind my back, whilst I carried on talking. Their faces remained unchanged, which was very professional of them. Apart from that little mishap, I think it had gone pretty well. Denise thanked me and asked me for a copy of the presentation. *Bugger.* I kicked myself for forgetting to give a copy out before I'd started. Never mind. I sat down and mentally prepared myself for the skills-based questions.

Eunice was trying to take a couple of paracetamol tablets without being noticed. I sat up straight, looking keen and expectant. Denise rubbed her temples, consulted her notes and asked me the first question.

"Kate, can you tell me about a time when you've had to manage a risk?" She and Eunice looked at me, pens poised.

Manage a bloody risk? I was there for a sales role. All my scenarios I'd been rehearsing were based on sales, and sales strategies; what had that question got to do with sales? I felt a horrible cold lurching in my stomach, and I couldn't think straight.

"Er, yes, of course," I said, trying to buy some thinking time. "Um, could you just repeat the question please?"

They exchanged glances. Denise said again, very slowly as if she was talking to the infirm:

"Tell me about a time when you've had to manage a risk."

I gathered myself together and waffled my way through a scenario where I'd identified that a process was incorrect, which had caused several customer complaints. I described what actions I'd taken to put it right and the resulting benefits. I hadn't rehearsed this example, so it was a bit stuttery, but I got through it. Whilst Eunice was nodding encouragingly as I was talking, I was very much being put off by Denise's body language, noticing that she wasn't making any notes at all, and she was just staring at me without any expression. At the end of my example, she cleared her throat and said:

"Well, that's all very interesting, but could you tell me about a risk you've had to manage?" *Shiiiiiiit.* She didn't think I'd answered the question at all!

"Well, Denise" I said, trying to sound confident. "I was describing the risk of having our customers complain, and therefore the risk of losing their business."

"Oh I see," she said, pursing her lips. "Well, let's move on then, shall we? Next question. Can you tell me what you've personally done to even out the peaks and troughs in demand?" *For God's sake, what has that got to do with sales? What does it even mean?*

This was a disaster. Again, I thought of an example, and managed to waffle my way through another scenario, but I wasn't prepared for this question either, nor the next one and my answers just didn't flow. I knew it was not going well, and that just made me more blustery and stammery. Denise was still staring and not writing, and it was so intimidating that I ended up addressing my answers to Eunice, who was at least smiling at me. I knew my face must be bright red from the pressure; my cheeks felt like they were on fire and my armpits were absolutely gushing.

I felt totally drained by the time Denise asked me her last question:

"What do you see as being the key challenges of this role?" I felt like answering:

"D'you know what love, I haven't got the faintest fucking idea but probably trying to get a smile out of you would be quite a significant one."

After almost two hours, it was over. I made my way back to the station feeling dog-tired and extremely depressed. The whole experience replayed over and over in my mind throughout the journey back. Those questions had been a total nightmare. As the journey progressed, I began to put things into perspective - maybe I was painting too black a picture of the whole thing. Ok, I wasn't prepared for those particular questions, but I'd still made some good points hadn't I? The presentation seemed to go down well, with the exception of the black-out of course. Perhaps it hadn't been as bad as I thought, perhaps everyone felt like this after an interview. I ignored the coffee cart this time. I couldn't face anymore, and I don't think the caffeine overload had done me any favours this morning. I felt like I was coming down off drugs or something. Not that I'd ever taken drugs. Well, only once, when I'd tried to smoke a joint but was too scared to inhale. My college friends had laughed at me, and one of them had performed a "blow back" on me - inhaling from the joint and blowing it down my throat. I hadn't minded because I fancied him and I knew this was the closest I was going to get to a snog. I didn't feel any different after this procedure, but pretended to be spaced out and acted crazily like everyone else was doing. Sauvignon Blanc was my current drug of choice, and I couldn't wait to get home and dive into a vat of it.

Chapter Twenty-One

I went to visit my Mum and Dad on Saturday morning. They were sat in the kitchen with my brother, who'd hand-delivered their wedding invitation.

"Here's yours, Sis," he said, proudly passing me a brown office-style envelope. "We're having to keep costs down so Kirsty nicked the envelopes from work. And the cards too, actually."

I opened mine up. The date on the invitation was the end of October *close to Halloween* with the service at 1 pm at the Registry Office, followed by a reception at The George pub. *Is it really going ahead then?*

"What's this bloody thing?" asked my Dad holding up a slip of paper. "We've got to get you bleeding Argos vouchers? I've never been to Argos in my life, I don't even know where it is."

"It's in Italy isn't it?" said my mother. We all looked at her.

"That's alright, Dad," said Stu, as if my mother hadn't spoken, "that's just if people want to buy us a present. We thought we'd get some new furniture for the house, so it's nice when Kirsty moves in..." His voice trailed off and he looked a bit sad, as if he was just starting to realise that his much-loved bachelor lifestyle was coming to an end.

"Won't she be bringing lots of her own stuff with her?" I asked. *Like her daughter, for example?*

"Yeah some, but we thought it would be nice to have stuff of our own, you know - too many memories attached to other things." He tailed off again. My father caught my eye and shook his head.

The kitchen was filling up with steam. Mum had put the kettle on to boil but seemed to have forgotten about it.

"I'll make the tea," I said, taking the kettle off the stove. "Got any biscuits Mum?"

"Oh yes," she said, "they're in the greenhouse. I'll go and get them." She went out into the back garden. I looked at my Dad and then at my brother.

"Dad, you really ought to get her to see a doctor," I said. "She's not right. You must see that."

"Oh she's fine," grumbled my Dad, "Just getting older. We both are."

"She does seem a bit confused, Dad" said Stu. "Perhaps you ought to get her looked at."

"Get her looked at? She's not a bloody car! I can't just lift up her bloody bonnet! She's fine, don't make a fuss."

He wouldn't listen. Mum came back in and picked up the wedding invitation.

"Oh, what's this?" she asked in surprise. I made the tea whilst Stu told her about the wedding - again.

Sunday

I had an argument with the Husband which started with me complaining about a dirty sock he'd left on the bedroom floor - *why couldn't you just pick it up, you've obviously picked up the other one, why did you leave one lying there, why? I know you've seen it, you've walked over it five times* - and culminated in him listing my many failings as a wife, which took a worryingly significant amount of time to reel off. He then stormed out of the house and slammed the front door, only to reappear, embarrassed, at the back door as he didn't have his car keys or wallet.

Oh dear. What a total over-reaction. Could it be his hormones? Did men suffer at certain times of the month too?

I didn't know where he'd gone or what time he'd be back, but he was currently keeping an eye on his Boss's house whilst he was working abroad so I guessed he may have taken refuge there. I took advantage of the peace and quiet and fetched the Sunday papers. I came across another article on Perypils in the finance pages.

Headline: Perypils: The Unacceptable Face of Insurance.

There was a picture of an unsmiling Big Cheese beneath the headline. The story had been written by a "whistle blower". This was a former member of staff, who no doubt had become "former" for a very good reason, and had gone blabbing to the press about the unacceptable standards at Perypils. They were accusing the company of failing to train its staff properly, and had sent the paper a 68 page Perypils training guide which they referred to as "meaningless, out of date gobbledygook". The writer said the team managers were lazy and incompetent and the senior management team were only interested in sleeping with each other, and boasting about how much they'd drunk the night before. There was a small picture of the Perypils head office building next to a larger picture of a glass of red wine. The caption read: "Life is a Cabernet".

The writer said the failure of the company to train its staff properly meant that the standards of customer service were extremely poor, and that the quality and competency scores were always very low - but none of the management team cared. The writer said that reams of management information is produced each month that no one ever looks at, and the managers just twisted the statistics into showing anything they wanted them to show. It was only a matter of time before the Financial Services authorities swooped on Perypils and closed the company down.

Although the writer had been kept anonymous, they had complained in the article that the company did not offer a Welsh-speaking service to its customers, so I assumed they had been employed at the Bridgend office. I wouldn't like to be working there on Monday morning.

A new working week and I was on tenterhooks, waiting to hear about the outcome of the interview. Every time my phone or mobile rang my heart started to race and I'd brace myself for news. When I'd arrived at work in the morning The Snake had presented me with a copy of Sunday's newspaper article, which she'd photocopied from the paper.

"I just thought you ought to see this," she hissed, her eyes glinting. "Everyone's talking about it this morning." I wondered how many copies she'd made. Not many of my team seemed to read or take any interest in the financial press, so if they were all talking about it, somebody must be encouraging them to do so.

"I thought it would have upset you Cynthia," I said, "you know, the bit about the incompetent and lazy team managers."

"Well some of them are, aren't they?" she replied, seeming to forget she was a team manager herself. "The writer was only stating what they experienced. What do you think's going to happen?"

"I don't know," I said *but I've no doubt the communications team will manage to spin it into a really good thing.* "But I do know if your team don't start to answer some of those calls that are queuing they are all going to have something in common with the writer - in that they're all going to become former employees."

I was starting to sound like the Big Cheese. She slithered off, back through the long grass. Hopefully someone morbidly obese would tread on her.

It was all quiet from the communications team throughout the morning, and then at lunchtime, everyone received an email message from The Big Cheese himself. He denounced the article in the Sunday press as being "a shameful pack of lies from a deluded and bitter ex-employee who couldn't personally meet the extremely high standards we set ourselves at Perypils." He said the company's lawyers were considering taking legal action against the paper. There was then a huge load of gushing blurb about our wonderful customer service standards, our world class employee training schemes and our exceptional expert analysis of management information to continually strive to exceed and out perform our competitors. It made me wonder who really was the deluded one.

I received an email from Brett the Boss. It read:
To All.

> *I have just been in a telecon with our Chief Exec. His directive is that every site's Quality and Competency figures must be at 95% by month end, and all sites must constantly remain above 95%. He stated that failure to achieve this target is "career threatening".*

I hope that's clear enough for everyone. If you have any problems give me a call, I'm always here for support.

Brett

Bloody hell, 95%? There was no way was I going to achieve that. Last month my department had scored 73%. This was because I had a number of new colleagues and it takes them a while to get fully up to speed. This month, I was on for a score of 79%, which was a good improvement and I felt really pleased with the progress. It was probably going to take the best part of six months before I was at 95%, and that was assuming I didn't get too many leavers. I phoned The Boss. He answered, sounded harassed and said he couldn't talk, could I email him? *Always there for support...*

I emailed:

Brett

    I'm afraid I'm going to struggle to get my Q&C score to 95% for a number of months as I have a high proportion of new starters. I am currently on 79% month to date, which is a 6% increase on last month's score, so we are making excellent progress. Happy to discuss.

Kate

I pressed send. Thirty seconds later he called me.

"Kate," he said, sounding panicky, "you have to achieve 95% this month. Kevin has made it very clear that it's not optional. If you don't, you and me are going to be out on our fucking arses!"

"But Brett, I'm nowhere near 95%," I protested. "And I

wouldn't expect to be with lots of new starters - no one would expect to be. It takes time and experience to achieve consistently high Q&C results-"

He cut me short. "It doesn't matter how you achieve it Kate, but it's an absolute no-brainer. You need to be at 95% by month end. End of."

There was an uneasy silence as I considered my next move.

"I just don't see how I can achieve it Brett, it's not possible. The only way would be by manipulating the quality sample by removing all the new guys and the numpties from the sampling, but we're not supposed to do that as it doesn't reflect the true customer experience and breaches the competency regulations."

"Do it." said Brett "Do whatever you have to, but for fuck sake hit 95%."

"I feel really uncomfortable about this, Brett," I said unhappily, "it's just not right, and no one in their right mind is going to believe I've gone from 73% to 95% in the space of one month."

He cut me off again. "Just do it Kate," he said. "It's what everyone else is doing. Just fucking do it." *Oh God, this had to be a joke.* I stayed until very late, waiting for everyone to go home before I started messing around with the quality sampling figures. When I'd taken out all the new starters and the Muppets whose quality was always poor, the score was still only 89%. Either I was going to have to enter a completely false score or I was going to have to get the team managers to only enter scores for calls that they knew would score very highly. Month end was approaching, so we'd have to get a move on. What would the team managers say when I tell them what we've got to do? Wasn't I always preaching to them about being open and honest and acting with integrity? I couldn't think how I was going to put a positive spin on this one.

I found it very difficult to get to sleep that night. I lay awake, tossing and turning, going over things in my mind. What if I got caught - I'd put colleagues on disciplinaries for falsifying their figures. What would happen to me? These figures got reported to the financial regulators; if they were found to be deliberately fudged I'd be thrown to the wolves. And saying "My boss told me to do it" just wasn't going to wash. I'd lose my job, I'd never get another one as my references would say I'd been dismissed for "gross misconduct", which any prospective employer would interpret as "she's a dirty little thief, don't touch her with a barge pole." We'd struggle to meet our mortgage payments and would have to move in with my parents, where we'd be forced to watch the Antiques Roadshow, eat corned beef and drink wine measured out from a thimble.

Brett's words swam around my head "It's what everyone else is doing." Why is everyone faking their figures? Where is the benefit to the company of pretending we're offering our customer's a better quality of service then we actually are? 95% isn't the real experience - 79% is. No wonder Perypils was in such a mess, pretending all was rosy, not bothering to get underneath what was going wrong and put it right. Were they really that short-sighted? So many questions were whirling around in my head but I kept coming back to the same one - what was I doing still working for Perypils? I must be mad - perhaps I was mad; perhaps I was actually clinically insane. How would I know? I got up and found an insanity test on the Internet. There were 100 questions, with your answers rated to show just how close you were to sticking pencils up your nose. I'd answered 93 of the questions before my suspicions about the authenticity of the test were aroused.

Question 93: Have you ever tried to fly?

Question 94: Did you die as a result?

I read on. Question 95: When talking to someone with the same name as you, do you sometimes get confused as to which one you are?

Question 96 clinched it: I'd been had. Do you understand the deeper meaning of Dannii Minogue records?

At work the next morning, I still hadn't decided how I would approach my team managers - I couldn't work out how to 'sell' the fact that we were going to fake our figures, so instead I confided in The Rock and told her the truth. She was really quite shocked, but quickly recovered herself and said in her usual manner: "I'd better go and find some 100% calls to listen to" and off she went to do just that. By the end of the day, she'd found enough to bring the score (the faked score) up to 93%, and we had another couple of days before month end so we should just about make it if she kept this up.

I was just preparing to go to a meeting with the other managers about resource requirements (what else?) when I noticed an email in my inbox from Eunice Jones. It was entitled: Strategic Sales Manager position. I opened it up.

To Kate.

> *Thank you for your interest in the above role. Unfortunately, on this occasion, your application has not been successful. I wish you all the best for the future.*

Kind regards, Eunice.

I stared at it in disbelief. I couldn't believe they'd sent me an email! They couldn't even be bothered to pick up the phone to tell me. That's disgraceful. Surely it would be common courtesy to call the candidates? How would they know I'd look at my emails today? I might not have even seen it for a couple of days, and by then I might have discovered the outcome from another source. *Cowardly bastards.* After all that time spent on the application and the interview preparation, I'd lost at least ten evenings and two weekends from my life. And they couldn't even be bothered to call. Is that how Perypils really treats its managers? It was just appalling.

I picked up the phone to call Eunice to protest, but stopped: it would sound like sour grapes because I hadn't got the job. I thought about complaining to Brett the Boss, but what was the point really? He wouldn't be interested. The wave of anger passed, and I sat slumped at my desk, disconsolate and trying to come to terms with my failure. Big Andy bounded over, coming to collect me, as I was late for the meeting.

"Come on Kate-Skate," he boomed. "Get your arse in gear." He saw my long face. "What's up?" I told him what had happened. He didn't know I'd applied for another job as I hadn't told any of the others about the interview. I hadn't wanted Cruella to find out and think I was running scared. Which I was.

"Bloody hell Kate, what the heck did you apply for that one for? Everyone knows that Lisa Hewitt was getting that job. The interviews were just a formality."

I stared at him.

"What, Lisa the big-busted weasley-featured project manager, that Brett was, well er, you know-"

"Yes that's the one! Brett promised her that role when he, well um, when things went a bit pear-shaped between them. She was always going to get it."

"Why was it advertised then?" I wailed. "Why let others apply for it?" Why didn't Brett bloody well tell me not to bother?

"So it looks genuine of course," he laughed. "Come off it Kate, everyone knows how it works round here! All the internal vacancies are a stitch-up. Christ, I hope you didn't waste too much time on it. Come on, let's get to this bloody meeting. I hear The Shark's waiting to tear some big lumps out of you!"

Oh my God. Why was I so naive? Bloody Perypils, bloody Brett, they owed me ten evenings and two weekends of my life. I'd never get them back. Not to mention the cost of my new suit and the power hair cut/fringe disaster. Perhaps getting the boot wouldn't be such a bad thing after all, this was just such bullshit. I traipsed after Big Andy, who was suggesting we hold The Shark upside down to put him into a hypnotic trance. I couldn't even raise a smile.

At month end I submitted our Q&C score as 95%. The real score had actually been 78%. Surely someone would query how my department had managed to go from 73% one month to 95% the next? Every time I passed The Rock she'd quip "That's magic!" in a Paul Daniels voice. I called her Harry Bloody Potter.

The Communications team issued a message from the Big Cheese. It said he was extremely proud to announce that all sites had achieved a quality and competence score of 95% for last month. He said it was "a reflection of the outstanding Perypils training and development programs, the fantastic quality of our people and the hard work of our management teams." There were quotes from several new employees (plants) saying how great their training had been and how quickly they had been able to achieve the required standards of their role. They also said they loved working for a company that was so customer-focused. There were a few pictures of these employees, showing smartly dressed, clear-skinned, white toothed individuals smiling broadly whilst speaking into their headsets. I looked across at the colleague sat in front of me. His trousers were very low slung, and the beginnings of a builders bum had appeared. I could have dropped my pencil down the crack. He was speaking to a customer whilst flicking around the internet and wiping his nose on the back of his hand. He examined the back of his hand closely. I had to look away.

Brett the Boss sent an email which said:

> *Well done to all on achieving 95% Q&C last month - this is a brilliant effort!*
>
> *Please say a big well done to all your teams and keep up the good work.*
>
> *You may buy cakes for your department as recognition from me on their superb achievement.*
>
> *Brett*
>
> *PS*
>
> *Go careful with the cake expenditure, get BOGOFs where you can. Sainsburys do a tray of 20 previously frozen doughnuts for £2, but*

you'll need to get there tonight.

Bloody hell. Did he actually believe his own lies? He knew the figures were completely fudged, had he convinced himself that this was a genuine achievement? And what about the Big Cheese - did he seriously believe every site had suddenly improved massively from the previous month? Surely he smelt a rat. It was farcical. It was all a load of big, hairy buggery bollocks. I had to get out of here.

CHAPTER TWENTY-TWO

Saturday

I awoke just before nine and dragged myself out of bed,
even though I felt I could have slept for another eight hours.
I could hear the Husband downstairs clattering around the
kitchen. Strange, I thought he was off out early to play golf. I
padded downstairs in my dressing gown and slippers.

"Morning love" I said rubbing my eyes. "No golf today,
or are you going later?"

"No, I'm not playing today," he said. He stood rather
awkwardly by the kettle. "Er, do you want a coffee? I thought
we could have a talk."

My stomach lurched. Not "the talk". Please let it be
about something mundane, like sorting out the garage, or
clearing the guttering. But I could tell from his face it wasn't
going to be anything like that. I sat down heavily at the
kitchen table, feeling sick. He was making us coffee, and the
kettle took an age to boil. He'd overfilled it as usual. Neither
of us spoke; the silence between us oppressive. At last he sat
down at the table and slid a mug over to me. It was a mug I'd
bought for him which had "Trophy Husband" written on it.
He stirred his coffee, still not saying anything and not looking
at me. I wasn't going to help him out, so I kept quiet, waiting.
He cleared his throat.

"Well, I'm sure you'd agree that things haven't been
great between us recently," he said, glancing at me to gauge a

reaction. He didn't get one. He took a deep breath "And I've not been that happy for some time." *What? How long is some time?* "So I was thinking it might do us both some good if we took some time out to, you know, give ourselves some breathing space, and, well, find ourselves again." *Find ourselves again? Why are you talking bollocks?* He was looking at me now.

"What exactly are you suggesting?" I asked, aware that my voice had gone a bit squeaky. "Do you mean you want us to book a holiday?" I knew he didn't mean that, but I couldn't help myself.

"Well no," he said, stirring his coffee again. I wanted to grab the spoon and shove it up his nose. "I didn't mean a holiday. You know I'm looking after Bruce's house whilst he's out in Hong Kong. I thought I would stay there for a while, you know, just for a few weeks to give us a bit of a break from, from, well everything really." *You mean from each other.*

"You're leaving me?" I think it must have been the manager in me, but I felt I really needed to be clear on what was actually happening here. I felt as if I was undertaking a factfind with a colleague at work.

"No, no," the Husband replied, but I noticed he did not look me in the eye. "Just a temporary break, just a few weeks to give ourselves a bit of head-space, and time to think and..." he tailed off. There was an uncomfortable silence.

"Won't you have to clear it with Bruce first?" I asked, ever-practical.

"He's fine with it," The Husband said, too quickly. *So he'd been planning this.* He realised he'd given this away and pathetically tried to cover it by adding, "Bruce said before he went away that if I needed to stay there it was no problem, in case I had a late appointment in that part of town, or something like that."

I didn't know what to say. I felt numb with shock - there must be hundreds of questions I should be asking, but I couldn't think what I should ask, or know how I should behave. Should I be angry? Sad? What would Madonna do in this situation? She'd probably throw her mug at his head and yell "Well get out then you mother f***** and don't come back. You wanna find yourself? Well find this!" and would pelt him with the Denby dinner plates as he ran for his life. But I didn't feel anger. I didn't feel anything.

"Well," I said, needing to break the silence. "You've obviously made your mind up. When are you going?"

The Husband looked hugely relieved.

"I thought I would get a few things together now and get off this morning," he said. *Bloody hell, don't hang about will you - can't wait to get out of here?* "I'm glad you're taking it like this, I knew you'd see it's for the best too. The best thing for both of us." *You justify it how you like mate, this is your decision and yours alone.*

He got up from the table. He looked about to say something else, but thought better of it and decided to quit whilst he was ahead. I heard him upstairs starting to pull drawers out, getting his things together. I stayed seated at the table, with my hands clutching my Trophy Husband mug. I hadn't drunk any of the coffee, I felt too sick. A thousand thoughts were whirling around in my head. Shouldn't I have seen this coming? I knew he was unhappy didn't I? Did I? I must have known, I just hadn't faced up to it. But I thought we were ok. Was this it, was it over or was he intending to come back like he said? What would I tell my parents, I was seeing them later. They'd be so upset, so worried for me. They had enough worries of their own.

I thought I'd keep out of the way whilst he packed. I wished I was washed and dressed and had put my make-up mask on so he'd at least think he was leaving behind something decent, not a mop-haired frump with morning-breath, wrapped up in a shapeless M&S dressing gown.

I heard him coming downstairs and going into the study. *My God, was he humming?* He was! The callous bastard, he was actually humming to himself, he was happy to be going! Was I that awful to live with? He'd been happy enough eating all the meals I cooked for him, or putting on a clean shirt that I'd ironed, or sitting in the garden that I'd weeded, and mown and dead-headed. I was angry now. A churlish thought struck me. He was bound to want to take the iPad with him. It was his after all, I'd bought it for his last birthday, partly because I couldn't think what else to get him and partly because I'd wanted one too. I'd make him beg for it though. The iPad was in the lounge so I went and got it, and sat back at the kitchen table pretending to use it. I heard him moving around upstairs and then saw him start to load up his car. From the mountain of stuff he was taking, it didn't look like he was going for "just a few weeks". I heard him go back into the study then into the lounge. I was sure he was looking for the iPad. He came into the kitchen and saw me with it. *Go on then you bastard, are you going to have the nerve to ask me to hand it over?*

He hovered for a moment clearly not knowing what to do. I ignored him, and focused on the iPad screen. I could almost hear his brain ticking over trying to decide what he should do.

"I'll be off now," he said. I looked up and nodded.

"Right," he said, looking at the iPad and not at me. "I'll, um, I'll call you later. Is that ok?" I nodded again. "And I don't think we should tell anyone about our, er, our arrangement," he said. "No point upsetting everyone is there?" He paused. "Not when it's just a temporary thing." *Temporary is it? You're a lying bastard.* Still, I wasn't sure how or what I was going to tell people - how humiliating to have to tell your nearest and dearest that your husband has left you because he was so unhappy - so I agreed I wouldn't say anything. He stood there for a moment, then turned and left. The front door closed behind him. I heard his car start up, and accelerate as he drove away. Then it was very quiet.

I walked round the house as if in a trance. I went upstairs to see what he had taken with him. There were a lot of empty hangers, all his best shirts had gone. Was he planning evenings out? Going to parties? I realised I didn't even know Bruce's address. From what he'd said about Bruce's house, it was a real bachelor's pad, with all the latest gadgets and gizmos and it had a hot tub. Had he taken his best swimming trunks, his stripy ones that I'd bought him from Quicksilver? I rummaged through his drawers but couldn't find them. Was it possible he was having a sort of breakdown, or mid-life crisis perhaps? Is it that he wanted to live like Bruce did; a single life with big butch brown leather furniture from John Lewis and a zillion-inch plasma television?

I went back to the iPad and tapped into History. The last items The Husband had looked at, apart from his infernal bloody Facebook, were:

- Various different sunglasses sites. *Why? It's virtually winter.*
- A site which converted units of alcohol into calories.

That's interesting, I should look at that myself later.

- Mobile phone tariffs. *Snore.*
- eBay search for tents. *Was he planning on going camping?*
- Wikipedia search on the lead actor from Bugsy Malone. *Is he going camp?*
- A website for protein shakes. *Building himself up? For what? For whom?*
- And NHS Direct - Haemorrhoids, how you get them. Oh no, that had been me, worried after I'd been sat on a cold stone bench for ages at the garden centre waiting for my mother to come out. It turned out she'd forgotten I was there and had gone for a cup of coffee and a sit down.

I tried to log into his Facebook page. I'd never looked at it before. Our usual password "Bollocks1" didn't work. He always used that. He must have something to hide. I tried "Bollocks2". It worked. *God, he was lazy.* He had 178 friends! Who were they all? Lots of women I'd never heard of. An endless stream of banal comments "I've just finished scratching my arse and now I'm thinking about picking my nose" etc. Why did people feel the need to share such boring trivial crap about themselves? Nobody cares!

I had a good poke around, but there was nothing particularly telling. I was surprised that he was friends with the Bunny Boiler, he'd never said. There was one message from her dated a few days ago that said:

"Hope u r lookin ford to the wedding not long now!"

He'd replied "Yes, me and the WOW are very much looking forwards to it!" Who was the WOW? Was it me? What did it stand for? I kept trawling through other messages and found one that he'd sent to Debbie referring to "The WOW". The message said: "I'll ask the WOW when I get home." That was it. What did it mean? Something nice or something nasty? Clearly both Debbie and The Bunny Boiler knew what it stood for. Were they all poking fun at me behind my back? Debbie's reply had simply said "Ok Goofy!" There wasn't much to go on.

The weekend stretched ahead of me, suddenly very long and very empty. I tried to process how I felt but I just didn't know. I didn't feel emotional or weepy, I just felt numb. Either I was cold and unfeeling or I was in shock. I felt very sick and couldn't face eating anything, which was most unlike me. Although it wasn't even midday, I had a large brandy. It was supposed to be good for shock. The burning liquid helped me pull myself together, and I decided I wasn't going to mope around the house all day like a sap. What would Madonna do? Get dressed up in her best gear and hit the town. Good idea. I phoned my parents to cancel, saying I thought I was coming down with a cold, and then I showered and dressed. I was going to go to Monsoon and spend a bloody fortune on a new outfit. Sod the Husband, sod bloody everyone.

Sunday

I woke with a headache having only managed a couple of hours of sleep. My kick-arse-Madonna-mood had been short-lived yesterday. I hadn't been able to find anything I liked in Monsoon, or anywhere else in town and I'd come home to an empty house feeling very sorry for myself. Even though I'd agreed not to say anything to friends and family, I'd phoned Karen and told her what had happened. I had to talk to someone. She'd come straight round and we'd gone to the pub. She thought it was possible that The Husband was having a mid-life crisis, so she Googled "the top tell-tale signs that your husband is having a mid-life crisis" on her iPhone. The responses were:

1. He says life is a bore. *Hmmm. He had asked if there was more to life, so I think this is a tick.*

2. He is suddenly making impetuous decisions about spending money. *He only makes impetuous decisions about spending my money, so I don't think this is a tick.*

3. Dramatic change in his style or appearance. *Nothing dramatic, although I had seen a tub of hair surf wax max appear in the bathroom.*

4. Drinking too much or abusing other substances. *Does Nightnurse count?*

5. He is thinking about or is having an affair. *He thinks about it every time he watches Hollyoaks.*

Karen had honed in on the last one and asked me if I thought he was seeing somebody else. That hadn't occurred to me, and I'd dismissed the idea when I'd been talking to Karen, but it had gone round and round in my head last night. Could he be seeing someone else? He'd had lots of evening appointments lately, but that happened in his line of work. Surely he'd have behaved differently, I would have noticed.

I couldn't get to sleep, looking at my alarm clock on the hour every hour, until 5.00 am when I think I must have eventually dropped off. The Husband hadn't called me like he'd said he would, but he had texted to ask if I was ok. I'd just texted back "I'm fine." What more was there to say?

I'd been onto his Facebook site again, but he hadn't updated anything or added any comments. Karen didn't know what "WOW" stood for. She told me that I must talk to him, openly and honestly. She'd offered to referee if I thought that would help. I knew she was right, but I couldn't face it yet. I was too much in the dark; I hated walking into situations unprepared. I wanted to talk to his friends, to see if he'd confided in any of them. I bet he'd spoken to Debbie and Paul but would they tell me anything? It would be unfair of me to ask them, not to mention humiliating.

I kept walking round the house, I don't know why. I wondered what The Husband was doing today. I was going to drive myself mad at this rate. There was nothing more I could do today, I needed to keep busy. My car could do with a wash and there was plenty to do in the garden. But what if the neighbours asked where the Husband was? Oh God, what should I say? I started to cry. I allowed myself a bit of a sob, then took a swig of brandy and gave myself a good talking to. *No more tears you wimp, you weed.* If anyone asks where he is just say "He's recovering from a surgical enlargement procedure." That should shut them up. I stood up with a sense of purpose and went to wrestle with the Flymo.

I managed to hold it together at work. Just about. I was so busy, there was no time to think or to dwell on things. I did have one "episode" after I'd been to the canteen at lunchtime to fetch a salad. Walking back along the corridor, I'd dropped the plastic container with the salad in it. The container burst open and the salad fell out on the floor. I shouted "Oh fuck it!" and kicked it very hard. The contents, which unfortunately included quite a lot of beetroot, splattered up the wall. Luckily there was no one around so I legged it, and phoned facilities when I got back to my desk, telling them "someone" had made a right mess in the corridor. I spent the afternoon worrying about if I'd been caught on CCTV, even though I knew the building didn't have CCTV. Must be a guilt-thing.

I'd got home on Monday night to find that the kitchen door was open, when I knew I'd shut it before I left the house. I always closed it, The Husband always left it open. I figured he'd been back to the house during the day. That hurt - why couldn't he have waited until this evening? He must want to avoid seeing me. I noticed that some things had been moved around - I bet he'd searched high and low for the iPad. Well, he wouldn't have found it, because I'd taken it to work with me. *Small victories.*

We hadn't had any significant contact, just exchanged a few texts. I checked his Facebook site every evening but he hadn't added anything at all and none of the messages he got from his 178 "friends" indicated that they knew about our situation. Karen called me frequently, wanting to know if we'd spoken and what I was going to do. She'd also asked what I was going to do about our bank accounts, and wasn't I worried that he would clear the whole lot out? I hadn't even thought about that. What should I do - wait for the two weeks that he said that he'd be away for to be up, or try and talk to him now? I was really torn. He said he'd needed some space, so perhaps I should give him that and leave him alone. But my mind was a complete whirl, I was struggling to sleep, and could hardly eat. At least some weight was coming off at last. I'm not sure I could go another week feeling this wretched.

My brother had called me about the wedding. *What was I going to do about the wedding?* Would I be going on my own now? What would I tell everyone? He asked me if The Husband could do a reading at the registry office. Apparently one of The Bunny Boiler's cousins had been going to do it, but now they couldn't make the service. Something to do with the terms of a restraining order.

I said I was sure he'd love to and that I would confirm in a couple of days. My brother was anxious to know straight away, and I could hear The Bunny Boiler in the background urging him to find out.

"Is it a yes or a no? Can't you find out for fuck's sake, the only other person I can ask is Uncle Stanley and he's got a stammer. The service will go on for fucking hours if he does it!" She was clearly feeling the stress of planning her big day. It was awkward, but I told Stu I'd let him know as soon as possible.

Friday

After a week of stomach-churning uncertainty and a totally scrambled brain, I decided I had to talk to the Husband. I started to text him, then scrapped the message and thought I'd call, but stopped myself. I needed to talk to him face to face. Neutral territory would be a good idea. He always finished work slightly earlier on Fridays and went to the gym without fail. His logic was he'd lose enough pounds during his Friday workout to counteract the excesses of the weekend. If I timed it right, I would catch him leaving the gym and we could go for a drink. If he had plans for the evening, tough luck, he'd just have to put them back a bit.

I drove there straight from work, and found a space in the car park where I could see the front door of the gym. I waited. After twenty minutes had passed, I wondered if I had got my timings wrong and had missed him. I was thinking about giving up, when the door opened and he appeared, carrying his sports bag and wearing his awful mud-coloured shorts, which were a bit too tight and a bit too short. I didn't know why he still wore them; I'd frequently made jokes about soldiers popping out of their barracks. I went to open the car door, but stopped. He was talking to someone, holding the door open for them. A woman appeared, dressed in gym gear. It was Debbie. I didn't know she went to the gym too. I watched them as they walked slowly towards the Husband's car. They were deep in conversation. Where was her car? He opened the boot and they both put their bags inside, then both got into the car. He must be giving her a lift home. The Husband drove them out of the car park.

As I couldn't think what else to do, I followed them. Did this class as stalking? Possibly. It was hopeless though, in the busy Friday night traffic I soon lost sight of them.

I made my way to Debbie and Paul's house, not really knowing what I was going to do. Maybe see if he'd gone inside, but then what would I do, go and ring the bell? Embarrass them all? I didn't know. When I reached the house, I pulled up outside. There were no cars in the drive and although it was a gloomy evening, there weren't any lights on. A newspaper was stuck through the letter box. It didn't look as if anyone was in. I waited for a while in the country lane, trying to think up an excuse for being there if they turned up. I decided I'd have to be honest. No one would believe I was 'just passing'.

I'm not sure how long I waited, but no one came. *Where had they gone?* Surely not for a drink, they were still in their gym gear, he had those horrid shorts on. And where were Paul & Chloë? Deflated, I eventually gave up and drove home.

There was a note on my door mat which said "We are at the pub, come up when you get home. Karen and James xx". I walked up the hill to the pub, and found them sat at a corner table. Judging by the tiny amount left in the bottom of Karen's bottle of Chardonnay I guessed they'd been there some time. I got the drinks in and told them where I'd been, hoping they wouldn't think I was deranged. I saw them exchange glances with each other.

"What?"

"Oh, it's nothing," said James quickly. "At least, it's probably nothing."

"What's nothing?"

Karen leant forward. "Kate," she said carefully, "do you think, I mean, could it be possible that there's something going on between them?" She looked at me closely. "He didn't drop her at home, so where did they go? He hasn't told you the address of where he's staying so you can't go round there and check up on him. I'm sorry, but it all seems a bit fishy to me."

The Husband and Debbie? Together?

"But they're just friends," I said, astonished, "as well as colleagues and anyway, she's got a kid. He can't bear children; don't you remember when he was godfather to Ann and Dave's kid? He didn't want to do it, but felt he couldn't refuse, and when he was asked to hold the poor thing for the photos he held it out at arm's length looking like he was holding up a soiled pair of underpants. I can't see him with someone who's got a sprog."

Karen was looking at me like Father Ted looked at Dougal when he'd said something particularly stupid. Was I being completely naive and idiotic? I could see she and James clearly suspected the worse, but I just couldn't believe it.

"Well, there's only one way to find out," said Karen, picking up her glass. "Call him, tell him you need to see him urgently and get the address. If he won't give it to you, he's up to no good."

"But it's late," I moaned. "What if he agrees? I don't want to go round there now."

"You see," Karen said to James. "She's in denial."

"Oh alright," I grumpily fished my phone out of my handbag. "I'll call him." The pub was noisy, so I went outside. I pressed his number, suddenly feeling nervous. Who'd have thought just a week ago I'd have felt nervous at speaking with my husband? It rang briefly, and voicemail kicked in. *Hmmm, had he seen my number come up and not wanted to take my call?* I left him a message saying I wanted to see him, could we meet up tomorrow and I suggested a coffee shop in town. I knew Karen wouldn't be happy with that, so when I went back inside I told her I'd left a message saying I needed to see him urgently. I felt overwhelmed with fatigue, and didn't stay at the pub much longer. When I got home, I received a text messgage from The Husband. It said: "Soz I missed ur call, ok 4 tmw, c u at 11.00?" I just replied "ok". Was he there with Debbie? I felt sick again. I had a message on my answer phone from my increasingly desperate brother. I deleted it. I felt a bit of empathy with the Bunny Boiler, I could see how these sorts of situations could easily drive you round the twist. Yet another sleepless night was looming.

CHAPTER TWENTY-THREE

I felt so tired on Saturday morning that it took every ounce of strength I had just to lift my head off the pillow. What looked back at me from the bathroom mirror was like something out of the Thriller video. Large dark circles under blood-shot eyes, set against a ghostly white face. It didn't look like me at all. It was going to take a serious amount of make-up to transform those features today. I don't know why it mattered what I looked like, but it did. I'd been awake half the night just thinking about what I should wear. In the end I plumped for a ditzy print tunic (purchased after Gok had said these were on-trend) and a soft pink cardigan that I knew the Husband liked for some reason. I'd spent the other half of the night thinking about what I should say to him. I was still not sure about this, so I was going to have to play it by ear.

I got to the coffee shop just before 11.00. It was very busy, but I found a table and ordered a double espresso - desperate times. He could buy his own. He arrived not long afterwards wearing a shirt I hadn't seen before and even though it wasn't sunny, a pair of Aviator sunglasses. He sat down and pushed them up onto his head. He looked a little apprehensive but he also looked, well, I think radiant was the word.

"New sunnies?" I asked. *How much did those cost?*

"Yeah, I got them off the Internet, what do you think?" He put them back down over his eyes, awaiting approval.

They might look good on Tom Cruise, a fighter pilot in Top Gun, but on a 46 year old financial advisor they just looked ridiculous.

"Nice," I lied. The Husband still had them on as he ordered a latte, *when did he start drinking lattes?* and I could see the young guy who took his order was trying to hide a smirk. When he got behind his counter he said something to his young girly colleague who looked over at us and giggled.

"So then," I said meaning *tell me what the fuck is going on?*

"So then," he repeated, removing his sunglasses and looking all sincere. "How are you?"

"I'm good" I replied automatically, then caught myself. "No, I'm not good. Not good at all. I know you said you wanted a couple of week's space, but I'm afraid I just need to know what's going on. I mean what's going on in your head. I don't even know where you're staying, you haven't given me Bruce's address."

"Haven't I?" he looked surprised, but didn't offer up the address. "But I thought we'd both agreed that this was a good idea, that we both needed some down time and it was a good opportunity whilst Bruce was away to take advantage of an empty house. You know it's only temporary. Bruce will be back on 27th." *The 27th? But that'll be three weeks not two.*

"And then what?" I asked.

"Well, then I'll be back of course," he said, but he wouldn't look me in the eye.

"Do you think you'll want to come back?" I asked, beginning to feel irritated.

He paused whilst his coffee was delivered and stirred it thoughtfully. *Buying himself some thinking time.*

"I really hope so," he said, looking at me with such false

sincerity I wanted to batter him to death with a piece of biscotti. "I'm sure I will want to." He looked at me and smiled. "You never know, you might not want me to come back!" *Yeah go on, make a joke of it, you twat.* You're basically enjoying doing whatever you want without a care, buying yourself shirts and idiotic sunglasses whilst I'm worrying myself into a frenzy. You're a selfish sod.

"How are Paul and Debbie?" I asked him.

"Ok," he said, taking a slurp of coffee. "Paul's in Japan again on business."

"That must be difficult for Debbie," I said, watching him carefully. "I mean she works full time doesn't she? Who looks after the Devil Child?"

"They've got a childminder," he said "and Paul's parents are very good, they live close by, so they have Chloë a lot." He quickly added "I think."

"How are Karen and James?" he asked, a swift change of subject. "You saw them last night didn't you? – Facebook," he added when he saw I was about to ask how he knew that.

"Yes, they're fine. They're worried about me of course." I looked at him. "They think you're having an affair."

"Do they?" he laughed and buried his face in his latte cup.

"Yes, they think you're seeing Debbie." I put it bluntly, fed up with pussy-footing around. I watched his face. There was a very brief glimpse of something - surprise, fear, guilt - I couldn't tell, but he quickly recovered himself.

"God, Debs and I are just good friends," he said, beginning to waffle. "We do get on very well, yes we do, we work together of course and have lots in common, not just work but other interests, she likes golf you know and, and, well just because we get on well doesn't mean, well people shouldn't think that..." *I think he doth protest too much.*

"So you're not seeing Debbie then?" I asked, aware he hadn't actually denied it.

"No, of course I'm not seeing Debbie," he said, looking me in the eye. "And I'm really disappointed you would even think that of me." *Oh, that's right, play the injured party now. Well, I'm not apologising.*

"It's difficult to know what to think," I muttered, picking up my cup. It was empty. There was an uncomfortable silence as neither of us knew what to say next.

"What are you up to tonight?" I asked eventually, just because I couldn't take the silence.

"It's your brother's stag night," he said, looking surprised. "I'm going to that. Aren't you going to the hen night? That's tonight as well - had you forgotten?" No, I hadn't forgotten, I didn't know about it as I hadn't been invited. Not that I'd have wanted to go in a million years but I'd still liked to have been asked.

"Oh yes, that's right" I said, vaguely. "Oh God, I almost forgot. Stu asked if you'd do a reading at the registry office service on Saturday. It looks like the wedding might be happening after all. I said I'd ask you and let him know."

"Yes, of course!" The Husband looked pleased and puffed himself up, inflated by his own self-importance. *I wouldn't get too up yourself mate, it was a toss-up between you or Stammering Stan.* "It would be my pleasure to do it." He looked at me. "I think we should go to the wedding as a couple, don't you? I mean, we don't want to upset the family or anything like that, and it would spoil the day for us if we had to keep answering awkward questions. What do you think?"

I felt too drained to argue that I thought we were a couple, so what did he mean by that - I realised I just wanted to get away from him. We agreed he'd pick me up next Saturday, he said he'd drive and not drink. That's a heck of a sacrifice, why was he being so obliging - guilty conscience? We asked each other a bit about work and then we got up to go. I remembered something as we were leaving the coffee shop.

"Can you let me have Bruce's address? Just in case of an emergency."

He had his back to me so I couldn't see his face. He said over his shoulder "Oh yes, I'll text it to you."

We got outside. How awkward saying good bye under these circumstances - do you kiss, hug, walk away, what?

He made my mind up for me by asking: "I was just wondering if you were using the iPad very much? I could really do with it for-"

I cut him short.

"Yes, I'm using it a lot I'm afraid, it's a bit of a lifeline for me whilst I'm on my own. By the way, why do you refer to me as the WOW? What does it mean?"

He did an impression of a goldfish. I'd given away the fact that I'd accessed his Facebook account, but I didn't care. He looked as if he was desperately attempting to think up something plausible but gave up and plumped for the truth.

"It stands for Work Obsessed Wife," he said, embarrassed. "It's just a joke, it's not meant to be nasty or anything."

Right. Is that what everyone thought of me? I shrugged, pretending not to care.

"I guess I'll see you next Saturday then." I turned and walked swiftly away.

I phoned Karen when I got home and relayed the conversation. Her view: "He's biding his bloody time to see if that Debbie bitch will leave her husband. He's just keeping his options open." She was furious I hadn't got the address of where he was staying because she wanted to "stake it out." She was still adamant I should do something with the joint bank accounts. I asked her if she thought I was work-obsessed. She shrieked: "For Christ's sake Kate, just because you work bloody hard doesn't mean you're obsessed. He'd be the first to moan if you didn't have a job and sat around on your arse all day watching Loose bleeding Women. He should support you, not go off and shag someone else."

Part of me felt she must be right. But part of me just couldn't accept that The Husband could lie like that to my face. We'd been married for almost twelve years, he wouldn't treat me like that, would he? How could he face me every day, sleep in the same bed, talk about fence panels if he was at it with someone else behind my back? And what about her, married with a young (devil) child. We'd shared meals, nights out, a weekend away together - surely you wouldn't do that if you were secretly bonking someone else's husband? How could you live with yourself, wouldn't you feel too guilty? I really didn't know what to think, I just knew I was fed up with thinking. I knew Karen was right about one thing, I did need to get the address, so if he didn't text it to me I'd have to find it out by other means.

I phoned my brother and left him a message saying that the Husband was thrilled to be asked to do the reading, and how much we were both looking forward to the wedding next weekend. I said I hoped they both enjoyed their hen and stag dos.

I drove over to see my parents. My mother opened the door, anxious to show me her outfit for the wedding. It was a pale green skirt-suit she'd bought in M&S. I told her it looked lovely. She said that Frank was very nervous about his speech. I asked her why Dad was making a speech - it should be the father of the bride not the groom. We both became terribly confused until I eventually realised she was referring to my brother, not my father. She'd just muddled up their names. I found my father in the greenhouse, shouting at a slug. There was a huge bird poo splattered on the roof of the greenhouse - it looked as if a pterodactyl who'd just eaten a vindaloo had flown over. It was a wonder the glass had stayed intact.

I asked if he was looking forward to the wedding and set him off on a rant:

"Waste of bloody money, why can't they just live together, they've got no bloody sense, no bloody sense at all, he's spent over a hundred quid on a bloody waistcoat! A hundred quid! They're a couple of bloody fools, no bloody sense those two."

I changed the subject and asked him how Mum had been. He looked a bit cagey. He said she'd not had a good week. Apparently she'd put his gardening shoes into a hot oven because she thought they needed warming up: "could have burnt the bloody house down." I looked down at his feet. He had his slippers on.

"Dad," I started, but he stopped me.

"I've made an appointment with the doctor, Tuesday

week. That's the earliest they could do, the bastards, disgraceful, got to wait over a week to see a bloody doctor. This bloody government, a total disgrace." *Thank God, he'd finally made an appointment.* I was relieved, but scared too, worried what the diagnosis would be, even though deep down, I thought I already knew.

"Do you want me to come with you?"

"No, no," he said, "we don't want a fuss." I watched him prodding about in his flowerpots and felt close to tears. Did he know he had some very difficult times ahead? He must do, he wasn't daft. He was going to have to accept some help at some stage. I went inside to make them a cup of tea.

I got home to an answer phone message from my embarrassed-sounding brother: "Hi Sis, great news about the reading, thanks a lot. Um, just so you know, Kirsty's decided, at the very last minute that is, to have a hen night. Er, tonight. Be great if you could make it. Let us know. They're starting off at the Red Square vodka bar in town at seven. Cheers then, bye."

Last minute my arse. Starting at the vodka bar, no doubt that was going to be a very messy evening. I deleted the message. There were no texts from The Husband - he still hadn't sent me his address.

Sunday

Performed daily check on The Husband's Facebook site. I saw a chain of messages about the stag and hen nights from different "friends". I read through them all, piecing together the story. It appeared that my brother's mates had got him a stripper. Someone took a photo and posted it onto Facebook. The Bunny Boiler had seen it, gone berserk and turned up at the bar demanding to see the stripper, whom she was going to "beat to a pulp". The stripper had already left, so the Bunny Boiler had set about my brother, whacking him with a large glittery pink stetson and then attempting to strangle him with a pink rope lasso. They'd all got chucked out. The Bunny Boiler had posted a message this morning which read: "To my ex-fiance have a nice life arse hole". I couldn't help noticing she'd missed out a comma, but her spelling had improved. Was the wedding off again, then? *What a nightmare.*

Still no text from The Husband.

Monday evening

My brother phoned to say that the wedding was off. I said "Are you sure Stu?" and he replied "Yes, definitely," then "hang on, she's just texted me." Pause whilst he read it. "Actually I'm not sure now."

I told him not to tell my parents anything until he was completely sure. No text from The Husband.

Tuesday evening - phoned my brother, but no answer. Texted The Husband "Please send me your address."

Wednesday evening - my brother phoned - the wedding was back on! I tried to sound thrilled and asked him to email the reading to me so The Husband could prepare. No reply from The Husband.

Thursday evening - popped into the hairdressers during their late night opening to see if they could fit me in Saturday morning. They couldn't. They could do Friday afternoon. I'd taken Friday off to get an outfit/gift/card/confetti, so this was a bit of a nuisance but I had to go for that. No reply from The Husband.

Friday morning (Wedding Eve)

I received a response from the Husband which he'd sent very late last night - he'd sent me his address! It was in the posh part of town and I forwarded it straight to Karen, just in case she had time to do any surveillance. I phoned my brother to remind him to email the reading to me. I could hear Georgia and the Bunny Boiler having a screaming row in the background, and my brother sounded extremely harassed. I asked if everything was ok, and he said "No" but he couldn't talk. *Oh God, was it all off again?*

I decided not to go and spend money on a new outfit, but instead spent a very pleasant morning with my nose in my wardrobes, and trying on lots of clothes to find something suitable just in case the wedding did go ahead. I eventually settled on a mid-length cream and brown silk dress, and a chocolate brown fluffy cardigan. Despite my recent worry-related weight loss, the dress was a little tight (*my God, I must have ballooned into a whale*) so I resolved not to eat any carbs or drink any fizzy drinks, caffeine or alcohol for the rest of the day. I'd get them a gift card from M&S on my way to the hairdressers later.

I decided to go for a "power" walk at lunchtime to try and chisel off a few extra pounds. I set off briskly towards the village, swinging my arms to burn off more calories. It was a lovely day - a beautiful blue sky, warmish sunshine and the fields a lush green. I saw a horse rolling around happily, waving its hooves in the air, as I passed the farm. It made you glad to be alive - I told myself that I really must do this more often. There was nothing to hear except bird song, until a large truck came up behind me and braked to a halt, noisily ripping through my solitude. Two men jumped out and jogged past me. *Oh great, it was bin day.* I tried to speed up to get away from them, but they kept pace: each time I overtook the smelly dustcart it would start up and go past me again, and I had to dodge the bin men who kept leaping on and off the truck, and rolling wheelie bins into my path. *Why does nothing ever go right for me, why?* There was no escape on the long road to the village, so I turned round and walked dejectedly back home.

I drove into town for my appointment at the hairdressers, stopping at M&S to purchase a £100 gift card. It would serve as a wedding present, or I could spend it on food if the wedding was called off. The hairdresser's was extremely busy, and they whizzed me through, washing my hair so violently that my brain rattled from side to side and I became quite dizzy. I hadn't felt like that since head banging to Status Quo at the youth club disco. I automatically said "yes please" when offered a coffee, but remembered I mustn't drink any caffeine in order to avoid bloating, so I had to sit there with a lovely fluffy cappuccino under my nose and I could only suck up the froth.

The Rock called me several times whilst I was having my hair done: once to tell me we'd stuffed up a customer's policy and it was likely to cost us "the best part of £15k in compo," then to tell me some of the systems had gone down, then to tell me that there were rumours of a major announcement next week - did I know anything about it, because everyone was asking? I didn't, so I told her to find Big Andy, he always seemed to know what was going on. I'd worry about all that on Monday. Well, Sunday night probably. My hair looked ok though, much tidier and nicely blow-dried. I'd have to sleep sitting up tonight so that it stayed like that for tomorrow.

When I got home my brother had emailed the reading. That was a good sign - perhaps all was ok again. I opened up the attachment and he'd sent a poem. It didn't seem like the sort of thing you'd have at a wedding. Thinking he'd sent me the wrong thing, I phoned him.

"Er Stu," I said, "Just a quickie. This poem you've sent over - are you sure you got the right one?"

"Yes I'm sure, it's Kirsty's favourite," he replied, sounding defensive. "What's wrong with it?"

"Oh, nothing's wrong with it," I said quickly, not wanting to cause any upset. "I was just checking; don't want anything going wrong on your big day!" I wished him luck. *You're going to bloody well need it, bro,* and we said our goodbyes. I forwarded the poem to The Husband without adding a comment, and enjoyed thinking about his face when he opened that email.

Cold chicken salad and no booze for supper. Sat upright in bed, starving.

CHAPTER TWENTY-FOUR

The Day of the Wedding

I got up at eight o'clock with a stiff neck. I didn't own a shower cap, so I had to shower very carefully so as not to get my hair wet. I definitely thought my stomach felt a bit flatter than yesterday. Checked both phones for messages, and there were none, so it looked as if the wedding was on! It was scheduled for 1 pm at the registry office and the Husband was due to pick me up at midday so we left ourselves enough time to get parked. I almost felt excited as I was getting ready. Karen phoned.

"Hi Kate," she said, "I know you've got your brother's wedding today, but I just thought you should know James and I staked out Montpellier road last night." *The Husband's address.* I went cold. What was she about to tell me?

"We sat in the car outside the house with some nibbles in our picnic hamper and watched Toy Story 3 on the iPad while we were waiting." *They'd made a bloody night of it!* "He was inside," she continued, "his car was there and we could see him moving about, until he eventually closed the curtains." *Yes, yes, what else?* "Well, it was all quiet for hours, but then at about ten thirty, oh hang on, what? Oh, James said it was ten thirty seven, a car pulled into the drive really quickly and went straight into the big garage."

"Did you see who it was?" I had that all-too-familiar sick feeling again.

"Well, it was all so quick. We're pretty sure it was a woman driving, and the car was one of those big four by four things with a child seat in the back." *Debbie drives a four by four* "But the garage door closed straight away and no one came out so there must be a door from the garage into the house."

"How long did you stay for afterwards?" I asked. *Was she there all night?*

"About another half hour," said Karen, sounding apologetic, *long enough for them to have sex at least once,* "but poor James' toes were getting cold and we were worried about his chilblains." She waited for me to say something. "Kate, are you still there hun?"

"Yes I'm here," I replied miserably.

"What do you think?"

I was trying hard to keep my voice from cracking.

"It doesn't look very good does it?"

"No," agreed Karen, "I'm afraid it doesn't." There was a pause. "What are you going to do? Have it out with him?"

What was I going to do? I'd already asked him outright and he'd denied it, saying they were just good friends. Would a "good friend" turn up at that time of night and hide their car from view? No, of course they wouldn't. I had to face the fact that there probably wasn't any other explanation. I thanked Karen and James for spending their Friday evening in such a manner and agreed to meet them for Sunday lunch.

I sat on the sofa, the excitement I felt earlier gone, replaced by nausea and a growing anger. He'd be here shortly, expecting to spend the day putting on an Oscar-winning performance as a devoted happy husband for the benefit of my family. I wasn't at all sure I could bring myself to go to the wedding. But I had to, my parents would be dreadfully upset if I wasn't there, and although my laid-back brother probably wouldn't be bothered, the Bunny Boiler would take it as a personal slight and would never forgive me.

I finished getting ready, and then sat in silence staring at the fireplace. Midday came - he was late. He turned up at quarter past, ringing the doorbell before letting himself in. No apology of course, just "We've got plenty of time" to justify his tardiness. I could hardly look at him.

"You look very nice," he said. *You rat-faced creep.*

"Right, let's go," I said, not returning the compliment. "You've got the reading?"

He looked surprised.

"I assumed you'd be bringing it." *Couldn't even print yourself a copy, you lazy tosspot.*

"Oh for God's... no I haven't." I started to flap. "I'll have to turn the laptop on, it takes ages to boot up, we'll be late."

"No don't panic, we've got plenty of time." He went into the study, logged into the laptop and turned the printer on. I was hopping from foot to foot, anxiously watching the clock in the hall. The laptop was painfully slow. *Why didn't you do this last night, you stupid bastard? Oh no you couldn't could you, you were too busy shagging your "good friend".*

A thought struck him.

"Of course, we could take the iPad and I could read from that," he suggested. *Nice try. I'd sooner chuck it in the canal that let you have it now.*

"You can't stand at a wedding service reading from an iPad," I said crossly. "It would look really wanky."

It was almost half past twelve. At last, the printer spluttered into life and churned out the poem. Had he even looked at what he would be reading? I didn't think he had.

We climbed into the car and were off. He started to say: "I just need to get some petrol-" but when I screamed "Are you *fucking kidding* me?" he looked very startled and decided there was enough in the tank after all.

We arrived at the registry office at ten to one, but the nearest car park was full. We drove round it twice and then the Husband said he was going to try the pub opposite, where we finally found a space. I got out with my head reeling from the stress. From the pub piled a group of about half a dozen guys, clearly part of the wedding party. Despite all being dressed in suits and ties, they still managed to look like they'd just stepped off the set of the Jeremy Kyle show. They must be the Bunny Boiler's family. They stood outside the registry office, laughing and pushing each other whilst they lit cigarettes.

There were two burly men stood outside the entrance to the registry office, hands clasped in front of them, who nodded us in through the doors like we were going into a nightclub. Inside there were about fifty guests beginning to take their seats. My brother stood at the front, sharing a laugh with his best man, very handsome in his suit and tails and a pale blue tie. I went to give him a hug and asked:

"What's with the bouncers?"

"Oh, that's a couple of Kirsty's cousins," he said matter-of-factly, like it was perfectly normal to have a couple of heavies at a wedding service. "We thought we'd better be on the safe side, just in case some undesirables turn up - you know what Kirsty's family are like." No I didn't know, but if they were anything like her, then nobody's pet rabbits were safe. *Flipping heck bro, what the hell are you getting yourself into?* It's not too late. Run, get out of here and flee to the hills...

I said a quick hello to my parents who looked extremely smart, my father saying, a bit too loudly:

"You two cut it bloody fine - waiting for it to be called off were you?" and then waving to various aunts, uncles and cousins as we found some seats. The Husband was looking at the poem.

"Bloody hell, Kate," he hissed, "have you read this?"

"Yes I have." *Why, haven't you?*

"But Jesus Christ, I can't read this, not at a sodding wedding!" He was panicking. I shrugged. I didn't want to be sat there with him, I wished I'd come on my own. The registrar asked us all to stand to receive the wedding party. Music started to play - Coldplay's "Fix You" filled the room. We turned to see The Bunny Boiler coming in on the arm of a grey haired man - I wasn't sure who he was, I knew she'd fallen out with her father some time ago. She was wearing a strapless long white dress which had an amazing sprinkling of silver bits on it, as if someone had shaken a pot of glitter over her. We got a good view of her barbed wire tattoo round her right arm as she passed and when she reached the front we could see she had a red devil tattooed on her back. Her hair was up, the top bit teased into blonde candy floss wisps secured with a sparkly tiara, the roots below much darker. Georgia bought up the rear in a sheer pale blue dress, which looked a bit like a long nightie. She looked absolutely freezing, but at least she was making an effort to smile.

The service began, and they stood at the front, the Bunny Boiler having to hoik her dress up at regular intervals whenever her breasts tried to peep over the top. My brother looked really proud and happy. They sat down for the readings and The Husband was up first. Shooting me a desperate look, he walked to the front and cleared his throat. He read out the title:

"The Four Candles."

There was a burst of laughter in the room. The Bunny Boiler shot a furious look over her shoulder. The Husband looked very uncomfortable, but composed himself and started to read:

"The first candle represents our grief; the pain of leaving you is intense...."

I could see the guests exchanging glances with each other and there were some thinly disguised snorts.

"The second candle represents our courage, to confront our sorrow...."

The guy sat behind me whispered loudly to his wife:

"Are we at a fucking funeral?" which made everyone around us get the giggles.

"For the times we laughed..." Someone whimpered. "The times we cried..." the woman seated in front of me buried her face in a hanky, her shoulders shaking.

"The silly things you did...." The guy behind me whispered: "What will they walk out to, the fucking funeral march?" which set everyone off again.

"The fourth candle... " A big cheer went up. The Husband, very red in the face, carried on.

"We light for our love...."

I caught the eye of the best man, Kieron, who was sat facing the guests and we both had to look away to hide our smirks.

"We light this candle that your light will always shine..."

A small boy sat near the front turned to his mother and

said so everybody could hear: "Is she dead Mummy?"

The Husband had to raise his voice above the howls.

"We thank you for the gift your living brought to each of us. We love you."

I knew the last line was: "We remember you" but he couldn't bring himself to read it out. Instead, he nodded to the bride and groom and slunk back to his seat, his face on fire. I had covered my face with my hand, pretending to scratch my nose so he wouldn't see me smirking. The registrar paused for a moment, as some of the guests were still convulsed. The bride did not look too amused, but my brother smiled and winked at her, and whispered something in her ear, which made her laugh. I looked across at my parents. My father's face was an absolute picture; my mother simply looked confused.

When the service was over, we all crowded into the small garden of the registry office for some photos and chucked confetti over the new Mr and Mrs Bunny Boiler as they came down the steps. The photographer and the best man did their best to organise everyone, but they had quite an unruly crowd to manage, and some of the bride's family appeared to have gone missing. I guessed they'd slipped away over the road to the pub. While I was stood smiling for the 'family of the groom' shots, the best man called over "Kate, can you get your hubby? We need him for this photo."

I called back: "Ok, we can always cut him out later!" which made everyone laugh.

The reception was being held in the function room of The George pub, which was a five minute walk away. I nipped to the loo. When I got there I found the bride in tears, wailing to a friend: "It's shit isn't it, I know it looks shit." She grabbed my arm. "Kate, be honest with me, does my hair look shit?" *Yes it does a bit.* I told her she looked absolutely stunning and gave her a hug. I came away covered in body glitter and headed to the bar. I chatted to my parents and to family members I hadn't seen in ages, all of us saying, as we always did: "Isn't it a shame we only meet up at these occasions?" The Husband had latched onto one of my brother's friends he'd met on the stag night. From what I could hear of the conversation, he was trying to flog him a pension plan. I saw him check his iPhone several times. *Missing her, are you?*

The room had been decorated with pale blue and silver heart-shaped balloons, with silver candles on the tables. As we were sitting down (unfortunately I had been seated next to the Husband) a young guy walked past our table and said very loudly to his mate: "Oh look, I can see one, two, three, four candles!" I shot a sideways glance at The Husband, who looked furious, but did not react. I so wanted to laugh but managed not to. We were sat with some of my brother's friends and their wives and girlfriends, and they were really good fun. The wedding breakfast was roast turkey "with all the trimmings" which was a bit bizarre, as it was October, with a sticky date pudding which was actually very similar to Christmas pudding. I was waiting for the mince pies to come round with the coffee.

I ignored The Husband and chatted to the couple next to me who were on the verge of emigrating to Australia, *the lucky buggers,* and they were extremely excited about it. Finally, we were all served with a glass of Asti *shudder* and the speeches began. The grey haired man who had given away the Bunny Boiler went first. It was her Uncle, Stammering Stan!

It was like a scene from The King's Speech. It must have
been such an ordeal for him, but he got through it, keeping it
very short, and we gave him a huge round of applause when
he'd finished. Then it was my brother's turn. He was
extremely nervous. I could see his notes shaking as he
clutched them. He said lots of gushing, sickly things about
the Bunny Boiler (she'd clearly written it) and described
Georgia as "a delight". *Who are you kidding?* He got emotional
at one stage, which was embarrassing, but he recovered and
finished off by presenting my mother and a friend of the
Bunny Boiler's with large bouquets of flowers. *Where was the
Bunny Boiler's mother then?* I thought she was going to be there.
Perhaps she hadn't made it past the bouncers.

The best man, Kieron, saved the day with a very funny
speech about my brother's exploits as a builder, even
managing to get the words "fork handles" in, which received
a massive cheer, though The Husband remained straight-
faced. Kieron also poked fun at the bride for choosing a
"white" dress, although I noticed he didn't mention anything
about the stag night. Probably very wise.

We all drank a final toast, and then to everyone's
amazement, a woman stood up and started shouting angrily,
gesticulating towards the top table. She was probably around
sixty, but was dressed quite youthfully in a tight fitting zebra-
affect black and white suit with a black hat which had a
feather in it. As she was shouting the feather bobbed about
furiously and the hat slipped slightly to one side. She was
clearly drunk, and I couldn't make out what she was shouting
because she was slurring so badly, but I thought I heard her
yell: "You're dead to me now bitch!"

Then several other guests got up too and joined in, and

suddenly it was bedlam. *What the hell was going on?* It was all getting extremely heated, and our table decided we'd move ourselves into the safety of the bar. Where were the bloody bouncers when you needed them? The Husband went to rescue my parents from the top table while I got a round of drinks in. There was lots of shouting still coming from the room, and then the sound of chairs being turned over and glasses smashing. Staff rushed into the room.

When my mother reached the bar she didn't seem at all shaken but said: "Well, I didn't think much of that last speech."

The bride came out of the room and rushed past us in tears, her friend close behind her. The commotion in the room next door eventually died down and my brother emerged to explain to us that the drunken woman was the Bunny Boiler's mother. She had felt snubbed because she wasn't on the top table and humiliated that she hadn't been given a bouquet of flowers. He said that she had done "precisely fuck all" towards the wedding so she hadn't deserved any recognition. She'd now walked out and taken half her family with her. We all said ineffective things like "Oh, families eh, what are they like?" and I got my brother a large whisky for his nerves. When my mother asked my brother why there hadn't been any crackers to pull, my father decided he was going to take her home.

The room was cleared for the disco, and the evening guests were turning up. The Bunny Boiler had recovered and was dancing with her friends, one hand holding her dress up. I saw Georgia tipping the dregs from discarded glasses into her own and downing them when she thought no one was looking. I pretended not to have seen her. The Husband was pontificating with another boring fart-arse about investment opportunities. Kieron, the best man, came over to me at the bar. I told him he'd made a great speech and he bought me a glass of wine.

He was very engaging to chat to, having worked for a long time with my brother in the building trade but had now set up on his own as an "odd job" man. He said it had been a scary move to strike out on his own, but he didn't regret it, he always had loads of work on. He asked if I could get him a quote for his buildings insurance so I promised to give him a call during the week and we swapped numbers. I said I hadn't seen his girlfriend, how was she, and he said they'd recently split up, which was a bit embarrassing. I told him I was sure he wouldn't stay single for long, and he fixed me with his lovely blue eyes and said: "I hope not." I half-wondered if he was trying to chat me up. It had been so long since anyone had it was impossible to recognise the signs.

The bride and groom had their first dance to REM's 'Everybody Hurts'. I stayed in the bar, fixedly talking to my Aunt so that I wouldn't have to dance with the Husband. I needn't have worried; he didn't have any intention of asking me. When things began to deteriorate into a drunken melee, we decided to go home. I said goodbye to the bride and groom who were holding each other up on the dance floor and we left the pub. Three women were sat outside on a picnic table, dressed in their pretty dresses and glamorous hats, and scoffing kebabs.

The Husband moaned all the way home about the wedding and the Bunny Boiler's awful family, saying my brother had just made the worst mistake of his life.

I nearly said: "It's a hereditary thing" but I stopped

myself. I managed to thank him for driving when he dropped me at home, our home, and asked if he wanted a coffee or if he was going straight back to the Shag Palace, oh no sorry, I meant Bruce's house. He didn't respond to the Shag Palace comment, but said he would get straight off as he was very tired. *Was she there waiting for him?* I said goodnight, and saw next door's curtain twitching as I walked up the drive. They must have been wondering what was going on. So was I.

CHAPTER TWENTY-FIVE

Sunday

I went round to Karen and James' at lunchtime for James' legendary roast lamb. We sat and discussed The Husband and what I should do. Karen was very much in favour of me "having it out with him once and for all" but I reasoned that I didn't have that much to go on - I once saw them leave the gym together and a car that may or may not have been Debbie's drive into Bruce's garage. Karen asked me what other signs I had observed that could be a clue. I couldn't think of any, so we Googled "tell-tale signs that your husband is cheating." The top five were:

1. Your husband has unexplained absences. *No shit Sherlock! Well, he's always at the gym, playing golf or working late. So nothing unexplained there.*

2. He receives and makes anonymous telephone calls. *Who makes telephone calls these days - how old was this site?*

3. He dresses up when going out. *As what? He's not a tranny... or is he?*

4. Your husband has a history of deception. *Yes of course he has, he's a Financial Advisor.*

5. If you believe your husband is cheating, he usually is. *That's reassuring.*

Not very helpful, but I thought it would be really useful if I could get hold of his iPhone and check his text messages.

I'd have to wait until we met up again and then try and have a peek. Karen suggested going through the pockets on the clothes he had left behind in case there were any clues, like receipts for meals, hotels or a pair of frilly knickers. God, how degrading this all was; was I really going to be snooping around my husband's possessions like some sad sap? I was furious with him for reducing me to this. Or was it my own fault? Had I driven him away, and he'd left because I was so awful to live with? Work-obsessed he'd called me. Did I neglect him? Possibly. Was it because I sometimes sang along to the Go Compare adverts? But as shameful and annoying as that might be, it was no excuse for shagging someone else. *If* he was shagging someone else. I was going to have to find out the truth, somehow.

The start of another crappy week. I dragged myself into work on Monday morning, my body like concrete. As I'd taken Friday off, I knew my inbox would be overflowing. Brett the Boss had clearly been working over the weekend again as the most recent emails were from him. One was entitled: DIARY CRASH. *Oh great.* I opened it up, and he'd booked a teleconference for 10.00 today. He didn't explain what it was about. I already had a meeting scheduled for 10.00, and then was back-to-back for the rest of the day - I'd have to reschedule everything. The Snake slithered over.

"Kate," she said in a hushed voice, "I don't really like to say anything," *But you're going to,* "but I thought you should know. When you were off on Friday there were lots of rumours flying around about a big announcement today. You weren't here to tell us anything and everyone's really worried about it."

I looked at Hissing Cyn. Just for once, could she not bring herself to say "Good morning" or "How was your brother's wedding?" or "How's your bum for spots?" - anything really, just to show that there was a human heart beating away inside the reptilian skin?

"Good morning to you too, Cynthia," I said. "I wasn't here on Friday, which I'm not going to apologise for, as even I'm entitled to a day off. There are other managers on site that you could go to should you ever need help with anything. Now, you're experienced enough to know that rumours turn out to be exactly that - just rumours." *Except of course, when they turn out to be spot on.*

"Well, of course I wasn't getting involved myself," *that would be a first*, "but it was all over Facebook at the weekend. Apparently, one of the sites is definitely closing, and as we're the smallest, everyone thinks it will be us."

"Honestly Cyn, I don't know where these things come from," I said, crossly. "This sort of gossip just isn't helpful. I have a meeting with Brett at 10.00 so if there's anything to be cascaded following that I'll let you know."

The Drain came over to join us, looking pale and sweaty. "I haven't been able to sleep all weekend," he said. "I've been worrying myself sick - what would I do without a job? I've got two kids to support. The wife said she can't do any more hours, not with all her social commitments. She's just joined a salsa group too, she needs new outfits for it. You wouldn't believe the cost of them, and then there's the shoes and-"

"Yes, it would be especially awful for you, wouldn't it?" said The Snake, rubbing it in. "And it's so difficult to get another job over a certain age, you just get thrown on the scrap heap in this country, it's absolutely-"

"Now look," I stopped her, "this is exactly the sort of scare-mongering we should be avoiding, because it's so unsettling for everyone. We don't know anything yet, so until we do, we've got to put on a united front for the troops and get on with business as usual. We've got customers to look after."

I sent them away but I was beginning to feel anxious myself. What was going on, were we closing? I went to see Big Andy, and he said it must be the restructure announcement we'd all been waiting for. He'd seen on Facebook that Bridgend thought they would be the site that closed.

I joined Big Andy, Cruella and The Shark in the meeting room at 10.00. They all looked worried, and nobody spoke as we dialled into the teleconference using the bat-phone on the table. The managers from Bridgend were on the line as well. We waited for about five minutes, and then Brett joined the call. He read out a briefing from the Big Cheese in a voice that sounded a bit gruffly, almost like he was purring. *Most strange.* The briefing informed us that this was a very exciting time for Perypils, with many opportunities to seize competitive advantages over other companies. As he was talking, there was a loud "Meow" in the background followed by a scuffling sound. We all looked at each other. Brett read on, telling us it was necessary to "streamline" our activities, get closer to our customers and make further reductions to our cost base. Was the paper clip amnesty not sufficient, then? So which site was closing? We all held our breath. There was a really loud, prolonged "Meeooooow". Brett continued to read. The Big Cheese was delighted to announce that there was no current need to reduce the Perypils property portfolio. We all looked at each in delight. No closures! Not yet, at least. Brett took a deep breath, then told us that in order to achieve the key streamlining activities, there would be changes made to the management structure. *Uh-oh.* He called it "the first stage in creating synergies in the management layers". There was a brief silence, then a Welsh accent asked: "What the bloody hell does that mean, man?"

"Well," said Brett, sounding uncomfortable, "what it means is-". An automated voice told us that "Brett has left the conference". We waited. He dialled back in. "Sorry, the bloody cat trod on the phone." *Working from home are you? Coward.* "Where were we? Oh yes, the synergies. Well, there's no easy way to say it. There will be a reduction in the number of managers. There's going to be a new structure across both the Cheltenham and the Bridgend sites, and a selection exercise."

"So we'll have to re-apply for our positions?" I asked.

"Yes, well, sort of. The positions will be different, in that they'll have additional responsibilities." *How could they possibly add any more!* "For example, there will be one manager for operations, who'll look after both sites."

We all saw the horrified look on The Shark's face. Brett continued: "There will be just one Finance manager for both sites..." We all looked at Big Andy, who shrugged, "and one manager who'll look after property policies," - *that's me* - "as well as customer complaints." *That's Cruella.* So the rumours had been true. Cruella and I were going head to head and would compete for the same position. I looked across at her, but she stared resolutely ahead, her witchy eyes black and narrow.

Brett hadn't finished. "The same exercise is being undertaken between Birmingham and Manchester. All these moves have been agreed by HR and the unions." *Those useless bastards.* "You'll each receive an application form, which HR will email to you later today. These need to be completed by Friday." *This Friday?*

There were howls of protest at the short deadline. Brett told us the forms were very simple and straight forward to complete, but he eventually backed down and agreed to give us the weekend as well.

"When will we know if we've been successful?" asked Big Andy.

Brett wasn't sure, he thought it would take several weeks. Someone asked if there would be any options for the unsuccessful applicants. *Yes, they can opt to fuck off!* Brett hummed and ha'd and waffled, but when pressed, said that he couldn't rule out forced redundancies. Cruella asked him what he meant by this being the first stage. He said this was "just for these four walls" *some hope* but that the second stage would be a reduction in the number of team managers. They'd have to go through a similar exercise once the departmental managers had been agreed.

I thought about The Drain. This would crucify him. There was a long silence on the line. Brett said he had to reapply for his role too, so he knew how we were all feeling.

A Welsh voice said "With respect Brett, you don't know how we are feeling because you're never around to notice."

Brett insisted that we were all in this together and told us he was always there for support. Someone at Bridgend snorted.

"There is one last announcement," said Brett. "And

that's that Amanda Fisher from Cheltenham will be taking up a new position as Kevin's executive support." The Climber! She was going to work for The Big Cheese? I couldn't believe it. Executive support? What did that mean exactly? Was she intending to move to Manchester? The others were all looking at me, but I had no idea, she'd not mentioned a thing to me. Why would she? I'm only her boss after all. How long had she been plotting this, who'd arranged it for her, Brett? Why on earth hadn't he told me?

Cruella snapped: "Is that a promotion Brett?" He stuttered and stumbled about it being a new "development opportunity" and didn't directly answer the question.

Someone in Bridgend asked angrily: "How the hell can you be creating a new position when you've just told us that half of us will be losing our jobs?"

Brett dodged this question too, saying we needed to focus on how great it was that no sites were to close and it was a real good news story to cascade. He said he appreciated we were "on the change curve" but that he could rely on us to get on with business as usual. No one responded. I think everyone just wanted to throttle him.

Cruella left the room immediately the call finished without speaking. I sat with Big Andy and The Shark as we tried to absorb what we'd just been told. The Shark said his opposite number at Bridgend, who was now his rival, was a good friend of the Chief Executive. He didn't rate his own chances of getting the job. He was probably right, but I didn't like to say so. Big Andy thought that they'd already decided who they wanted to give the positions to, so the whole exercise was pointless anyway and he wasn't going to lose any sleep over it. We all agreed that just having a week to complete the application form was ludicrous and totally unfair.

Cruella came back into the room. "I thought you should know that it's already on Facebook that we've got to apply for our roles and that the Team Managers will be next." *Oh shit.* Why had someone done that? People deserved a proper communication from their manager, not Facebook gossip. I went back to my department and called a smug-looking Climber over to my desk.

"Amanda," I said, "Brett's just announced that you're leaving us."

"Oh, he's so naughty isn't he?" she laughed, flicking her hair back. "I wanted to tell you all myself but he's jumped the gun. Oh well. Yes it's true, I'll be leaving in about three weeks I think, unless Kevin needs me sooner." She laughed again. "And we can't say no to Kevin can we?" *Clearly you didn't.* I had so many questions - what, when, why, how - but I couldn't be bothered to ask her, and I doubted she'd tell me the truth anyway. I called the other team managers over. They had an abundance of questions about their own positions, but I couldn't answer any of them. The poor Drain was in a dreadful state, and they were all aghast when the Climber told them that she would be leaving and wasn't being replaced. TLS George asked who was going to manage her team. I suggested we split it up and share the staff out between the rest of them.

"But that's another five people each," said The Snake in dismay. "How are we supposed to cope?"

Only The Rock asked me how I was feeling. I decided to be honest and said I didn't know. I was in a bit of a lose-lose situation - either I'd have double the workload or I was out of a job altogether. I wasn't sure which was worse.

The Climber trilled, "Oh never mind you lot, if it gets too bad here I'll try and find you all a job in Manchester!" The Snake fixed her with her cold eyes. I sensed a strike was imminent.

"I don't remember seeing that job advertised," she said icily, "What exactly did you have to do to get that position - under Kevin?"

The Climber ignored the insinuation.

"Well Cynthia, Kevin has wanted me to work for him for some time now, well, since he met me and was so impressed that he's been looking for the right development opportunity for me. Obviously he wasn't going to advertise it as he only wanted me for that position." *Which, missionary?*

I could feel a scene brewing, so I quickly said we faced a difficult time ahead and we needed to stick together and support one another through it. I did manage to make them laugh by telling them about Brett's cat joining in the managers' teleconference and cutting him off. The Climber didn't laugh.

"But Brett hasn't got a cat."

I suggested he may have been looking after it for someone. She still looked concerned, and The Snake, never one to miss a trick added:

"I think Lisa Hewitt has a cat. Do you think he could have been staying at her house?" The Climber went the colour of a thundercloud, so I called time on the meeting, promising to keep them updated with any new announcements.

Back at my desk, my email inbox was overflowing. HR had emailed the application form to the managers, but no one could open it, triggering a whole chain of emails between HR and numerous managers. My head was buzzing. I had a whole string of meetings planned in for the rest of the day, so there wasn't time to think. I'd think on the drive home.

Monday evening

HR still hadn't been able to send an "openable" version of the application form so I didn't know what information was required. I was in a quandary - apply for a role I didn't want, or take a bullet and ask for redundancy. I hadn't worked out what redundancy sum I would get, but I'd been with Perypils for twelve years, so it would probably be enough to keep us ticking over until I found another job. If I could find another job. I really needed to discuss this with the Husband, but it was so difficult, given our situation. What a time for this to happen! What if he didn't want to come back? I couldn't afford the mortgage on my own and I wouldn't even be able to rent somewhere if I didn't have a job. *Oh God, what a nightmare.*

When I got home, I received a text from "The Best Man":

"Great to see you again on Sat. Don't forget to get me that quote. Give us a call if you need details. Kieron."

I was impressed - he hadn't used any text-talk, and he'd used punctuation and capital letters! A man after my own heart. I made a note to get a quote for him tomorrow. I didn't feel like eating anything, so poured myself a generous vodka and tonic. I picked up my phone to call the Husband and tell him about my job situation. Just as I did so, my phone pinged and a text came in from him:

"Hi there, hope u have recovered from the w/e! Just to

let u know that Bruce will not be back until 15th next month so I will stay on here till then. Hope thats ok with u. I picked up some stuff I needed this morning. C u soon."

Oh no, the iPad! I'd forgotten to take it to work with me this morning. I rushed into the study, but it had gone. He'd taken it. *You bastard.* I burst into tears and sat sobbing on the floor of the study. I wanted to crawl under the desk, curl up and stay there. I had been expecting him to return this weekend, now he wouldn't be back for another two weeks. How could he just send a text? Why didn't he have the decency to phone me? What a cowardly bastard. Was she there with him? I began to wonder if I really knew him at all.

Sobs subsided and were replaced by anger. What the hell was I doing sat blubbing on the floor? Get up and fight! I was going to have it out with him. I grabbed my bag and car keys, almost changed my mind when I remembered there was a double edition of Corrie on, but decided I could watch it on ITV 1 + 2 + 2.

It took me a good forty five minutes to get across town and reach Bruce's house, which was situated at the end of a rather grand avenue. The Husband's car was parked in front of the house - *good, he was there.* I just drove straight in. The double-fronted garage was closed, and I jumped up at the windows to see if I could spot another car in there, but it was too dark to see.

I pressed the doorbell and could hear its pretentious chimes tinkling inside the house. The Husband came to the door. He did not look too pleased to see me.

"Oh, hello," he said "What are you doing here?"

"Well now, let me see," I started, trying to keep calm. "One, I'm still your wife, believe it or not, two, you've texted your wife to say you're not coming back for another two weeks and you couldn't even be bothered to phone, three, you think you can just come back to the house and take things without any consideration for me-"

"Right, come in, come inside." He ushered me in, glancing around outside anxiously in case any of his snooty neighbours heard raised voices and called their friends in MI5.

Bruce's house was something to behold - beautiful oak-panelled flooring, fancy modern art sculptures, Paul Smith rugs. I caught sight of myself in one of the mirrors in the hallway - *oh dear*. My mascara had run during my crying fit and I quickly scrubbed at my face as The Husband led the way into a shiny stainless-steel kitchen. I could see that he had left his mark, with stains on the work surfaces and dirty mugs queued up at the sink waiting for the mug fairy to wash them. There was the bloody iPad propped up on the breakfast bar!

I perched on one of the bar stools and faced him. He looked uncomfortable, and leant on the breakfast bar, saying rather vaguely "Er, would you like a coffee or something?" his tone implying 'you're not intending to stay long are you?'

I declined. I was looking round for traces that a woman was there or had been there - a handbag perhaps, or a pair knickers hanging on the radiator. I couldn't see anything obvious.

"Right," I said, taking a deep breath, "I want to know what's going on and I want the truth. I was expecting you to come home at the weekend and I'm pissed off that you texted a casual message to say you wouldn't be back for another fortnight - you couldn't even be bothered to call me. How do you think I'm feeling about all of this? You just don't seem to care at all about my feelings. You come back to the house when you knew I wouldn't be there, and pinch the bloody iPad which, alright, I know technically is yours, but I told you I really needed-"

"Whoa," he broke in, "I haven't pinched the bloody iPad, what are you talking about? Don't tell me you've lost it!"

"What's that then?" I demanded, pointing at the iPad sat innocently between us on the breakfast bar.

"I bought myself another one," he said. "I thought that was the most sensible thing to do as we both needed one."

"You bought another one?" *So where the hell is mine?* Oh God, it's probably in the bedroom or something. "But they're about five hundred quid! You should have discussed it with me first. Why didn't you?"

He got defensive. "It's my money," he said snootily. "I got a sales bonus last month, so I used that. I work bloody hard for it you know, it's not easy in this economic climate. We *are* in a recession - perhaps you hadn't noticed."

You patronising twat.

"Well, when I got my last bonus, can you recall what I spent it on?" I asked him. He clearly couldn't remember. "Bloody fence panels!" I spat. So you're quite happy that I spend my bonus on us, on our house, but you're not going to do the same with your bonus, you're just going to spend it on yourself? Do you think that I didn't work hard for my bonus, too?"

"Oh yes, well, we all know how hard you work, don't we?" he said, throwing his hands up in the air. *Who's "we"? Who was he talking to?* "You're always ramming it down our throats. You've always got your head in your lap top, you don't get home till God knows what time, we can't go out at weekends because you're 'catching up', (*He actually made the speech signs with his hands, the wanker*) "and you're always complaining that you're tired. I don't know why you still do the job, you obviously hate it and it makes you, well, you know..." He tailed off.

"No, go on, it makes me what?"

"Irrational," he said, triumphantly. "It makes you behave like this - turning up here, in a state, accusing me of stealing from you. You're so ungrateful! I spent my weekend taking you to that bloody awful family wedding of yours, and I couldn't even have a drink when, God knows, I bloody well needed one. Having to read that ridiculous poem.... It just proves the point that we could use a bit more time apart, give us both a bit of space, just like I said in the first place. And you agreed." *No I bloody didn't.* I realised I'd played right into his hands, I was on the back foot.

"I didn't accuse you of stealing, don't exaggerate. And my job might not be a problem for much longer. I've got to reapply for my shitty job and if I don't get it, I'll probably be made redundant." He looked shocked. I told him that it was me versus Cruella and I didn't much rate my chances.

"Bloody hell," he said rubbing his chin, and I could see his mind racing. What was he thinking - how would we afford the mortgage, or how would I cope if he left me, or if he would be entitled to some of my redundancy payout? Was he already thinking of ways he could spend it?

"You're better than this other person though, surely?" he asked. "She sounds like she hasn't got any people skills at all."

"She hasn't," I agreed, "but I don't think that Perypils particularly want managers with people skills anymore. They want bullying, hard-nosed, humourless bastards, and she wins hands down on that front."

There was a silence between us. I decided I may as well get it all off my chest.

"Has Debbie been here?"

The Husband looked surprised. "Why do you ask that?" Did he look a bit shifty?

"Just answer the question."

He stood up straight and folded his arms. "Yes, she's been round a couple of times," he said, looking at me directly. "She's a friend, why shouldn't she call round?"

"Does Paul come with her, and Chloë?" I asked, watching him closely.

"Now look," he said impatiently. "This is ridiculous. Debs is a work colleague and friend, nothing else. I've told you that before, you're being ridiculous." He got on his high horse. "And quite frankly, offensive."

I stuck to my guns. "So, from that answer, I guess she comes round on her own." I nodded to myself. "I see. Does she stay the night here?"

He exploded. "This is insane! You need to have a serious word with yourself Kate - you turn up here looking like Alice Cooper, and first off you accuse me of stealing from you, then you tell me you might be losing your job and now you're accusing me of sleeping with someone else! You're off your head. No, for your information, she doesn't stay the night. She's a respectable married woman. With a child." He turned and started to rummage in the massive American fridge-freezer, possibly searching for some beer or was he hiding his face? "Honestly," he said, slamming the door when he couldn't find what he was looking for, "we really need this time apart, I'm glad Bruce has delayed his return - in fact I'm relieved. You need to sort your head out, you really do."

"Ah, I knew it would all be my fault," I said, getting up from the stool. "For your information, Debbie was seen turning up here very late one night, so you'll have to excuse me being a bit, what did you call it? 'Off my head', as I thought that was quite unusual behaviour for someone who was just a colleague - and a friend." That wasn't exactly true, but I wanted to see his reaction. I thought I saw him flounder momentarily, but he quickly recovered his self-righteous indignation.

"Well whoever it was who thought they saw something was clearly mistaken. Debs doesn't turn up here late at night, who said she did?"

"Facebook," I said wearily. This wasn't true either, but I wanted him to spend the rest of his night fruitlessly searching through the hundreds of banal, pointless comments of his Facebook friends, in the attempt to find something incriminating.

I started to leave. "Perhaps you'll do me the courtesy of phoning when you're next coming to the house; or coming back home or staying here for good," I said sarcastically. "It would be quite nice to know. And in turn I'll let you know if I've still got a job or not - you know, just small little issues that we need to talk about, thankfully nothing too significant."

I'd reached the front door and wrenched it open. He'd followed me, but didn't say anything. I drove home feeling wretched. The anger had gone, and I was beginning to feel I'd made a right fool of myself.

I phoned Karen when I got in and relayed the

conversation to her. I told her I hadn't seen any evidence of Debbie at the house. She snorted:

"Well of course you wouldn't, Paul's back from Japan. She'll be at home playing happy families. Shall we go and have it out with her? I bet you anything Paul doesn't know she's been round there while he's been away."

It was tempting, but I couldn't face it. I could still be completely wrong, and at this rate I was going to end up looking like a psycho. They'd have me sectioned, handing an easy victory to Cruella. Perhaps The Husband was right – maybe I was irrational, insane, off my head. That made me think about my mother - she had her doctor's appointment tomorrow. I thought about phoning to wish them luck, but stopped myself, it was getting a bit late now. I hunted around the house and eventually found the iPad under the Next Directory. Oh well. Might as well order myself something I don't really need while I can still afford to.

Chapter Twenty-Six

Tuesday

We were still unable to open the HR application form and all the managers were up in arms, saying the time we had to complete it was just getting shorter and shorter. Emails were flying all over the place. I kept out of it. I was finding it difficult to concentrate, wondering how my mother had got on at the doctors.

My team managers were being very needy. I thought I should have a travelator built past my desk, so they could just step on and ask their inane questions as they glided by, without stopping. TLS George surpassed himself. I'd spent over an hour with them all this morning running through a large document called the EBP - Emergency Business Procedures. This was a list of actions we had to take if the building was inaccessible, if it burnt down, for example. *Oh, happy release.* I walked them through it, page by painstaking page, and they all said they fully understood everything. This afternoon, TLS George had come up to my desk and said he'd received an email from the communications team asking if he'd been briefed about the site's EBP. He said he'd never heard of it, so he'd replied "no."

He was a bit taken aback when I shouted: "You stupid shit George! You've got the memory of a fecking goldfish!"

"What?"

"Do you actually remember this morning? It was the bit

of the day which took place before you went to lunch. I spent well over an hour of my life taking you through - no, spoon feeding you the EBP, which you told me you understood. That was at eleven thirty. How come it's now two thirty and you're telling me you can't even remember it? What's wrong with you? Am I just wasting my bloody time?"

"Oh that," he muttered sulkily, "I didn't know what it was called." *What a waste of bloody space you are.* Now the Communications team would think I hadn't briefed my team, and that I was incompetent. Sure enough, one minute later, I received a bollocking email from Brett the Boss, saying it was a "must-do" communication and I had to "make it happen".

He copied Cruella into the email, congratulating her on her successful team briefing. *Great.* One nil to her. Was there actually any point me applying for this role? I replied to Brett saying sorry and confirming that I had now briefed everyone. I decided that telling him I *had* already briefed it, but one of my team couldn't recall it five minutes later would have sounded worse.

I got home at seven, itching to call my parents, but had to wait until quarter past, as I knew they would be listening to The Archers. When I phoned them my father answered. He told me that "those stupid bastards next door" had already put their Christmas lights up, and it looked like the "bleeding Blackpool illuminations". He rumbled on about them for quite a while, until he began to run out of steam, and I managed to dive in and asked how they'd got on at the doctors.

"Had to wait forty bloody minutes to see him."

"Yes, but what did he say about Mum?"

"Well, not exactly thorough are they? He couldn't wait to get us out of his bloody room. Asked her a few questions, gave her a prod and said we'd have to go and see someone else at the hospital. Christ knows when that will be. He said an appointment would come through, but I won't hold my breath."

"But what did he say Dad, what did he think about Mum?" It was like pulling teeth. There was a pause.

"He thinks it could be the early stages of dementia," my Dad said quietly. "But it might not be, he didn't know. He didn't know anything at all really - useless. The hospital will tell us more."

I couldn't speak. I had a huge lump in my throat.

"Are you there Kate?" my Dad asked. "Now, don't you go getting upset, you know your mother wouldn't want a fuss. She's perfectly ok, look, here she is to say hello."

"Hello love," my mother said brightly. "How's Luke?"

Luke? Who the fuck's Luke? I used to go out with a Luke about twenty years ago. He was the one and only bearded man I'd ever been out with. Once, during a snogging session, one of my bogeys had got caught up in his moustache and I'd retched. He'd called an abrupt end to our relationship, saying, not unreasonably, that he wanted a girlfriend who didn't throw up when he kissed her.

"Er, he's fine Mum," I said, not wanting to upset her. "How are you doing?"

"Oh good, good. How about you, how's things, any news?"

Well Mum, it's like this - my husband has moved out for a while because he can't stand to be near me, he's possibly having an affair with a woman who gives birth to devil children, he's spending money willy-nilly without consulting with me and I'm about to lose my job to a woman who is universally hated and feared by all, but she'll still be considered a better choice than me, so I'm not really sure what that says about me.

"No, no news Mum."

We chatted for a bit and she didn't mention the visit to the doctors, so I didn't ask her about it. Anyway, I wouldn't have trusted myself not to blub down the phone. That wouldn't have been very fair on her. I Googled "dementia". The word itself is taken from Latin, originally meaning madness. It was a depressing read, describing the illness as a 'long term decline'. I felt a glimmer of hope when I read that in some cases the symptoms were reversible, but this only occurred in less than 10% of cases.

I thought about calling my brother, but decided not to. Why ruin his evening, too? He was probably still enjoying his honeymoon period. I'd talk to him about it when he next called, or after Mum had been to see the specialist and we had more information. Why was this happening to my Mum; couldn't my parents just have the trouble-free, silver-lining slide into old age that they so deserved? Life was so bloody unfair. For the second night in a row, I sat on the floor and cried, before slapping myself in the face - *wimp, weed* - and putting the TV on to watch Homes From Hell. May as well wallow in someone else's misery for a while.

Wednesday

HR managed to email a version of the application form that we could actually open. Brett had said it would be simple and straightforward to complete. It didn't look it. The first half of the form was very similar to a CV, and you had to describe your last three jobs, along with your key responsibilities and achievements. Then you had a free format space to complete to say why you were a suitable candidate for the role. *Because I've been doing it for 12 years and no one's ever complained?* Then there was a section entitled "Key Proficiencies". This listed certain skills such as communication, leadership, influencing, arse-licking etc. and you had to give examples of times when you'd demonstrated these proficiencies. *My God, it was going to take forever.* Protesting emails started to fly around from managers saying the timescale (Monday) was ridiculous, but HR wouldn't budge, saying the deadline was "paramount" to the Perypils restructuring programme. At least I had the weekend to complete the form. It wasn't as if I had anything else planned.

In the evening I started to read as much as I could about dementia on the internet, including checking to see if it was hereditary and then feeling guilty for thinking about myself. Received a text which read: "You haven't forgotten me have you?!" It was from the Best Man. Oh God, I had forgotten. And forgetfulness was one of the major symptoms. Had it started already? I texted back, saying: "Yes! Very sorry. Will call you tomorrow evening if that's ok." I wrote it down on my Things I Really Must Do list, under Make a Will and Phone Auntie Jane, which had both been on the list for about a year.

Thursday

Bad weather had closed in, and the building was being buffeted by gales and lashed by driving rain. I got asked the question I always got asked in poor weather conditions, usually the second a snowflake flutters past the window: "Will we be sent home?" I told them if they saw a cow fly past the fourth floor window like in Twister then they could go home. There was a lot of grumbling at this point, and I could hear the admin team saying things like "the end is nigh" and making references to The Day after Tomorrow. I was dreading going home to see if my fence panels were still intact.

I received an email from Cruella which said Brett the Boss had asked her to arrange an emergency resource meeting with the managers so we could have the usual bun-fight over who gives up people to help the claims team in Bridgend. *Why did he ask her and not me?* Was she in charge now? It felt as if she had already won. I asked The Rock to attend for me. I couldn't bear being answerable to Cruella just now.

The pressure was getting to everyone. The Drain came back from the canteen flushed and angry after having had a stand-up row with one of the canteen ladies over the pieces of chicken in his chicken curry. He said there were only five, and refused to pay the £2.90 unless they gave him more chicken pieces. The canteen lady refused, saying that she was only allowed to dish out five pieces to each customer. The Drain had put down his curry and walked out, saying he'd never eat in there again. I said I thought he always brought sandwiches in for his lunch. Apparently his wife was spending every evening practising for a salsa competition and wasn't getting home until very late. When he'd suggested to her last night that she might be neglecting him and the children, he'd found a parsnip and two ping pong balls when he'd opened his lunch box. She didn't take kindly to criticism. He went off to devise a strongly worded letter to the canteen manager.

It was dark when I got home, so I took a torch out to the garden. There were no holes where the fence should be, which was a result, but I could see that one of the panels was flapping about in the wind. *Oh bugger, that would need sorting.* I remembered to phone Kieron. He was very chatty, and we had a laugh about the wedding, the dreadful song choices and the festive wedding breakfast. He wanted quotes for his buildings and contents insurance so I took lots of details from him and promised to get one of my guys to give him a call with some figures. He said he hadn't been able to work today because of the awful weather. I told him I had a wobbly fence panel.

"I could have a look at that for you if you like. Unless your husband can fix it of course, I wouldn't like to tread on his toes." *You can tread on his dick if you like, I don't care.* I told him that would be great if he could, and we arranged for him to call round on Saturday morning. Hooray! How brilliant, I might be able to get something fixed without having to wait weeks for the Husband to do it and having to chase him over and over. Kieron might be a very useful person to know.

Friday

The Snake had a glint in her eye and a jaunty slide in her slither. She told me that Lee Halfpenny had failed the final part of his progression plan as he hadn't met his quality targets - could we dismiss him now?

I told her to email his plan and any notes to HR and get them to arrange a final hearing. We might be getting somewhere at last.

I got caught by The Office Bore, who proceeded to tell

me without stopping to draw breath about her new three-piece suite, her grand-daughter's ballet lessons (she's the new Darcey Bussell apparently, although I've seen a photo and didn't realise Darcey was so rotund or squinted quite so badly), her friends' bed and breakfast, her husband's gout.... I almost screamed in her face: "Shut up shut up shut up! I couldn't give the tiniest shit!" but stopped myself by clenching my fists and digging my fingernails into my palms. Why did no one ask me how I was feeling? I was on the brink of losing my job. Why hadn't Brett phoned me to see if I was ok? Or texted, or emailed? It wouldn't have killed him. Come to that, why hadn't the Husband been in touch? I'd heard nothing from him all week, not since Monday when I'd accused him of stealing from me and sleeping with another woman. *Hmmm*, perhaps I shouldn't really expect to hear from him anytime soon.

Karen wanted to meet up for a drink in the evening but I was too drained from the week. I just wanted a glass of wine, a bar of Dairy Milk and the remote control. Flopped on the sofa. *Actually, this wasn't so bad, I could get used to this.* I might have to soon.

Saturday was another foul day, cold and wet and miserable. Kieron turned up and braved the rain to sort out the wobbly fence panel. I made him a coffee when he'd finished and we sat in the conservatory chatting and dunking my favourite Choco Leibniz (*chocolate lesbian!*) biscuits. He was such a nice guy, easy to talk to and very easy on the eye with his floppy fair hair, high cheek bones and lovely twinkly blue eyes. I half wished The Husband would turn up and fly into a jealous rage when he saw I was entertaining a good looking man in our house. Oh, who was I kidding? He probably wouldn't have cared less. Even if we'd been rolling around naked on the sheepskin rug he'd have just stepped over us, asking "Have you seen my trainers anywhere?"

Kieron had asked me where The Husband was. I'd said "Er, he's playing golf," and I could tell by the way he glanced outside at the sideways rain that he wasn't convinced. He wouldn't take any money for fixing the panel, but instead said I could buy him a drink sometime. As he was leaving, he said he was going to see a local jazz band play at The Mill that evening. Without thinking I exclaimed: "Oh God, how ghastly for you, I just hate jazz, it always sounds to me like a load of random instruments being tuned up!" He looked a bit crest-fallen and I could have kicked myself for being so crass - he was obviously a fan and he'd been so helpful. *I am a complete buffoon.*

I drove over to see my parents in the afternoon. My mum opened the door looking worried.

"Oh Kate, it's your father, he's not well at all." Was she confused? Did she think my father was the one that was ill and not her? I went to find my Dad. He was sat in their lounge with one of his legs propped up on the pouffe, his ankle wrapped in a bandage.

"Oh Dad, what have you done?" I cried.

"Those bloody doves!" he said, grimacing in pain. "All pecking the bloody lawn to pieces. I slipped on the steps and went arse over tit. Bloody ankle turned right over."

"You were chasing the doves?" I asked, examining the bandage, which had been very crudely applied.

"No, I was chasing a bloody cat that was chasing the bloody doves. Sodding things, they're a complete menace, those bloody idiots next door, couple of complete imbeciles."

I went to get some stronger pain killers from the pharmacy. Honestly, it was probably worse than having kids.

Sunday

There was nothing for it. I had to complete the application for my own job, tomorrow was the deadline. I got set up in the study with a percolator of strong coffee gurgling away in the kitchen. At least my CV was up to date after the sales manager debacle. The most difficult part was saying why I was a suitable candidate for the role. It's not easy to complete this for a job that you didn't actually want. I wrote:

"I have been in this role for 12 years, and could be considered to be performing well, although my boss does not speak to me very much or give me any feedback, so I've had to assume that no news is good news. I don't want to do the job anymore as it would be fair to say I've grown to detest the company, but I desperately need to keep in paid employment as my husband may be about to leave me high and dry and I don't want to have to live in a bed-sit that smells of cabbage. I can't stand the buggery bollocks bullshit spin from above, the stupid politics which I don't understand but often fall foul of, the willy-waving Boys' Club of which I'm obviously not a member, or the constant scape-goating in this no-blame culture. I know that in some jobs, although the role itself may be despised, its saving grace is the great people that you work with. Unfortunately, this isn't one of those jobs. The fact that I am having to complete this application makes me feel sick to my stomach with self-loathing and hatred. I am, however, excellent at disguising contempt, both for myself and for others, and I feel it is this skill that makes me the perfect candidate for this role in the Perypils management team."

I left that paragraph in place whilst I got on with the rest of the form. I would, of course, be deleting it later, not quite having the balls to submit it, but it felt good to have it there. Not that I should have worried - nobody would actually be reading the bloody form.

The box-filling took all day and into the evening. I finished it about midnight and went to bed, but couldn't sleep as my mind was still too active. Kieron had texted me to say "Thank you for introducing me to chocolate lesbians, it was my first time and I'm going to be having them more often from now on!" which had made me chuckle, but I'd heard nothing from the Husband all weekend. *Was that it, were we finished?* I realised I hadn't snooped around his Facebook pages for almost a week, and shocked myself by thinking that perhaps I just didn't care what he got up to anymore. Did I still love him? If I had to write an application for the position to remain as his wife, what would I write? Would I even want to apply?

CHAPTER TWENTY-SEVEN

All the managers had sent their forms to HR. I sat with Big Andy and The Shark in the canteen and had a good old moaning session. We'd all spent our Sundays completing the bloody form. Cruella was off sick, which was most unusual.

Big Andy boomed: "Well it can't be from stress, she's got nothing to be worried about!" and dug me in the ribs. *Cheers mate.* It was alright for him, nothing ever fazed him. The Shark was worried sick. He looked completely grey and he said he'd put his CV onto some job websites; he reckoned he'd be out of here soon. I made myself a note to do the same when I got home.

I asked if they knew when we'd hear anything, and Big Andy said that HR had told him the 23rd, which was weeks away.

"No point in worrying about it," he reckoned, "nothing we can do now. Just got to get on with it." He was right, but we all agreed it was so difficult to focus on anything with this bloody great thundercloud hanging over us.

The Husband called and left a message. Bruce was returning over the weekend so he would be back home on Saturday morning. He hoped that was ok with me. He suggested we went out for a meal on Saturday night so we could "have a talk". The arrogance of him, just assuming I didn't have any other plans! I didn't as it goes, but I decided I

325

would do now. The Climber was having her leaving do on Saturday night, and although I hadn't been intending to go - I could hardly think of anything worse - I thought it would be a good reason to get out of the house for the night. I phoned Karen. She said:

"So you're just going to let him waltz back in are you? Well, at least kick him out of the bedroom for a while, make him suffer. Don't let him back in until he's taken an aids test."

"What?"

"He may have picked up an STD. You can't be too careful Kate, you don't know where he's been."

Oh God. I could just imagine having that conversation with him, he'd go loopy. It was a good idea about separate bedrooms though, at least initially - it would seem a bit weird getting into bed together when we'd barely spoken in weeks. For some reason, I felt the urge to make sure the house was immaculate. I had been keeping it tidy anyway - it's so much easier with just one of you - but I wanted to show him how well I'd coped. I dusted, hoovered, and shiny-sinked as if my life depended on it, and put fresh flowers in vases around the house. I moved the clothes that he'd left behind into the spare bedroom and made up the bed. I was sure he wouldn't be very happy with this arrangement, but tough titties.

I didn't know what time he would be home on Saturday, but I went out early into town, so he wouldn't think I had nothing better to do than to wait around for him. I left him a curt note saying I thought it was best if he slept in the spare room for now and that I was going out this evening. I spent the morning window-shopping in town, which was crammed full of Christmas shoppers *how utterly depressing* and then went to see my parents in the afternoon. I got home around four, thinking I would breeze in, get myself ready to go out and breeze out again. Nonchalant; that was the impression I wanted to give.

His car was in the drive. I opened the front door, and the hall was already in a mess - he'd left several bags and pairs of shoes lying around, and his wash bag was sat on the stairs, waiting for the magic stair-fairy to carry it up. I found him in the study, hunched over his laptop.

"You're back," I said, not smiling.

"Yes, hi," he said, rising to give me an awkward dry peck on the cheek. "I found your note. Actually, I found it after I'd put all my stuff back in our room, so I had to take everything back out again." *Ah, poor you.* Your first sentence since you arrived back home and you've already blamed me for something.

He gestured towards the laptop. "I thought as you were going out tonight and we won't be able to talk, I'd start on a list of things I wanted us to cover." *You're not serious?* "When I've finished, I'll print it out so you can have a read and we can discuss it, you know, when you've got the time."

I looked at the screen. I could make out the title at the top which read: "Things I'd like us to change". The list looked pretty long already.

"Right, well," I said brightly, "I'll look forward to receiving that then. I might make my own and then we could compare. I daresay I'll see you sometime in the morning, but I may be feeling a little rough. I've got a big night out planned."

"I'm playing golf in the morning," he said, turning back to the lap top, not interested in my arrangements. "I don't know what time I'll be back."

I didn't say anything else. I made myself a cup of tea without offering to make one for him, which I'd never done before. Had I expected him to slink back into the house with his tail between his legs, declare his undying love for me and beg for forgiveness? Perhaps I had expected that. Instead he'd swaggered back into town like a gunfighter in a bad western, declaring "Things are gonna change around here." The note had obviously got up his nose, but I'd intended it to. I knew I wasn't helping myself, but I wasn't going to be a bloody doormat. And now I had to go and spend the evening with The Climber and a load of my pissed-up staff. *Nose, Face, cut off.*

I got dressed up in the 'youngest' outfit I could find, a black tunic (or it might be a dress) with a purple paisley pattern on it (Monsoon, where else? I really ought to broaden my horizons a bit), thick black tights and black stilettos. The tunic/dress felt a bit too short, so I slipped a short black skirt on underneath. I tried to make my hair look a bit funky by scrunching up the ends using some ridiculously expensive moulding gunk I'd bought on a whim from the hairdressers. It looked like I'd been dragged through a hedge backwards - then forwards, then backwards again. I blasted it with hairspray. If anyone struck a match near me I'd be lit up like a fecking Christmas tree. I looked at myself in the bathroom mirror. Had I achieved a young funky look? *Had I buggery.* A crazy-haired, forty-something peered back at me through tired eyes, which had far too much eye liner round them. *God, I looked knackered.* I applied another lashing of Touche Éclat under my eyes, then another. I wouldn't be able to afford this stuff when I was out of work. I'd have to make eye liner out of bits of charcoal found at the bottom of the barbeque and use red Smarties as lipstick.

I ordered a taxi to take me into town, which was decadent, but it was bloody cold out. I went to the loo before I left, noticing too late that the toilet roll had run out and not been replaced. *Typical.* I left the house without saying goodbye. *Sod him.* As I entered the pub, I instantly felt over-dressed. Two girls pushed past me, both dressed in very short denim shorts, bare legs and huge great block-heeled shoes they could hardly walk in. Another girl stood at the bar wearing a jazzy-patterned pair of leggings and tiny cropped top. She'd catch her death of cold, surely. The Climber was sat at a table with about ten others from work. Although it was only six thirty, I'd say they'd made a very early start. My arrival was met with the roar "The manager gets the drinks in!" so I went to the bar to get a couple of bottles of wine for the table.

The pub was very busy with most tables already full. As I waited at the bar, I saw a young guy seated at a table to my left put his head down on his arms and throw up on the floor. His vomit was completely blue. I looked away, feeling queasy. I ordered the wine - unbelievably it was buy one bottle get the other free. The miserable barman said it was happy hour until seven. That explained why the place was packed. The blue-vomit guy had been quickly marched out of the pub by his friends. A group of girls came over and quickly sat down to nab the table. They obviously hadn't seen. As I walked past, I heard one of them start squealing in disgust. *What a classy place.*

I put the wine down on our table and poured myself a large glass. It was a bit vinegary, but I didn't care. I couldn't get through tonight sober. I poured a glass for The Climber. She was full of herself as usual, telling us all about all the amazing nightclubs in Manchester she would soon be going to and how she would be rubbing shoulders with footballers and celebrities. As well as wine, they were all drinking something called Jäger Bombs. They tried to get me to have one, but I refused after I got one of them to look up the number of calories on their iPhone. 158!

I asked The Climber if any of the others were coming. She said that Martin couldn't make it as he was at a 50th birthday party at the community centre, Cynthia couldn't make it as she had "one of her groups", whatever that was and Jan couldn't make it as she'd said she was too old to be out on the town. I knew what she meant. I asked about George.

"Oh yes, he's here somewhere," said The Climber, reaching out to pour herself more wine. I looked round and saw TLS George stood at the far end of the bar, passionately snogging a young girl. I squinted at them.

"Who's that he's trying to eat?"

"Oh I don't know! He's always at it with some little tart or other. Someone else's girlfriend usually."

I looked a bit closer. Was that... no surely not. It was, it was Georgia! For Heaven's sake, she was only fifteen! She shouldn't be in here. Was she drinking? It looked like it. What should I do? Should I go and break it up and tell George how old she was? Phone the Bunny Boiler, or my brother? I had to be careful, Georgia was capable of making a right old scene when she was drunk. I decided to text my brother. He texted back saying that the Bunny Boiler was in town too and he'd let her know. I kept my head down.

Ten minutes later, the Bunny Boiler came storming in. She picked out her daughter and pushed her way through the crowd at the bar, grabbed Georgia by the hair and wrenched her backwards. Georgia shrieked and tried to wriggle free. TLS George looked stunned. The Bunny Boiler aimed a punch at George, screaming "Paedophile!" and wrestled Georgia out of the pub to general hoots and cheers. I sincerely hoped Georgia didn't find out it was me who'd dobbed her in. George and Georgia. *Oh my God.* What a pairing that was.

The evening limped on. I had hoped we might go somewhere for a nice meal, but none of them showed any signs of wanting to eat anything. All I wanted to do was go home, but I couldn't face going back early. I was determined to pretend to the Husband that I was having a great time without him. I ended up playing chaperone to the seriously drunk Climber. She was making a right show of herself, stumbling around knocking into people and getting very lairy when they protested. She fell right over at one point, and I had to help her up, which wasn't very easy. She was also attracting a great deal of predatory alpha male attention, and I was constantly swatting groping hands away from her. She missed a call on her iPhone at one point and squinted at the screen.

"Oh look, it was Brett. Shall I call him back and tell him what a tosspot he is?" When I told her that wasn't such a great idea, she passed the phone to me and said, "You tell him Kate, go on, call him and tell him he's a tosser!" *I would have loved to have made that call.* Still, probably not a good time, with my job still hanging in the balance. I told her I'd do it after the jobs had been announced. She said "Oh you'll be fine, Brett really fancies you. He told me." *Really?*

"Well, he said if it was a choice between you or Clare he'd do you." *Charming.* How professional. To my shame, I felt a stab of happiness that Brett found me more attractive than Cruella. I really was a very sad individual.

It was almost 2.00 am before I managed to get The Climber into a cab and persuade TLS George to go with her and make sure she got home safely. He wasn't keen - she was almost certain to be sick on him. I gratefully got into my own taxi, not feeling a bit drunk, just worn out with playing the mother-hen all evening. I wasn't cut out for a nurturing role, that's why management suited me so much.

The house was in darkness when I got back and I made as much noise as possible when I got in. Childish I know, but small victories.

I got up extremely late on Sunday morning. The house was quiet, The Husband had gone out to play golf. I munched a bowl of cereal as I drifted through the downstairs rooms, which had been in pristine condition yesterday, but were now a complete mess again. In the spare bedroom - The Husband's room as I could now call it - he had bags and bits of clothing strewn everywhere. Yesterday's socks lay on the floor. That always drove me mad. Why couldn't he just pick the bloody things up, it only takes a second. Oh dear - had I become a nagging wife? Is that why he'd had to get away?

I went into the study, and saw on the printer a page listing the things he wanted to talk to me about. I had a read:

"Things I'd like us to change - a discussion document":

> ➤ Work life balance - a maximum of one hour per evening to be spent on work, and two hours at the

weekend. It is not acceptable to 'build up' credits, i.e. if you do not work on a Monday evening you cannot carry this hour forward, you lose it. *So you're dictating how I should spend my evenings and weekends? Are you going to be stood over me with a stop watch?*

➢ Holidays - each to have one separate holiday/weekend during the year when we are free to go away with friends, or on our own. One joint holiday which will be a two week block. During the joint two weeks, we must experience one new activity i.e. sky diving, white water rafting, sailing etc. *You're having a fucking laugh.*

➢ Going out - we will try one new restaurant each month, and use this as an opportunity to discuss how things are going and air any problems or issues. *Ooh, that will be fun.*

➢ Washing the cars - we are responsible for washing our own. *You lazy bastard! That's the only thing you do for me! Why haven't you mentioned the housework, the gardening, the weekly shop? Shall I just mow one half of the lawn next time? Clean half the bath? Just shop for myself? Cut the soap in half?*

➢ Car maintenance - we are responsible for maintaining our own. *Oh great, I'll probably put oil in the screenwash again.*

➢ Use of the study - it is not practical for both of us to use the study at the same time, so a rota needs to be drawn up - and kept to. *I hardly ever use it! You're always in there. You're just referring to the one time about a year ago when I was in there and you got the hump because you couldn't play online carting with James.*

➢ Finances - 25% of any bonus or additional earnings to be placed in a joint savings account to be used on house/garden repairs. *That's hardly fair is it? You know I get more bonuses than you do.*

➢ Maintaining a healthy size and weight - we are responsible for ourselves, but should consider our diet - suggest two meals per week protein only (no carbs) and no chocolate to be kept in the house. *Now you've gone too far. And is that a dig at my protruding stomach and mysterious back fat? I can still get into my size 12 clothes you know, the same size I was twenty years ago. Perhaps they do make the sizes bigger now, but that's not the point.*

I sat and looked at the list. Separate holidays, sky diving for Christ's sake, rotas, regimented work hours, protein-only meals - had our marriage really come to this? Plus it was all on his terms. I was surprised he hadn't added anything about sex, such as "We'll have one session on our own, or with friends and then one joint session which will be a two minute block. During the two minute block we must experience one new activity, such as muff-diving, donkey-punching, rimming etc."

I thought about creating my own list, but whilst it would have made me feel better, I knew it would be counter-productive. Instead, I phoned Karen and read the list out to her. I thought she'd be her usual militant self and suggest I ripped it into tiny pieces and stuff it into his big gob, but she was strangely reserved.

"Well, it all sounds a bit self-centred, Kate, but at least you know what's on his mind now, the things that bug him, and it seems as if he's trying, well, you know, he wants to discuss them at any rate. Gets it all out in the open. That's what you've got to do - if you want to carry on together that is."

I was silent.

"Kate? Do you want to carry on with him?"

"I don't know," I sighed. "I just don't know. I'm still suspicious about him and Debbie, I don't know if something went on or not. He says not, but I don't know if I believe him. And I think I've got quite used to being on my own over these last weeks, and you know what? It's not that bad. I've been part of a couple ever since I was fifteen - once I'd discovered eye liner and push-up bras I was never short of a fella and I've been scared of being on my own. But I reckon it's better than being unhappy. Miles better in fact. I even managed to get a fence panel fixed within a couple of days. It would have taken him months to get round to it."

"Well, your head's probably all over the place," said Karen. "Don't forget you're worrying about work too, and your Mum. Best not to make any rash decisions. That would be my advice. I think he was doffing Debbie - the way she would turn up at the pub, pretending it was a co-incidence. What bullshit. They'd planned it, I bet you any money you like. But you need to get some real evidence. Have you managed to look at his text messages yet?"

"That's the point though, Karen, I don't want to be in a relationship where I have to look at text messages, go through pockets and all that crap. I can't stand uncertainty. And life's too bloody short."

"Why don't you see what happens with your job, and get Christmas out of the way? See how it goes and use the New Year to start afresh - either together or on your own. Don't make a snap decision now."

She was right of course. But I liked to make snap decisions, I couldn't bear indecisiveness. I wasn't able to settle to anything for the rest of the day, and found myself continually glancing out of the front windows, waiting for his car to pull into the drive. I made up a beef casserole and put it in the oven to cook slowly - call it a peace offering. He arrived home just as it was starting to get dark.

"Hi," I called from the kitchen. "How was golf?"

"Dreadful," he said grumpily. "One of the worst rounds I've ever played. My back was aching very badly, so I couldn't get my swing right. I think it's because I had to sleep in the spare bed last night, that mattress is rubbish." *Yes of course, that would be my fault then.*

"Oh dear," I said, feigning concerned sympathy. "Well, we can always swap the mattresses round if it helps. I've made us a nice casserole for tonight, and I thought we could open a bottle of red. You never know, that might help ease the pain." He shot me a look to see if I was being sarcastic but I smiled warmly back. He went to select a bottle of wine and came back to the kitchen to open it.

"I read your list," I said, attempting a light tone.

He looked surprised. "What list?"

"You know, what you want us to change. It was on the printer. Where you left it."

"Oh, I must have printed it out by accident. That wasn't the finished version, it was just a start." *Bloody hell.* I accepted a glass of wine and took a big gulp.

"So do you want to talk about it then? I mean, what you've written so far?"

"Oh no, not yet," he frowned. "No point until it's

finalised. Then we can have a proper chat about things. What time will the casserole be ready? I've got some stuff to do, I'll be in the study." *Have you checked the rota, is it your turn to use the study?* He was impossible to talk to when he was in a bad mood. However, three glasses of wine later and he'd mellowed. We sat down to the casserole and I told him all about work and what was happening with my mum. He was sympathetic, and halfway through the second bottle, he was getting a bit sentimental, saying that he was glad to be home and how much he wanted to make things work. He started rubbing at his back and making "ooh ouch" noises, but I stood my ground and said we should stick to separate bedrooms and take things slowly. He looked a bit sulky but was forced to agree that this seemed sensible.

And so we fell back into our routine of sorts. I felt like I was treading on eggshells all the time, mindful of 'the list' and taking care not to get caught doing too much work in the evenings. After a week or so had passed, I asked him if he had finished the list, and he said almost, and suggested we used it to form our New Year's resolutions. He was probably just too lazy to finish it off.

CHAPTER TWENTY-EIGHT

Work was horribly hectic. With The Climber gone, the others now had larger teams, and what with a spell of bad weather, volumes of calls were through the roof. We were all feeling the strain. It didn't help that Martin The Drain was off sick again. I phoned him to see what was wrong. He said he was suffering from an anxiety attack - his wife had told him she was in love with her salsa teacher and was leaving him. They'd gone to a 50th birthday party where the DJ was a big Ricky Martin fan. He'd called his wife up onto the dance floor to show them all her salsa moves. She couldn't dance a step. The DJ had dragged her round the floor like a rag doll. When they got home he'd confronted her about all the lessons she'd been having and she'd broken down and confessed: it was mainly horizontal dancing that he'd been teaching her. All the new outfits she'd bought were just so she could dress sexily for him. The Drain was in bits. I checked he had the Perypils counselling number, which of course, he knew off by heart, but there was not much else I could do for the poor sod.

TLS George also had a couple of days off sick, and returned to work with a black eye and bruised hand. He said it was a footballing injury, but The Snake told me that a jealous boyfriend had caught up with him. At least, that was according to Facebook.

On the 23rd, I came into work expecting to hear about my job. I hadn't slept a wink and my stomach was churning. I kept nipping in and out of the loo. By lunchtime, there was still no news. I phoned Big Andy. He hadn't heard anything either. At around 3 pm, HR sent an email round to say that the job announcements would be put back a week. They didn't give a reason. *God, after all that.* Emails started to fly around saying it wasn't fair, managers making the point that we were given less than a week to complete our applications but HR could take as long as they wanted to make a decision. Brett the Boss didn't call me, or email me. Had he called Cruella? She was keeping her head down. She probably already knew she'd got the job so was keeping out of my way.

A week came and went. Another email from HR told us we would have to wait until 13th December. They blamed the unions this time, accusing them of dragging their feet. That was going to be a great Christmas present. What did Santa bring you this year? Well, let me see, redundancy followed by mortgage arrears, followed by homelessness, followed by prostitution.

Lee Halfpenny's piss-poor-performance hearing was set for the 4th December. Darren, one of the managers from Bridgend was coming down to do it. On the morning of the 4th, Lee phoned in sick with a stomach upset.

I called Darren who said: "But I've just driven over the bridge - I'll have to pay six fucking pounds to go back over it now." I didn't really know what to say to that. We rescheduled the hearing for 11th.

I was getting worried about Christmas Day, as at the moment, the plan was it would just be me and the Husband. My parents were going to my brother's for the day. I think the Bunny Boiler was going to be knocking up a rabbit stew. I hadn't bought anything yet for the Husband, I didn't know what I should do. We were usually quite generous with each other, but this year it didn't seem appropriate, it would seem false to shower each other with gifts. I'd have to talk to him about it. I'd phoned my Dad to see what they wanted for Christmas.

"A shot-gun for me and a trip to a Swiss clinic for your mother." Not exactly helpful. He had at last received a hospital appointment for my mum to see a specialist in January. He told me he'd phoned to check that they meant "this bleeding January and not the next."

11th December - Lee was still off sick with a mysterious stomach virus. I rescheduled the hearing for 18th December after doing battle with HR, who told me that Perypils did not like to dismiss their colleagues so close to Christmas, and therefore the hearing would have to wait until the New Year. I told them no way was I going to pay that useless little shit any longer than was absolutely necessary.

The snotty HR woman said to me "Do you realise how serious it is for people to lose their jobs?" *Ha ha!* I told her I was about to find out, and that Perypils seemed to have no problem announcing management redundancies so close to Christmas. Why don't the usual rules and courtesies apply to managers too? No contact from Brett the Boss. Was he still alive?

15th December. I arrived at work, nerves in tatters. First stop - the loo. I jumped every time the phone went. Just before 11.00, Brett called me on my mobile. *Oh no, here we go.* I braced myself. I'd decided I was going to be very adult and professional about this, and I would not break down and cry and call him a knobhead.

"Hi Brett." I knew I had a wobbly sheep's voice.

"Kate, hi," he said. "I'm calling everyone today with the outcome of the recent applications following the restructure." He paused. "It's really tough you know, I'm having to have some really difficult conversations today." *Oh poor you! Are you seriously expecting sympathy? Just tell me, you spineless piece of crap.*

"Yes, well," he continued when I didn't say anything. "It's been extremely difficult, and we're having to lose some really good people." *Here we go.* "However, good news for you Kate, I'm very pleased to tell you that your application was successful and I can confirm you in the role." *I'd got the job? Had I heard that correctly?* That was the last thing I'd expected him to say - I was absolutely astounded.

"Of course, it will be a stretch, I know that," he was still talking. "You'll be doubling your numbers, and taking on customer complaints, which is an extremely demanding department. But I know you've got the capabilities to do this Kate, you're far and away the best person to take on this challenge. I've always known that. And remember, I'm always here to support you."

I stammered out some thanks. He asked me not to discuss it with anyone until after an official announcement was made by the communications team at midday. Had he phoned the right person? Would he phone me back in a few minutes and say, "Oh sorry about that, I thought I was talking to someone else." My head was whirling. *On my God, I'd got the job!* It was a job I didn't bloody want, and it would be a completely impossible job to do, but I still felt on top of the world that I'd got it. I'd beaten Cruella! It was a victory for people skills over the cruel lemon-lipped bullies. Hoorah! Perhaps the Perypils hierarchy was changing after all; maybe it would become a really great place to work, like it says on all the posters.

I was dying to tell everyone, but I had to wait for the announcement. I wondered how the others had got on. Just after midday, the communications team sent an email round detailing the new management structure, which would come into effect on the first of January. Brett was keeping his job, *how, how?* The Boys Club at work of course. Big Andy was in, but The Shark was not on the structure. His rival and totally coincidentally close friend of the Chief Exec was named instead. Cruella was missing too, of course. The email had gone out to everyone, so my phone was soon ringing with congratulations and my inbox filling up. I felt I really ought to go and see Cruella, but decided that today was too soon. It was very awkward. Perhaps I'd try and see her tomorrow. What would I say? *Tough shit loser!* No, no, I would be gracious, she must be distraught.

I received an email from Cruella's deputy, Mini-Me:
"Hi Kate.

As I understand you are to be our new manager, I would be grateful if we could discuss the team's shift patterns at your earliest opportunity. The shifts are causing much tension between the teams and badly affecting morale. Also I should like to request the weeks commencing 4th and 11th July as my two weeks holiday next year. Clare has turned this request down once, but I felt this was extremely unfair and I would like you to reconsider. Can you please let me know as soon as possible, I wish to book my flights to Poland and arrange a tour of Auschwitz. Thank you."

She was going to be trouble. And shift patterns, I hated dealing with shifts. I'd get The Rock to sort them out; she was great at things like that.

My guys all came up to say well done. I knew they were hugely relieved not to be working under Cruella. I phoned Big Andy with congratulations. He told me to stay away from The Shark as he'd "kicked off big time" when he'd been given the bad news and was not taking it at all well. I said I would steer clear.

Then he said: "Good news for you Kate. That was a stroke of luck about Cruella, wasn't it? You must have been pissing yourself."

"What do you mean, a stroke of luck?"

"Oh come on Kate, don't tell me you didn't know!"

"No, know what?"

"That she's pregnant! It was the worst kept secret in the building. She tried to cover it up under baggy jackets and huge great handbags, but you could see she's got quite a bump there. And she kept taking time off with morning sickness. They were never going to give the job to a pregnant woman, that's why she did her best to hide it. But it seems word got out. You know what this place is like."

I was speechless. So I didn't get the role because I was "far and away the best person". I got it because Cruella was up the duff.

"But that's, that's immoral!" I said, finding myself outraged on Cruella's behalf.

"Yep," he said, "It sure is. She's fuming of course, says she's going to sue them." He paused. "Do you think it happened by immaculate conception? I mean, someone would have had to have sex with her otherwise. I can't think of anyone who's that brave. Or do you think she used a turkey baster? Perhaps she advertised...."

He twittered on, but I wasn't listening. Brett was a lying little sod who'd shafted Cruella because he knew she was pregnant and made me think I'd been first choice all along. I'd been his only choice. I hoped Cruella did sue them, sue the bloody arses off them. I felt stupid for thinking I'd got the job on merit. So much for the Perypils hierarchy changing for the better. It was only getting worse. *The bastards.* I seriously thought about handing in my resignation. No, not today, but I'd do it in the New Year. I had to get another job first. I would put my CV on every jobsite I could find and get out of here as soon as I could. Enough was enough.

At home The Husband opened a bottle of champagne and we had a Chinese take-away by way of celebration. I didn't tell him about Cruella being pregnant, I wanted to feel successful for once, even though I knew it wasn't real.

CHAPTER TWENTY-NINE

18th December - Lee Halfpenny's hearing was due to take place at 11.00 am. The Snake appeared at my desk at 10.30 am holding out a letter. He'd resigned. *Oh, deep joy!* What a relief. Hissing Cyn was desperately disappointed that we wouldn't be sacking him.

"But can't we go ahead with the hearing anyway?" she wailed. "After all that effort, the time I've spent on him and his, his issues, all those file notes, meetings - he just gets away with it? So he can go and do the same at another company?"

I had complete sympathy for her. But I couldn't change anything. She slid despondently back to her desk, and was completely hidden behind Lee's mountainous HR file. I phoned Darren in Bridgend who was coming to do the hearing. He had already reached Cheltenham.

He said "Oh for fu...." and then his line broke up.

Most of my online Christmas shopping had turned up, but I still hadn't got anything for The Husband. I thought I would search online for some iPad accessories. They wouldn't be delivered before Christmas, but I could always say I'd ordered them but they hadn't arrived in time. I could show him the pictures on Christmas Day. He had an evening appointment so he was out of the house. I went into the study and lifted the cover from the iPad. The screen icons looked different. That was odd. Oh, it must be The Husband's new one, I hadn't used it before. For some reason

I turned it over. It was engraved on the back with two small words: "For Goofy".

I stared at the words. Why had he had that engraved? Why Goofy, who called him Goofy? I felt as if a cold bucket of sick had been thrown over me. *Debbie*. Debbie had called him Goofy when we were surfing in Devon. "For Goofy". So had she bought him the iPad? That was five hundred quid at least. You wouldn't spend that amount on someone unless... unless they meant something really special to you.

I sat motionless in the study. So was it true after all? There was something going on between them. Was there any other explanation for that engraving? I didn't think so. How long had it been going on for? Did she want me to find out, is that why she'd gone for the naff free engraving service when she'd bought the iPad? Or did she think he wasn't going to be returning home after our "trial separation"? I put my head in my hands to make it stop reeling. I couldn't stand all these questions, I hated this feeling of nausea that just kept swelling up from my stomach.

I didn't deserve this, it wasn't fair, *it was Christmas*. I fought off the tears. *No. No more wimpy weedy behaviour*. I had to stop feeling sorry for myself and be strong. He said he had an evening appointment, but possibly he was out with her. Perhaps they were exchanging gifts as they wouldn't be together at Christmas. I phoned him. It went to voicemail. I left him a message: "Can you come home as soon as possible. We need to talk." Two minutes later the phone rang. It was him. I let it go to voicemail. He left a message, sounding a little apprehensive:

"Er, are you there Kate? No? I think you just called me. I'm just finishing my appointment. Should be home in about twenty. Ok?"

Twenty minutes. About the time it took to drive from Debbie's. If he was there. Where was Paul? Away again? Night out? The Devil Child presumably went to her doting grandparents. I wondered from room to room, and took a big swig from the brandy bottle to fight off the nausea. I was seated at the kitchen table with the iPad in front of me when I heard his key in the lock. He came in, looking round the kitchen for signs that I'd cooked him some supper. I hadn't.

"Hi," he said, sounding a bit unsure of himself. "Everything ok? What's the plan for tea?" *The plan is to see if I can fit this iPad up your arse. If I can shove it up far enough you should be able eat that.*

"You need to explain this to me," I said bluntly. I showed him the engraving on the back of his iPad. He read it and went white. Had he actually noticed it before?

"Er well, it's what they call me at work." He was flustered.

"Everyone at work calls you Goofy?"

"Yes, that's right."

"So who bought the iPad?"

"Well I bought it, well no actually, it was a gift from work. Part of my bonus." *That was quick thinking.*

"That's very unusual isn't it? Did everyone get one?"

"Er, yes, no, I mean I'm not sure if everyone got one. It depended on how well you'd done, against your target."

"You told me you bought it for yourself, out of your bonus."

He sat down opposite me at the kitchen table. I drummed my nails on the pine surface and looked at him. He looked at me. He looked defeated.

"Did Debbie buy you the iPad?"

He didn't respond.

"I'll take that as a yes then," I said. My heart was racing. "And as it's such a generous gift I guess you were giving her something in return."

"It was just a present," he said feebly. "She and Paul are loaded, you know that, it's not a great deal of money to them."

"Oh, so it was a gift from Paul too? So if I call him he'll confirm that will he?" I picked up my mobile.

"No no, don't do that!" The Husband, horrified, tried to grab the phone from me. "It's late, Chloë will be in bed. You'll upset them."

"I'll upset *them*?" I was angry now. "Have you thought for just one second how I might be feeling? I can't believe you're still trying to deny it and wriggle your way out of it like a, like a-" *(dammit, I couldn't think of anything that wriggled)*, "like a wriggly thing. Why can't you just grow a pair of balls and tell me what's been going on? Debbie bought you that iPad, didn't she?"

Silence. "Well, didn't she?"

"Yes." He looked down at the table top.

I took a deep breath. "And she did that because you are more than just friends. Aren't you?"

"It's over," he said to the table.

"Sorry, what?"

"It's over." He looked up at me, putting his hurt little boy face on. "There was something, but it's over, finished. I'm sorry."

So there it was. *At last.* A confession. I'd hoped and hoped it wasn't true, I'd been in denial, but it was true, it had happened. Of course it had happened. I wanted to be sick.

He was trying to gauge how I was going to react, what I was going to do.

"It was nothing really, I mean it meant nothing," he was saying. "We were both a bit unhappy, you know, unsettled, both you and Paul work such long hours-"

"So you thought you'd fill in some time by shagging each other?" I spat at him, "Don't you dare blame me and Paul for your disgusting behaviour! You're pathetic."

I stood up and filled the kettle. God knows why, I certainly didn't want a cup of tea but I just had to do something.

"No, no, of course I'm not blaming you," he said, like he was talking to a four year old. I wanted to scream. "I'm just trying to explain to you why it happened. We didn't mean it to, we tried our best to fight it-"

"When did it start?"

"Well, I can't really remember. It's not important. What is important is that it-"

"It is bloody important to me! When did it start? Before Devon? Afterwards? Earlier?"

He thought for a moment, clearly trying to decide if he should be honest or not. "It was probably around Devon I think, maybe a bit before that, I don't know."

"Oh my God! So we spent the weekend with them and you were already at it! You'd both planned it, so you could take a holiday together. How could you be so sly, so devious? Weren't you sick from shame? Their child was there too, and Paul's parents. You're disgusting, both of you."

He tried to back-track. "But nothing had really happened up until then - it was that weekend, she told me how she felt, but we kind of already knew. We couldn't stop ourselves, we did try..." *Those late nights drinking brandy together.* With a wife and a husband and a daughter asleep in the same house. *How very classy.*

I held my hands up. "I don't want to hear any more. You know, it's not so much the thought of you two together that sickens me as much as you lying to my face. You making me feel like I was a piece of shit for thinking the worst. We've been married for twelve years and you could just lie to me like that. You're a bare-faced liar. What else do you lie to me about? What else are you capable of? I don't think I really know who you are anymore."

"You're being over-dramatic–"

"Oh am I really?" I brandished a coffee mug at him. It had 'I'd Rather Be Surfing' printed on it. "I don't think so. I think I'm entitled to a bit of drama when I find out that my husband is a lying cheating deceitful rat. Does Paul know anything? No? Thought not. I bet you two have had a right old laugh behind our backs, what a pair of bloody mugs we are."

"You're not going to tell him are you?" The Husband looked scared. "I can't see what good it would do now, you don't want to split a family up surely? There's no point now, not when it's all over and done with. It's not fair on the kid." *You really are a piece of work.*

"Did you think about the kid while you two were at it like rabbits?" That sounded very wrong, I hadn't meant it to come out like that. "And it might be over and done with in your mind, but it's not in mine. I want you to leave."

He looked at me in alarm. "Leave? But where would I go? Look, I know you're angry, yes you've every right to be, but can't we talk about this? I know we can get through this. Other couples do you know, it doesn't have to be the end."

"Yes it does," I said. I suddenly felt very calm and clear. "I want you to leave. *Now.*"

"God, this is so typical of you," he said getting up, the little boy lost act disappearing. "Always over-reacting, making a drama out of everything. Well, I'm not going to leave. I've every right to be here. It's half my house and it's Christmas for God's sake."

He caught himself and tried to soften his manner. "Look love, I know you've had a shock and I'm truly sorry. But it was just a bit of silliness, and it's over. I suggest we get through Christmas and try and start afresh in the New Year, yes? Let the dust settle a bit. See how you feel then. You don't want to spend Christmas on your own do you? And it would upset your parents, your poor Mum, she'd be ever so confused wouldn't she? She wouldn't understand what was happening. Don't let's be hasty, you may always regret it. What do you think?"

"I think you're a total shit. How dare you use my mother's illness to try and emotionally blackmail me? Just how low are you prepared to sink?" I picked up my mobile again.

"Either you leave now or I'm going to call Paul and tell him what you've been doing with his wife," I said. "I don't care about their Devil Child, I don't care that it's Christmas, it's just another day in the sodding calendar. And I don't want to spend another day of my life anywhere near you. It's your choice."

He looked trapped. Was he going to stay and risk me phoning Paul? He was desperate for Paul not to know, probably scared he'd get beaten to a pulp. He came to a decision.

"Well, if you're quite determined to split up a family, *at Christmas*, just out of some kind of petty revenge then I guess you've given me no choice but to go."

"Do you really believe you hold the moral high ground here? When did you become such a knob? Oh just go will you, just get away from me. You make me sick."

He paused, waiting for me to change my mind. I brandished the phone at him. He turned on his heel and stormed up the stairs. I heard him banging around in his room, opening and slamming drawers, getting some things together. He still had some stuff in bags that he hadn't bothered to unpack since he'd come back from Bruce's, so that would save him some time.

For something to do, I opened a bottle of wine and started to make myself a Philadelphia sandwich, and although I wasn't hungry, forced myself to eat it. He came into the kitchen to snatch up his iPad and to glare at me, but I ignored him. He eventually started to take some bags out to his car. When he'd finished he came back to the kitchen to double-check that I hadn't changed my mind. I hadn't.

"I'm going to Keith's," he said. I looked blank. "Keith from golf. He says I can kip in his spare room. It's just a tiny box room..."

I shrugged.

"Well, have a happy Christmas then, won't you?" he said, sarcastically. "And don't go changing the locks because I should remind you that it's my home too and I'm not leaving for good. Just for, well, just until..." he tailed off. He waited again for me to say something, to change my mind, to say everything was all right, but I didn't. He turned and left, slamming the front door so hard that the whole house shook. His car was revved up angrily, and then the house was silent again, just like the time he'd left to go to Bruce's.

But it was different this time. I felt different. It felt right that he was gone. It was like some horrible dark presence that had been lurking in a corner, had finally been exorcised. He'd made a fool of me, and as much as I hadn't wanted to believe it, I think I'd known it all along.

I felt such relief - I wasn't going mad, I wouldn't be boiling anyone's bunnies today. Although that fake, false trollop Debbie had better lock up her hutches. She could expect a visit from me sometime soon. She wasn't going to get away scot-free, *no way*.

I realised that for the first time in my life, after 42 Christmas's, I would be spending this one totally alone. *What bliss. What joy.* I could curl up on the sofa in my jim-jams and watch wall-to-wall crap telly. I wouldn't have to get all red-faced and sweaty cooking a great big roast, and open presents with a fake smile on my face. I could have a Christmas cheese toastie if that's what I felt like. I could even put some Marmite on it now – I no longer had to listen to the Husband making sick noises whilst I ate it. Thank goodness I hadn't splashed out on a Christmas present for him. Instead, I could treat myself to something fluffy and frivolous from Monsoon. Perhaps one of those hairy jumpers he hated so much, because the fluff got up his nose.

I wondered into the spare bedroom. A stray sock looked reproachfully up at me from the floor. I scooped it up and threw it straight into the bin. *Gone. For good.* I wrapped my arms protectively around myself. I would be starting the New Year as a single woman. It was scary, but it was exciting too. I would try really hard to exercise and lose my second stomach and back fat. I'd have to start after Christmas of course, but by Springtime, I would be running through wild flower meadows looking slim-waisted and bronze-limbed. I would find myself a new man. Maybe one that thought I was actually "wow", and not just an acronym. If I searched enough institutions I was bound to find someone sooner or later. Perhaps I'd have a chance encounter with James Martin who'd fall in love with me and let me smear him with Angel Delight night after night. I would find myself a new job too, a better job, one I could feel proud of. My new colleagues would be cheerful and competent with perfect bowel function. Yes, I was really looking forward to Christmas this year.

At work, the call volumes were dropping off and spirits were high as they always were during Christmas week. The whole department was covered in sparkly tinsel and every flat surface held tins of chocolates and boxes of mince pies. An email had gone round asking the person who had sent Stalin Stan a card with a picture of Santa wearing a swastika armband to own up. There was no budget this year for staff Christmas presents so I bought bottles of wine for everyone out of my own money and held an "austerity" Christmas raffle (top prize = a day off, bottom prize = the Perypils official calendar). I presented The Rock with a huge box of Thornton chocolates and begged her not to retire next year. She grinned and said, through a hazelnut praline, that she had "forty two days, three hours and twelve minutes" left to work. She'd marked up a daily countdown on the whiteboard behind her.

I was just on my way to tamper with her whiteboard when I noticed that the admin team had gathered together to give each other their Secret Santa gifts. I watched the first guy unwrap his present to reveal a huge tub of Vaseline, a man-size box of tissues and a Farmers Weekly magazine. *Oh God.*

ACKNOWLEDGEMENTS

With grateful thanks to Josie Clement for all your excellent advice, support and infinite patience and thank you to my lovely husband for being nothing like Kate's!

ABOUT THE AUTHOR

Jo Edwards lives in Hampshire with her husband, in a village they selected for its abundance of fine pubs. She is always delighted to hear from readers – visit her at www.jo-edwards.com.

For more information and links: